THE SUMMER

OF THE

OSPREY

by Elisabeth Ogilvie

Down East Books / Camden, Maine

BOOKS BY ELISABETH OGILVIE
*Available from Down East Books

Bennett's Island Novels
The Tide Trilogy
  High Tide at Noon*
  Storm Tide*
  The Ebbing Tide*

The Lovers Trilogy
  The Dawning of the Day*
  The Seasons Hereafter*
  Strawberries in the Sea*

An Answer in the Tide*
The Summer of the Osprey*
The Day Before Winter*

Children's Books
The Pigeon Pair
Masquerade at Sea House
Ceiling of Amber
Turn Around Twice
Becky's Island
How Wide the Heart
Blueberry Summer
Whistle for a Wind
The Fabulous Year
The Young Islanders
Come Aboard and Bring Your Dory!

Other Titles
My World is an Island*
The Dreaming Swimmer
Where the Lost Aprils Are
Image of a Lover
Weep and Know Why
A Theme for Reason
The Face of Innocence
Bellwood
Waters on a Starry Night
There May be Heaven
Call Home the Heart
The Witch Door
Rowan Head
No Evil Angel
A Dancer in Yellow
The Devil in Tartan
The Silent Ones
The Road to Nowhere
When the Music Stopped

The Jennie Trilogy
  Jennie About to Be*
  The World of Jennie G.*
  Jennie Glenroy*

Jacket illustration © 2000 by Jim Sollers
Printed and bound at Versa Press, Inc.; East Peoria, Illinois

5   4   3   2   1

Down East Books; P.O. Box 679; Camden, ME 04843
BOOK ORDERS: 1-800-685-7962

ISBN 0-89272-498-6

Library of Congress Catalog Card Number 99-89168

4094 8967 7.14

1

On that lustrous June afternoon, all work on the wharves and all play around the shore stopped when the strange boat came in. This was not the fairly ordinary occurrence of a yacht's search for a night anchorage or a small dragger limping in with engine trouble. The boat's broad stern was stacked high with wire traps; they were lined up three traps high along the washboards past the house on the port side, and on the starboard side they reached as far as the two tall propane gas cylinders standing upright by the canopy, before the rise began toward the high bow.

This boat was not coming in for directions or to stop off for a night on her way somewhere else; there was no other place to go beyond Bennett's Island but the Rock and then Spain. She was coming *here*.

Courteously slow, her engine barely heard, she made her way among the moored boats toward Foss Campion's wharf on the eastern side of the harbor. Two men could be seen over the traps along the starboard side. The man at the wheel wore a Greek fisherman's black cap and a white sweater. The other, smaller, seemed eclipsed under an old felt hat with a floppy brim. He had his shoulders hunched up and his hands in his pockets as if he were cold. Both men wore dark glasses, and both looked straight ahead.

Three children fishing for flounders from a skiff tied astern of Rob Dinsmore's boat stood up to get a better view, and Rob yelled between his hands, "Set down!"

They did, but the passage of the boat barely stirred the water or frightened the eider ducks with their collective flock of ducklings. She was a good forty-five feet, and the robin's-egg blue hull and white decks, canopy, and house had the luster of fine china. She towed a white skiff that looked as never-stepped-in as virgin snow. The house roof sprouted a radar installation with its thick white disk, the Loran and VHF masts, and forward of these a short pole topped with a cherry-red and yellow-green pot buoy, like a surrealistic parrot on a perch. The same brilliant colors gleamed through the dark mesh of the traps.

The name of the boat was lettered in black on either side of the flaring bow, *Drake's Pride,* and as she passed the wharves, the watchers saw her name again across the stern, and beneath that, peremptory as a shout, the words *Bennett's Island.*

Nils Sorensen said softly, "Well, well."

"Jesus," said Jamie Sorensen, just above a whisper.

"Jamie," his mother said, but it was more of a reflex than a reproof. She couldn't take her eyes off those words. The bubbly purr ceased, and the boat swung in an easy arc across the end of Foss Campion's wharf, leaving only the sounds of the water lightly swashing around the spilings, and the soft smack-smack as boats bowed and nodded in the gentle wake of her passage among them.

The slighter man climbed out past the gas cylinders and stepped onto the wharf to make the bow and stern lines fast. Cartons were handed over, and two large plastic water containers. Then a dolly was hefted up; they had timed their arrival perfectly for transferring the gas cylinders from washboard to wharf at high tide. One was rolled onto the dolly, and the skinny man in the floppy hat wheeled it up the wharf. The captain carried a carton under one arm and a water jug with the other hand. They took the path among the ledges to the small, prim white house, and the man with the carton unlocked the front door, went in, and shut it behind him.

The other man wheeled the dolly across the ledgy side yard to the kitchen door, at the angle where the shed joined the house. The gas fitting was there, as everyone on the island knew. He twisted the heavy cylinder off the dolly and went back for the other. When that was in place, he took a wrench from a hip pocket and attached the tanks to the fitting. All the time he never looked away from what he was doing; when he went to and from the wharf, he seemed to be staring rigidly ahead. When Terence Campion's dog barked from her doorstep, he didn't look around. He could have been stone-deaf and wearing blinders. He carried the rest of the things to the house and went in by the back door; now it was as if the house stood as silent and as empty as before.

For the watchers, it was like a visitation in a dream, except that the boat was still there with its load of gear and its gaudy, insolent buoy. Then there was that place-name unequivocally presented to the islanders in shouting black on pale blue.

BENNETT'S ISLAND.

With halibut and potatoes baking, and dandelion greens simmering, Joanna Sorensen had walked down to the wharf to stand around while her husband and son finished getting ready for tomorrow. It was an ordinarily quiet time in early June. With everybody in, the harbor business was limited to the fishing children in the skiff and the fishing shags at the harbor mouth, their erect snakelike necks black against all the blue and the sun glitter, and the medricks diving among them, weaving their intricate flight patterns as fast as light. Their rasping cries pierced the bright air.

Safe inside the harbor the communal flock of adult eider females and ducklings dawdled back and forth, the mothers constantly commanding or warning in low voices, shepherding their whistling and diving puffballs. Whenever a blackback gull flew in low over them, the quacking became loud and fast, and the ducklings were gathered up into a tight cluster among the adults, who angrily stretched their necks toward the villain, and their voices rose into a furious crescendo of threats until the blackback flew away.

"I dunno what those damn blackbacks are good for," Jamie Sorensen said. "Except to gobble down ducklings like popcorn. I'm going to keep my rifle down here."

The herring gulls peacefully sat on fishhouse ridgepoles or paddled above their reflections, looking contemplative. One walked familiarly in and out of the Sorensen bait shed. He was a brownish gray yearling, still black of bill and eye, raised by the Dinsmore girls from a chick they'd found wandering around on Sou'west Point. It had taken great dedication, because he needed so much to eat. They had named him Prince Henry the Navigator, Hank for short, and he was a great nuisance, but tolerated for the sake of his foster mothers.

"Here you are, Hank," said Nils, tossing him a salt herring. Jamie sighed, and Nils winked at Joanna behind his back. On the next wharf their daughter, Linnie, and Steve Bennett's stepson, Eric Marshall, were helping Rosa Fleming load clean dry traps aboard *Sea Star*. Linnie had been home from college only three days and had her fifty traps all set out. She was euphoric.

"'And what is so rare as a day in June?'" she chanted. "'Then, if ever, come perfect days.'"

"God, it used to be some peaceful around here," Jamie said from the bait shed.

"That's what you said when we brought her home from the hospital," his father said.

"He really adores me," said Linnie, "but he'd die before he'd admit it. What's *that?*"

That was the explosive impact as an osprey crashed into the water just off the end of the breakwater. They all watched the hard beating of great sooty black wings as the bird struggled to lift itself and its prey from the water. Then it was clear, dipping again, but rising higher the next time, the fish glittering in its talons. It flew off toward the Eastern End, calling excitedly as it went. Two others cruising at different altitudes answered, and went on with their seemingly effortless coursing and watching, far above the lightning maneuvers of the medricks and the cruising shags.

"Daddy, can we row out there and fish?" Diane Dinsmore shouted from the stern of *Beautiful Dreamer*.

"No, you can't!" Rob called back. "Wouldn't be nothing anyway. They won't bite when something's driving 'em. You'd likely tangle up with a dogfish. . . . Looked like a mackerel, he had," he said aside in his normal voice. "Lord, I'm some hungry for a good mess."

"Remember the Gloucester fleet that used to come for the mackerel?" Nils asked Joanna.

"Yes," she murmured, mellowed by the memory of the black boats with saints' names and the men who spoke English to the islanders and another language among themselves, rapid and tuneful as a running brook. A couple of older men had helped Karl Sorensen to mend a huge hole torn in a seine; it had been spread out on the big wharf, and the needles were swift as medricks in their brown hands. One had been dour; the other had laughed and talked constantly. He had been stout, with merry eyes.

"That's when I ate my first sea urchin," Joanna said. "And my last. That man talked me into it."

"His crew was his family," Nils said. "They'd argue until they sounded ready to murder, and then they'd all burst out laughing. I thought that was about the nearest to heaven anyone could get."

Jamie glanced around at his father, who said without self-pity, "You'd have to grow up in a house run by Gunnar Sorensen to know what I mean."

"Sometimes I think I've been cheated," said Linnie. "When did they stop coming?"

"With the war," said her mother. "I wonder how many of those boys survived it. I wonder how many of them remember this place."

"Well, I may have missed out on all that," said Linnie, "but Rosa and I couldn't have gone lobstering in those days. I wonder what special memories I'll collect this summer." She and Rosa lifted a trap together and carried it to Eric aboard the boat. "It doesn't look like much so far."

"Cheer up, you never can tell what the next tide'll wash in," said Eric. Joanna watched the three on the next wharf: Linnie, lanky in her jeans and striped jersey, her fair hair rainwater-washed, floating to her shoulders; Eric, thin-faced, lean as Linnie around the middle, looking older than twenty-six but with a cowlick standing up from the crown of his mouse brown head as she'd first seen it when he was a weedy little boy of eight. The back of his head and neck still had that vulnerable look, giving the lie to the new lines in his face.

Compared to Linnie and Eric, Rosa looked large, but without flesh to spare. Her broad forehead and wide-set gray eyes gave an impression of serenity and self-assurance. She loved *Sea Star* as if the boat were her own flesh and blood. She loved lobstering. Most of the men had gone to wire traps, but Rosa still kept her wooden ones, which she'd built herself. The gear brought in lately from deep water was lined up in rows on the wharf, giving off the sweet-and-salt pungency which, like the smell of good bait, pleasured island noses.

"'Who knows whither the clouds have fled?'" Linnie inquired. "'In the unscarred heaven they leave no wake; and the eyes forget the tears they have shed, the heart forgets its sorrow and ache.' Don't you love that, everybody?"

She didn't need an answer but went on into the next verse. Jamie sighed loudly. His family often made him sigh, as if he were the only solidly consistent one in the bunch. Eric was waiting for another trap, and Joanna surprised on his face an expression that cast the first cold dark over the warm effulgence of the afternoon. It was only for an instant, and then she couldn't be sure that she had seen anything; but still, the impression stayed, like a blot on your vision after you've taken a quick look at the sun.

Maybe unconsciously she'd been thinking the hour was perfect and she should knock on wood. She did, surreptitiously, against the hoisting mast behind her. Now Eric was laughing at something she'd missed, and it had taken years off him. She looked in at Jamie, who was stolidly stuffing bait bags. Nils had finished and was wiping off his hands, whistling contentedly under his breath.

June could have disturbing associations for Jamie, a year after Eloise. For herself, it was the time of year when Alec had died. When the wild strawberries were coming and the new birds hatching out, with every-thing beginning, including their child, Alec had ended in this harbor.

The eyes forget the tears they have shed, the heart forgets its sorrow and ache. Your own, that meant. Then you watched your children go through it. You had not the slightest comprehension of what it meant to be a parent, until you were one.

This was when the strange boat came so quietly up Long Cove that they hadn't known she existed until she was coming around Eastern Harbor Point. The watchers seemed spellbound until the two men had disappeared inside the house.

"What in the hell was *that?*" Hugo Bennett yelled from farther along the row of wharves. The three young fishermen headed in, Robin Bennett pulling mightily on the oars.

"Foss Campion never said he sold to a fisherman," Joanna said indignantly. "He claimed it was some rich man who wanted to get away from it all."

"Looks as if he's bringing it all with him," Rosa commented.

"Yup, that's a hundred-thousand-dollar job if I ever saw one," Rob said. "Maybe more." Over beyond him Ralph Percy stood staring at the new boat as if for once he couldn't think of anything to say.

"There was something familiar about the skinny one," Eric said. Jamie walked up the wharf, wiping his hands on a piece of burlap bag, and Hank flapped, squawking, out of his way.

"Where you bound?" Nils called after him.

Jamie didn't turn; he was very stiff and square of shoulder. "I can't get my hands on Foss Campion's neck, but I can call him up and find out what the hell's going on around here."

"Come on back," said Nils. "We'll soon know. Waste of time and money trying to raise Foss."

"You're right, he'd just fall all over himself. I'll go over and ask the son of a bitch himself."

"No, you won't," said his father. "We're going home to supper."

"Who's got an appetite after *that*? Didn't you *see*—" It was as if he couldn't put words to the outrage.

"I did, and I don't think anybody else missed it either. But you aren't tearing over there all winged-out and wild-eyed."

For a moment it looked as if Jamie would ignore him and go anyway. But Nils did not often speak as he had just spoken, and when he did, his children heeded him, whatever their private resolutions might be.

"You come on up, Rosa," Joanna said. "You can't go home and eat alone after all this excitement. You're welcome too, Eric."

"They'll be looking for me at home, but thanks, Aunt Jo." His thin face creased more deeply with his smile. "Look at Robin. She's leaning on those oars like a dory fisherman on the Banks, hurrying to get back to the schooner before the fog shuts in. She'll run all the way to the Eastern End to tell the news, with a detour at Hillside in case Uncle Owen doesn't know yet."

His young half-sister was yelling at him as the skiff came in. "Hey, Eric, wait for me!"

"My devoted public," he said with a wry little grin.

The last of Rosa's traps went aboard. Rosa thanked her helpers and stepped down into the cockpit, started up the diesel, and took *Sea Star* out to her mooring.

"I'll wait for Rosa," Linnie said to her mother. "Boy, I can hardly wait to find out about this. Who does he think he *is*? How does he dare say she's a Bennett's Island boat?"

"No law against it, far as I know," said her father. "If he's bought Foss's place." Jamie gazed across the harbor at the robin's-egg blue boat, biting at the inside of his cheek. Nils put a hand on his shoulder. "Let's put for home. My mouth's been set for that halibut ever since you and Hugo brought it in."

2

The island men and their wives collected at the Sorensen house after supper. Time was when the women never came to these meetings, and it was said that on Brigport they'd still be excluded. Of course, a spontaneous gathering in someone's fish house was a different matter, but this meeting had an unusual formality about it. Jamie had given the Percy and Dinsmore children fifty cents each to see that the word got around.

The older and younger Fennells came from up the lane beyond the clubhouse, with Peter Fennell, the island's only baby, sleeping in his carriage. Ralph and Marjorie Percy came from next door to Rosa, Mark and Helmi from the house up on Western Harbor Point above the store and the big wharf; the Dinsmores from the Binnacle; Philip and Liza; and the Bartons and the Terence Campions from around the harbor, past the house into which the mysterious strangers had disappeared. Hugo and Charles came down from the Homestead, and even Mateel, who hardly ever left her house and garden. Owen and Laurie were there, with Tommy Wiley, Owen's helper; Tommy was radiant with excitement at being included. Steve and Philippa walked up from the Eastern End. Eric didn't come with them, and Robin stopped off at Terence's, where the harbor children were playing, and Vanessa had left small Anne there.

Earlier, while everyone was busy with supper, one of the strangers had emerged long enough to put *Drake's Pride* on Foss Campion's mooring.

"There she is out there, big as Billy-be-damned," said Owen when he walked into the sun parlor. "By God!" He laughed in astonishment at the brazenness of it. "'Bennett's Island' right across her arse!"

8

"That's what we're here to discuss," said Jamie tersely, "so let's get to it."

There was more room in the long sun parlor than anywhere else in the house, so chairs were brought out from the other rooms, and the young men sat on their heels against the wall, as fishermen have always done.

"We electing a chairman?" Ralph Percy asked. "How about Charles? He lives in the Homestead, and back in the old days that'd make him the head hooter around here."

Charles said, "If you'd called me the top senior citizen, I'd have wrapped your leg around your neck and strangled you with it." He was the oldest man on the island since Foss had left and saw no honor in the position.

"What do we need a chairman for?" Owen demanded. "He's here, isn't he? We were told it was some rich bastard who wanted a quiet place for the simple life. So he shows up loaded with gear. No taking soundings. No coming in like a little gentleman, hat in hand, and asking permission to come aboard. *No!*" He slammed his hand flat down on the table. "Shoves it into our face, down our throats. My God! Time was when anyone showed up like that, he would've been met by a delegation when he stepped ashore. So what in hell do we need a chairman for? We're all here. Let's go."

"I second that!" Jamie was on his feet.

"Hold your horses," said his uncle Charles. "We're here to find out how everybody feels about this, and there's quite a few more here to speak up, unless they've all got paralysis of the vocal chords."

Jamie flushed, making him look about sixteen, but managed to mind his manners. "Okay, then, we take a poll."

"I know where I stand." Hugo spoke up. "Who gave the guy a right to say he hails from Bennett's Island when he's never set foot on the place before today, never even talked to a Bennett's Islander?"

"Well, he sure talked to Foss," said Barry Barton.

"Hypnotized him is more like it," said Terence. "I don't think Uncle Foss pulled anything on us. This guy, Felix Drake, approached him, said he'd like a place on a real remote island with no summer people. He'd had a new boat built and would take himself back and forth. No mention of lobster traps."

"Anybody spoken to him yet?" Mark Bennett asked.

"We went kind of slow past the house on the way around here tonight," said Barry, "so he could come out and make himself known. But they're lying low."

Kathy spoke up. "I saw somebody putting the boat off, and I tried to shove Terence out to meet him when he came back ashore, but you know what *he's* like." Terence looked unoffended and unrepentant.

"Let's all go over now and have a little confab," Hugo urged.

"You just hold up there," his father said. Hugo indignantly opened his mouth, and Charles said, "And don't tell me what I'd have done forty years ago. In those days nobody ever brought the law in unless there was bloodshed. Nowadays you give a man a hard word, and he sues you for harassment. Two fellers give a man a hard look, and it's conspiracy."

"Well, there are ways and ways," said Owen with a mildness that deceived no one. "No bloodshed, no hard words, not even a hard look. Nothing anybody can put a finger on. When he comes out with his next load of gear and starts to haul the first batch, they've all disappeared. That's what happens when you don't know the bottom." He shook his head in sad concern. "You're likely to lose a lot of traps down deep holes."

"Where's this famous Bennett's Island friendliness that folks go away and write about?" inquired Steve Bennett.

"You mean the folks who come in here in trouble or get storm-stayed or fogbound?" Owen scoffed. "Hell, they aren't figgering on moving in with us. They're no threat. That's not like letting the camel into the tent."

Steve was amiably persistent. "Listen, it might be this man's ignorant of the way he's supposed to do things. He's bought a place out here, so when he's having his new boat painted up pretty, he thinks why shouldn't he say she hails from Bennett's Island? Sounds good, and it's not breaking any laws. And why should he come out here first, hat in hand"—he nodded at Owen—"and ask if he's welcome? It's all cut and dried, isn't it? He owns property, he takes it over. . . . I'm just trying to think like him," he explained. "Supposing he comes around tomorrow introducing himself and asking how people feel about him. What are you going to say to him? Get the hell out?"

"Why not?" Young Matt Fennell spoke up so fast that everyone was surprised, and his parents looked a little worried. "It's honest, if that's the way we feel."

"And that's the way everybody feels, isn't it?" Jamie stood up. His blue eyes briefly scanned each face. "Any objections?"

"You look at them like that, as if you had a knife up your sleeve, and nobody'll dare object," said Linnie.

"I know nobody who isn't a fisherman is supposed to say anything," said Joanna, "but so far we've only heard from a few of them. So while we're waiting for the rest, I'd like to say something. I know wives are only allowed in as long as they keep their mouths shut—"

"Letting you in on any conference is a calculated risk," said Owen, "so we might as well bow to the inevitable."

"My, you talk some fancy." She gave him a syrupy smile. "Well, I feel just about like everybody else, that he's pretty brazen. It's like a stranger walking right into your house without knocking, and dumping his luggage in the middle of the floor. But in all fairness, I have to agree with Steve. You might say we have a pretty tight-knit society out here, and in some ways moving here is like going into a foreign country. He can be just plain ignorant, and if we're going to hold that against anybody—" She shrugged.

Steve picked it up. "And as far as him calling himself a Bennett's Islander, no harm in that. It won't make him one. Takes time to get naturalized out here."

"If the cat has kittens in the oven, that don't make 'em biscuits," said Maggie Dinsmore. Everybody laughed except Jamie, who saw his earlier advantage sliding away from him.

"Let's get back to business," he said austerely. "So far there's been a lot of backing and filling, and not much else. We taking care of Drake first hop out of the box, or not?"

Matt Senior cleared his throat. "I don't like this anymore than you do. Yes, I think the man's got one hell of a nerve. And it looks like he's going lobstering for a hobby, so his fun will interfere with our livelihood. But Charles is right when he talks about the law. And the law also states that if you have a license, you have a legal right to set lobster traps wherever you want."

"A legal right, sure," said Jamie. His cheek bones were glowing again. "But what about a *moral* right?"

"Yeah, what about that?" said Hugo eagerly. "He'll be catching lobsters that belong to us, because we depend on catching lobsters for a living. He's got no moral rights here."

"Forget moral rights." Nils's quiet voice cut in. "You can argue that till kingdom come. How about the fact that we all had a chance to buy the place from Foss?" He nodded across at Jamie. "You personally or anyone else on the island. Foss offered it at a fair price before he put it on the market. We could have all gotten together on it. But nobody wanted to tie up any money."

"We'd been through a tough year," Ralph said defensively.

"Yep, we had," Nils agreed. "So we let Foss sell it where he could. Either to summer people or a new fisherman. We could absorb another one. Agreed on it, didn't we? So I don't see that we've got a leg to stand on."

"Neither do I," said Mark.

"Hear, hear!" Owen said maliciously. "The big buyer sees a chance to get more lobsters and makes more money."

Mark's sidewise look without turning his head was typically Bennett. "Seems to me I've been hearing that he'd catch lobsters you fellers would otherwise get. So it'll be the same amount of lobsters for me, just divided up different."

"Christ, don't you have any loyalty at *all*?" Owen asked.

Jamie said abruptly, "I think we have the right to tell him and his partner they're not welcome. This is no rich man's playground."

"I don't figger we have to worry about being taken over by a batch of playboys," Ralph Percy observed. "That property isn't big enough to turn into a colony."

"Too bad," said Barry Barton. "Might liven the place up. Happy Hours on the wharf. Girls in bikinis perched up on the bow—"

"Heck, Barry, I could go hauling in a bikini if that's what you think the place needs," said Linnie. "Rosa, are you game?"

"I don't think the island's ready for me in a bikini," said Rosa placidly.

"We'll never know till we get a look, will we?" said Owen. Jamie gaveled the table with his fist.

"Okay, it's a damn big joke, but he's on the island with one load of gear, and you can be damn sure it's not the last. And nothing's been decided here. Just a lot of laughs. Can't I get some straight answers? Sure, we know what the senior statesmen think," he said sardonically, "but how about hearing something straight out from every fisherman here?"

"Fisher*person*," said Linnie. "Because you have to include Rosa and me."

He ignored that. "Matt?"

"I'm with you, Jim," young Matt said earnestly, "but what's the question? Whether we tell him straight out or take the indirect approach?"

"You mean like cutting off his traps?" Tommy Wiley blurted out. He was joyously incredulous, as if he could hardly believe his luck at getting in on something like this.

"I should've left you home," Owen growled at him. "Don't you know you never *ever* come right out with anything like that? You mention any of this outside this house and I'll cut off your tail behind your ears."

"Yup, but you said when we first come in—"

"He says a lot besides his prayers, son," said Charles. "You ought to know that by now."

Jamie scowled while he waited for this to be over with, and Joanna was irrepressibly reminded of him with his infant eyebrows drawn together in silent displeasure. Tiny blond eyebrows then, like little feathers from a warbler.

"The question *is*," he said in the measured rhythm of patience maintained with difficulty, "who wants to get rid of him, no matter how, period."

"Question mark," said Linnie, and Tommy giggled.

3

One result of the poll was an agreement that Felix Drake had put everybody's hackles up by his arrogant entrance into their lives. Like all lobstermen they resented the part-timers, the men who had well-paying jobs or other income to live on and went into lobstering for the fun and excitement of it. These men didn't have to pay for new boats and gear out of what they caught; they were in the clear from the first. A bad year was no threat; they never experienced the gut-chilling moments of wondering just how much longer the lobstering would last, and what—if anything—could be done to save their particular world for their children.

The second result was a majority decision to see how the stranger worked out. The law was on his side, and there was nothing to be done about him as long as he behaved himself.

"If he had a big enough piece of the island, he could bring out a batch of hired fishermen," Philip Bennett said. "That would be another kettle of fish. But he's outnumbered here. As long as he doesn't foul us up with a thousand traps—and we can let him know the limit—he'll be no more than a mosquito."

"This is a pretty rugged way of life except for a few months in the summer," Nils said. "He'll find out. In the meantime, we're not going to starve because of what he catches."

"We were half prepared for another fisherman anyway," said Terence Campion.

"And that didn't worry us none," Rob contributed.

"But he'd have been a real honest-to-God fisherman like us," Jamie began in frustration. He gave up and ran his hands violently through his short fair hair. "It's the *principle* of the thing." He still kept searching the faces with fierce eyes, but he was opposed except for Hugo, young Matt, and his uncle Owen. Yet he wasn't giving up, not in front of everyone. He'd nailed his colors to the mast.

Joanna ached for him and was annoyed with him at the same time. When she and Nils had suggested he buy the Campion place for the time when he'd have a wife and want his own home, he'd said, "*Wife?*" in an aghast, if not outraged, voice, and walked out of the house. Now he was furious because someone had taken what he'd refused, and he was trying to build his mistake into a cause.

She stood up and said loudly, "I'm going to make a gallon of coffee."

The deadlock was broken. With relief the other women straggled out after her, and behind them male voices broke into earnest or deliberate conversation. Chairs shifted. Someone laughed, and the atmosphere was suddenly free from tension. Joanna didn't look around to see if Jamie had dropped to his heels beside the other boys or had walked straight out the back door. She didn't want to know that.

The women scattered through the kitchen and dining room. A little knot gathered by the baby carriage to admire the sleeping Peter. When Kathy began taking down cups and putting them on a tray, Joanna realized that Linnie and Rosa must have quietly departed.

"I guess the crisis is over for the time being," Kathy said. "Wow! Terence was feather-white when he saw that load of gear. I don't know if he can even be civil to the man when he meets him face to face. He thinks he took advantage of Uncle Foss."

"Well, they'll likely all sleep better tonight for hashing it out now," Nora Fennell said comfortably. "Land of love, I didn't think that boy of mine could sound so warlike!"

"It's the name on the boat that gets me," said Marjorie Percy. "Not *Drake's Pride,* but the other."

"Philip was really stung when he saw it." Liza was still marveling. "I couldn't get over how he reacted. My old easy-does-it boy was anything *but.* I thought I knew all the ways that prove islanders are a breed apart, but today I found out something new."

"Nils wasn't too charmed either," said Joanna. "Just said, 'Well, well,' but that spoke volumes, as the saying goes. Stung me, too. Silly, isn't it? Because when you boil it all down, it doesn't amount to Hannah Cook. How many cups do we need?"

"None for me," said Vanessa. "I don't know about Barry, he's so wound up he could go on for hours. I'd love to stay, but I have to put Anne to bed."

"I guess I'd better go along, too," Kathy said, "though God knows I'd love a wild night on the town."

Owen's voice cut across the others, large and buoyantly imperious. "Got anything cold out here besides water?"

"Nope," Joanna answered without looking around. "All we've got is pure, sparkling Adam's ale." Then she did look around, and her throat stopped up at the sight of the two taken by surprise face to face in the doorway. In the space of the next breath they had turned away from each other as if in mutual loathing. Vanessa's back was toward Joanna, but she had seen the life leached out of Owen's face so that he looked like one of those coarsely powerful sculptures hacked from dark wood.

Vanessa had gone into the dining room and picked up a book from the sideboard. In the next moment Owen had disappeared from the doorway, and Vanessa was intently reading in the Swedish-English dictionary from which Linnie was collecting a vocabulary.

"That coffee smells heavenly!" exclaimed Kathy. "If this Finn doesn't get out, she'll never make it."

"I'm with you," said Van coolly, putting down the book. *Did I really see what I* thought *I saw?* Joanna wondered.

Jamie announced that he had herring to catch, and the seiners left, Tommy with them. Eventually only the Bennett brothers and their wives were left. The family settled around the dining room table with second cups of coffee, in lamplight, because Joanna liked to bypass the generator whenever she could.

"Did I tell anybody I saw Simon Bird over at Brigport?" Charles asked. "He's going on a two-man dragger. Bald and scrawny now, with a beard birds could nest in. Greeted me like a long-lost brother." He sat back in his chair, folded hands on his chest, and rapidly rotated his thumbs. "He asked for everybody in the family. Real touching, I thought, considering we ran that whole crew off the island."

This set off a storm of recollections, in which Joanna was as silent as the women who had come much later to the island. She was remembering the Birds with a chill in her stomach that she drove away with too-hot coffee. The chill did not come from remembering that Simon Bird—so handsome then, too; she couldn't imagine him bald and scrawny—had attempted to seduce her when she was fifteen; he'd probably thought she was less innocent than she was. But when she was newly widowed, not much older than Linnie, and pregnant, he had come to her and told her he owned her house. Alec had gambled it away.

It had taken the Fennells to turn the house back to a place she could bear to enter or even look at in passing.

A screen door quietly opened and shut, and Eric came into the dining room, his eyes narrowed against the light. "I just saw the seiners off," he said. "Tommy didn't make it again." He went to the kitchen and filled a mug with coffee.

"What's he doing?" Owen asked. "Not that he can get into much trouble around here, but I always like to be ready for surprises."

"He's rowing Linnie around the harbor in the twilight and giving her his life story. Of course, she knows the last five years of it, but you couldn't tell."

"I wish she'd use some of that tact on her brother," said Joanna. She pushed a plate of mincemeat squares toward Eric. "Eat up and give the cook a good name."

"How was the skipper's mood when they cast off?" Nils asked.

"Rotten," said Eric. He stirred his coffee, staring down at the small dark eddy as if seeing a face or a message there. "*Willy,*" he said suddenly, and everybody looked at him.

"Will he what?" asked his stepfather. "Will who what?"

"Willy Gerrish. That's who Drake's friend, or helper, reminded me of."

"*Our* Willy?" said Philippa.

"Yes. When he climbed out of the boat and just the way he walked up the wharf. I've seen Willy do that often enough when he lived at the Eastern End, so it hit me all at once today. But it's probably only a coincidence."

"I dunno," said Steve, his stepfather. "Willy was living around Limerock last year, going sternman for somebody fishing in the bay. I met him on the street, and he wanted to buy me a cup of coffee. He told me he'd always regretted letting Gina talk him into leaving the island. She left him anyway within a month."

"Poor Willy," Philippa said. "He was such a good, eager boy to have around. Most of the time I felt like wringing Gina's neck, the way she treated him. And he adored her."

"I let him down as easy as I could," Steve said. "I told him I'm not handling that much gear now. None of us are. Our own conservation plan and so forth. He was some disappointed. So he could be back, if he had the chance, and he knows the bottom around here. That'd be useful for Drake."

Owen slammed his hand down hard again, as if he had to strike something, anything. "Jesus, can't you hire him away from Drake? He'd go with you faster than a gull can gaffle a herring!"

"I don't need him," Steve said. "I've got no room for him. And Drake's likely promising him a hell of a lot more than twenty percent and all found. If it *is* Willy."

"It's him all right," Owen said savagely. "I can feel it in my bones. *I'd* hire him if I didn't have Peter Pan on my hands till death do us part or he gets married, whichever comes first. You know Willy'd rather be with a Bennett than anybody else."

"I don't know anything of the sort," said Steve with a smile. "Might be Drake beats us all hands down for charm."

"Let's see how long you think it's a big thigh-slapper," Owen said ominously.

"Why don't you shorten your sails and start acting your age?" Charles asked him. "It's bad enough to have the kids spoiling for a fight without your wanting to get right in there with them, stirring everything up with a stick. You wait till that boy of yours is a dite older; you won't take kindly to him agitating for trouble or being shoved into it by somebody else."

"He's a Bennett's Islander, isn't he? How many generations since old Jamie got this island to have and to hold?" His dark eyes raked them all, scorning them for going soft. "If my boy wants to hold on to his heritage, he'll have to fight for it."

"I don't see one fisherman, rich *or* poor, as an invading army, dear," said Laurie.

"But maybe we should ask Rosa to compose a national anthem for us, just in case," said Joanna. "We could design a flag, with Owen and Jamie rampant like those rearing lions, standing on a couple of lobster traps, with crossed bait irons between them."

Everybody laughed, and the lamp flames shivered in the chimneys.

Eric's face lost the haggardness that had come new to it this year. He had entered this family as a thin, anxious, little boy forever conscious of having lost his father, and he had acquired Steve, five uncles, a collection of cousins, Jamie for a best friend, and the island.

All their lives they'd been sitting around tables, laughing like this, or fighting, or grieving. Wasn't it rich that it still went on, all of them still here? Wasn't it *good*? But what about another year? How she'd hated those lines of verse when she first saw them, and she still hated them.

> *Time goes, you say? Ah, no!*
> *Alas, Time stays, we go.*

None of us will ever be ready to go, she thought fiercely. Never, never, never!

Unheard in their approach, Robin and young Mark came suddenly into the lamplight as Eric had done. Robin was carrying the black and white cat, who looked over his shoulder at the roomful of people. The eyes of the three young creatures glistened as if with their own luminescence.

4

Rosa and Linnie had walked out together into the bronze ambience of the afterglow. The hour was pierced by the flute notes of the white-throated sparrows singing in the dark woods. The children's voices rang out in occasional excited bursts across the harbor, above the muted drone of a distant engine. No generators muddied the purity of the evening.

The scents of flowers and drying mown grass lay heavily on the motionless, damp air. Already the dew was soaking into sneakers. "Let's go for a walk, Rosa," Linnie said. "Let's walk around the harbor and knock on the door over there and tell them we're lost and ask for directions."

"You do it," said Rosa. She yawned convincingly. "I'm about dead on my feet."

"Well. I've got to do something with a night like this," said Linnie, "and there's nobody to walk to Fern Cliff with. Let's wait at the shore to see the seiners off. Jamie hates that."

"Have some pity on the poor cuss," Rosa said. "He's already had a hard night. I'm for bed. So long." She turned off onto the path toward home.

"Night!" Linnie called blithely after her.

Once Rosa was behind the big spruces whose boughs laced into a screen at the foot of her lawn, she breathed more freely. Jamie was so imprinted on her consciousness after an hour or so of watching him, and she had wanted so much for him to win out in spite of his wrongheadedness, that now she felt tired and irritable, but she could not yet endure going inside. She walked faster, past the house and into the dusky woods, out to Barque Cove.

The sea was a pale but dimming glass all the way to the horizon, which was invisible; there was only a blending of sky and water, a few stars, a distant set of lights lower down like moving stars. Soon she heard *Valkyrie* leaving the harbor, the seine boat charging along behind her, going away past Long Cove. "I've got to do something with a night like this," Linnie had said, but it was half a joke with her. Linnie was in love not with a person but with the idea of being in love, so that the nearly unbearable beauty of an island summer should not be wasted.

For Rosa the velvety touch of the night air against her skin, scented with the sea and grasses and spruces still warm from a day of hot sunshine, was at once pleasure and burden. She sat for a long time, until she saw no lights on the horizon but the familiar ones of distant lighthouses, and the engine sounds had ceased to be audible. A little breeze ruffled the water as the tide turned, and it made gurgles and miniature splashings down below, like those of the ducks. She sighed, stretched as hard and as tall as she could, and felt her way home through the now-silent woods.

She brushed her teeth out on the back doorstep and started for the stairs without a light. Passing the shelf where her radio sat, she turned it on before she thought. Instantly the night was filled with voices near and far, which always struck her as a kind of miracle, as if the voices and their cynical or serious or joking conversations came from supernatural beings who populated the skies. She put out her hand to turn it off, still trying to hold on to the mood of Barque Cove, but Bruce MacKenzie of *Hannah Mac* boomed in her ear.

"Dryer'n a cork leg out here, and we've been cruising since sundown. Where the hell are they?"

"Same over here." Jamie's voice was slightly distorted, and made heavier, it resembled his uncle Owen's voice. "Might as well put for home and crawl under the kelp."

"Aye-up. Hey, what about that big fancy craft over there in the harbor? Lad got a look at her stern this afternoon when she went past him off the Black Ledges. Who's the rich guy among you Bennett's Islanders? Somebody discovered oil in the pasture?"

"Funny you should ask," said Jamie. "I've been wondering myself."

"That's Felix Drake!" a strange voice broke in.

"Who dat say dat?" asked Bruce.

The man identified his boat and himself. "You fellers roosting out on those rocks don't know about high society. He's got a big place down near Coates Cove. He was raising Morgan horses for a spell, and I dunno what all. Looks like he's found a new hobby. Heard nobody took kindly to it down there, so those fellers will be real happy for you to have him. My brother-in-law built that boat for him. My nephew laughed himself silly painting 'Bennett's Island' on her stern. Says, 'They'll get a surprise when they see *that!*'"

"Well, he was right," said Jamie with commendable restraint. "Of course, I haven't met the gentleman yet."

"Oh, he'll be glad-handing you." There was a croaky chuckle. "Big bundle of charm, he is. Real nice to the peasants."

Silence. Then Bruce said dryly, "Well."

"Ayuh" said Jamie. "Well, I'm gone." He gave his name and numbers. "Over and out."

She turned off the receiver and went up to bed, completely awake now, and lit a lamp and read until she heard *Valkyrie* coming in. She blew out the lamp and a little while later she heard the murmur of good-nights as Matt and Ralph separated in the lane; in a minute or so the Percys' back door opened and closed when Ralph went in. She knew in her bones that Jamie would not be coming here tonight. He had rented his uncle David Sorensen's house, between Nils's place and Philip Bennett's, so his comings and goings wouldn't disturb the family, and in her mind's eye she saw him approaching it, shucking off his boots in the entry, washing up in the dark that was never really dark, just a deep gray dusk. Then he would go upstairs, shedding his clothes as he went, and lie awake, staring up at the shadowy rafters. Between Drake and the missing herring, he would be too angry to sleep, and he wouldn't give her a thought.

And the hell of it is, she told him, if *I* stop thinking about *you*, you won't even notice. And if you did, you wouldn't give a damn. All that matters to you is what opposes you or what you can't have. You're more self-centered than Conall Fleming.

She went to sleep finally and woke a few hours later with the first light. The whitethroats were beginning again. She put on a wool bathrobe against the chill and ate her breakfast looking out across the island to where spruce tops were inked in against a peach-colored sky.

The first gulls were coming in, and out in the lilac beside the back door the catbird was indefatigable. Barn and tree swallows shot past the windows and chattered from the eaves.

She filled her thermos bottle with coffee and took two hard-boiled eggs from the water in which they'd cooked, wrapped them, still warm, in foil, and put them in her lunch box. She dressed in jeans and a cotton shirt with a turtle-neck sweater over it, pulled on a pair of bright yellow neoprene overalls and her deck boots. She wished she could pull on this bright, shadowless hour and wear it around her like armor against the rest of the day. Last night, along with the gut-and-bone knowledge that he would not come to her, there had come the other knowledge that she had reached a crossroads where she could not lallygag any longer.

She didn't look toward his windows on the way to the shore, but when she came out on her wharf, she saw that he had already gone out. Hank swept down on her, banking so close that his wings fanned her hair, and rose to land on her fish house ridgepole. The tide was up, and quiet, and her skiff lay motionless by the ladder. A raven flapped across from the woods behind Hillside Farm, noisily pursued by three crows.

The sky was now barred with blue-lavender and dusty pink, and the harbor reflected it with the sheen of taffeta, crosshatched by the silver wakes of paddling birds. *Drake's Pride* looked enormous out there on her mooring, floating on the brimming high tide. She was only about five feet longer than most of the island boats, yet her intrusive presence made her loom almost twice as large.

Rosa had set her bait aboard yesterday, before putting *Sea Star* back on the mooring with her load of traps. She untied the skiff painter and held it in her hand with the lunch box handle while she went down the few rungs. A sense of moving largely and freely in her own element almost always came to her whenever she walked out onto the wharf, with *Sea Star* lying off there like a faithful charger awaiting her whistle. But that sense was often missing these days, and she feared and hated what had taken its place: a truth like a presence which had crept up on her, walking in her footsteps, making no sound, snapping no dry twigs of warning, making no cataclysmic pounce from ambush. One day she had simply realized that it was there, and in its close companionship she found everything else altered.

She rowed out to *Sea Star* with quick, short strokes. Hank remained on the ridgepole, balancing with his wings while he abused any other gull that violated his air space. The skiff seat was wet, cold through the waterproof overalls, and the oars dripping with dew. If she believed in omens, she would see one now in the fact that Jamie Sorensen had been the first person she met when she entered this harbor two years ago: suspicious, antagonistic, his eyes the intense cold blue of shadows on snow. Now he preoccupied most of her conscious hours and her sleeping ones, too, and to no profit. So much for her devout oath never to victimize herself again, so much for her confidence in her own integrity.

Well, it was never too late. There was something in knowing when to give up instead of struggling on, clawing at bare ledge with bloody fingers, digging in with bruised toes, and then sliding back in a shower of battering stones.

One thing, she thought, I won't stuff myself with food again, the way I did after Con.

The skiff nuzzled along the side of *Sea Star*. She slid her oars under the middle seat, stood up and set her lunch box on the washboard, and swung herself into the cockpit. She fastened the skiff painter with a couple of half hitches to a ringbolt in the deck and started the engine. The instant response always gave her a gratified surprise. She took the skiff painter and walked up on the wet bow deck to fasten the skiff to the mooring and then cast off.

Overhead the sky was turning the blue of *Drake's Pride*, and the east was blindingly bright. Rosa jumped down into the cockpit, ducked under the canopy and put the boat in gear, and headed out. Nothing yet could quench the euphoria this moment always gave her, the Presence hadn't learned yet to cross the water. If only she could hold on to this heady knowledge of her own self-sufficiency when she was ashore. Why couldn't she? Damn it, if alcoholics could reform, so could she.

She headed down the west side and around Sou'west Point. Beginning work, she loose-ballasted each dry trap with flat rocks from the two crates in the stern, to hold it down until it had soaked up and the built-in ballast would be enough. She fastened in the stuffed and juicy bait bag and slid the trap overboard with a little good-luck pat, letting the new warp run out and tossing the clean bright blue and yellow buoy after it. She could have had the radio for company, either fisherman talk or music, but she preferred the sound of the engine and the wash of water along the boat's sides.

Nils passed her with a wave, and then Matt Senior. She was jogging

along toward Bull Cove when she saw *Drake's Pride* just going behind
Brig Ledge; he must have come around by way of the Eastern End. She
was tempted to turn on her radio and see if he was talking or if Ralph and
Terence, who were working near by, were discussing him. But the
temptation quickly faded away. She didn't really care. She felt detached
to the point of indifference; she didn't give a damn what Drake did or did
not do. The blue boat had now disappeared behind the high ledge. She
had only two traps left and planned to set them in Bull Cove, if
everybody hadn't got there ahead of her. She swung the bow toward the
cove, and there was *Valkyrie* lying just inside Schooner Head; Jamie sat
on the washboard, watching her. He was bareheaded; he always was
unless the sun got in his eyes, when he put on a very ancient duck-billed
cap. He lifted one hand in a solemn salute, not a wave, when he knew
she'd seen him, and she felt a shameful rush of hope. *He's been waiting for
me.* They had always met here, wind permitting. Then she thought
sardonically, How'd it happen that he remembered it, with Drake just off
there behind Brig Ledge? But she knew she was pleased, and she hated
that.

When she came slowly alongside and shut off the engine, he linked
the boats loosely together amidship with a length of potwarp. It was so
calm that *Valkyrie* was anchored to a lobster trap and lay there as docile
as a skiff. Birdsong and the warm pungence of the woods drifted out over
the cove.

"Going to drop them in here?" he said, nodding at the two traps.

"Might as well." She poured coffee for herself and peeled an egg.

"You see Drake farting around Brig Ledge?"

"Couldn't miss him."

"Like a hayseed in your eye," he said. "I hope they'll all get their
bellies full of him. If it wasn't for the chance of him getting fouled up in
my gear, I'd hope he didn't have a cage on his wheel, so he could get
them all good. I hope nobody's told him yet about the trap limit, so he
really plasters the place."

All he wanted me for was to hear him growl, she thought. Solemnly
she ate her eggs and drank her coffee, watching the light waves shimmer
upward endlessly over the spruces. Jamie lit his pipe. "You had your radio
on?" he asked abruptly.

She shook her head.

"Well, everybody's been talking about him. Everybody meaning half

of Brigport, and some guys from Stonehaven, and a couple from Coates
Cove. If he was listening, his ears must be burned down to nubs. Or else
he's been enjoying it. Probably that," he said morosely. "Money's no
object with him. I hear he's tried everything but running a chain of
whorehouses, and maybe he's done that. Who knows? Now he thinks
he's just bought himself an island for his private lobstering preserve."

Oh, Lord, Jamie, you can be so damned tiresome, she thought.
"Well, he hasn't," she said. "Just one very small piece of harbor
frontage."

"Have a doughnut." Gloomily he held out his lunch box. "We could
stop him in his tracks tonight. It's already happened to him once, I hear.
He thought the waters off his mainland place were his own. Lobstermen
around there taught him the difference. But he probably thinks we're a
bunch of inbred morons out here. You know, to hear 'em talk last night,
you'd never guess what they used to be up to. He wouldn't be the first
man to set traps out here and never see them again."

"But he might be the first man with the money to keep on setting
more gear till you get tired of cutting," said Rosa. "So he has the last
laugh. That's what he'll have bought—seeing you make a fool of
yourself."

He said with a wintry smile, "I'd swear you've been taking lessons
from the old man."

"I've got work to do." She put away her thermos bottle.

"What's the hurry?" he asked, surprisingly. "It's summer, and there's
no wind blowing." She began to get one of the traps ready to put
overboard. "Something eating you?" he asked.

She thought of several outrageous things to say, but settled for a
slight quirk of the lips and brief hunch of one shoulder. She slid the trap
along the washboard away from *Valkyrie*, strung in the bait bag and
fastened the door, then tipped the trap overboard, let the warp play out,
and threw the buoy after it.

Jamie smoked his pipe and appeared to watch her, but she could bet
that his thoughts were aboard *Drake's Pride*, which was now heading east
toward the Seal Ledges.

She got the last trap ready and went to start the engine, but Steve's
Robin B. was just coming around Schooner Head and approaching them.
Steve's face showed through the windshield, and Eric stood in the stern,
bareheaded like Jamie and wearing dark glasses.

The boat came in alongside *Sea Star*, and Eric held on with a gaff. "Is this a private talk?" he asked.

"If it is, we don't intend to stay long." Steve put one foot on a crate and leaned his folded arms on his knee. "Wouldn't dream of it. Just thought I'd tell you it's Willy all right. The gentleman lobsterman spoke to us when we were leaving the cove this morning. Introduced himself, all smiles, strong handshake, looks you right in the eye. Man to man. He said it was a real privilege to meet one of the original Bennetts. I told him they were all up in the cemetery."

"Meanwhile, Willy was trying to disappear into the bait box," said Eric. "I never saw such red ears. I sang out, 'Hello, Willy!' and he jumped and took off his hat and called me Reverend. Then *I* had the red ears."

"Poor Willy," Steve said. "I told him to drop in and have a cup of coffee and a piece of strawberry pie with us someday, and I thought he was going to cry. You can't be mad with the little cuss. I guess he was so crazy to get back here he didn't realize how it would be after he got here. He's no fool; he knew there was a meeting last night."

"He was probably scared shitless," said Jamie. "Thought there might be a lynching. But once he got a kind word from you, he was ready to show Drake all the sweet spots."

"Not all of them," his uncle said. "Willy learned a lot out here, but he didn't learn everything. I wonder if Drake's going alongside everybody he sees this morning, wanting to shake hands." With a common thought they all looked out toward the Seal Ledges; *Drake's Pride* was up alongside Philip Bennett's *Kestrel*.

"Jesus, I'd like to hear *that* conversation," said Jamie.

"Maybe he's thinking of running for governor when he gets tired of lobstering," Eric suggested.

"I wouldn't vote for the bastard for hog reeve," said Jamie.

Perversely changing the subject, Rosa said to Eric, "Why did you get red ears when Willy called you Reverend? I should think you'd be used to it by now." Then she thought she'd been rude and added, "Don't answer if you don't want to."

"I'll answer it," he said candidly. "I've never gotten used to it, that's all. I still look at letters addressed to the Reverend E. J. Marshall as if they were somebody else's."

"But you earned it. It's not as if it happened to you overnight."

"Unless he's been kidding us all," said his stepfather, "and he's been doing something else all these years and got his diploma for five dollars through the mail."

"That's it," said Eric, hanging his head. "I can't live any longer with my guilt. But not even torture will make me tell you what I've been really doing when you all thought I was in college."

"Playing piano in a whorehouse," said Jamie at once.

One of that chain of Drake's, Rosa almost said, but she didn't want to bring Drake back again, even in a joke. Eric struck his forehead with his fist and said hollowly, "Don't ever tell my mother."

"But is it true they all have hearts of gold?" Jamie asked.

"It's time we left," said his uncle.

As soon as they had circled away, Rosa started her engine, and Jamie knocked out his pipe and loosened the line that held the boats together.

"Do you think Eric really likes being a minister?" she asked him.

"Oh, sure. He always wanted to be one because his father was." He started his engine. There was no leaning across washboards to kiss her, and there never had been, even if they'd slept together the night before. She kept *Sea Star* in neutral until Jamie had turned around and headed out, with an offhand wave. She thumbed her nose at his oblivious back and waggled her fingers, wishing he'd caught her at it. But she felt better, she didn't know why.

She set the last trap in the cove. Jamie already had three there. "Ah, togetherness," she said aloud. "His and hers. Sweet."

5

It was a boat day, and Joanna came early away from the store and the mail-time sociability; she had a letter from her older daughter and was anxious to read it. Linnie was down on Mark's wharf, yarning with *Clarice Hall*'s engineer, while a summer boy from Brigport, dressed like a rodeo cowboy, wordlessly admired her from a distance. She'd been out and hauled this morning, and her sixteen-foot lapstrake *Dovekie* was back on the haul-off. Rosa was just coming back in. Across the harbor *Drake's Pride* lay at what was once Foss Campion's wharf, with Willy washing off any signs of toil. Doubtless picking off herring scales with eyebrow tweezers, unless Felix Drake had brought out some more exotic bait unavailable to the common man.

And there was Drake himself, coming past the fish houses with a springy step, immaculate in pale chinos and a blue turtleneck. His gray hair would have been curly if it hadn't been cropped so short; it looked like a silver fleece, in pleasant contrast with a ruddy tan. Tiger rushed barking from the Binnacle to confront him, and he dropped to his heels and put out a fist for the dog to smell. Joanna stayed where she was by Nils's fish house, so as not to interrupt the negotiations.

Head bent forward, voice confidential, hand scratching the braced back, Drake was clearly winning the suspicious terrier. Finally he told Tiger he was a good watchdog, and then he came to his feet without visible effort. His height was average, his back was straight, and he was youthfully flat of belly. She could imagine him jogging so many miles every morning, or playing killer tennis.

Then he saw her, or appeared to have just become aware of

her. "Mrs. Sorensen!" He came toward her, his hand out. "I'm Felix Drake."

"I was pretty sure you were," she said, and he laughed as if she'd delighted him with her wit. His eyes were a clear light hazel, shiny as the dog's. They narrowed when he laughed and creased attractively at the corners; she wondered if he knew that, and worked at it.

He had a robust voice, surprisingly deep. "What a pleasure this is! I've already met your husband, out on the water. A *fine* man. He told me some things I need to know, the trap limit everyone has agreed on, and so forth. Very sensible."

I wonder if he's waiting for me to welcome him to Bennett's Island, she thought. "Will you be bringing your family out?"

"I'm afraid not." Frowning with earnest regret. "My wife has so many things going on that she can't be pried away from home, and the same with the youngsters. They think *I'm* crazy!" Merry laughter. "But it's such a beautiful place I'm hoping to coax them all out to see it. That little schoolhouse over there is a real gem! Do they really ring the bell in the morning?"

"Oh, yes, at half past eight."

"I was out setting my traps, so I missed it." He sighed. "I can't help wishing my girls had been able to go to one of those wonderful old one-room schools. What memories you all must have! What memories these children will have!"

"Yes," Joanna murmured, trying to think of a way to break this up. But he did it.

"Well!" he said vigorously. "I'm just on my way to meet the postmaster, lobster buyer, and storekeeper, all three in one man, I understand." His eyes sparkled at her from among the creases. "Another of those famous Bennetts."

Famous for what? she wanted to ask. "Oh, he's there all right," she said brightly, "along with quite a few of the citizens." They separated with friendly nods. The man had to be ignorant rather than arrogant, bouncing around like an eager dog, unless the bounce was as calculated as the eye crinkles could be.

She stopped at the well to fill the empty pail she'd left. The lean young black-and-white cat was waiting for her by the gateposts. The old collie Rory Mor had died in the fall, as quietly and courteously as he had lived. Linnie had been at school and thought she had gotten her mourning over with before the Thanksgiving weekend. But there would still be that moment to be faced when she went through the gate and Rory was no longer there, as he had been since she was seven years old. So she brought home the leggy kitten they'd been feeding at her dormitory.

He had jumped out of his box into a houseful of strangers, and within fifteen minutes he had made it, and them, his own. He was as exuberant and social as a puppy and so loquacious that nobody ever had the last word with him. Linnie had named him Pip because he had such great expectations, and so far nothing and no one had disappointed him. He adjusted cheerfully when Leo and Tiger hadn't responded instantly to his hail-fellow-well-met approach but had become Scylla and Charybdis to keep him from getting past the well to the wharf. He had even liked the veterinarian when Joanna took him to Limerock in the late winter; cats have no great expectations of growing up to be mothers or tomcats.

Now he talked fervently to Joanna before she reached him, and then wrapped himself around her legs so she picked him up out of self-defense, and he put his cool black nose in her ear. She went straight through the long sun parlor and out the back door to sit on the step by the lilacs, still damp and morning cool. The cat sniffed the letter all over as she opened it and then stretched his length beside her thigh, lying on his back and staring at her with his speckled golden eyes, his front paws kneading space.

Ellen had been home for a week in late April, and there'd been a spell of warm weather then so they could sit out here watching the baby trudge around the yard in her overalls and boots. She would stand for long minutes, studying the hens, and they would collect at the wire and study her. The swallows had just returned, squabbling noisily about their houses and diving at the cat.

Ellen had two stepchildren, and she wrote now that their mother was dying; by autumn they would be living with her and Robert. They had often visited and got on well, but she was sensitive enough to know the new arrangement would not be easy, especially for children eight and ten who had lost their mother by death.

"It may help them to know that I lost a parent," she wrote, "even if I never knew him. I remember that talk we had about him. We were a long time getting to it, but I'm so happy that we had it at last."

"Do you mind if I call him Alec?" she had asked that morning, eyes on her baby daughter. "It makes him more accessible. You never knew this, but when I was little, he was my father which art in heaven. I knew that was really supposed to be God, but I didn't know what God looked like, and I had pictures of my father, so I used to say my own words. 'My father which art in heaven, Alec be thy name.' I missed him even with Grandpa and all the uncles, so that way I felt I was really talking to him. I talked to him a lot. I told him everything, even what I wanted for Christmas, like Santa Claus. I put him into the hymns. 'He walks with me, and He talks with me, and He tells me I am his own—' Does this shock you?"

"No!" Joanna blew her nose. "But the older I get, the easier it is to get tearful. *I* used to talk to him. But you were always such a cheerful little tyke, and here you were having this secret life. . . . So was I, thinking I'd never get over it, trying to keep it to myself, but it used to rise to such a pitch I'd think I was about to shatter like glass. And we were away from the island, all of us, and I was working to support us in a place where he'd never been. Seemed to make it worse. . . . Well, the edge dulls after a while. Life is meant for living. I hitched a ride on a dragger one day, just to get a look at the island, and the rest is history."

"Nils was here," said Ellen delightedly, "living all alone and lobstering from a peapod. If we couldn't have Alec, how lucky we were to have Nils. I convinced myself Alec would be glad for us, and I remember explaining to him that when I started to call Nils Father, it was to set a good example for Jamie. And then I didn't talk to him so much. Sometimes I felt guilty about it. Then all at once I was older than him. How do you talk to a father who's still a boy and you're a grown woman?"

"Did you ever actually say good-bye?"

"No." She asked shyly, "Did you?"

"The night he died, I kissed him and said—" She couldn't say it now. "But it wasn't real. Nothing was real to me until you were born. . . . I don't suppose there's a day when I don't think of him. Not mourning, but just some little thing, like with everyone else who's gone. You're reminded of what someone used to say or do, maybe because you say or do the same thing. And there are hundreds of little pictures flashing up. In a place like this, the influences stay. The island's like one of those old castles full of ghosts collected through the centuries."

"I'd like to meet up with some of the earlier ones."

"You've heard your Sorensen uncles swear Gunnar rules this house. But he's never bothered me."

"He wouldn't dare," said Ellen. They both laughed. The conversation had slipped easily away from the dead, but it had bothered her for the rest of the day and when she waked in the night, up against Nils's back. Not for Ellen's sake, but for Alec himself. For the pathos of his dying so young, and so needlessly, and without his ever knowing he would be a father. "A father who's still a boy." It was like grieving for a son.

Ellen's letter brought it all back, and she was in no mood to stay around the house. She went in to put up a lunch, intending to walk to Sou'west Point. The cat accompanied her conversationally between refrigerator and counter. Then he was suddenly distracted by a sound outside and at once turned into a stalking panther. Eric came in the back way, putting his sunglasses in his shirt pocket.

"Thank Providence, an oasis!" He headed for the water pail in the kitchen. "I started out in the cove below the house, went around the Head, and climbed the rocks all the way to Goose Cove, with no shortcuts. By that time I was ready to strike out for the nearest settlement." He took a long drink. "Ah!" he breathed. "Good and cold. There's no water like island water. Except at the Eastern End, of course. I stopped at the Homestead, but nobody was there except the dog."

"Mateel's going in on the boat this morning." She put the teakettle on the gas stove. "How about a cup of coffee and a crabmeat sandwich? Kathy's picking out crabmeat to earn herself and Cindy a trip to Boston next fall."

"I'm happy to help out the cause." He sat down in a rocking chair in the sun parlor, and the cat jumped into his lap with a chirrup and tried to roll. Rocking and stroking, while the cat's purr rose in volume, Eric said, "I didn't go out with Dad this morning, thinking I'd work all day on my dissertation. But after three hours of staring at the typewriter, I broke out, and here I am, without a useful thought in my head."

"If I don't ask you about it, it's not that I don't care," said Joanna. "It's only because I wouldn't understand it."

"I'm not sure I understand it either," said Eric. "I seem to be doing everything but working on it. Sooner or later," he said cheerfully, "I've got to come to grips with it."

"Why did you pick such a difficult theme if you—I don't know how to be tactful about this—if you don't know enough about it to write it?"

He put the cat down and followed her to the kitchen. "Well, I did know. At least I thought I did. My ideas were striking, original, opened new doors, cast new light, offered fresh visions, and any more clichés you can add. I started off like the front runner in a marathon. Now, not only does it seem nonstriking and nonoriginal, stale, locked into the same old echo chamber, but so do I."

"I'm sorry, Eric. How about some of my first lettuce in your sandwich?" The cat agitated piercingly for crabmeat, and she put some in a saucer for him. "There, that'll shut you up for five minutes. I never had such a mouthy cat."

"He's a Bennett's Island cat. Was there ever a really taciturn Bennett's Islander?"

"Not in the Bennett family anyway." She made the sandwiches very thick with lettuce and fresh crabmeat and cut them diagonally with a slim sharp filleting knife.

"I'll never fade away with despair; my appetite never gives up," said Eric.

"*Are* you in despair, Eric?" She said it lightly, pouring the coffee. "I thought June on the island was a sure cure for everything."

"It should be, shouldn't it? No, I'm not in despair. I *have* been," he added unexpectedly. "But hasn't everyone at some time or other? And a few have had more than their fair share of it." He took the tray and carried it out to the table. "Seems as if it's part of the rites of passage, losing your first love. Something you pray won't happen; but it does, and then you pray to survive it."

She sat down opposite him, carefully maintaining an air of friendly but not avid interest.

"Jamie went through his hell last summer," Eric said. "If there are different degrees of hell, mine was on a different level. Tame, actually. Wishy-washy, compared to all the Wagnerian drama surrounding Jamie."

"That's a nice way to put it," said Joanna. "I thought it was pretty squalid myself."

He used a whimsical manner which she was sure he had perfected for self-defense. "Yes, but fire, fury, threats, jealous lovers—how many did the girl *have*? Thunder and lightning roaring and crackling around the old Viking. But *I* get a letter written in elegant calligraphy like a work of art on her best pale blue stationery with a gold monogram, telling me she is sorry, but she knows she can never be a minister's wife. She left it for someone else to mail at the airport as soon as she boarded the plane for California. And nobody would give me an address or a telephone number."

She listened silently, swallowing back her instinctive reaction: rotten little slut.

"And you feel like such a fool, you know? You're standing there with your mouth open saying, 'But—but—' But *what*? You don't know." Disarmingly he smiled at her. "Look, Aunt Jo, she was right. She'd have been a disaster. But she was—*is*—" He went on with his face half turned away. "There were things that had nothing to do with the sort of minister's wife she'd make. The things that you don't forget in a hurry, and you think you never will."

The cat hurried out from the kitchen, and Eric gave him a piece of crabmeat. When he straightened up again, he said, "The point is, I never had any opportunity for violence. I know, I'm supposed to be agin it, like sin, but a man's a man for a' that, as Burns said in another context. I was cheated out of a confrontation. I couldn't rage to her face or to anyone else's. And I've never told anyone about this until now. My mother and Dad know there's something, but they won't ask. You got it out of me with your crabmeat sandwiches."

"As far as I'm concerned, nothing's been said. But this is the reason you can't put your mind on your work?"

"My work should come first right now. If I were a fundamentalist, I could say 'God's work,' though I can't quite see my dissertation as that. God's had so many millions of words offered up to him in the form of treatises and manifestos and learned explanations of what He's all about, I can't believe He's hungry for a few thousand more from me." He got up and went into the kitchen for more coffee. Thin and long-legged, but not awkward, and soundless in sneakers. His voice came out to her. "I might as well go the distance, Aunt Jo. That crabmeat's powerful stuff. . . . The fact is, she stirred up something that must have been smoldering for a long time and started it blazing. *Doubt*. I don't know what sort of minister I'll make. I don't know how completely I'm committed."

"Maybe she's done you a favor if you really had doubts."

"I wouldn't admit their existence before. There couldn't be any doubts. I was going to be a minister, as my father was. Now I'm haunted by him as well as by her. Whose commitment am I honoring, his or my own?" He came back, portraying humorous dismay. "In the small dark hours I even think words like *betrayal* and *traitor*. You'd think I could pray about that, wouldn't you? But it doesn't seem to be the sort of thing to bother God with. The more you call for an answer, the more remote the possibilities of one. I'm glad I have my own quarters at the Eastern End. I get up in the middle of the night and go out to see what the island will do for me."

"What does it do?" she asked.

"It never lets me down. When I'm on my feet and moving, the specters go away."

"I don't think your father would want to be a specter in your life any more than Ellen's father would."

"If only I could remember him," Eric said, gazing out the windows. "If only he'd left me something—written me a letter—but I don't think he expected to die when he did. This isn't self-pity, Aunt Jo. I'm just thinking out loud."

He sipped coffee and watched a goldfinch drink from the birdbath against the alders.

"Do you suppose that deep down you're wondering if you gave it up you might get her back?" Joanna asked.

"It's me she doesn't want. The minister bit was just a handy excuse. Maybe she couldn't bring herself to be brutally honest. And I don't want her." He spoke without emotion. "There are things I can't forget, but I still don't want her. You're right, though, maybe she's done me another favor besides not marrying me. I've got this summer to discover the truth."

"I hope you do, Eric." She got up to let the cat out. She was so moved by Eric's confidences and so distressed for him that she was afraid it would show.

"Jamie looks the same as ever to me, but how is he?" Eric asked. "I'm not trying to gossip behind his back but, close as we were, I can't see us exchanging our battle stories and displaying our scars. I care about him, though. He's as much a brother as anyone could ever be."

Her shakiness left her. "All I can say is that I don't know. It's been a year, and he knows that poor Darrell came off worse in it—not that that should be any consolation. I don't suppose he ever gives a thought to Bron.

"My mother wrote about her. She liked her."

"We all did. But like you, she wasn't exciting enough." Her smile had no humor. "It was exciting enough for *us* when he moved in with her. It almost started a trap war."

"You see what I mean about Wagnerian drama?"

They both laughed. "He tried to tell me it wasn't serious with him and Bronwen," Joanna said, "but I've always had this suspicion that she was in love with him and he was too damned innocent—or stupid—to see it."

"Now Rosa's in the picture," he said tentatively.

"I don't know about him and Rosa. You certainly can't tell by the way they act when you see them together, but now that he's living next door he could be spending all his nights with her and I wouldn't know."

"You say that mighty calmly, Aunt Jo."

"After Eloise, I can be calm about it, even thankful, thinking he'll never come to any harm with Rosa. But it's not very fair to her. That niggles at me, same as with Bron."

"Rosa looks unflappable," said Eric.

"She's been badly burned once, and she's no fool. She seems to take Jamie just as he is, and that calls for a lot of patience and forbearance, which I am short in." She went back to the kitchen and got a tin of chocolate chip cookies. "Here's your dessert."

"Talk about your first-aid stations." He waved a cookie at her, then ate it in two bites.

"You looked at me then exactly as you did when you were twelve," she said.

"I *feel* twelve. My kid sister's taking me fishing after school in the old *Sea Rover*. She acts as if I don't know anything or I'm so old I've forgotten it all. When I told her that Jamie and I went lobstering together at her age in *Sea Rover* and had a running feud with the MacKenzies and we used to pitch herring at each other, she looked at me with absolute awe, as if I were talking about some time before the Flood."

"It *was*," said Joanna solemnly. They both laughed. He got up to leave and put his arms around her and kissed her cheek. She could not remember when Jamie had last done this, and she felt a very slight twinge of envy of Philippa. She hugged him back.

He took a handful of cookies on his way out. "See you later, Aunt Jo. And thanks for listening."

"Any time, dear."

"Any time what?" Linnie called, coming in at the harbor end of the sun parlor, with the cat over her shoulder. "What did I miss?"

"You'll never know," Eric called back, and kept on going out by the barn.

6

"Wait till I tell you!" Linnie ordered her mother. "Don't go anywhere." She went into the kitchen to make a sandwich and brought it to the table. "You'll never guess what I just heard!"

"The boy in the cowboy hat is the heir to oil millions."

"The boy in the cowboy hat comes from Arlington, Massachusetts, and his father's a dentist. I'm not talking about *him*. It's what Duke told me about this Drake. When he saw the boat on the mooring, he whistled. Then we saw Mr. Fancy Pants himself coming around the shore. What'd he say to you?"

"Gracious greetings, I guess you'd call it," said Joanna. "He's already met with your father. I'd like to be a gull on the canopy when he meets your brother."

"Me, too." Linnie gave the picture a few moments' attention while she ate part of her sandwich. "Duke told me that all his money comes from his wife. And she's handsome, Duke says. Built like a brick you-know-what." The mail boat's engineer was a dedicated gossip. "The girls are into horse shows, all that kind of rich stuff. Oh, and he says Drake found Willy for a helper because Willy has relatives at Coates Cove, and Drake's a friend of Henry Coates, a big lobster dealer over there."

"Now there's a name from the past," Joanna commented. "Henry Coates used to run a lobster smack out here now and then, years ago."

"Then he probably put Drake on to Foss's property because of that, and he probably told Drake if he was so crazy to go lobstering this was the place."

"Probably, probably." Joanna teased her. "Duke's full of those."

"But it stands to reason, doesn't it? Nobody will let him fish inshore; he must have lost about a thousand traps, Duke heard, because he kept setting out and losing them. But he's used to doing what he wants, so *somewhere* there has to be a place where he can indulge himself, and this is it."

"What have we ever done to be so lucky?" said Joanna.

"Yup," said Linnie happily. "It should be *so* interesting. Any good mail?"

"A letter from Ellen." Joanna gave it to her.

That afternoon, about the time when most of the men were coming in, *Drake's Pride* left the harbor and headed for the mainland. Even after she had disappeared, she remained an indelible imprint on the collective retina. Absent, she still took up space in the harbor because she would be back. Drake's lime-green and cherry-red buoys insolently floated on island waters, each one a fresh insult or annoyance, depending on the viewer. He'd set a discreet distance from other traps so as not to risk a snarl; but he was there, wherever you turned, and he could still set another hundred traps or so if he intended to fish up to the islanders' two-hundred-trap limit for the summer fishing around the rocks. He could also set more gear farther out.

Rosa, encountering three of his buoys in one of her choice spots, understood the nearly intolerable compulsion to slash. Well, at least her reaction showed that she was still alive, she thought cynically. She had not yet turned into a mush of self-pity. She wondered how long it would be before the clean sweep—Paddy's Hurricane—took place, with the seiners out half the night during the dark of the moon. Three of them wanted action. Ralph was more cautious; he said that Drake's enthusiasm wouldn't last past the easy shedder season. The first bad weather of the fall would spoil his fun, and then they'd be rid of him.

The high school students came home that week. Owen's Holly and Charles's Betsey each brought a friend. Owen's Richard and Philip's Sam, being each other's best friend, were concerned only with getting their traps out as soon as possible.

Linnie and Rosa were picking wild strawberries on the high land beyond Barque Cove when Sam's fifteen-foot outboard rig went by, Sam standing up to steer so he could see over his load of traps. He didn't notice the women.

"Farewell, peace," Linnie said with a sigh. "He's looking for my buoys. Well, I had it to myself for a few weeks anyway. Now Sam will be buzzing around me like this bumblebee, setting as close as he can manage, so we can have nice cozy chats while we try to sort out snarls."

"How's it feel, being his first older woman?" Rosa asked.

"Claustrophobic," said Linnie. "I have this feeling he thinks he'll marry me when he grows up. I love him, he's cute as a seal pup, but— *phew!*" She blew hard.

"Cheer up, he's just had his first year in the big world, and maybe he's in love with some fourteen-year-old Kewpie doll, so now you're over the hill for him."

"Thanks. You know, a hundred years ago at my age I'd be considered a desperate old maid." She sat back and pensively nipped the berries off a perfect spray.

"Are you desperate?" Rosa asked, amused.

"No, but I wish there were some single and attractive males on the island who weren't relatives."

"You ought to go over to Brigport with Hugo when he checks out the summer material."

"I've seen what they have to offer so far. My God, beside *him*, Sam is sophisticated."

It was an easy afternoon, and the warm turf smelled of strawberries and other pleasantly aromatic growth. Rosa felt contented in this hour. By rearranging her work pattern, she'd managed for three days to miss meeting Jamie at Bull Cove. Now, lulled by the sun and the music of the light breeze in the spruces, she could almost convince herself that she didn't care if he hadn't missed her. Between the absence of herring and the presence of Drake, she didn't even exist for him, and right now she could even think, recklessly, Well, to hell with *you*, chum.

"If we had to have a playboy," Linnie was saying, "I don't know why he couldn't have been young and single."

"Maybe he has some friends like that." Gulls rode the upper wind currents, around and around as if hypnotized, and the ospreys' voices rang through the sky. The western sea twinkled in diamonds and sapphires.

"I wouldn't be able to stand them," Linnie said. "I can't stand him, and I don't even know him. For once I agree with Jamie, but I'm not going to let him know it." She snickered. "Boy, I'd love to go out some night and paint 'Bennett's Island' right off that stern. I'd use bright red. Will you come with me?"

"Nope," said Rosa.

"I didn't think so. I suppose the council of elder statesmen are right about ignoring him."

In the early evening Rosa sat on her back doorstep, trying out tunes for a new song. She hadn't done this for a long time, just another of the things she'd allowed Jamie to knock out of her mind, and it had always been one of the great pleasures of her life.

The birds were outdoing themselves with their evensong, and a normally shy thrush was picking around under the trees at the edge of the woods; she watched him while she plucked at the guitar strings. An old song took over, and she hummed the melody to the words in her mind.

"The waves were white, and red the morn,/ In the noisy hour when I was born:/And the whale it whistled, the porpoise rolled,/And the dolphins bared their backs of gold;/And never was heard such an outcry wild/As welcomed to life the ocean child."

The thrush flew suddenly into the woods, and Jamie came around the corner of the house. The unexpectedness of it demolished in one blow all her gains. There was a commotion in her innards like the onset of a virus. She tightened her belly against it, nodded at Jamie, and bent her head over the guitar again, plucking as if she knew what she was doing, but both words and the melody were gone like the thrush.

Jamie sat down on the chopping block and took out his pipe. Supposing he had come to ask her why she'd been avoiding him? With a weary distaste she recognized hope like a new shiny growth of the poison ivy on the brow of a beach back home. You dumped on the stuff sworn to kill it, and next year it looked healthier than ever. What got it finally was a winter of bad storms, surf constantly flooding it and tossing the beach rocks back six feet into the marsh, burying the plants.

So what could she expect to accomplish in a week? "Well," she said moderately, laying the guitar aside. He considered her with those blue eyes, and hope shot out fresh glossy sprays. Then he took the pipe out of his mouth and said, "Drake is nothing but a goddamned pimp. He's using the island for a whore."

She could have laughed at her disappointment. Instead, she yawned.

"Am I boring you?" he asked with rather stately dignity.

What if she said yes? "He's going to be a fact of life around here till the new wears off it for him," she said. "So why torment yourself? Forget him. Or at least ignore him."

He looked honestly bewildered. "How can I? I am what I am, and I can't help it."

"Look, can't you see him as no more than a nuisance? If he wants to call himself a Bennett's Islander, that's a compliment. He's like a kid trying to be an old frontiersman. He's like that boy hanging around Linnie, the one who dresses like a rodeo rider. When he gets tired of it he'll go away, and you'll kick yourself for getting all fouled up about nothing."

He was making an effort to keep his temper. "That's everybody's line, but I thought you'd see what I see. He's dangerous."

"Why, because he has a little money? Or a lot of money? It doesn't make him God."

"No, but he thinks he's halfway there." He didn't smile when he said it.

"You're making him into a villain, and he's nothing but a show-off." She picked up the guitar. "Why don't you get obsessed with something else?" Me, for instance. Last year he'd been obsessed with Eloise Robey, and she'd take Drake over that any time. But why should she take anything? Her head drooping low over the guitar, her fingers searching for chords, she said, "What can he do to the island? It's been here since the world began. Practically."

"I *told* you!" Without raising his voice he seemed to be shouting. "He'll use my—our island for his whore to make money off. He won't be any part of this place; he'll just come out to haul and rush back in again. He'll never spend a dollar in the store. He won't sell to Mark. He'll get his bait ashore, gas up ashore, take his lobsters ashore."

"Okay. Annoying. I'll even grant infuriating. But not dangerous."

"You don't know what else he thinks he can use the island for."

"Sure I do," she said. "He might rent his place to summer people for a few thousand dollars a season, just to keep him in cigarettes and gas. We rich folks have to watch our nickels and dimes just like the poor folks."

"And we can have the kind of dirt here we never had before," he argued with passion. "A drunk who could set the island on fire. A child molester. A bunch of drug addicts."

"Ayuh, and a clan of those mass murderers that look mild as milk and commit massacres," she said. "How about that? Jamie, why are you always borrowing trouble?" she asked wearily. "When I was down, you were always up, telling me life was pretty damn good and I'd better start living it."

"I'm not *down!*" he said indignantly. "I'm a realist! And damn it to hell, I don't want to be proved right! I don't want there to be a chance of it!"

Ralph came around the back of the house, trailed by his boys. "Thought I heard the skipper's dulcet tones. We going or not?" His broad freckled face was carefully innocent.

"We're going." Jamie stood up. "But another goddam dry run, and I'm quitting."

"Hey, where's that old Viking spirit? I hear they've struck over to Metinic."

"That old Viking spirit wants to chase something else besides herring," Rosa said.

"Don't we all? But cheer up, blackfly time passes, and so will this. Let's get out and slay them herring." They went away with the children in their wake, Ralph slogging along in his rubber boots and talking, Jamie never looking back at Rosa.

A year ago Jamie had astonished everyone who knew him by having two affairs within six months, as if he had suddenly decided he had better commit some youthful foolishness while he was still youthful. The first one hadn't mattered much except possibly to the girl involved. The second had been different. He had committed himself entirely to Eloise Robey, so much in love he'd considered the world well lost, and finally he had been devastated like a coast swept by a tidal wave.

Rosa believed he would never again allow himself to be so vulnerable. So all the passion and adoration had been thrown away on a little slut far more dishonest than any professional prostitute.

Rosa had been just as enthralled and then victimized by Conall Fleming, and she had briefly made a fool of herself over another man in something she preferred never to remember except as a degrading experience in a bad dream. She understood what had happened to Jamie; she had been strong and eager to help him as he had helped her. But being there for someone could be taken to extremes, passing from affectionate concern to a growing irritation like a blister starting on the heel. Does he think that's all I have to do with my life? Be there for him when he feels like dropping in for some sympathetic agreement? *I thought you'd see what I see.*

Apparently that's just what he did think, and had no reason to believe she wasn't content to live in the compartment where he kept her until needed. She'd never told him, and it was time she did. A year was long enough. He'd probably be dumbfounded when she said it, and she wouldn't be able to make him understand, and she'd wish she'd never started it. While he watched her with those unclouded blue eyes, she'd fall all over herself in rage and humiliation because she couldn't come right out and say, I want to be more than a convenience for you.

Finally, when she had trailed off into flustered silence, he would walk away from her without a backward look, the way he had just done. She could see it all so clearly that it gave her a pain in the belly, the kind that reminded her of what she'd read about hara-kiri. How long did those people live before they toppled forward into their own blood?

"Oh, my God!" she said aloud. "You are so far gone on the wrong track, woman, that you'll never get back on course."

She put her guitar in the house and walked across into the Percy yard to spend an evening with Marjorie.

7

Joanna woke very early in summer, before daylight. Usually she would hear the erratic clanging of the bell on sunken ledges beyond Sou'west Point because there was always the ocean surge and swell out there, but at rare times there was utter silence until the first bird began. She would lie there listening to one bird after another joining in, until it was like a line from one of Philippa's favorite poems. "And long notes of birds, violently singing until the whole world sings."

All the land birds were familiar, down to the tiny kinglets, and among the gulls' calls she sometimes thought she could distinguish Hank's voice; she was sure the Dinsmore children could.

Lying there listening, not sure if Nils was awake because he slept so quietly, she would often drop off again for another nap, but that wasn't happening much these days. If she didn't rouse herself up by planning out her day or remembering dolefully that she'd promised herself to clean a closet, she would think at once of Eric, and wonder if he was walking through this dew-drenched hour before daylight trying to come to terms with his grief and rage before he had to face anyone.

Her compassion was almost a repetition of what she had felt for Jamie last summer after the Eloise business, though it was not as intimate and poignant as it had been for her own child. Eric will get through it all right, she assured herself. Eric is not weak; he has other strengths to sustain him. But she recognized her selfishness; she couldn't enjoy her own summer while knowing one of the family was miserable.

Jamie's wrath about Felix Drake didn't count as misery. Jamie wrathful was preferable to Jamie in black despair.

Eric would be all right, but now there was something else to come into her head at these undefended moments, like a mosquito which has slipped into the house unnoticed and begins singing about your ears just as you settle down to sleep.

Vanessa. Owen. That encounter in the doorway. She'd tried to say it was nothing, but it would not be thus wiped out. Nils, of course, would tell her it was all her imagination. He would be nice about it, but positive, and she didn't intend to let herself in for that.

The incident wasn't the first she had seen. That was at a dance last summer, and she had almost said, "Don't you two *speak?*" She'd intended to make a joke of it, but a sixth sense had kept her quiet. Later she wondered if they'd had some disagreement when Van was knitting trapheads for Owen, though four years did seem an ungodly long time for holding a grudge with nobody else's knowing about it; an impossibility on the island. She wasn't about to bring it into the open, so she put it out of mind.

This was the dance to which Darrell Robey had brought Eloise to show her off, thus the beginning of Jamie's disastrous escapade.

Joanna believed she had completely forgotten the other small incident, that silent encounter and turning away, until it happened again a little while ago. And now that she had seen it twice, she would not be able to shove it out of sight. It was somehow shocking to her that such enmity could go on unseen but vigorous for years. She gave them credit for keeping it to themselves, thus forcing nobody to take sides. But now someone did know it, herself, and she wished she didn't.

Common sense intervened; it usually did after she'd dragged everything out and strewn it around in broad daylight, like the contents of that closet she should clean. You don't have to watch for it to happen, she lectured herself, but if you do see it, you don't have to dwell on it. Whatever the trouble was, it is none of your business. *None of your business,* she repeated like an incantation. *None of your business.*

"Boo," said Nils softly, and she jumped.

"You sneak!"

"Are you saying your prayers to the ceiling or calling down curses?"

"I'm making a list," she said. She turned toward him, into his arm, and put her own across him and hugged him. Because she was always making lists, he didn't ask her what this one was for.

"Let's stay here all day," he mumbled against her temple. "That

would create a sensation, wouldn't it? Stand the whole place on its ear.
They'd even forget Drake."

"Maybe we should try it," she said. "You think it would work on
Jamie?"

She felt him laughing without sound. "He'd be shocked. At our age
it's indecent, didn't you know that?"

"Linnie thinks it's terrific." They kissed and lay there in comfortable
silence for a few minutes, watching the light fill the room. An engine
came to life in the harbor, and then another. Nils sighed.

"Well, this won't buy shoes for the baby or pay for the ones he's
wearing," he said. They kissed again; she gave him another hug and let
him go. They dressed quickly in the morning chill, and Nils was
downstairs first. Linnie wasn't up yet; she'd spent the evening up at the
Homestead and hadn't come home until midnight.

Pip was waiting and spoke eloquently to them. While they ate
breakfast at the small table in the sun parlor, the cat went impartially
between them, always spending just so much time on morning sociability
before he went out the back way to his own kingdom, the belt of woods
and alder thicket and the Homestead meadows where Leo and Tiger
never went.

Joanna walked down to the shore with Nils. Everyone was ready to
go by the time he was rowing out to his mooring, everybody but the
seining crew. They'd go out to haul later, after they'd had some sleep.

Nils towed the skiff in again for her to use later if she wanted it; she
might go rowing when it had warmed up and dried up a bit. She waited
until he had turned the boat away from the wharf and headed toward the
harbor mouth. They waved, and as she left the wharf, Hank sailed past
her head and flew up onto the Binnacle roof to wait for the first Dinsmore
child to come out.

Sam, short, stocky, round-headed, clumped down his front steps
with his rubber boots hauled up to his hips. Liza came out on the porch
behind him. "Have you got your license?"

"Ayuh!" He touched his hip pocket. "Hi, Aunt Jo!" He headed for
Philip's wharf, always on the run even in his boots.

Liza shook her head fondly. Joanna said, "He's in for a disappointment. Linnie isn't up yet."

"Oh, well, there's always tomorrow. Lord, it's so quiet around here
without him, and when he's home, I feel as if I'm trying to keep up with
quadruplets. He's wonderful. . . . Coming in for a cup of coffee?"

"No, thanks. I'm walking off my breakfast." Joanna went on past the beach to the big anchor half sunk in the marsh, and followed the spongy black path through the field toward the schoolhouse. In a few hours school would be in session. In the meantime, the small white building was like a hopeful little entity waiting for the flow of life to return to it. The wet white clapboards took on the tints of the sunrise, like the gulls' breasts. She crossed the yard, passed the island-made swings and jungle gym, and went over the seawall and down into Schoolhouse Cove.

The tide wasn't quite up, and sandpipers ran in and out of scallops of foam edged with the fine lace of the light surf. Joanna was at once beatifically relaxed and full of enthusiasm for the day ahead. The sea was so flat that, as the islanders said, you could roll a marble all the way to Spain.

She left the beach at the western end of the seawall, where rugosa roses grew in great thickets, rooted in sandy soil, surviving winter gales and spray. A few were open, a deep rose color and heavily fragrant. She poked her nose into a yellow-powdered heart and breathed deeply with her eyes shut.

Then she heard an engine coming instead of going, and she knew it was none of the island's boats. By the time she reached the anchor, the blue boat had arrived at her own wharf. The traps on the washboards on either side, as well as on the broad stern, obscured the activities in the cockpit, but she saw Willy, in his old hat and surplus army fatigues, come up onto the wharf and make bow and stern lines fast. Then he went to the head of the ladder and began lifting off some of the big four-headers and swinging them over to one side. He had always been surprisingly strong for his size.

Joanna was about to walk on toward home when she saw the woman going up the few exposed rungs, with Drake close behind her. Willy smiled nervously under his floppy brim as he reached out to half-lift her onto the wharf. She wore a long full cloak of some dark material, with a hood dropped back; her hair was a flyaway bush of bright auburn, which, as the sun struck it, flamed like fire. Beside that, the Percy red hair was dull as ancient rust.

She stood looking around her; her face seemed very narrow and pale between the dark cloak and the fiery hair. She put up a hand to shade her eyes.

Had he got his wife to come out and take a look at the place which, according to Duke, she'd paid for? And where was Kathy, for heaven's sake? Why wasn't the dog out, sounding off to the sky by now? Joanna could only hope that Kathy was an invisible but intense spectator at a front window.

Drake had gone back aboard, and now he handed up to Willy three matched pieces of maroon luggage. Then he joined the woman on the wharf. She took the little case, he took the next size, and with his free hand under her elbow he walked her up the wharf. Willy slid down into the boat, and cartons and water containers began to appear on the wharf.

It was the woman, gazing all around her as she walked, who saw Joanna across the milky blue loop of high tide filling up the curve of the beach. She spoke to Drake, who stopped so suddenly Joanna guessed he was startled; he'd been acting as if he and the woman were all alone in the world.

He spoke over his shoulder, and Willy popped up on the wharf with a folding chair, which he snapped open with a flourish, and the woman sat down on it. Drake came springily around the beach to the anchor. He took off the Greek fisherman's cap, and his unshaded smile was so broad it gave the impression of reaching her before he did.

"You're just the person I wanted to see!" Somehow he was squeezing her hand and she didn't remember giving it to him. "I'd have come around to your house if you hadn't been here."

She didn't believe a word of it. "Why?" she asked agreeably.

"I wanted to explain about this young woman I've brought out. She's been through a very rough time, and she needs complete peace and solitude." He turned properly somber. "I know island people are very friendly, but she isn't ready for that. Maybe you could, uh, make it clear?" He was still holding her hand.

"I thought you'd coaxed your wife out for a day."

"Oh, no, no! Just a tenant for the summer, or however long it takes her to recover." He studied the ground, shaking his head and sighing. "*Gifted* young woman. *Brilliant.* Partner in a decorating business in Boston. She had a traumatic experience up there, and if she can't make herself go back, it may have destroyed her whole career."

Rape. You heard the word too often these days. "Well, an island summer can be healing," Joanna said, "and I'm sure everyone will respect her privacy."

"I got her out here early, so she could arrive invisibly, if you follow me." He was still holding her hand.

"I'm sorry I spoiled that."

"But you're the right one, you see!" He pressed her fingers again. "Her name is Susanna Baird—I wanted you to know that—but she won't need anything, so you don't have to give her a thought. I'll bring out everything, even drinking water, when I come out to haul."

"As long as she isn't nervous about being alone. Some people are really thrown off by the island nights. No streetlights, just the breakwater beacon."

"She'll love it. It was the city that nearly did her in."

"All right, then," said Joanna, trying politely to get her hand back. "I'll pass the word around that the kindest thing we can do for her is to leave her alone."

"Thank you, thank you!" He tucked his cap under one arm so he could make it a two-handed grip. "The Bennetts must be very special people if you're a sample. She'll be so *grateful.*" But she's not to have a chance to tell me herself, Joanna thought, while her hand wriggled in futile motions toward freedom. She was tempted to ask him if he wanted the Bartons and Campions to detour along the back path and out around the schoolhouse instead of walking past the house, but she was afraid he wouldn't recognize sarcasm.

She said, "I must be going."

"Yes, of course," he said eagerly. "So must I. Thank you." He gave her hand another squeeze. With a quick widening of his smile he turned and went back at a brisk military clip. She walked on to Philip's.

"I'll take that coffee now," she announced. "I need it."

Liza was having a tranquil breakfast. Leo, the large yellow cat, sat in a chair beside her, having bits of bran muffin. Liza put her book away, poured fresh coffee for Joanna, and put warm muffins on a blue willow plate.

"Did I see a third and female party hatch from the robin's-egg?" she asked.

"You sure did. He made a special trip around the shore to tell me she's his tenant for the summer, she's getting over something very bad, and she needs to be completely ignored. God knows what hideous thing could have happened to her. But that man sets my teeth on edge."

"I know. Just short of smarmy."

"His smile opens and shuts as if he's got all these automatic settings for it." Joanna lifted her hand and examined it back and front. "I thought I'd lost it forever. First he reminded me of a big eager dog; now I think *he* thinks he's irresistible. However, I wasn't asked to meet her even if I *am* one of those very special Bennetts. I was just asked to keep people away."

At times Liza's oval face had the other-world serenity of a Madonna in an old Italian painting. Dreamily she said, "I wonder if she's the Drake's duck."

"That never occurred to me!" Joanna protested. "What I did think, when he mentioned a traumatic experience in Boston, was that she might have been raped."

"Well, I hope it isn't that," said Liza. "Maybe it's a messy divorce. Or . . . listen, excuse my dirty mind, but wouldn't this be a great place to stash a mistress?"

"Now *that* sounds dirty," said Joanna. "Like something you can do anywhere, you don't have to come to an island for it. A motel room would do."

"That man gets richer in every story they've been passing around on their boat radios," said Liza. "You know how they gossip."

"According to what Duke told Linnie, the money comes from his wife. This is Duke's story, remember, so I'm not repeating it as gospel. The wife is good-looking, too. At least Duke thinks so. Built like a brick you-know-what, as my daughter tells me, to spare my old ears."

"How nice for Felix," said Liza sedately. "A rich wife and a handsome one. But even so, he could still appreciate a new duck. It's a holdover from my days on the magazine. You never knew who was sleeping with who—whom—so there were lots of guessing games all the time."

"Well, I don't care if he has a harem," said Joanna. "We've all wasted too much time on him. My son is the worst. Talk about paranoia!" She chucked Leo under the chin, and he gave her a languorous look, a miniature lion half-drowsing in the sun on the veldt. "We aren't going to waste the summer on him, are we, Leo? It's too short to foul up even one day of it."

"'And summer's lease hath all too short a date,'" said Liza. "Practically the only thing I can remember from high school Shakespeare except for 'Is this a dagger which I see before me' and 'To be or not to be.' . . . What does she look like? I saw that gorgeous hair."

"I couldn't tell about her looks, except that her face is thin and pale. You know that white skin some redheads have. Her name's Susanna

Baird, and she is partner in a decorating business in Boston." She got up. "If I don't go home right now, I'll hate my morning chores even more than I do."

Liza walked onto the porch with her, and they stood looking out over the harbor, quiet again after the early-morning surge except for the fishing ospreys. "I'll pass on what he said," Joanna said. "But it might be she'd appreciate someone like Kathy, after she's had some isolation. Anyway, if she pokes her head out of doors, somebody's bound to speak to her. I can't stop that."

"How do you suppose he got her all the way into the house before Kathy could bounce out, coffeepot at the ready?" Across the harbor Drake's engine started up. Liza said with appreciation, "I can tell a good engine when I hear it. That's a lovely one."

"Probably a Rolls-Royce," said Joanna. The blue boat moved gracefully across the harbor with her stacked traps. "I wonder what he does if a gull drops something on that paint. Probably sends Willy up *at once* to scrub it off. Thanks for the mug-up, Liza."

The rest of the island was stirring; she heard children's voices in the Dinsmore house, and Tiger was out sniffing frantically through the grass as if something wild had passed by in the night. He gave Joanna a preoccupied wag. Hank sidled from one end of the ridgepole to the other, watching for his foster mothers.

As she approached her house, she smelled bacon. Jamie was getting breakfast for himself, attended by the cat, who wound around his legs, emitting long, impassioned cries.

"Morning!" said Jamie heartily. "I hope you don't mind. My cupboard was bare."

"My cupboard is your cupboard."

He put his eggs and bacon on a plate, carried it to the sun parlor table, and went back for coffee and toast. "Want some?"

"No, thanks. I've just had a mug-up with Liza." She sat down at the table with him. He did look at peace with himself and the world this morning, and there could be only one reason.

"How'd you do last night?" she asked.

"Stavin'." He broke off bacon for Pip. "Watch those claws, old stocking. We stopped off Goose Cove. We're guessing at about eight thousand bushels. The carrier's coming out, but we can fill everybody's orders, too."

"Jamie, I'm so glad," she said from the heart. By her euphoria she realized how contagious Jamie's tensions were; there were all sorts of bonds, not especially comforting ones, between a child and even a nonpossessive parent. And wasn't it astonishing how his disposition could improve overnight because he'd found herring? She sat with her chin on her hand, trying not to watch him too obviously; she kept shifting her gaze toward yellow warblers fluttering around in the lilac bush, but she was taking in the way his hair grew back from his temples in sun-bleached little whorls and the blueness of his eyes when he looked up at her. She admired his eyebrows and the neat shape of his nose, like Nils's, not the big Bennett one, and the beautiful cut of his mouth when he was composed.

Sometimes she tried to imagine herself with five sons, and her admiration for her mother had grown every year until it was reverence. What must have saved her parents' reason many a time was the fact that Philip and Steve had more equable temperaments than the other three. Philip said he was quiet because there was no use trying to compete with Charles's lungs; Steve claimed that his disposition came from being at the bottom of the heap. "I never wanted to call attention to myself," he said. "Somebody was likely to give me an order."

But he'd been nobody's shadow, any more than Philip had been; each balanced a stormy brother, who was his closest friend. Owen was the middle one, the singleton who'd had no counterweight, and had given himself and everybody else the most trouble of all.

"So the prince is back," Jamie said, startling her. "With more gear."

"Aye-up! And he's rented the house for the summer. We now have our first official summer complaint. A very quiet, shy lady who needs to be quiet because she's getting over some awful experience."

"How come you know all this?" He stopped eating to stare at her with aggressive surprise. "You actually had a cozy chat with that"— visibly he changed course—"that character?" Even Jamie must get tired of saying son of a bitch or horse's arse, she thought.

"I did," she said. "He had to explain the situation because there I was in full view by the anchor, watching him set her and her dunnage ashore. She's to have no company, and he'll bring out everything she needs."

"So he's renting the place," Jamie said with bleak satisfaction. Pip, hanging on to his knee and searching his face, was ignored. He wailed, and Joanna took a piece of bacon from Jamie's plate and gave it to the cat; but even this didn't break up Jamie's concentration. The good herring catch was now forgotten.

"It's the truth, he's using this island like a whore," Jamie said. "He'll keep on renting the house for an arm and a leg, and he'll make himself a good handful of money catching lobsters that belong to us. That's all the island means to him." He didn't raise his voice. "And we're just a bunch of peasants who had to fit ourselves out for a damned expensive business. Some of us are up to our necks in debt—a bad year could drown us; we need every dollar we can get." He shoved away from the table and stood up so abruptly that his chair fell backward. Pip scampered, but not far.

"He turns my stomach! I can just hear him bragging to his friends—if he's got any—about this goddamn rugged place he's discovered and got a foothold in. Jesus, I'd like to get him down and ram his mouth full of herring so rotten the gulls wouldn't touch it!"

"Jamie, *shut up!*" said Joanna. "Just listen to yourself! *Just listen to yourself!* And you're as red as a boiled lobster. Now you stop working yourself up into conniptions about this man. I agree with you about him, everybody does, but nobody's so close to ruin out here that what he catches this summer is going to tip anybody over the edge. If he suspected that you were going into the high fantods every time he showed up in the harbor, he'd be laughing himself foolish. Now you just remember *that* and get on with your own life. Start thinking about your own future, and stop turning into a fussbudget or worse."

"Worse?" He cocked an eyebrow at her, looking uncannily like his uncle Owen.

"Yes. If you don't mend your ways, nobody'll be able to stand you in another five years. People'll dodge when they see you coming."

He went absolutely blank, as if he'd gone into hiding behind his face, and she was sorry for that. She warmed and slowed her voice. "Jamie, you're letting that man get the better of you already, and it's nothing to do with how many lobsters he catches or if he rents the house. I hate to see you like this."

"Like what?" Very slightly he smiled. "Listen, Ma—" That was deliberate, because he knew she hated it. "I'm not alone in this, you know."

"We all feel the same way about the man. But think about what I said. Don't give him power over you."

"You forgot to say something else."

"What?"

The corner of his mouth curled up even more. "'I'm not your Ma!'"

"I wish you weren't too big to take a lath to!" But she had to laugh. "I'm getting out of this house and going for a good long row." On her way for a jacket she lightly cuffed his head, and he looked around at her with a challenging grin, sat down, and began to finish his meal.

8

Felix Drake and Willy had slept two nights aboard his boat, hauled around once, and had gone back to the mainland. Everybody who had bought herring from the seiners had it already salted away in the butts, and in an early-afternoon lull Rosa and Linnie were alone at the shore, baiting up. Everyone else was still out, except Barry Barton, who had caught a kink in his back and was doing light chores around his fish house. The village was abnormally quiet; it was the last day of school, and the students, the teacher, and several mothers had gone to Sou'west Point for an all-day picnic. The high schoolers had joined the party.

Except for occasional sightings of Barry on his wharf, there were no signs of life on that side of the harbor. The Foss Campion house looked vacant, all shades drawn as Helen had left them; she was always afraid of the sun's fading something, and the house had been sold furnished.

The day was mysteriously suspended in crystal, a weather-breeder. The sea lay cerulean to the deep violet line of the western horizon. Brigport, eight miles of green fields, dark spruce forest, and marble-pale rock, seemed to float as lightly on the ocean as foam on a wave. High over the waters between the islands the three ospreys drifted on black wings. A few shags were fishing; others perched on a ledge off Eastern Harbor Point, holding their wings out to dry. But the noisy, speedy medricks were absent.

Linnie tossed Hank a herring. "And that's the last one today," she told him as he gobbled it. "I can't afford this. I have to pay for my bait, you know. My brother is tighter than the bark to a tree. I'll bet *he* never gives you anything."

"I've seen him do it a couple of times when he thought nobody was looking," said Rosa. "Sort of sneaked it."

"He must be afraid of spoiling his image."

Talking about Jamie, even foolishly, was becoming difficult. Rosa was finding it hard to say his name in a normal tone of voice, though she knew no one else noticed. She kept expecting that even saying "he" or "him" would send her voice tremulous and cracking like an adolescent boy's. She forced it now. "Doesn't he even give you a family discount?"

"With the Scandinavian Scrooge, money's thicker than blood any time." Linnie stood in the bait shed doorway; she wore a long oilskin apron over her jeans and jersey, and her fair hair was pinned up on top of her head. "Hey, does he give *you* a rake-off? Or a bushel of free herring now and then, the way mainland guys who aren't skinflints take their girls out to dinner?"

"Are you kidding? I'm not his girl. That's everybody else's fantasy."

"I thought so," said Linnie grimly. "He'll probably have his kids working for their board and room by the time they're three. After they finish paying for the doctor, that is."

Hank lifted off with a great flap and wind of wings to scream warnings at two gulls flying over, and then hurried back to where he could guard both bait sheds. Linnie dropped a pail on a rope overboard, hoisted it up half full, and scrubbed her hands with yellow soap.

"Well, all the excitement about Sir Francis Drake died out fast, didn't it?" she said. "Except with Jamie, that is. Hugo can't stop thinking about women long enough to stay mad, and Matt's got Carol and the baby. Jamie ought to be married."

She stopped, but Rosa refused to break the silence or even look around. You're a free woman now, old sock, she told herself, so start breathing like one. Let her wait till hell freezes over.

Linnie resumed so briskly it was almost funny. "Of course, if he's really lucky, Drake will get snarled with him so he can have an excuse to cut off a few traps. You know, when my mother was a girl, all my uncles were wild as hawks. There was some activity around here then. It's an awful tame bunch now."

"Don't sound so envious," said Rosa. "You're tempting Providence."

The crystal was shattered by the boat coming fast past Brigport on a straight course for the harbor. The flared dark bow reared aggressively between two arcs of white water.

"Now what?" Linnie said, looking and sounding like Jamie.

"Drake has some little friends," Rosa suggested.

"They're going to shoot in here like a—a torpedo or something! Gorm!" she yelled between cupped hands. "Chowderhead! You come into this harbor like that, brother, and I'll—"

"Always the perfect lady," said Rosa.

"But they make me so mad! The minute everything's perfect, some stupid pea-brained lowlife has to destroy it, and they don't give a damn!"

The last word was a shout rising through silence; the engine had suddenly shut down just off the breakwater, and the boat came quietly in. She was a large, heavy, lobster boat of the distinctive Nova Scotia build, broad-beamed, with a high bow dropping back to low sides and stern. She was painted dark red with buff decks and house and had a dark red dory in tow. She was not elegant like *Drake's Pride*, but she was strong and seaworthy. Her name stood out in large white letters on either side of her bow: *Sweet Helen*.

Her house roof carried the usual electrical equipment, and the regulation potbuoy for identification was wine and buff like the boat herself, in broad vertical stripes.

She moved slowly toward Mark's wharf; there were two men aboard. "Well, she's not carrying traps," said Rosa, "so I don't think this one is moving in. Maybe they're short of gas."

"*Sweet Helen*," Linnie murmured. "That's pretty. Sounds familiar, doesn't it?"

"Not to me."

No one was moving around the long wharf under Western Harbor Point, where the big lobster car with the scales and a few dry crates identified the heart of the island's business. Mark would be up at the house, having his dinner nap, to which he never admitted, and the store would be closed until two.

Suddenly the man at the wheel caught sight of the women and turned the wheel. The high bow came around, and *Sweet Helen* headed for the Sorensen wharf.

"Here they come," said Linnie. "Well, I suppose somebody has to answer their foolish questions."

"And find out who those stupid pea-brained lowlifes are. Besides being gorms and chowderheads, that is."

Linnie grinned. "Sounded just like my brother, didn't I? I'd better watch it." She pulled the pins out of her topknot with one hand while the other felt for the comb in her hip pocket. She stepped back into the bait shed, combed her hair, and came out again with it tumbling softly to her shoulders just as *Sweet Helen* slid murmurously along the spilings.

The man at the wheel halted the boat by hooking his gaff over a rung of the ladder. The other one walked up on the washboard to the bow, which set him eye to eye with Linnie.

"Hi!" she said sociably. "I like the name of your boat."

"Thanks, dear," said the man at the wheel. "I like the reception committee." He had reddish hair and beard, short and curly. His broad face was young, deeply dimpled in each cheek; as his eyes moved from Linnie across the gap to Rosa on the other wharf, the dimples deepened, and his eyes nearly disappeared behind thick reddish lashes. "Holy mackerel, it gets better 'n' better!"

The slim dark man standing on the bow was silent as a shadow through this. Now he said in a quick soft voice, "Where can we find the harbormaster?"

"He's probably taking a nap," Linnie said, "but there's the deputy. Old Hank up there." She pointed at the gull watching them from the bait shed roof. The man at the wheel grinned.

"Check us over, will he? Look at our documents and all?" He was burly in bib overalls over thick freckled shoulders and red-furry chest. "Watches out for smuggling, too? Say, can he sniff out dope, like one of them police dogs?"

He shook with laughter at this, and Linnie said, "He's so good he ought to have an official cap, but his head's too small." She began laughing herself, and in the midst of this the man on the bow was immobile, gazing at nothing, his lips tight. He was lean to near gauntness, very dark, with prominent cheekbones and a humped nose. His face narrowed down to the thin mouth and long jaw. Straight black hair fell across his forehead and untidily about his ears. His eyes were deep-set and looked coaly black; Rosa remembered Gypsies coming through Seal Harbor one year, she had talked with one at the door and noticed the same dead blackness that seemed to give nothing back.

He said without raising his voice, "What do we do about picking up a mooring? Or don't you people let strangers in?"

"Usually we have an armed patrol boat guarding the harbor mouth," said Linnie, "and if anybody did slip in, well, the harbor's mined. But since you made it this far without blowing up, take the mooring nearest the breakwater, the one with the orange buoy. It belongs to Mark Bennett. You can talk to him at the store after two."

As he ran back along the washboard and jumped down into the cockpit, his friend said winningly, "Thanks, dear. What's your name?"

Linnie smiled back at him. "Who wants to know?"

The dark one said, "Come on, let's get tied up and ashore."

"Roy and Pitt Bainbridge, dear," Redbeard said. "We're Selina Bainbridge's brothers. He's Pitt." Jerk of the thumb. "William Pitt Bainbridge. Now ain't that a corker? With a name like that he'd ought to be a politician, but he ain't got the manner for it."

"Somehow I guessed that," said Linnie. "I'd never hand him a baby to kiss. He'd probably bite its ear off. I'm Linnea Sorensen, and this is Rosa Fleming."

"Linnea and Rosa," he repeated. "That's some pretty. Sounds like a bokay. Where's my sister live, dear?"

"I think you've got the wrong island," Rosa said.

"To hell with this," said the dark brother. "There ought to be somebody who'll talk straight."

"She's talking straight," said Linnie haughtily. "There's no Selina Bainbridge. We never heard the name before in our lives."

He turned his back on them and stood staring across the harbor. Roy looked entertained. "You ever met up with a feller named Drake?"

"Oh, him. Yup."

"Well, he's got a—I guess you'd call it a tenant, hasn't he?"

S. B., Rosa thought. Simultaneously Linnie exclaimed as if just discovering gravity or electricity, "Susanna Baird your sister?"

"If she's got red hair, she is, dear."

"Nobody else has seen her but my mother," said Linnie, "but she's got red hair all right."

"That's my Sheena!" Roy said. "Susanna Baird? My, oh my." He gave Pitt a nudge in the ribs. Pitt didn't turn his head, and Rosa thought, That is a furious man.

Linnie was pointing out the house to Roy and the mooring that went with it; Drake's skiff was fastened there. "Thanks, dear," Roy said affectionately. "I guess we can tie up at the wharf a spell before we have to put her on the mooring. Deep water there?"

"Plenty," said Linnie. He lifted a meaty hand as if conferring a blessing. The boat backed away from the wharf and then headed slowly across the harbor. "*Sweet Helen, Coates Cove,*" Linnie read off the stern. "I wonder what 'My, oh my' means."

"How about those rosy cheeks and those dimples and the way he uses them?" asked Rosa.

"I don't know, de-ah. But at least he's got manners." She watched them tying up at the Campion wharf. "The other one— Pitt is the right name for him. Black as the pit. He acted as if he had to brace himself before I climbed aboard him. What makes him think he's so desirable that any woman who's just ordinarily friendly and polite is burning with lust for him?"

Rosa looked at her with surprise, and Linnie colored and gave her a sheepish grin. "My God, the way I'm reacting you'd think I *was* on fire for him. And he probably isn't all there. He doesn't even know how to carry on a decent conversation."

"Well, we've found out that the Lady of Shalott isn't somebody exotic from faraway Boston. At least she started out in Maine. Selina Bainbridge. What a name! Sounds like a Gothic novel."

"Listen," said Linnie. "Cindy and Robin are half-convinced now that she's an honest-to-God heroine in hiding from a murderer or sadistic guardian, and that name'll prove it to them."

The men were walking up the wharf, each carrying a carton. Roy rolled along as if he were on a streaming deck in a gale. "The bear that walks like a man," said Linnie. Pitt was a neat, dark, attenuated shape behind him. Because of the school picnic, not even the Campion dog was at home on that side to see them, and Barry had gone back into his house, presumably to rest his lame back.

Not a curtain twitched in the Foss Campion house. The brothers went around to the side yard, which was mostly ledge with pockets of grass and daisies, to the kitchen door. They didn't seem to knock, just simply disappeared inside.

"Oh, fiddle," Linnie said in disgust. "I thought maybe she'd rush out and throw herself into their arms."

"Maybe she saw them coming and she's hiding in a closet. Maybe she wanted to get away to get over her troubles in private."

"That sounds from the heart," Linnie said.

"It is," Rosa said.

Linnie was embarrassed, which wasn't characteristic. "I've never set eyes on Conall Fleming, and I don't know how you feel about him now; but I know I'm glad you came to Bennett's Island. And right now you have something on your mind, I can tell, and I'm not being nosy."

"Yes, you are," said Rosa. "You're the nosiest critter on God's green earth. After Kathy." They both laughed, and she returned to her own baiting up, but Linnie persistently talked to her back.

"You do have things on your mind, though. Your aura's different."

"Have you been talking to Maggie? Why don't you consult her Ouija board?"

"Come on, tell me," Linnie urged. "What are friends for? Besides, I'm practically a relative. You're closer to our family than to anybody else on here, so admit it."

"Well, with the Bennetts and Sorensens being about ninety percent of the population, I don't have much choice, do I? You'd better see what Hank's doing in the bait shed."

Linnie shooed the gull out, each squawking at the other, and shut the bait shed door. "Oh, come on," she urged. "All I started to say was that anytime you want to talk about something, I'm a good listener, and I know how to keep my mouth shut, even if nobody else believes it."

"Thank you," Rosa said without sarcasm.

"Hey, it's not Lillebror, is it?"

Rosa expected her hands to shake, but they went on working without a tremble. "I thought you weren't calling him that anymore. Since he isn't your little brother."

"I know, but it's such a pretty word. And speak of the devil, there he comes past the breakwater."

Rosa just managed not to look around. "Well, I'm about done for the day," she said, as if she hadn't heard. "And believe me, it's been a long one. I wake up with the dawn chorus, of which Ralph Percy is the loudest whistler." She took off her long oilskin apron and wiped her hands on an old shirt kept there for the purpose. "I guess I'll go home and scrub up. I never get a good lather with salt water."

You're talking too much, she thought. Just *go*. . . . Could there really be such a thing as an aura?

Behind her Linnie whooped with joy. "Oh boy, I can't wait for this! He sees *Sweet Helen*. He can't take his eyes off her!"

If she ran now, which her body was straining to do, she'd give herself away to Linnie. She drew up a pail of salt water after all, sat on a crate, and worked away with yellow soap and a nailbrush. *Valkyrie* was heading straight for her home wharf, everything rocking in her wake. Busily scrubbing, Rosa said, "Well, at least this boat doesn't say she's from Bennett's Island."

"No, but she's *here* and connected with Drake. Oh, brother, I can see the blue lightning!" *Sea Star* was rolling now, and Linnie's little *Dovekie* wildly cavorting, and Linnie shouted, "Hey, watch it, Sorensen!"

9

*E*ric Marshall leaned out from under the canopy and waved his old school baseball cap at the girls.

The side of the boat thudded against the ladder, and Jamie was up on the washboard at once.

"Who's *that?*" Thumb over his shoulder and a backward jerk of his head. His eyes accused them both of conspiracies. Rosa stood up and emptied the pail off the far side of her wharf.

"Gee, I hate to be the one to tell you guys this," said Linnie, "but the Russians came in that there vessel. Quite a few, but they're a lot smaller than you'd expect."

Jamie blew hard through his nose and slitted his eyes at her. "Are you sure they're Russians?" Eric asked. "They could be Evonians. In fact there's a strong theory—very hush-hush, of course—that most Russians *are* Evonians by now. Evonia's way out there beyond Venus, so it took the first colonists some years to get here. There's a big hole in Siberia where their spaceship landed."

"Ah, Evonia!" Linnie clasped her hands to her breast. "The homeland beyond the stars!"

"They probably keep trying to get back there," said Rosa.

"Like salmon going up the river to spawn," Eric said.

"All right, you three smart-arses," said Jamie. "Who the hell is it? If Drake's sending out hired fishermen—"

"Oh, relax, Lil—lovey," said Linnie. "They're the Lady of Shalott's brothers, and they dropped in to bring her a few groceries. It just dawned on me," she added brightly. "Maybe she's a drunk or a drug addict, and she's trying to go cold turkey."

"Ayuh." Jamie was cynical. "They just dropped in to take a good look around. They'd better not show up here next time with a load of gear. Drake's shore privilege means just him. They might all have to find out the hard way."

"Doesn't change much, does he?" said Eric fondly. "God help us all if the old Viking in him ever takes charge."

"I'm giving serious thought to it," said Jamie. The ice had gone out. "We need a little blood-and-guts excitement around here."

"Just what I've been saying," said Linnie.

"Listen, they're agreeing!" Eric said to Rosa. "Make a mark on the stovepipe!"

"You going to the car with me or not?" Jamie asked Eric.

"When I signed on for this voyage, I swore to go to the end with you, Captain Ahab. Sail on!"

"Make us a pot of coffee, Lin," Jamie called as *Valkyrie* backed away.

"Who was your slave last year?" she retorted. "I'll make a pot of coffee because Father's at the car, but he'll likely let you have a cup." He put a hand behind his ear and pantomimed deafness.

"That one," she said to Rosa. "He can make me so mad, and then he makes me laugh. And last year he made me cry. What a critter. Come on home with me, Rosa. You could drink a cup of real coffeepot coffee and eat a molasses doughnut, couldn't you?"

"Mm," said Rosa. *Coward.* But she shouldn't make an issue of it before the family.

Liza Bennett was reading in the hammock on her front porch and spoke to them, but they saw no one else as they walked up to the Sorensen house; Maggie Dinsmore and the girls and Tiger all had gone to the picnic.

There was no gate left to open into Gunnar Sorensen's front dooryard, only the posts. But Rory's ghost was there, stiff-legged, gray-muzzled, dim-eyed, the collie tail welcoming. Rosa felt a prickling in her nose and eyes, and there was a small sniff from Linnie. Then Pip raced toward them, a black-and-white streak, and Linnie swung him up over her shoulder where he clung to her jersey, smelling at her hair and then blinking his speckled eyes amorously at Rosa.

"Hello, Pip," she said, and he at once leaned toward her to be taken.

In her arms his lean body vibrated with the force of his purr. I could get me a cat, she thought. Something to hug.

Joanna wasn't home. Linnie put doughnuts in the gas oven to warm, and a teakettle of water on to boil, and Rosa was carrying mugs and spoons out to the sun parlor when she saw Jamie coming. He stopped next door, kicked off his boots and left them on the back doorstep, and went inside. It still wasn't too late for her to go, but she stayed, folding paper napkins as if for a real meal. Linnie and Pip were saying, "We-e-ell?" to each other in identical tones.

When Jamie crossed the yard, he had washed up, combed his hair, put on a clean T-shirt, slacks, and moccasins; he looked all dressed up, and she knew just how his skin and hair would smell.

Why weren't you slammed amidships by some quality of character rather than the color of someone's eyes and the way he carried his head? Yes, and smelled, so you wanted to breathe it in like Pip. Con's beauty, or what had been beauty to her, had tormented her long after she had discovered just what he was. Quint, buried in her head and seldom disinterred, had been warm brown life in her arms. She'd known what he was, too, in a very short time. But any revulsion she felt now was for her own stupidity. Men were simply what they were, she was what she was, and she had finally forgiven herself her weaknesses. No one, least of all God, expected you to go on flagellating yourself forever.

There was no comparing Jamie to those two. But her acceptance of the situation between them, which perhaps wasn't even a situation to him, bore a family resemblance to the other acceptances. And she was not the same woman now; there should be no compulsion to degrade herself by snatching at crumbs.

"Where's Father?" Linnie called from the kitchen.

"Barry Barton held him up. Little man's talking about a new boat and wants advice. He's been asking everybody, and now it's the old man's turn. Eric's gone off somewhere." At the sound of his voice Pip ran out to him, and he picked the cat up and slung him around his neck like a scarf.

"Eric's got something on his mind," said Linnie, coming in with the coffeepot and a plate of doughnuts.

"Yeah, and don't be asking what it is."

"What do you think I am? Stupid?"

"Yep," said Jamie.

"You want this coffee in your cup or over your head?" They all sat down at the table, Jamie with the cat still lying around his neck, vibrating noisily and trying to reach the doughnuts. Rosa wished she hadn't come. She felt as timid and flustered as she'd ever felt in her green youth, but she knew she didn't act or look it. Now if only Linnie had forgotten about her damned auras.

"It gowels me right to the bone, thinking of those strangers across the harbor," he said.

"Don't be so xenophobic," said Linnie loftily.

"How long you been waiting to use that word, turdheels?"

"Ever since I first discovered it and thought, That's the perfect word for my darling brother."

"Fancy name for being a suspicious bastard, huh?"

"Don't be so smug about it," Linnie said.

"Well, somebody has to be suspicious around here. Tell me about those guys."

"Pitt and Roy Bainbridge. Pitt's the strong silent type like you; Roy's the charmer."

"He charm *you?*" Pip batted at the doughnut in Jamie's hand. He lifted the cat off his neck to the floor and gave him a piece of the doughnut.

"If he did, I know better than to tell you. Besides, it was Rosa he kept looking at." She was meticulously offhand. "Couldn't keep his eyes off her—"

"I hope they don't think they can make this their base just because their sister's out here."

Linnie put her chin in her hands and stared at him. "You really are a xenophobe, you know that? I don't know how you ever got along in the Navy, the way you suspect everybody you haven't known since you were two. You even thought I was an impostor when they brought me home. You said, 'What's *that* doing in our family?' It's a wonder I wasn't permanently marked by it."

"Bullshit," said Jamie. She threw a piece of doughnut at him. It fell on the floor, and Pip pounced on it. "What I said was the truth. 'No more peace and quiet around *here.*' I was ready to move out."

"It took you long enough to leave the nest. Most men are married and have a family started by your age. If you and Hugo want to hold on to this island, you'd better start thinking about your posterity."

"It's taken you so long to grow up I can't see cluttering up my life with another kid."

"Lucky for the kid," said Linnie. "With you for a father he might as well be an orphan."

Rosa felt as if the doughnut she'd eaten was about to make her sick. She drank half a mug of very hot coffee too fast, and the result took her mind off nausea.

"These fellers young?" Jamie asked.

"These fellers young," said Linnie. "I hope they come often to check on sister Sheena. The only males on the island to follow me around are Sam and Richard, and apart from being my cousins they're only fourteenish."

Jamie pushed back his chair, and she said, "You don't have to rush across the harbor now and hew the Bainbridges down with one sweep of your battle-ax. I wasn't thinking about nookin' and knollin'. Not yet."

"I'm getting cold water for my coffee," he said. "And if you want to make a goddamn fool of yourself, that's your privilege." He went into the kitchen.

"Gee, sport, that's generous of you." She winked at Rosa. "But I'm not looking for anybody to make a fool of myself about," she called after him. "I just thought it would be nice to be walked home from the dances by someone who wasn't a relative. And who's grown-up."

He didn't answer, and Rosa wondered what she had never stopped wondering: if Eloise was a destructive parasite in his blood. After a moment he said, "Here comes the old man."

The moon was growing, so the seiners did not go out that night, but Jamie didn't come up. Rosa was angry with herself for being sleepless. She had wanted it to go one way or the other, no mistaking it, hadn't she? Well, it had happened. But she'd planned to do the saying, not to be dropped like a tool that had permanently lost its edge, or an old skiff beyond repair, hauled up to die in the beach peas and sow thistles.

She got up finally, dressed, and went out for a walk. It was after midnight, and the village was asleep, the boats like passive dreaming beasts in a pasture. *Sweet Helen* was out on Drake's mooring, her tender astern. There was a light in the cabin. So the brothers weren't sleeping in the house. The moon's light was dull and deceptive, not really bright yet, but not dark enough for the stars all to show. She liked starlight the best. There was something weird about moonlight; you had to keep reminding yourself that day would come and the familiar would safely return, because you could hardly imagine there had ever been anything else but this dead white light.

She walked along the path toward the school, making no sound on the soft marshy earth. She was considering whether to go out on Windward Point by walking the road to Hillside Farm first, or to go down into Schoolhouse Cove and follow the shore around, when she thought she saw someone sitting on one of the swings in the schoolyard.

It startled her heart into a violent beating, but in the next instant she muttered, "Optical illusion." An odd one; no matter how she stood, she couldn't recapture it. She hurried forward and found the swing moving in a windless night, and the seat was still faintly warm. She walked to the back of the schoolhouse, and looked into the tunnel of the lane that led through spruces behind the houses on that side of the harbor. She sensed movement deep within it.

So the Lady of Shalott left her loom and crept out of her tower at night. Rosa was positive of it, and sorry she'd frightened her and spoiled her walk. Maybe she'd been looking forward all day to having the island to herself, coming out here to Schoolhouse Cove as Rosa had come, away from houses and the atmosphere of other people.

We could have gotten together, Rosa thought with irony. Two lost souls comparing stories. Then she was repelled by her self-pity. Only God and Felix Drake knew what this woman had been through. It could be ghastly enough so that in comparison an indifferent male was nothing at all, a bruise you'd get over, a disappointment you'd survive.

She walked quickly home through the sleeping village. She took off her dew-soaked sneakers and socks and rubbed her feet warm. Please don't let me be sorry for myself anymore, she said solemnly to herself as she got into bed, like a child who wants very much to be good but finds it difficult. Then she fell asleep.

10

Joanna was rowing down Long Cove at sunrise. The wind seemed to blow ninety percent of the time around Bennett's and Brigport, so she tried not to waste whatever calm there was. This dry, fine spell wasn't going to last much longer. It was a prolonged weather breeder which would end up with a grand old baister of an easterly or southeasterly. Except for the damage to gear, Joanna thought that the overture was always worth it.

She rowed in liquid fire opal as bits of sunrise caught in the gray water and flickered like flame about her oars, dripped from the lifted blades. The wooded land rising between Hillside Farm and the Eastern End was still in dense velvety shadow, but luminous mists floated over the treetops and melted away in the brightening sky. Thrushes sang deep in the woods, which in this light and this hour were like woods where she had never been, still damp and dark with leftover night.

When she was a child living in the Homestead, she had often looked out just before dawn or in the middle of the night toward the woods across Goose Cove, and imagined that these were not her trees, which she knew as individuals, but an enchanted wilderness, which each night replaced the other one between sundown and sunup. If only you could get out early enough, you'd catch the alien forest before it could vanish. The trouble was that if you walked into it, you might never come out on the other side. But who knew what you might not find deep inside?

She remembered this often; in fact, none of these things were ever forgotten. They were part of her, and most of them were pretty entertaining, but kept to herself as she'd kept them to herself back when they dominated her life.

The gulls were coming in, engines sounded in the still air. She could see Brigport boats at work to the east. But she felt happily solitary, except for a couple of sea pigeons, guillemots, off Eastern End Cove: little black-and-white birds with their bright scarlet feet clearly visible as they paddled along. Steve's boat was gone, and she briefly considered going ashore for coffee with Philippa, then decided not to break up this hour.

She rowed out around the Head through a confetti spatter of varicolored buoys. Several of Felix Drake's were there. She put him out of mind and looked up at the huge mass of the Head as she rowed. There was always a raven's nest somewhere near the Head, and she could hear the young birds. The ospreys also had a nest at the Eastern End, but she couldn't see it from far down here on the water.

Now she met the ocean swell, the sensation of great strength, gentle for the moment, lifting her up, and then the slow descent as if the sea were falling away from beneath her. Gulls rode the swells with her, and the inevitable eiders. The wet buoys flashed and dazzled in the rising sun. She saw Steve's boat rolling in the surge off the Hogshead, off to the east, and Barry Barton and Owen were out by Green Ledge. The swells were deepening, and she turned to row back. If the wind came up, the swells could begin to crest, and she didn't like following seas lifting and driving her along and hissing past her on both sides. Not when she was in a low-sided ten-foot skiff.

A perfect hour had gone by, and along with it the illusion that this was all hers. She wondered if every islander had this secret, guilty, never-admitted desire to have his own island all to himself. She knew that Jamie did.

Joanna and Nils had exercised enough control at the supper table last night to keep Felix Drake and the newly arrived Bainbridges away from the meal. It meant that Jamie was silent the whole time, and Linnie had to think of something else to talk about, obviously a hardship. After supper Hugo, Eric, and Tommy Wiley came by, and Jamie went with them to the clubhouse to play pool. She expected that he would stop off at Rosa's after the game; she wished very much that he'd marry Rosa and begin raising a family. She was afraid of his turning into an eccentric, self-centered, and always suspicious bachelor. Oh, good Lord, she thought, he's one already! How did Nils and I ever produce *that?*

Linnie had done the dishes and prepared to walk around the harbor to the Bartons' to return a book. "Want to come?" she asked.

"No, thanks," said Joanna, knowing what was expected of her. While they were getting supper on the table, Linnie had sputtered on and on about the incredible rudeness of Pitt Bainbridge. Now she was hoping for an accidental encounter to see if the same thing happened again. Joanna knew; she'd been through it all herself.

She and Nils were in bed reading when Linnie came back, and she called out a good-night and went to her room. In the morning she left the house before Joanna came downstairs; she was always hoping a very early start would give her the edge on Sam. When Joanna returned from her row, Linnie was still out, and *Sweet Helen* still rode placidly on Drake's mooring.

She went home to a fervent welcome from Pip, who'd been prowling around his private wilderness since he'd been let out at first light. They both were ready for a mug-up. She left him sleeping it off in a rocking chair, and walked to the store shortly before the mail boat was due.

Linnie had just come in and was putting *Dovekie* on her haul-off; when Joanna reached her, Linnie was snapping half hitches over the stake and yanking them viciously tight.

"What is it?" Joanna asked. "No lobsters, too many sea urchins, or what?"

Linnie sat back on her heels and scowled. "One big sea urchin! That *Sam!* If his traps were set any closer to me, he'd have to sit on my lap to haul. So of course, we had one grand John-Rogers snarl, and he acted as if it was more fun than the Fourth of July, giggling like a lunatic, and I'm trying to be nice to the child while I feel like shoving my bait bucket over his head." She stood up. "And then—wouldn't you know it?—Richard came zooming down, yammering about having a dance they can charge money for, and by the time we got our traps sorted out, with the two of them crazy as coots, I was fit to be tied. I wish to God somebody'd have some adorable little thing come to visit that they both could fall for, and then they'd see me as this hag they wouldn't come within a mile of."

"You could blacken your front teeth," Joanna suggested, "and paint in some lines and age spots."

"And grow a few whiskers." Linnie relented, and as usual the change dazzled, at least in her mother's eyes. "It wasn't the kids. I was rotten before I went out."

"Thanks for sparing me that this morning then. Why were you rotten, or can't I ask?"

"I met *them* last night, just after sunset when I left Van's." The gesture with her thumb and the jerk of her head toward *Sweet Helen* were exactly like Jamie's. "It was perfect timing, me walking past when they were coming out. Roy was ahead, and Pitt was still at the back door. I didn't see *her*, but I know she was there because Pitt was saying something, and he was smiling. I couldn't believe that smile! Marm, it was so *nice* it transformed him! I saw it for just this one instant; then Roy saw me and hollered, 'Evenin', de-ah!,' and ruined everything."

"How?"

"Pitt's head snapped around, and when he saw me, the change was absolutely insulting. As if I were loathsome. I was so mad I'd have tackled him then and there about it except that I couldn't think of anything to say, and my throat felt closed up." She laughed angrily and scrubbed her hands over her red cheeks. "Me with no words. Jamie would never believe it. Well, anyway, I made up my mind that he's got to give me at least one decent look. Just one! I don't ask for the smile. Probably only his mother and his sister ever get that. But one glance at me and maybe a polite word, like 'Hello,' and I'll never give him another thought."

"Well, let me know how you manage it," said Joanna. "Both the look and the not-another-thought. Come along, and I'll buy you one of those big, thick, expensive candy bars. Isn't that supposed to be consolation?"

"My life," said Linnie dourly, "is one candy bar after another. I should be as big around as a hogshead by now. I wish I'd blown my savings on a trip to Sweden this summer." She stalked in silence behind her mother. Not only in some random gestures was Linnie like Jamie.

The Fennell baby lay in his carriage outside the store, solemnly watched by Anne Barton and Danny Campion and guarded by a large hairy mongrel with warm eyes. The older children were down on the wharf waiting for the mail boat to whistle outside Long Cove. Not all the women were at the store, but there were enough for a quorum to discuss the plans for the Fourth of July. Charles Bennett's two oldest were coming home with their families and bringing fireworks, and the community picnic was always on.

"Should we send Miss X a special invitation?" Marjorie Percy asked.

"I think that would be *real* nice," said Maggie Dinsmore.

"I just want to know what happens if she comes out and sees her shadow," said Marjorie. "Does that mean six weeks more of summer or what?"

"Six more weeks of Felix Drake," Lisa suggested.

"Susanna Baird, Selina Bainbridge," Van murmured. "Both of them sound made up."

"There's Bainbridges over in that Coates Cove section from way back," Mark said from behind the post office window. "When we were dragging, there was a Micah Bainbridge hailing from there. He had a dragger called *The Tillson Girls*. I heard he was married to one of 'em. He might be father or uncle to these three."

"Susanna Baird could be her professional name," young Carol Fennell offered.

"Whatever it is," Maggie said, "it doesn't seem right to ignore her. I almost sent the kids over there yesterday with a batch of new yeast rolls, but then I thought, Better not. I wouldn't want the kids snubbed. What's anybody to do?" Maggie was distressed. "It's just not our way out here to pretend somebody doesn't exist."

"I guess we all think the same way, Mag," Joanna said. "But that's what she wants. Besides, her brothers are here now, and Felix Drake's running back and forth. So she's not isolated."

Suddenly Champ began to bark, and Roy Bainbridge boomed at him, "Hush now, you fierce dog. I can tell by your tail you're some ferocious. Gonna take a leg off me, are ye?" He moderated his voice as he looked into the carriage. "Guarding the baby, huh? My God, look at that fist! All ready to fight the world. That's some handsome baby. What's his name?"

"Peter Matthew Fennell," Danny piped.

"See, I knew he was a boy! He your brother?" he asked Anne, who gazed up at him in silence.

Roy was trying to cajole her into talking, with the dog frisking around him, and Danny volunteering information, when Pitt drifted up behind them, silent as a leaf.

Beyond Roy's thick, bare, freckled shoulder, the narrow face of his brother showed like a dream image. Between the heavy black forelock and the gaunt cheekbones his eyes had the glint of anthracite. His lips were thinned almost to invisibility, as if by a barely tolerable exasperation that could explode at any moment.

"You actually saw him smile?" Joanna murmured to Linnie.

"Hard to believe, huh?"

Roy filled the doorway, all dimpled radiance. "Good morning, ladies! And that must be Mr. Mark Bennett in there. Good morning, sir!"

"Morning." Mark looked at him over his glasses. "Your father ever run a dragger called *The Tillson Girls?*"

"He sure did!"

"Thought so." Mark went back to work. Pitt retired silently to the shadowy niche between the cracker and cookie shelves and the wall of the post office section, where the official notices were tacked up.

"Hi there, dear!" Roy hailed Linnie. "Now that's a pretty face I know!"

"Hello, Roy and Pitt," Linnie said. "Everybody knows who *you* are, so I'll tell you about us." She began naming the women off, and Roy bobbed his head at each one, his grin untiring. If Pitt nodded, it was not perceptible. When the introductions were over, Roy braced back against the candy case, with his thumbs hooked in his overall straps.

"How's your sister feeling?" Nora Fennell asked.

"We don't want to bother her if she doesn't feel like seeing anyone," Maggie said. "But we don't want her to think we aren't friendly out here."

"Hell, I mean heck, I don't see how anybody could think that. I felt the friendliness the minute I came into the harbor."

"It must have been the way I yelled at you to slow down," said Linnie.

"I never heard that!" he protested, laughing. "And I mean what I said. Some places you go in you can feel everybody watching you like you're carrying the plague. But not here."

"Maybe because nobody saw you come in but Rosa and me."

"Well, I don't see any uncivil faces here this morning. Except maybe this feller you forgot to introduce, Linnie." He pointed at the store cat, who sat very tall in a nail keg beside the cold stove.

"Oh, that's Louis," Linnie said. "I'm sorry I ignored you, Louis." She gathered up the big gray tiger, and over his broad head her gaze moved from Roy to Pitt. Carrying the cat, she wandered toward the notice.

"You go offshore lobstering?" Mark asked from the post office. "From the size of that boat I'd think so."

"Yup, got trawls out on Cash's. Four of us in partnership. Two boats, so there's always somebody out there with the gear. We take turns running in with the lobsters and picking up supplies."

"Good out there?"

"Fair," said Roy, speaking as a true lobsterman. No one would ever admit to more than fair lobstering. "We run in a pretty good load of crates. Course, you can't tell what the next load will be. Could be not enough to pay for the gas. . . . Hey, Linnie! You won't find us up there on the wall. The latest ones ain't been printed yet."

"Some of them look meek as milk," Linnie said, "but they're supposed to be dangerous." She went closer to Pitt as well as the posters, Louis heavy and complacent in her embrace. She put a finger on one subject. "Don't approach this man yourself, it says. Call the police. What do we do out here if we recognize him getting off the mail boat someday?"

"All fall on him," said Marjorie. "Mark can call Limerock while we bury the crook beneath a ton of female flesh."

"What a way to go!" said Roy. "Almost makes a feller want to take to crime."

"Oh, we'd probably get some harmless little embezzler like that one." Linnie touched a weak gentle face. "I wonder who and what he embezzled for."

"You'd be surprised what some fellers want a lot of money all at once for," Roy said. "It's not always women. This little guy might've been a secret gambler, lost a lot of money on the horses. Or maybe he had some big project he believed in, thought it was a sure thing, and he'd get the money put back before anybody caught him. Now that boat of ours—"

"You mean you embezzled for that?" Joanna asked. "Are we looking at the fruits of sin out on Foss's mooring?"

Roy slapped his solid thigh and laughed as if she were the great wit of the century. "Gorry, I'm sorry to disappoint you, dear. But we never had to turn our hand to crime yet. Ask and it shall be given to you, like the Bible says, and we were brought up by the Good Book. Cap'n Micah Bainbridge is a God-fearing man, so we were a Micah-fearing pair. You can ask Pitt here."

"But would he admit anything?" said Linnie, looking straight at Pitt. "Even that? Nope, it might incriminate him." Pitt was as inscrutable as Louis.

"You got him down to a T, dear. He don't even like to say 'good morning' for fear somebody might ketch him up on it. Better safe than sorry, that's my brother's motto. . . . Mr. Bennett!" he called across the room in a quarterdeck voice. "You must know Henry Coates. He used to run a lobster smack out here when he was young."

"Sure, I remember Henry," Mark said. "He wasn't one of our regular dealers, but he'd come out here from time to time when he needed to fill special orders, and lobsters weren't coming too good."

"Ayuh! Well, he's the big man in Coates Cove and all around there. He had the money, and he was willing to take a chance on us, because somebody took a chance on him once, and look at him today! He's making money out of more pies than he's got fingers to put in, and one of the biggest is peddling fish and lobsters." He shook his head in awe. "God, he's got routes going everywhere. Even got one in New York State now. They want seafood, they want it regular, and they want it fresh from Maine waters. They'll buy it to load their freezers, too. Now he's got a couple of small draggers bringing in the fish, and it's sorted and loaded and on its way and sold within twenty-four hours. And Judas, *how* it sells!"

He was so naïvely, innocently proud that everyone looked kindly at him. "Same with lobsters," he went on. "Henry buys all we can bring in, and damned if he don't sell every one. He don't charge all out doors either. You buy a half dozen, you get a discount, see? He's got hundreds of folks, miles from the salt water, living like kings and counting on their weekly lobster feed. Think of that!" He marveled. "Henry Coates has changed their life!"

There was a moment of silence, since nothing could come up to this inspiring statement, and then Roy broke it himself. "That cat's been staring at me like I was three sheets to the wind and raving." Louis returned the scrutiny without embarrassment from Linnie's lap.

"Or else he thinks I'm better than a circus," Roy went on. "Course, you can't tell if a cat's laughing. They got a real poker face."

So had Pitt. Joanna wondered if he ever wished Roy would shut up. Perhaps he simply turned him off inside his head; during a lifetime of Roy he must have learned that, if only from an instinct for survival. She caught a glimmer of what intrigued Linnie; she had never seen a human face that expressed or gave away so little. She could not imagine a smile. It would be like a glass shattering in all directions.

Clarice Hall whistled as she came past Tenpound; Mark locked the post office and left with Louis at his heels. Everyone streamed out behind him like rockweed changing direction when the tide turned—everyone but Pitt, who lit a cigarette and read the posters, and Linnie, who frowned over the glass bulge of the candy case as if trying to make a life-and-death decision between Mars Bars and Almond Joy. Good luck, kid, Joanna thought.

On her way out she met Helmi coming in to tend the store, tall, white-blond, green-eyed as Louis, her knitting basket over her arm. "Did I miss anything?" she asked.

"Tons," said Joanna, "but I don't think it'll make or break your day."

The southeast wind had freshened enough to swoop down over the woods and wrinkle the harbor. Out on the wharf children jockeyed for the best places to catch the lines; would the boat tie up at the end or beside the lobster car? The suspense increased as *Clarice Hall* came in past Eastern Harbor Point with a bone in her teeth.

"This is some beautiful place!" Roy exclaimed, breathing deeply and expanding his chest. "You people got a little hunk of paradise out here, you know it? You—"

He stopped as if a gag had been thrust into his mouth. Not everyone noticed, in the stir as the mail boat approached the wharf; but Marjorie Percy glanced past him at Joanna, and Joanna returned the subtle signal. They both looked in the same direction as Roy, and saw *Drake's Pride* slashing across the mail boat's wake.

"Hey, there's that Drake jerk!" a youngster yelled.

Roy spun around with a dancer's lightness and headed between Joanna and Marjorie as if they weren't there, and up through the long covered shed to the store, walking fast, no jolly rolling now.

"Well!" said Marjorie. "Why so sudden, I wonder?"

"I don't suppose we'll ever know," said Joanna.

The mail boat eased into place along the outer end of Mark's wharf; across the harbor *Drake's Pride* was moving slowly now toward her own wharf.

Everybody followed Link, Mark, and the mailbags up the wharf except the children, who wanted to watch the unloading of freight and be teased by Duke. Joanna found Linnie sitting on the bench outside the store, watching eiders and ducklings in the narrow sheltered slot between there and the Fennell wharf. She looked bemused.

"Well?" said Joanna.

Linnie looked up over her shoulder. "Well, nothing. Helmi was doing something in the back room, and I was trying to think up a remark he'd have to react to, like 'Your fly's unzipped,' and Roy came in all a-fluking and said, 'Drake's here!'" He was as red as those buoys." She pointed to the heap on the Fennell wharf. "Pitt shrugged, said, 'So?' and sort of shepherded him out. They went away some fast, and Roy wasn't stopping to orate about the scenery. You know, I've been thinking of Pitt attached to him like the shadow Wendy sewed onto Peter Pan. But without touching Roy or saying a word, he was in charge. Weird, isn't it? Everything looks so plain and simple on the surface; but it never is, and I don't know why I'm surprised at anything, at my advanced age."

11

In about a half hour *Sweet Helen* had left the harbor, and Felix Drake and Willy went out to haul. The Sewing Circle met that afternoon at the Homestead; they worked in the big living room which looked out to sea from one row of windows and down to the harbor and across to Brigport from the opposite row. Most of them were open, bringing in the scents and sounds of summer. Linnie didn't often choose to stay indoors on such a day, but she was there and had been given a place at the quilting frame. Liza had designed the quilt, and it would be raffled off at the fair they put on with the Brigport women each August. Every woman on the island would have contributed some stitches to it.

During the desultory talk in the first few moments of settling down, Kathy Campion was remarkably subdued. She kept her eyes on her work but was seen to tap her thimble nervously on the arm of her chair when someone wondered aloud what was keeping Philippa. The signs that she had something to tell were obvious.

Philippa came in and explained her tardiness, Robin's goat had opened a gate and begun grazing in the richest patch of wild strawberries in the field. She had to be lured home by new chocolate chip cookies still warm from the oven. "Nobody ever told us goats had such refined tastes," Philippa said. "Robin thinks it's a sign of her aristocracy. She waits on her hand and foot, as if Gambler's really a princess in disguise."

Robin had named the Toggenburg kid Gambler because in stories goats gamboled on the green. Steve said the name suited because the doe was forever taking a gamble on her chances of survival to elderly goathood.

Kathy's thimble finger tapped in little convulsive bursts during a chain of animal anecdotes; then came the pause she was waiting for, and she uttered a single dramatic *"Well!"* and got everyone's attention.

"I stayed home from the boat on purpose this morning," she began with the leisurely precision of the gifted storyteller, "not just to do some baking. I did bake, to salve my conscience and convince myself I'm not really a snooper. Well, I thought now that her brothers are here, I could make a dent. Be neighborly, you know." Her mouth quirked up at that. "Anyway, as soon as my kids all went to meet the boat, I farmed over there with a warm raisin loaf and a pot of fresh coffee, thinking I was irresistible. Or at least the loaf was. But there wasn't a sound in the house; you'd swear it was empty, that she wasn't there and never had been. The brothers had gone out when I wasn't looking, and I had the feeling she was standing pressed against a wall, holding her breath. So I was going to leave the loaf on the kitchen table; but the back door was locked, and the shed door was locked, too. Can you believe it?"

She looked as astonished as she'd often been at fourteen, when most human conduct constantly astounded her. "Well, I wasn't about to leave my good baking on the doorstep for that Hank to get. I swear he knows when you're carrying any kind of food, no matter how it's covered, and he came zooming straight across the harbor and perched on the chimney, watching me. So I took my raisin loaf home again and made a pig of myself. Just managed to save a slice for each of the kids and a good piece for Terence's mug-up when he comes in."

"Gosh, Kath," Linnie said. "I thought you had more to tell than that. You should have been at the store when Drake came in. Roy took off out of there as if he'd just stepped into a hornets' nest."

"I *saw* Drake come in." Nothing could shake Kathy's sense of theater. "And I just *happened* to be looking with the glasses when the grand duke saw that boat on *his* mooring. For a minute there I thought he was going to ram her amidships, but he slowed down just in time." She chuckled. "Willy was sort of cowering in the stern, like Becky when I'm giving one of the kids a hard time and she's looking for cover."

"Why would he be mad because his tenant's brothers came to see her?" Maggie Dinsmore wondered.

"And that *still* isn't all," Kathy assured her. "I don't want my kids ever to hear me talk like this, or the next time I tell Cindy she's nosy she's likely to tell me she comes by it honestly. Well, I wasn't *sneaky*. There they were out in the face and eyes of everybody, if everybody wanted to look. Roy and Pitt came tearing around the harbor and hit the wharf about the time Drake tied up. You wouldn't believe that Roy could move so fast."

"Just out of curiosity, was Pitt moving fast, too?" Joanna asked.

"Oh, yes, he was coming right along, but he looked calm. Roy was some flushed; you could hardly tell his face from his hair and his beard except that the reds clashed. Gorry, I wish I could read lips! Drake was furious. No arm waving or foot stamping, but I could tell. Roy talked back. He waved his arms some, and I could hear his voice but not what he said because the hoisting engine was going over on the big wharf. Pitt looked off into space, and Willy walked straight up by as if they weren't even there, carrying a box of groceries that was all he could heft. It must've been the strength of desperation. . . . My Lord, I'm some dry."

Mateel hurried to bring her a drink of water. Kathy thanked her and drank it all, unhurried, complacent, sure of her audience.

"The next thing I knew," she resumed, "Pitt and Roy went up to the house, Roy with his head down and charging like a bull and Pitt sort of floating along with his hands in his pockets. They passed Willy coming back, and he gave 'em a wide berth and scuttled by with his hat down over his ears. He looked like a grasshopper under a mushroom." She waited graciously for the laugh. "Felix stood there with his hands on his hips, staring at the house. They came past him as if he weren't there, climbed down into their dory, and rowed away without a backward look. Not even a wave to Sister in case she was peeking out around a curtain. How's that for drama?"

"Frustrating," said Philippa, "because we'll never know what's behind it."

"What if they aren't her brothers?" Laurie asked. "Maybe she doesn't want them anywhere near her, but they found out where she was, so Drake is just protecting her rights."

"Or if they really are her brothers, maybe they're part of her troubles," Van said, "and she came out here to get away from them."

"When we tried to talk about her to Roy this morning, he got us off the subject some fast," Marjorie Percy said.

"Well, I'm not so curious I'll die of it," said Kathy. "If she drops dead in there, Drake'll find the body so she can have a funeral. I've got other things to think of, just as long as she doesn't set fire to the place when she's drunk or full of pills."

"How's your Boston trip coming along?" somebody asked, and the conversation left Drake and the Bainbridges for the rest of the afternoon, even when *Drake's Pride* returned from hauling and dominated the view of the harbor.

When they stopped work for tea and wild strawberry tarts, Linnie came to where Rosa stood watching Richard and Sam fishing off Goose Cove Ledge. "Well, that's that," she said. "I'm a failure, and so young, too. I never got a smile from him or even a decent, kindly glance. I'll bear the scar forever."

"You can't win 'em all, to coin a phrase," Rosa said. "Maybe that enigmatic expression is all he's got. There may not be a thing behind those eyes but space."

"Well, we'll never know. Old Felix ran 'em off. Isn't it fantastic? A man moves in on us without an aye, yes, or no, and the next minute he's ordering somebody off the island." Linnie finished her tart and licked her fingers. "These are good." She went away to get another one.

Rosa managed to get away first from the meeting, and she took the meadow path that led to the woods behind the Sorensen place. There was a minor uproar of scolding and alarmed birds among the alders and birches, on account of Pip, who sat placidly on a shoulder of ledge. He took off in a long, flowing leap and ran to Rosa, who was too preoccupied to pick him up until she nearly fell down trying not to step on him. She passed the barn and the hens with him clinging triumphantly to her shirt and rubbing his head against her ear. When she tried to put him down beside the house, he hung on, and while she was detaching him, Jamie shouted at her. He set down a pail of water and came through the gate.

"*Damn,*" she whispered. "You're a blasted nuisance, cat." She should have been walking home while Jamie was still at the well, and he'd never have known she was on the other side of the spruce windbreak.

He came toward her like a man with a purpose. Maybe it was on his mind that she hadn't been meeting him for coffee these days; any other man would have noticed. But then Jamie Sorensen wasn't like any other man. He'd have made a good early Christian hermit, she thought, living in the desert and ignoring the women who came out to tempt him. Who was that one who lived on top of a pillar? . . . Still, he might have missed her. Dimly.

Voices from out behind the barn. That would be Joanna and Marjorie. Pip leaped from her arms and headed for the voices. She put her hands in her pockets and said, "Well?"

"Did Drake come alongside you this morning?"

"No." She took a few steps toward home, and he came along beside her.

"He's been so damn thorough with his politicking I didn't know he'd missed anybody. He got me today. Hadn't had a chance to meet me around the shore, he said. Didn't want to miss out this time."

Rosa looked around at the garden, overhead at the scaling gulls, anywhere but at him. The soft, sarcastic voice went on. "Hands across the washboards, good, hard grip. Looks you straight in the eye. Too damn straight. When anybody fixes you with an eye like that, you know damn well they're trying to hypnotize you into not smelling the stink."

What would happen if she yawned in his face? She was almost desperate enough to try it, almost hungry for a good row so as to end everything clip and clean.

"I asked him," said Jamie, "why he put 'Bennett's Island' on his boat instead of 'Coates Cove.' He said he owned property here and goes lobstering, so that makes him a Bennett's Islander. The hell it does, I says, and he didn't even get mad, not that you could notice. He gave me all this barnsalve about how he understood, he was Maine-bred and born and raised; he'd been in love with the island ever since he first heard of it and saw the pictures, and when he sailed into the harbor the first time, it was like coming home. Jesus, it almost gagged me. I swear he managed to get his eyes wet and forced a tremble into his voice." A snort of incredulous laughter. "Now he wants it to be home, and he won't rest till he's won his family over. He's always heard great things of the Bennett's Islanders, and so far, until me, he hadn't heard any objections."

"But you fixed him," said Rosa. "Struck this trusting soul straight to the heart."

"Funny, huh?" he said acidly. "Because nobody else gives a damn. Sure, they'd come to the meeting—humor the kid—and that's all. Looks as if I'm the only real islander in the bunch, and that includes my own family. Hugo and Owen were with me at first. We'd have cleaned him out the minute those traps went overboard, and then he'd know for sure he had his arse in a sling. But you were there; you heard it. Nobody'd say 'shit' if their mouths were full of it."

"Kind of difficult under the circumstances, I always thought," said Rosa. They had reached the lane, and she stopped and faced him. "If they aren't all obsessed with Drake, it's because they've got other things to think about that are a hell of a lot more important."

"What could be more important than the island?" he asked with such indignant innocence that she wanted to shout at him, *Me*, you numbhead, you idiot, you—She forced a few deep breaths, and he didn't even notice that. He was still talking.

"You don't know who he can sell out to when he gets tired of it. You don't know what we could get in here, like some disease infecting everything. It's already begun, for God's sake! *Her*, whatever she is. And those brothers, if that's what they are. They could buy him out, or he'd let them come in with him, and that means three new fishermen throwing a few thousand pots overboard like mad." His face was flushed, his eyes wild. "Can't you see it? Can't *anybody* see it?"

"For heaven's sake," she exclaimed, "they've been here only once, and you read all that into it?"

"They stayed long enough to look things over, but they already knew about the place. They think it's a gold mine out here. Plenty of grounds and only a handful of fishermen. You wait and see, they'll be dropping in every five minutes like it's the corner bar. Roy holding forth to the women, flashing his goddamn dimples—"

"You noticed them, too!" She clasped her hands under her chin.

He looked as if he wanted to slap her. "And my sister babbling about that wooden Indian who's probably not even right in the head." He stopped, too furious for words.

"Like brother, like sister," she said. "One-track minds, both of you. She has to have a mystery to ponder over, and you've got to have something to stew about while the nights are too bright for seining. What else can you do, unless you go hunting with Hugo over at Brigport?"

It was deadly, but he deserved it.

"If I haven't been up," he said, "it's because the last time I darkened your doorstep you looked bored as hell."

"Jamie Sorensen," she said in a voice made more ferocious by its low pitch and even cadence. "If you knew just half of what you think you know, you'd be a hell of a lot smarter than you think you are. Because you don't know *beans*. Talk about a wooden Indian. You're solid pine between the ears. Nobody else really exists for you, you're so taken up with all your suspicions and fixations. Everybody else is just a paper doll pasted on a mirror." She wet her lips, got more wind, and began again; he watched without blinking, either fascinated or utterly amazed.

"We don't have any brains; we don't have wants and ideals and obsessions of our own; the only way we can be real for you is if we think exactly as *you* do. Be your reflection, your echo. You don't hear anything people say about themselves. You don't even wonder what they're thinking about when they're quiet. If they're not falling all over you telling you you're a hundred percent right, they must be damned stupid. Or—they're boring as hell."

The Percy boys were war-whooping home on the other side of the windbreak, Tiger skylarking at their heels. Rosa said softly, "Of course, if people dare to argue with you, you know they're alive all right, but you don't think they should be."

"I'll concede," he said stoically, "that I've got a one-track mind and I'm a stupid, insensitive son of a bitch."

"I couldn't have put it better myself," said Rosa. She walked across the lane to her own land and looked back at him. "And you know what the worst of it is? You're proud of it."

She kept on going, and the trees seemed to close in silently behind her. Her head was spinning. Did I really say all those things? Where did they come from? Well, that fixes it. That takes care of everything. Approaching her back door, she felt as if she could set out now and walk to Sou'west Point and back without a stop.

Funny, you expect everything to look different. After she'd gotten the word from Con that he'd been having an affair and wanted a divorce, she'd been surprised because everything was still the same outside her. The birds hadn't been blasted off the earth but acted as if nothing had happened; in the town the stores, the post office, the garage, and the wharves all were in their proper places, and people went about their business with the same faces and seemed to think hers was the same she'd always worn, while to her it felt like a death mask.

She took a kettle of lobster chowder from the refrigerator and put it on the gas stove to warm slowly. She was so ravenous she picked out a couple of chunks of pink and white meat and ate them cold. The difference between then and now was that now she didn't believe she was going to die, was already dying, and mustn't let anyone know. One doesn't die so easily. The business with Con had been a good vaccination. She'd run away from Seal Point; but she would never run from

Bennett's Island, and she wasn't going to get fat again either. When she was over the worst of this, it would be a life of single blessedness instead of a life of double cussedness. There could be worse things.

But as she waited for her supper to heat, she was realizing that Jamie hadn't followed her and that one weak corrupted little bit of her had been hoping he would.

12

She turned off the gas under the chowder and went out. The Percy place, hidden from Rosa's by a fringe of spruces and old apple trees, vibrated audibly with life. She heard the breathless, choking laughter and hilarious threats of the two young boys wrestling in the yard, Ralph whistling and hammering at the same time, and Marjorie calling above all the noise, "Ralph, I'm going over to get Rosa to have chili with us tonight."

Rosa ran into the woods and didn't stop until she reached Barque Cove. On her first night on the island she had walked out here in the night and the fog, by flashlight along the strange path in a silent, dripping world as foreign to her as a tropical rain forest. She had stood here high above invisible water made evident by only the smallest sounds when it gurgled through crevices and sighed like a sleeper as it washed over the pebbles. She felt then as if her life had been blown out, and she had been atomized and then reassembled in a limbo of perpetual mist and deathly stillness.

Then she had gone back to the house, slept, and woke after midnight to remember her boat with a pain that was very much life. She went down to the harbor past sleeping houses and found that someone had put *Sea Star* safely on a mooring.

Jamie Bennett had done it for the boat's sake, he told her, censuring her for possessing a boat she could neglect like that. But later he had treated her as tenderly as he handled *Sea Star*.

Well, that was a long time ago. No night and fog hid Barque Cove now; it sparkled in the light wind and early-evening sunshine, and it was also in plain view of the young Fennells' house, which hadn't been there when she had needed Barque Cove for a refuge time and time again. She could find herself another one, but she was done with brooding and moping. If she never admitted to wounds, there'd be no wounds to lick.

She went back to the house, to the evening song of her thrush and the catbird's virtuoso performance. Marjorie had left a note on the table, inviting her to supper and to bring along her guitar. Rosa took both guitar and banjo and went across the yard.

Inevitably their music drew an audience of teenagers and children, and parents who came to collect the small ones stayed awhile. Everybody sang. When Hugo suddenly appeared, swept up a speechless Cindy, and swung her off her feet, Rosa wondered if Jamie was behind him. But only for that instant. Jamie wasn't there, he wouldn't be, and there were no wounds. Remember that. She was shaking her hands and blowing on her fingers between numbers now; but she played on, and she slept that night as she hadn't slept for a long time.

It was a good omen, she thought in the morning. Maybe she was actually relieved, not bereaved. To celebrate her new freedom, she decided not to go to haul today; it was no skin off anyone's nose but her own if she skipped a day.

She made a lunch and a thermos of tea, put them and some plastic containers into her pack basket, and went down the west side to pick strawberries. By the time she reached the steep slopes at Sou'west Point, Linnie had either finished with the traps there or was hauling outside first. On the way to the point Rosa had seen Sam working his way back; he wasn't allowed to go out around.

So for the time being there was no one to hail her from the water; she shared the point only with the gulls that kept the cliffs as their own, the sparrows that claimed the fields, and a family of ravens. She could hear the invisible young ones' harsh yet infantile voices from the high nest just inside the woods. She heard the engines all around, and whenever she stood up to rest her back or to move to a different spot, she saw boats; but she and they were occupying different worlds this morning. Jamie's gear was all off the outer shores, ledges, and shoals, so she wouldn't have seen *Valkyrie* anywhere from this northern slope below the ridge, but she felt so pleasantly insulated she was sure the sight would have been no more than a pinprick.

In the late afternoon, with all her containers filled with wild strawberries, all her food and drink gone, she went up to the ridge and across open ground to the old wood road which led back through the woods to Goose Cove. The shade was cool, sprinkled with little speckles of sunlight that flickered like sequins when the rising wind moved the treetops.

From above Goose Cove she crossed the island again, through the woods on the rise behind the Fennell house, and came out above Barque Cove. She walked home through her own woods. It was quiet at the Percy house, but that would not last.

She put all her containers but one on the cold earth floor of the cellar; before she'd started home, she had sat down and hulled this one dishful of berries. Upstairs she put the chowder on to heat while she washed up. She ate her meal with pleasure, still comfortably padded with indifference toward the rest of the world. "The rest of the world" meant Jamie; just because she didn't care to keep thinking his name didn't mean that she wasn't facing facts.

She finished off her supper with a dish of wild strawberries, lightly sugared. She ate slowly, crushing the small sweet berries between her tongue and the roof of her mouth. One never hurried the year's first taste of wild strawberries.

She went outdoors to hull the rest of the berries. She had knocked together a table of driftwood boards laid across crude sawhorses, and for benches she used old lobster crates, which, like the boards, had come into Barque Cove; she had wheeled them home through the woods. She brought up the berries from the cellar, turned out the first lot onto a platter, and began to hull them into a deep kettle. It was now suppertime for most of the island; everyone was indoors, and the village was quiet, given over to the cruising gulls whose occasional cries of greeting or warning echoed across the empty places of the sky.

She worked steadily, wiping her hands on a wet washcloth when they became too sticky. In time the village was stirring again. The Percy boys washed the supper dishes, uproariously, and then chased each other down the path, barking and howling at Tiger like a couple of wolf cubs. *Finest Kind* went out, voices and laughter rising above the sound of the engine. Hugo was taking the teenagers out for a ride around the island, probably down to Pirate Island and out to the Rock, with a sunset sail home. She wondered if Jamie was going. She couldn't imagine it, but all signs failed in a drought.

Anyway, even if he should follow her sarcastic suggestion about Brigport, it was nothing to do with her. The shy thrush began to sing as the shadows grew darker in the woods. She was down to the final quart of strawberries.

"Hi, Rosa!" Linnie came up from the lane. *No*, Rosa protested at once. She would not forfeit this comfortable, fatalistic detachment. But she didn't say it aloud, and Linnie had seen nothing strange in her face and manner.

"I wondered why you didn't go out to haul today. I thought you were sick, but my father said he saw you picking down at Sou'west Point." She sat down opposite Rosa. "Listen, I know now where *Sweet Helen* comes from! I don't mean Coates Cove, but the name." She took a folded paper from her shirt pocket, smiling with the pleasure of a child who's found a whole and workable toy in the rockweed. "Eric brought it up; he found it in one of Aunt Philippa's books. It's from *Doctor Faustus*, by Christopher Marlowe. He sold his soul to the devil so he could have all these visions, and one of them was Helen of Troy. Listen to *this*." She read aloud in a low voice accented with dramatic pauses:

" '*Was this the face that launched a thousand ships,*
And burnt the topless towers of Ilium?
Sweet Helen, make me immortal with a kiss.' "

She lowered the paper. "Isn't that beautiful? And can you believe it? Those two, with a boat named out of a poem like *that?*"

"It's beautiful," Rosa agreed, "but do you honestly believe they named their boat after Helen of Troy?"

"Maybe one of them reads," Linnie said hopefully. "Not Roy, he couldn't take the time off from talking, even if he can sound out words with more than one syllable. But I think Pitt's different." She was very offhand.

"Or else Henry Coates has a daughter," Rosa said, "and she found the name. Maybe she's a Helen. She probably launched the boat, too. Broke the champagne over the bow and everything."

"Spoiled rotten," said Linnie. "Daddy's girl. Water-skis in a bikini and drives an Audi. *If* she exists, and I have a stinking suspicion that she does. God, I hope it's Roy she's after. That will give Pitt a chance to breathe." She began to hull berries with nimble fingers, talking all the time. "I've figured it out. He's been in Roy's shade so long he can't believe the sun will ever shine on him. Of course, he's clearly the brains, but Roy has the charm. He's so big you can't see anything else, and he's got those damn *dimples.*"

"You planning on being Pitt's sunshine, his only sunshine, and so forth?"

"I never said that! I just thought that if he believed a medium attractive girl found him worth speaking to—and I'm being modest, I hope you notice—it would do him good. It would be," she continued loftily, "an act of kindness on my part."

"You bet," said Rosa, and they both burst out laughing.

"Anyway," Linnie said, "I'll probably never see him again, if Dapper Dan has his way. Well, he can't keep them out of this harbor even if he does think he's just bought it. And if they do show up, I'm not going to make a big thing out of it. I'm nice, I'm not repulsive, and I just want to be friendly."

"How friendly?"

"Just ordinary-civil-human friendly. I didn't take one look at him that day and think, This here frog is my prince in disguise. Twice in my life I thought he'd arrived; but I was wrong, and I don't plan to be swamped again. The best time I was in love, the most beautiful, was long before those two." Linnie's voice faded, and her fingers stopped moving. She gazed past Rosa into the twilight under the trees.

"That's when I was in love with love. I was simply in a state of being in love. That's when it's purest, before you find out how black it is on the other side of the moon."

"Amen to that," said Rosa.

"When I was thirteen," Linnie went on in that remote voice, "and Aunt Philippa had the school, she and Uncle Steve took all the island kids to Portland for a week, and one thing we did was go to a circus. Our first one, and we knew it just had to be the best. Nothing else could *ever*—well, anyway, there was this family of acrobats, and there was this boy who walked the high wire. He was slender and dark, and he wore white tights and a bright red shirt with full sleeves and sequins, so he was all sparkling and twinkling up there. For a long time afterward he walked in my dreams. Both kinds, sleeping and waking."

The last word disappeared into silence. Rosa hulled steadily. When she stopped to wipe her hands, Linnie said, unusually shy, "Did you ever have dreams like that?"

"Yup. Not about an acrobat, because I'd never seen a circus, but there was a warden who always used to wink at me when he was talking with my father, and he'd say, 'Hi, there, honeybunch.' Oh, God. Apollo in a green uniform. For him I was almost ready to give up ice cream."

Linnie laughed. "But you see what I mean about it being pure, don't you? You're worshipping from afar, and all you dream about is hearing him say your name as if it's something special, and you can call him by *his* name. . . . I can remember the last dream, the last sleeping one, as if I'd just dreamed it last night. I remember every detail, and I can still feel the clutch in here." She pressed a fist into her midriff. "As if some big hand had reached in and grabbed and *twisted*. He came walking above the bay from Limerock to Bennett's, and I saw him when he started. I can remember how purple the mountains looked behind him, and I watched him all the way. The water was rough below him, all tossing blue and green streaked with white. Clouds would rush past the sun, and the water would turn to that dull, cold, wicked silver. Then it would brighten again. Gulls were flying all around him like an escort, and he just came steadily on and on over the waves. I could hear those combers hissing as they leaped for his feet. And he was smiling at me."

She stopped. Rosa, who had been seeing it all, asked, "Then what?"

"That's when the clutch comes in." Linnie turned her head away. "That's when the fist grabs and twists. I woke up before he reached me. I tried to dive back into the dream; but I couldn't, and I cried and cried, because I knew it would never come again."

"I'm sorry," Rosa said, as if it had been an actual bereavement. Well, it was.

Linnie said with a sudden, jeering laugh, "I don't know what the connection is with now."

"Pitt Bainbridge looks like the high-wire walker," said Rosa.

"It's crazy anyway," Linnie said harshly. "And I'm not going to get all mystical and supernatural about it." She crushed a berry in her fingers, looked surprised, and licked the pulp from her thumb. "But I saw that smile, and I'd like to see it again, just once. Maybe it won't be quite what I thought. But I'm going to find out." She looked Rosa in the eye. "And if you tell my brother any of this, I'll kill you."

"Don't worry," said Rosa.

They finished the berries and piled the containers in the sink and washed their hands. "Come on up and play pool," said Linnie. "I don't think any of the male chauvinists are up there, hogging the place tonight."

"How come you didn't go on that sail with Hugo?"

"With all those *kids*? I never knew sixteen was so young. I wanted to think. And now I've thought. How about it?"

Rosa shook her head. "To tell you the truth, all I want is to go to bed and read awhile and get a good night's sleep. Thanks for helping out."

"Okay. Thanks for listening. . . . Anyway, we'll probably never see them again. Maybe this will be one of those brief encounters that you never forget. Ships that pass in the night and all that kind of junk."

"'I did but see him passing by,'" Rosa sang. "'And yet I love him till I die.'"

"All right for *you!*" Linnie said. She laughed and ran.

Rosa measured sugar and strawberries together in her biggest mixing bowl and put it in the refrigerator for the night. She always made a batch of jam for the Websters and kept a few jars for herself, to eat in deepest winter. She laid everything out for the morning and went to bed while the swallows were still shooting past her windows, and the windows on the far side of the harbor were aflame with reflected sunset.

There was still plenty of light for reading. Everyone's books went the rounds; you wrote your name in yours if you wanted them back, and sooner or later they arrived home again. Marjorie had handed Rosa a shopping bag full of paperbacks last night, and she had started one; but after the evening of music she'd been too sleepy to get far and didn't remember anything about it. She picked it up again tonight, one of those thick volumes so hard to hold open, and discovered that the plot was nonexistent, and the characters could barely contain their lust during the dull chapters inserted for convention's sake between the bizarre couplings, which occurred at regular intervals, like a clock striking every fifteen minutes. The author must have had a timer, Rosa thought. Bell goes off. *Let's see, how'll they do it this time?*

After a while the only reaction to the sex scenes was a mild curiosity as to how many ways the characters could fornicate without repeating until they should have died of exhaustion.

Rosa threw the book across the room and picked up one with Nils's name in it, *The Sea and the Jungle* by H. M. Tomlinson. There'd been nothing written in the other one, and no wonder; who'd want to be seen claiming it? She suspected it had come home with one of the high school girls who'd been happy to get it out of the house before a parent spotted it.

Two pages into Nils's book, she began to relax.

She woke up with a start in a dark room, with her book turned down open across her chest. She was so wide-awake she could have had a night's sleep, and everything she'd kept at bay all day was coming at her from the dusky corners.

When she was a child, there'd been a short spell when she believed something was lurking under her bed in the dark, ready to grab at a dangling foot. Kid, you didn't know what was just waiting for you to grow up, she told that child.

It was a little past midnight. She got up and dressed and went out. The moonlight was bright, and in spite of the uneasiness it always caused her, to be moving around in it was better than lying in bed trying not to think. She walked out on her own wharf as if to assure herself that *Sea Star* was there. The boat was a comforting presence, something both tangible and responsive that was hers. She sat down on a crate to contemplate the harbor. Sleeping boats in the moonlight did not have the slightly menacing mystery of sleeping houses.

Philip's cat, Leo, appeared and sat on the crate beside her. He was usually aloof during the day, a small but dignified lion. She took no liberties now but enjoyed the way he treated her as an equal.

Hugo's boat was back on her mooring, and Rosa'd been sleeping so hard she'd heard nothing. *Drake's Pride* looked enormous on the brimming high tide, the moonlight reflected off her glossy side as if from glass. She heard a variety of tranquil little noises, oddly companionable; water splashed gently under the wharves, and someone's skiff knocked softly but persistently against a spiling. Then she realized that this set of sounds was too regular, the rhythm too familiar; she had been listening to oars.

She stood up, using her rampart of drying traps as a screen and tried to see without being seen. Maybe it was the Lady of Shalott; the sound came from that side of the harbor. Then she saw the gleam of the white skiff moving away from *Drake's Pride*. Living light danced about her waterline, the oars both shattered and scattered light, and a sparkling wake was left behind.

The man was rowing with quick, even strokes. It was Felix Drake. He wasn't wearing his cap, and his gray head was silver. He was heading for his wharf. Rosa moved out past the traps and watched him reach it, go up over the end, and walk rapidly toward the house. He went around to the kitchen door. It couldn't have been locked, or else it was opened to him, because in an instant he had disappeared.

"So that's the way it is!" she whispered. "I'll be damned. The old fox."

She waited a few minutes, but he didn't come out. Leo heard something under the fish house and went to see what it was. She sat down again, wondering what went on, behind shades drawn to keep out both sun and moonlight. "Your business, folks, not mine," she murmured. She'd keep it to herself, but how long before somebody got it out of this Willy? Felix Drake couldn't very well keep him under lock and key. He'd already been down to the Eastern End for supper. Steve and Philippa weren't the kind to pump him, but somebody like Kathy or Hugo wouldn't mind in the least.

She shrugged it all off and walked home. Through the black shadow of her spruces she emerged into her moonlit yard, where the table sat like a large, waiting, but docile beast. "Make me immortal with a kiss," Linnie had read across it. No one would ever cry that to Rosa or say it in silence against her lips. But Jamie must have thought, for a little while at least, that Eloise had heard it from him and granted it.

She smelled Jamie's pipe before she was into the kitchen. Then she saw his silhouette against the moon-bleached landscape outside the front windows. She stood still just inside the door.

"Turned into a moon howler, have you?" he said. "I thought you'd left home for good."

"I was thinking about it. Spain seemed like a good idea." She leaned against the sink, her hands behind her gripping the edge. There was a faint tap as he put his pipe in an ashtray. The tiny red heart glowed in a well of blackness. He came without sound and put his arms around her. When she didn't respond at once, he cupped her chin and turned her mouth toward his.

"Jamie," she said against it, trying to hold her head away.

"Sh, sh," he murmured.

"No, but—Listen, there are things—"

"No talk tonight. I've heard enough talk, and made enough, to do me for the rest of my life."

13

Before dawn a southeasterly breeze was blowing and picking up all the time. The sound of the building rote came in at bedroom windows, and curtains slapped against screens. The rising wind found familiar chinks and cracks to wail through, arousing winter memories in island dreams. By full daylight the turbulent sea looked frigidly gray and white under a ghostly sun which, five months back, would have been described as wading through a snowdrift. It disappeared as the clouds came thicker and faster on a wind reaching gale strength.

Nobody went to haul, and Felix Drake didn't head back to the mainland with his catch but floated his crates off his mooring. The rain came, beating hard across the island, and in the short, deceptive lulls the combined roar of surf and the wind through the trees filled the air so that when you were outside the house, you had to shout to be heard by someone ten feet away.

The storm lasted for all day and half the night. The next morning the wind had gone around to the northwest and had become merely a brisk breeze, which would flatten the seas. When Joanna walked down to the harbor with Nils, Linnie had already gone, after making a devout promise to use common sense and leave certain of her traps until a quieter time. *Valkyrie* was still in, no sign of Jamie, but Rosa was just starting up *Sea Star*. *Drake's Pride* was leaving the harbor, Willy pulling on his oil pants in the cockpit.

"Going to haul around again before he goes ashore," said Joanna. "There's something about that man Drake that makes me wish all his gear has either been dragged into deep holes and lost, or piled up and buried in the rockweed."

"Sorry, kid," said Nils, "but that doesn't happen much with wire traps. It's the wooden ones that travel."

"I know, damn it. Does the sight of that boat bother you?"

"Not the boat. She's able enough; she knows what she's about. Pretty, too." The skiffs had been hauled up to the brow of the beach yesterday and turned over. Joanna took hold with him and helped to turn his skiff right side up. "But he's no fisherman, not even a mainland one. He's learned the motions and knows how to go through them, he's got Willy to do the dirty work, and he thinks if he calls everybody Skipper or Cap'n, he's putting the natives at ease."

Drake's Pride had disappeared around Eastern Harbor Point. Rosa left her mooring and headed out. Nils slid the skiff down over the damp coarse sand to the water, and the nearest eider group, busy around Linnie's haul-off, began to move out of the way. When the skiff was waterborne and Nils straightened up, Joanna handed him his dinner box. He said with wry amusement, "I haul these days with my ears laid back, trying to look all ways at once like Pip figuring on how he's going to cross the backyard without the swallows getting him. You never know when Drake's going to shoot into view and come up alongside wanting a *gam*. His word, not mine."

"Where do you suppose he got *that?*" It was the old whaling term for a social conversation at sea.

"Oh, he read it somewhere, probably, and thinks it's real salty. Whalers, lobstermen, what's the difference? They're all in boats."

"Deep down do you feel like Jamie, that he's using the island like a whore?"

"I guess we all do, don't we?" he said. "We live through the good and the bad, for richer, for poorer, in sickness and in health, the whole works, and our dead are buried here. He buys himself a shore privilege, throws traps overboard in the best weather, scampers out long enough to haul them, and then he goes back ashore and doesn't even sell his lobsters here first. I'm not about to let it curdle me, one in the family is enough, but if I was of a mind to be irritated, Felix Drake could do it."

"Why don't you let him know it next time he hails you? Oh, all right," she said resignedly. "You wouldn't."

"I'm goddamned tempted to let him know I'm not all overcome by the honor of being called Cap'n."

"Why, Cap'n, what language," said Joanna. They kissed and he stepped into the skiff and pushed off. Joanna watched him reach his boat and get aboard, then turned back to the path for home, not intending to stay there after being kept in the house all day yesterday. Jamie was coming off his doorstep. He waved at his mother with unusual good cheer.

"I'll bet you're hoping that Drake's in a snarl with you so you can whack him off like mad," she accused him.

"Me, molest Felix the Fart and litter good bottom with lost traps?" he said virtuously. "Not to mention the lobsters caught in 'em and lost to the rest of us? Marm, what are you *suggesting?*"

"Even your great-grampa Gunnar couldn't manage to look as pious as you do right this minute. So mind your failings."

He grinned and went on, as if his rubber boots were as light as moccasins. No sense wondering why; just be thankful for small blessings. She was in the house, trying to decide where on the outer shore she would go and if she'd take a lunch, when Laurie tapped on the front door and came in. She was a sturdy, compact woman who could easily have put on extra flesh and become stout over the years if she'd been careless. As it was, at first glance she didn't look much older than the girl who'd come to Bennett's Island to teach in her first school.

"Come on with me, Jo," she said. "I've been dying to get out while there's still some good surf. The girls aren't up yet, they were out half the night with Hugo, and Richard's gone with Owen and Tommy."

"Decisions, decisions," said Joanna. "Shall I put on boots and cook my toes or keep on soaked sneakers and have cool feet? Yep, that's it." She tossed Laurie an orange and put one in her own pocket.

Pip enthusiastically led the way out past the henyard and the barn. The path across to Goose Cove was soggy underfoot, and Pip took it in long leaps.

Heat came from a hazy sun, and warmth rose from the tawny pink granite terraces where the women walked. From the steaming woods rising on their right, a moist, resinous scent swept down to them on erratic gusts of breeze; on the left there arose a cold, briny emanation from the seas which broke below them. Fresh rockweed flung ashore during the storm glittered in bursts of light as the sun strengthened, and carnival flashes of color came from occasional buoys bobbing in the surf, where traps were being dragged ashore.

Pip was as happy and excited as a dog. He ran ahead, darted up into the woods for a little wilderness exploration, rushed at gulls picking in the rockweed and watched them fly, crept up on menacing objects— long ropes of kelp draped like serpents across the rocks and old driftwood stumps shaped like mysterious beasts drowsing in the sun. If the women got ahead of him, he bounded after them, his cries lost in the noise of the water.

"He's such an extrovert he ought to be named Richard," said Richard's mother. "Did you know that darned kid invited the whole freshman soccer team out here for over the Fourth? Thank God they all have to be in a parade, or they don't want to miss some carnival, or they're tied up with family reunions."

"Cheer up. He'll get them out here sooner or later. The thing to do is have some big project for them, like painting the house or digging up half a field for next year's potatoes."

They stood among the spruces on the high promontory of Schooner Head, watching the boats that worked offshore, rolling in the silvery surge. The two Fennells were together today, in case some heavy work called for four hands. Owen's *White Lady* rocked near Brig Ledge. Owen was at the wheel and operating the hauling gear. Tommy took over when the trap came out of water; he brushed off the sea urchins and crabs, took out the lobsters, throwing back the shorts and measuring the others. Richard took out the old bait bag and put in a fresh one and fastened the door. The boat circled so Tommy could slide the trap overboard where it should go, and Richard flung the buoy after it.

"Richard's having so much fun he may not want to go back to solitary lobstering," said Joanna.

"Oh, he's too much of a Bennett to want to be somebody else's crew, even his father's," Laurie said. "Besides, Owen says it's hard enough to watch out for one of them in the boat. The two together drive him crazy. He says they both regress to about age eight."

"Do you think you'll ever lose Tommy?"

"Not if his parents have anything to do with it. They act as if he wouldn't be on the mainland a month before some girl got him pregnant." They both laughed.

"Another few years," said Laurie, "and I may be driven to finding

Tommy a wife. Oh, he's a good kid, willing and lovable, but I don't see myself keeping house for a willing and lovable old bachelor along with my husband in my sunset years."

"Strange, but that's what I think about Jamie sometimes," said Joanna. "Leaving out the 'willing and lovable,' unless he mellows. . . . He was on the sunny side this morning," she added thoughtfully. "I wonder why."

"A nice dream about millions of herring?"

"That could do it," Joanna agreed.

They went down into Bull Cove and sat on an old timber like a house beam, half buried in the beach peas and sow thistles. It had been there a long time.

"I wonder where this thing drifted from," said Joanna, "and how many conversations have taken place on it. I'll bet just about everybody on the island has sat here at some time or other. Good thing it can't talk, huh?"

"Mmm," said Laurie peacefully, her chin in her hands. Pip made a token dash after a sandpiper and went poking around in the windrows of fresh rockweed. The two women sat silent, watching the cat against the dazzle beyond him.

White Lady came into view, and they knew when Richard spotted them and spoke to Owen. He leaned out from under the canopy and swung his arm in a broad salute. The women stood up and wigwagged back.

"They're all three happy as clams out there," said Joanna. "I can see the grins from here."

Laurie didn't answer, and Joanna glanced at her. Her blush was that of a young girl, and so was her smile. She hunched up her shoulders, hugging herself, and never took her eyes off the boat. It was as if Joanna weren't there.

"When's the engagement to be announced?" she asked, and Laurie said without looking away from the boat, "I'm as much in love with him as I ever was, and sometimes it's almost as painful as it was in the beginning. I still can't take my eyes off him whenever he's around."

"We've noticed," said Joanna. "We all think he's pretty lucky. And so are you, I guess, to feel that way still."

"I don't know," said Laurie. "You'd think that after all these years I could take something for granted, wouldn't you?" The boat was moving away now. Laurie put her hands in her pockets and dug sand with the toe of her boot, intensely fascinating Pip, who began to help dig. This made her laugh, and she sat down on the timber again.

"Why should it be painful?" Joanna asked. "Do you worry all the time about something happening to him? Or does it jump out at you just when you're feeling happiest and punch you in the belly? Or show you some horror you can't describe, you can only feel?"

Laurie braced back to look her in the face, surprised. "You say that with an awful lot of feeling."

"Because I know what it's like."

"All right, I'll tell you," said Laurie decisively. "I used to think he was—well, I simply couldn't imagine anything bad happening to a *Bennett*. It had no *right*; it wouldn't *dare*. And I guess he felt the same way, till he got the scare about the heart attack, five years ago. We both were terrified, Jo. We tried not to show anyone, but the warning to take better care of himself was the same as a death sentence. We'd cling to each other all night like stranded mountain climbers in a blizzard, trying not to slide down an icy slope into a crevasse."

"My God." Joanna shuddered, and Laurie smiled.

"Don't forget I come from that kind of country, and I know about these things happening. My father was in plenty of rescue parties. . . . Anyway, Owen and I got over it, as much as anyone does. But you're right, the terror is still there. I've had my moments when I've tried to be hard-boiled and plan what I'd do without Owen. I owe it to the kids, and to him, too. But I'd get sick to my stomach. It wasn't that I couldn't cope, because I keep the books, write the checks, do the taxes. It's just that life without Owen in it is unimaginable, and I couldn't even begin to think about it."

"I know the feeling," said Joanna. "That's what I mean about the ambush and the fist in the gut."

Laurie clasped her knees and hunted for words. "You know, there was a time before the heart scare when he—well, on the surface he was the same, but he *wasn't* the same, if you know what I mean. There wasn't anything I could put my finger on, but I'd have this feeling that he wasn't with us. With *me*. I'd have this sensation that I was talking into outer space. No, it was more like across miles and years all contained in one room."

Fine chills ran delicately up Joanna's neck into her scalp. "At night," Laurie continued, "when we were in bed, it was as if his body was there but he wasn't. I thought I was going crazy. Premenopause paranoia. How's that for scientific?"

"Impressive as hell. How long did it last?"

"Till he thought he was having a heart attack and took off for the mainland that day right in the middle of hauling, without telling anybody. When I had something real to worry about, I knew I wasn't headed for the booby hatch. And oh, boy, was he scared when he came back. He told me about it when he could find the words, and I was scared, too, but at least we were together in it. And we *have* been, ever since."

She picked up a stick and drew his name in the sand. Pip pounced on the stick and scrabbled out the letters, and she laughed and pulled his tail. "He must have been having premonitions, sensations, for a while before he had the actual pains, so that explained the distance I'd felt between us. You may think this is an awful thing, Jo," she said with an appealing glance, "but I'd gotten it into my weak head that he could be involved with another woman. Now you're shocked."

"No," Joanna protested. "But nowadays there aren't many chances for hanky-panky on Bennett's."

"But it could have been somebody on Brigport," she argued. "And I've been over there often enough with Owen to know what an impression he makes on the rusticators. You know that as well as I do. Even at fifty-five he can still do it without trying, and I'm not just being a besotted wife when I say that. The girls bring home their friends, and Tommy gets tied up in knots of frustration while Mr. Bennett gets all the attention. And it's nothing to him. Some men would have their heads turned front to back by all this juvenile adoration. Or be embarrassed by it," she added.

"Nothing can turn a Bennett man's head because Bennetts are born sure of themselves; it's in the genes. And for the same reason it's practically impossible to embarrass them. I know. I've tried."

"Well, let me tell you, God can shake them up," said Laurie. "Or fate, or whatever it is that gives them the first hint that they aren't immortal."

"So I've noticed. Tell me about your suspicions. Did you have anybody in mind?"

"Well, it's so foolish to talk about now, but I built up a real case around this woman who was sitting on the Brigport breakwater one day, like the Lorelei, only she wasn't combing out her long golden hair, she was painting. Owen called to her—used her first name—and ordinarily I'd not have given it a second thought, because he went to Brigport plenty of times without me and could have been introduced to her in the store. But this time I thought at once, She's the one." She gave Joanna a shamefaced little grin. "I hid it pretty well, I was really good at that. Then he went away for a few days. He had a good reason; he said his eyes were bothering him. Honestly, Jo, it sounds so soap opera-ish, I'm embarrassed."

"Listen, you're giving me gooseflesh, so don't stop now. Besides, it will be good for you."

If Laurie only knew how many times the more cynical of his brothers had suggested in earlier days that if Owen was being straight-up-and-down faithful it was only for lack of opportunity to be otherwise.

"Well, all right," Laurie said dubiously. "But I feel like such a fool.—I didn't believe it about his eyes, I wanted to find out if *she'd* left Brigport at the same time, but I didn't know how to ask. I was too proud anyway. But when he came back, I was actually surprised. After two nights of no sleep I was sure he'd left me. Run away with a summer complaint. Never mind practical considerations like how would he make a living, how would he even survive away from the island—and I had all the bankbooks. Oh, gosh, this is all so *foolish!*"

"No, it isn't," said Joanna stubbornly. Pip flattened, ears laid back, tip of tail twitching. There was nothing that Joanna could see except for an odd, small hump in the rockweed. Either he thought it was something alive, or he was pretending he thought so.

"Anyway, he came back," Laurie went on in a small husky voice, "and said he didn't need glasses. But he was still preoccupied. So I thought they'd made their plans and he was trying to decide how to tell the kids and me."

"And then came the day when he thought he was having a heart attack." Pip was inching forward on his belly.

"Yes, and that was it." Laurie spread out her hands. "The heart scare was the real menace, and it wiped out everything else. For a long time I didn't even have the chance to be ashamed. But it was there all right, and been there all along, and I never thought it would pop out like this."

"This is when some folks would go for a cigarette or a drink," said Joanna. "This is the best I can do." She handed Laurie a jackknife to peel her orange. Laurie's embarrassed giggle sounded very young. Pip left off stalking the unknown and strolled up to them with his tail straight up, blinking benignly. He rubbed his cheek against their knuckles and gave the knife a close examination.

Joanna said, "Tell me something, just for curiosity's sake. Why the resignation? Why didn't you think, The hell with this! I'm going to bring him up with a round turn.—Were you really going to strike your colors and give in without a fight?"

"Joanna, don't you think I know that Owen married me out of duty?"

It was a jolt. "Talk about being brought up with a round turn, you just did it to me." Joanna grasped for certainties that weren't there. "Damn it, Laurie, I—How can you be *sure?* What makes you—Good God, you've done it. I'm speechless." She tried to laugh, but it was a failure.

"You're speechless because you know that's the truth." Laurie was no longer shy and abashed. "You all knew it at the time. Look, I wasn't the type of woman he'd pick to fall in love with, the deep, desperate kind of love that pulls you up by the roots—which is the way I fell in love with *him.*"

"And you couldn't hide it." That at least was a certainty. "You were as innocent, probably an awful lot more so, than these girls Joss and Holly bring home. You were practically downy. And you came to this place in a beautiful September. You were in love with everything, and here he was. If ever an older man took advantage—"

Laurie shook her head vehemently. "No, no! I wanted him. I'd never felt that way about anyone in my life before. He was the most beautiful man I'd ever met, he melted my bones, and he could have had me the first day. No, he never seduced me, Jo. But if you want to call it that, I made it very easy for him. You know that song of Maggie's—'O whistle, and I'll come to you, my lad.' Well, he didn't even have to whistle."

Neither did Alec, Joanna thought. "And our girls wonder why we worry about them," she said aloud. "As if we didn't know anything about it."

"I didn't expect him to marry me," Laurie said. "I'd never have demanded it. To me he was—well, anyway, I was worried about the baby, what I'd do, how I'd tell my parents, and so forth, but I knew all the responsibility was mine."

"The rest of us didn't see it like that," Joanna said, "and I still don't.

The child was half his. Well, he had the accident to his hand and knew it could have killed him, so he saw the light. Scared again. You have to terrify these Bennetts to get any concessions from them."

"But you see, he married me because he felt he had to, and that's been on my mind all these years. So when I began having these delusions, it must have been my guilty conscience. He's been a wonderful man to me, a wonderful father for the kids, but what have I done to him? What if I've kept him from having the one great love affair of his life?" She was mocking herself, but the thorn was there.

"To be brutal about it," said Joanna, "if it hadn't been you, it'd have been someone else, and you were a relief."

Laurie's laugh brought Pip running again. "Jo, you can always throw cold water when it's needed."

"And sometimes when it's not, they tell me. But don't ever think you've cheated Owen, out of anything. I'd say you've given him everything he needed."

"*Need* is different from *want*." Laurie's voice flattened. "Hey, you won't mind forgetting this conversation, will you?"

"It's forgotten. But I hope it's been useful."

"I guess it has." She threw a periwinkle shell for Pip and watched him pounce. Joanna watched her. You wish you'd never said anything, she thought. But they'd been in the same family for enough years to keep it from making any lasting difference between them.

"I'm *glad* I talked," Laurie said suddenly. "Maybe this was something that should be out to the air, like diaper rash."

"Wow, *that* comparison would take old Owen down a peg!" Joanna said.

Laurie rocked backward in laughter that squeezed tears from her eyes, and nearly fell off the timber. Joanna doubled up over her knees.

14

Fog came in the night, and Joanna woke often, disturbed by the heavy, moist, lifeless air. The moon was shining through the fog, so each time she woke she thought daylight was coming. . . . The foghorn at the Rock mooed through the night, and the bell beyond the southern end of the island clanged unevenly in the deep swells. When at last it was well and truly dawn, the birds were starting up, especially that indefatigable robin. She could think of nothing but a cup of strong, hot coffee. She was trying to slide cautiously out of bed when her wrist was seized in an unbreakable grip, and Nils pulled her back into bed, pushed her onto the pillows, and kissed her. His body pinned her down, his face poised over hers, laughing in silence, challenging, possessive; the private Nils, hers alone.

She took his head in her hands and kissed him all over his face with loud, smacking kisses. "There!" she said, a little out of breath. "And you'd better let me up quick if you don't want an accident."

He rolled off her onto his back. "What a wet blanket, and no pun intended."

"It *was* intended and it's a rotten one." She ran her hand through his rumpled fair hair and kissed him once, quietly and lovingly, and got up. There was nothing to see outside the windows as she dressed; the fog was right up to the screens, filling them with moisture. Her clothes felt damp.

Nils didn't seem in any hurry to get up, and that nagged at her, like the first sign of sensitivity in a tooth. "I'll bring you a cup of coffee if you feel lackadaisical this morning," she said.

"No, you won't. Coffee in bed isn't my idea of high life."

"What is?"

Seriously he studied the ceiling. "Tearing out into the fog thick as dungeon isn't it either. Keeping my wife in bed all day *is.*"

She leaned over and kissed him again, on her way to the door. "Know what? I wouldn't trade you for a farm down east." He smiled and said nothing more.

Pip scratched on the other side of Linnie's door, and Joanna unlatched it with hardly a sound. The cat hurried out, talking.

"I'm awake," said Linnie in a muffled voice. "He's been trying to pry my eyes open for the last half hour, and when I put my head under the covers, he tunneled in." She sighed pleasurably and seemed to sink back into half-sleep.

The cat thumped down the stairs on loud little catfeet, not like Sandburg's fog. Joanna still missed Rory's standing at the foot of the stairs looking up at her, and she supposed she always would. "I'm glad you're such a noisy cat," she said to Pip, who agreed. She let him out the back door and went into the bathroom. She tried to treat this as any foggy summer morning on Bennett's Island, but yesterday a woman on Stonehaven had gone upstairs to see why her husband hadn't followed her down and she had found him dead.

The men had got the news on their boat radios, and Nils had told her at suppertime. The fisherman had been alive when his wife got up, they had talked about the day, and fifteen minutes later he was dead. Nils must have been thinking about that this morning, and she hadn't even remembered it until now.

She resisted calling up to him when she came out of the bathroom, but started the breakfast. Wasn't it too quiet upstairs? The mantel clock had gotten much too loud; it was all she could hear. When Nils came down the stairs, she was swamped with happiness, and knocked on wood.

"What was that for?" he asked.

"Just taking care of things. After yesterday. You know."

He nodded and went into the bathroom, and she laid strips of bacon in the iron spider. Balance had been restored. She and Nils were all right for another day—or all right so far, if you wanted to be extra cautious.

Nils came out of the bathroom, drying his face. "Just whose spirit were you kicking out? Grandpa's? Remember all the texts he had hanging up all over the house? All about vengeance and retribution and hellfire. Took me quite a while to find out that nobody else's God was a giant version of Gunnar Sorensen." He returned the towel to the bathroom. "After he died, Grandma told me once that when he was young, he was the life of the party. Singing, dancing, oh, light as a feather, she said, with her eyes all shining. I couldn't believe it, but she swore to it."

Pip clawed at the screen and yowled. Nils let him in.

"Did she say what happened to change him?" Joanna asked.

"He met the devil one day." Nils took down plates from the cupboard and silver from the drawer. "Horns, tail, and all. Told Grandpa he was waiting for him to dance and sing his way to hell."

"But *where* did he meet him? So I can avoid the place."

"Right up in our bedroom. You moving out of it now? He was having pneumonia. Grandma heard his part of the conversation. She said he was scared foolish and promising everything. Afterward he told her just what the devil looked like. . . . How about scrambling those?"

"Anything you say, Cap'n." She cracked the eggs into a bowl. "I'd say the devil took him over then, wouldn't you? When he stopped singing and dancing?"

"I don't know, but while I still hated the old man, I was sure he was going to hell anyway, and it would've been a lot easier on the rest of us if he'd gone by way of his singing and dancing."

"Doesn't it say somewhere in the Bible that the Lord loveth a merry heart, or am I thinking of a cheerful giver?"

"Who's a cheerful giver?" Linnie asked from the stairs.

"You're full of sunshine this morning," said her father.

"I'm always full of sunshine. Besides, I played cribbage with Uncle Owen last night and skunked him. I understand his own kids don't dare."

"He's probably still sulking," said Joanna. Yesterday's talk with Laurie passed only lightly through her mind, and she hoped Laurie hadn't heard about the Stonehaven man.

She walked down to the shore with Nils and Linnie. The village was ghostly in the fog. Hank was walking around in the field; when he saw them, he took wing and reached the fish house first, forever hopeful, but this morning no herring came his way. There were oars in the fog, voices, engines starting up, as familiar as the voices. *Sea Star* was hazy; *Valkyrie* was barely visible, with Jamie an apparition on her bow to cast off the mooring. Anything beyond him was unseen.

While Nils was rowing out into the wall of mist, Linnie brought *Dovekie* to the wharf and loaded her buckets of filled bait bags aboard. Hank came to the top of the hoisting mast for a better look.

"Throw him one from me, Marm," Linnie said.

"Yep." Joanna lifted the two half-hitches off a spiling, coiled the painter, and dropped it neatly into the bow. "Hug the shore," she said automatically.

"Don't worry, Marm," Linnie said indulgently. "I won't get out on the freeway where the big trucks go. I'll feel my way along with one foot on shore. And they won't let Sam go to haul in this, so I'll have it to myself."

She leaned over and started her outboard motor. It answered at once. *"That's* always a nice surprise."

She headed out, and Joanna didn't watch to see her vanish into the fog. Resolutely ignoring the harbor, she went to the bait shed, and with Hank coasting by her ear like a witch's familiar, she took out two herring from one of the big butts. Jamie's, she thought with a little grin. I wonder if he'll miss them.

At home and sitting down with a second cup of coffee and Pip sprawled across her lap, she remembered her moment of terror early this morning. Not that she'd really forgotten it; she'd only put it aside.

"A good way to go," Nils had said when he told her about the Stonehaven man. "But it was too soon."

Last night they had gone to sleep in each other's arms, like young lovers. They had agreed long ago that neither of them should be taken away from the island to die. For Joanna it was not a morbid promise but a comforting one. They had traveled, enjoyed it, and would travel again; they weren't grown fast to the ledges like barnacles. But they would never live away from the island or die away from it if they had any choice whatsoever.

"I'm going for a walk," she said to Pip. "And *you're* staying home."

Immediately he jumped down and went to the back door and looked over his shoulder at her, blinking seductively.

"No," she said. "I'm not in the mood to play hide-and-seek or praise you every time you climb a tree." He became even more winsome.

She said firmly, "Come on, I'll give you some more breakfast." She left him eating. She wanted to be alone with the island, and even the cat's innocent presence would be in the way. She crossed the Homestead meadow unseen from the house up on the rise, and went into the woods beyond the cemetery and onto the old road; she loved it in the fog, with the woods all dark and silent except for the steady drip off the branches and the wraiths of mist floating among the wet-blackened trunks. There were small, sudden flurries of bird life, crossbills chattering unseen in the treetops, the silent flight of a small hawk only glimpsed from the corner of the eye. And there was the unexpected gift that convinced her she'd been meant to take this walk, and without Pip: an indignant little crowd of chickadees scolding a tiny saw-whet owl that sat like a toy on his birch branch. He was hardly bigger than a robin, and he refused to be flustered.

She stood watching, not shifting a finger even when she felt a mosquito on her neck. The indignant chickadees ignored her, and the little owl, barely blinking his round eyes, was not about to take wing and show her his soundless flight. She backed carefully away so as not to make any sudden motion, and at a little distance along the path she turned homeward.

The scene had put a crown on the day, the earlier intimations of mortality burned off as the fog was burning off.

When she emerged from the woods at Goose Cove, luminous layers of mist thickened and thinned over water of the same fragile blue as the sky. By comparison, the color of the blue flag in the little marshy patch was as sharp as a shout, and in the meadow the daisies had the whiteness of snow. A bank of buttercups that had been bowed and sodden when she passed them earlier were now shiny as yellow metal amid the glitter of diamonded cobwebs.

She shed her sweater as she crossed the meadow, and hot herbal pungency rose from the earth around her. When she reached the house, she was hot and thirsty. Someone had let Pip out, and he was off about his own affairs. Linnie's turtleneck was dropped on a chair. Joanna had a long drink of cold water, combed her damp, short hair without the usual closer look at the whitening over the ears and the here-and-there glints through the black.

"It's still there," she said aloud, "but so *what?*"

Everyone had collected mail and groceries and gone home, the hoisting engine chattered on the wharf, and only Helmi and Louis were in the store for the moment, the cat a large, striped, slumbering heap on the counter. Joanna walked through the long shed out to the wharf, where freight was being unloaded from the mail boat, assisted or impeded by a clutch of youngsters with whom Mark was remarkably patient.

White Lady was tied up on the outside of the *Clarice Hall,* and Owen was aboard the mail boat, supervising the transfer of lumber from her deck to his own; Tommy, Richard, and Sam were doing the work.

Drake's Pride was at the lobster car being gassed up, and Willy was holding the gas nozzle to the tank. When he saw Joanna, he touched the floppy brim of his hat in a bashful little salute. Drake stood on the car with his billfold in his hand, watching the meter on the pump. He was dressed for the mainland in cream-colored corduroys and an argyle pullover.

"That's it, Willy, my lad," he said, and Willy withdrew the nozzle and returned the hose to its place. Drake came lithely up the ladder. "Mrs. Sorensen!" he exclaimed.

"Mr. Drake!" she answered, and they both laughed.

Behind them Mark said with noticeable restraint, "Why don't you young ones start wheeling and lugging some of this small stuff up to the store?"

Aboard the mail boat Owen said, "No, you chumps, don't lay it that way, unless you're figuring on dropping off one board at a time astern all the way around the island so somebody can find you in case you get lost."

"God, how I love these people," Drake said to Joanna. "I'm proud to be called a Maine lobsterman."

Just who does call you that? Joanna silently asked. "How's Miss Baird coming along?" she asked aloud.

"Oh, she seems to be responding," he said in a low and confidential voice. "She really appreciates the privacy. I have you to thank for that."

"None of us would push in where we aren't wanted."

His ruddy color deepened a bit, and he said hastily, "I'm sure of that; it's not what I meant—"

She wondered just how she was looking at him, and smoothly interrupted. "It must have been nice for her to see her brothers."

"Oh, that!" His voice dropped even more, and he leaned toward her. "Sometimes your own people are the last you want to see. The boys meant well, but they upset her. I had to tell them. It was my duty toward my tenant, she had certain rights, but she couldn't bring herself to send them away, poor girl."

"That's too bad," said Joanna.

It seemed like a good all-purpose answer and it satisfied Drake, who said, "Yes, well, that's the way things go. But time heals all wounds. Life goes on. It's always darkest before dawn."

She found herself solemnly nodding while trying to keep from saying, Yes, and a stitch in time saves nine, doesn't it? That's so comfortable to remember.

Owen saved her by yelling up from the mail boat, "Hey, Jo, you got any soul-and-body lashins at home? How about a cup of coffee?"

"It'll be ready when you get there," she called back. "Good-bye," she said to Drake's smile before he could tell her how colorful Cap'n Owen was, and walked fast up the wharf.

15

"When you get all this stuff aboard," Owen was saying to his men, "get yourselves some cold soda. It's on me."

"The last of the big spenders," said Mark. "He said it before witnesses, too. He can't take it back."

Owen caught up with her by the Binnacle. "Mark's set up for life now. He'll never have to worry. Drake's buying gas from him."

"Well, a rolling stone gathers no moss," said Joanna, "and it never rains but pours. Here today and gone tomorrow, and it's a long lane that has no turning. How about, Talk's cheap, but it takes money to buy rum?"

He grabbed her by the shoulder and swung her around, to face him. "For God's sake, Jo, you parted your fasts?"

"I've been listening to the Great I Am. Is he *real*, or are we all dreaming him?" She laughed aloud at Owen's expression and patted his cheek. "No, I'm not losing my mind; I've still got both oars in the water. Let's get that coffee. Let's raise hell and use the strong stuff and not the decaf."

"Don't say that word too loud," he cautioned her. "I wouldn't want to spoil my image." They reached the gate, and he scooped up a delighted Pip. "How goes the battle, old stocking? . . . What's this about Felix the Fart? As he's known in certain low circles around here."

"Is he an honest-to-God fool, or does he think he's making fools out of us? He has the weirdest effect on me."

"He doesn't leave you speechless, that's for sure. . . . Take that cold nose out of my ear, cat." He put Pip down, and the cat rushed ahead of them into the house.

Owen leaned in the kitchen doorway while she made the coffee. "We had a fine old snarl yesterday, right after I saw you and Laurie at Bull Cove."

"With *him?* Jamie was hoping for one."

"Ayuh. I get all the luck. Oh, he was full of regrets and excuses and scared of me getting close enough to scratch his paintwork. Willy was working his guts out, trying to clear the snarl, so I told Drake to grab on to it, which he did. When we got the snarl cleared out without much cutting, he was all flushed with manly toil. Then he popped into the cabin and comes out with a bottle of Chivas Regal and offers me a drink. I guess he thinks that's how you do."

"Like calling everybody Skipper or Cap'n."

"Yup, I got that, too. I thought Richard and Tommy were going to bust a gut, but they managed to restrain themselves."

"Did you accept the drink?" Joanna asked.

"Nope. I thought of saying I was fussy about who I drank with, but I'm not the rough character I used to be. I told him I never drank on duty, but I thought Willy'd appreciate a swallow, the way he'd been working. Like to killed Drake, handing his expensive booze over to the hired help, but he did it. Didn't quite say, 'Here, my good man,' but anyway, Willy was grateful," he said complacently. "He'd leave Drake in a flash if anybody crooked a finger at him. I've got half a mind to do it, just to see what Drake does next, except I wouldn't know what to do with Willy afterward."

"You'd better leave well enough alone. You don't know what Drake could show up with if he lost Willy." She poured coffee into mugs. "Want a doughnut?"

"If you made them, sure."

They went out to the sun parlor table, and Pip took a chair for himself, his speckled golden eyes fixed on the doughnuts. Joanna broke some up for him. Owen stirred his coffee for what seemed a long time, gazing out the window. In the clear white light his swarthy skin showed the seams and creases from years of weathering, and his black eyes looked deeper-set than they used to be. They were always restless eyes, even when he was sitting still; but in this prolonged pause they were as quiet as his body was, and it was as if he had forgotten he was stirring his coffee, or as if he had moved so far away in spirit it was only an illusion that he was here at all.

She was used to Nils's long silences; they had always been a part of him. With Owen it was disturbing, especially only a day after the talk with Laurie. Just as she was about to break the spell, trying to think how, he said suddenly, "Well, sister mine, here we are."

"We certainly are," she said with relief. "Here. Yes. I thought you'd gone into a trance."

He ignored that. "It's funny," he said thoughtfully, "you see the gray in your hair, but you're the same inside as when you were a kid. You get to know more things, go through more experiences, get scared shitless a lot more times, but inside you're the same as you always were. Even when you have young ones of your own, you don't automatically turn into somebody else, this big grown man, a stranger."

She nodded.

"One day it hits you just how many years have gone by, and you think, That can't be right! Hell, I'm just getting ready to live!—You've been getting warmed up to it all this time. You're still waiting for it, whatever it is you've been working toward." His doughnut was ignored, and Pip reached out a cautious paw. "Then, all of a sudden, there's no time for *it* at all. So what's happened to it? Where the hell is it, and when did you miss it? *How* did you miss it?"

He looked accusingly at her. "Listen," she said, "I know what you're getting at, but just what is it you've been waiting for? Do you know?"

"I'll be damned if I do!" he said angrily. Pip, extremely intent, began drawing the doughnut toward him. Joanna saw, but didn't want to risk shattering the moment.

"All I know is," he said, "is that I've wasted my life expecting something that never showed up. Not to stay," he added as if to himself. "But up to a few years ago I couldn't break the goddamn habit. I'd wake up with more hopes and expectations, feeling almost as young as my kids, and then I looked in the glass one day and thought, Who are you kidding, you old buzzard, with the white hairs coming? And your wife doling out the food so you won't get a potbelly? Just who the hell do you think you're kidding?" He tipped back his chair and laughed long and loud.

Pip swept the doughnut onto the floor and jumped down after it. Owen brought the front legs of his chair down with a crash, shaking his head and wiping his eyes. "Well, nobody can say that I don't appreciate a good joke, even when it's on me."

"And how do you wake up now?" she asked. "Not feeling like an old man, I hope. Because I've never seen any signs of it."

"Jesus, no!" he said vigorously. "I still have my moments. Unsinkable Owen, that's me. But sometimes I think it would be a hell of a lot easier if a man started feeling and thinking like an old fub in plenty of time to be ready for it, instead of wanting to yell like his kids, 'It's not fair! I haven't had my turn yet!'"

"Everybody must feel like that, sometime or other. You *would* be an old fub if you just sat around completely satisfied with everything, your whole life long. That feeling of wanting, hoping, expecting—I know what it's like." This was an incredible conversation, and she prayed for no interruptions. *Linnie, stay away.* "But what happened a few years ago to shut you off? Something real, like the heart scare, or was it just—" She couldn't think how to describe it and waved her hands vaguely.

"Well, it sure as hell wasn't *that*," he said, "whatever it was. What's this represent?" He mimicked her gestures. "The rum horrors?" His laughter this time was completely natural and took years off him. "Nope, I wasn't ever like old Gregg, seeing furry monsters with tusks and wings coming over the foot of the bed. . . . Where's my doughnut?"

"Pip took it, and he's eating it under the table. Have another."

He ate half at one bite, and she said, "Speaking of monsters, Gunnar saw the devil. Talked with him."

"We always knew who he was working for, the old reprobate. Wouldn't you like to see him eyeball to eyeball with our new citizen?" He tucked his thumbs in imaginary suspenders, narrowed his eyes, nodded his head, and said softly, "Yaw, Mr. Drake, it seems your compass is wrong. I will point you home again."

She wouldn't allow him to get away from her direct question. "*Was* it the warning?"

His gaze turned opaque. He drummed his fingers on the table. "You could say that. Yep. Gives a man a hell of a jolt. Everything else gets jettisoned. Then there's nothing to wake up for but relief because you made it through another night, and then you can start being scared again."

"But that wears off, doesn't it? It seemed to, with you."

"Sure, those fellers who defuse unexploded bombs get so they can sleep, too." He took his mug out to the kitchen.

"Are you all right?" she called after him. It was easier to ask when they weren't face-to-face. "If you're having some pains or any weird feelings at all, for heaven's sake—no, for your family's sake—don't be a fool and suffer in silence. Go to the doctor *now. Today.*" He came back and, passing her, put his hand on her head, and said soothingly, "Darlin' mine, I'm fine. No aches, no pains, no bruises. I'm not a hero; I never could suffer in silence. I'm a coward. Always was."

"I remember," said Joanna, "one time when Siggie was drunk and thought you were after Leonie. He called you yellow because you wouldn't fight with him, and you stood out there in the moonlight bawling, 'Sure, I'm yellow! I'm yellow as a goddamn buttercup!'"

They erupted into laughter. Joanna felt the tears spurt into her eyes and knew the laughter was a kind of mourning. Then they sat in reminiscent silence for a few moments. Under the table Pip was heard eating his stolen doughnut with noisy gusto.

"So," Joanna said mischievously, "all that ails you is change-of-life blues."

"Maybe that's it."

She didn't trust his amused agreement, but she wouldn't ask him anything else. His health was supposed to be the problem, and they'd taken care of that.

Suddenly he said, "Sometimes I feel like making a change. Go away down east, learn new waters. That'd be a challenge, such as it is."

This time she went for more coffee. But talk about a jolt! "Alone, you mean?" She sounded casually curious. "Like the way you went away for years? And then showed up one day like the Ancient Mariner?"

"Christ, no!" He sounded genuinely startled and followed her into the kitchen. "But there's times, like when Drake came in here and we had the big powwow with nothing to it, sure, I sounded off, but afterward I thought, What in hell was it all for? There'll always be fishermen here. What does it matter whether they've got Bennett blood, or Sorensen, or Fennell or Campion, or what? It's just rocks and spruce trees after all."

"But it's an island," she said, "and it's *our* island. How many people in the world have an island? How many would like to? We've got one, and that makes us more than rich; it makes us different."

Leaning in the doorway, he gave her that cynical sidewise look and the lift of an eyebrow. "You may be bored," she said, trying not to fire up, "you may be tired of it all, may be restless, but what about your kids? Or didn't you mean all that highfalutin talk about their heritage?"

"What about my *wife?*" He gave her a dazzling smile. "She's a convert, and that's the worst kind. So, apart from the fact that a new fisherman moving in anywhere is viewed the way we see Drake, and even if I got through all the protocol and set some traps, I'd probably never find them again. Apart from that, my wife and my children are rooted here in solid granite. Oh, Laurie'd go anywhere I went, but the kids would divorce me. 'We get the house and the dog and the island, Dad. So long. Write sometime.'"

He pulled her into his arms and gave her a massive hug. "God, if you could've seen your face!" She pinched him viciously in the ribs until he yelped and let her go.

"I've got to get back to the boat. Those three are likely foundering in soda by now and running up the bill as fast as they can."

"I'll go with you." She had to get out of the house and talk to someone else, think about something else. She wished he had confided nothing to her, yet she always wanted to *know.* You can't have it both ways, she scolded herself. Talk about still being a kid inside, you're still trying to have both ends and the middle. You think life is so fine at the moment, you're all hawsed up if everybody else doesn't feel the same way.

"What are you looking so ugly about?" Owen asked her as they left the house. "Want a few nails to chew?"

"I'm still peeved at Drake," she lied. "The way he practically gave orders for nobody to go near his tenant. Just the sight of that boat irks me."

"Hell, don't blame the boat; it's not her fault. Tell you what, he's gone by now, so you run right around the harbor and tap on Miss Mouse's door and tell her the cat's away, come out and play."

"Why don't you do it? Give the old charm a workout. Do you good."

"Could be dangerous. The kids brought home some book they've been giggling and shuddering over, about vampires in Maine, so the latest scuttlebutt is that the lady's a vampire who flaps around after dark looking for necks to bite. In my day that kind of goings-on didn't have anything to do with vampires."

Tiger rushed around the Binnacle, shrieking at them, and Hank hallooed from the chimney. Owen took hold of Joanna's elbow. "Thanks for the mug-up and the ear, Jo," he said in a low voice. "And keep it under your hat, huh?"

"What do you think I *am?*"

"Okay, okay! I apologize!" He squeezed her arm. "Remember Indian sunburn?"

"Don't you try it or I *will* talk. I'll tell everybody you're in your second childhood."

Tiger was now ecstatically smelling Owen's rubber boots as if they brought news from another world rich in titillating scents. Back along the road Danny Campion came running past the fish houses. He was barefoot and wore only cutoff jeans. His head was yellow as his mother's used to be.

Maggie was sitting on the front steps of the Binnacle, scowling at a paper spread out on her knees and muttering to herself. Her glasses had slid far down her short, freckled nose.

"Maggie, me love!" Owen hailed her. "What's got under your rose petal skin today?"

She looked up, pushed her glasses back with a forefinger. "You two come along just in time. I was about to use some awful language. I sent off for these instructions for a real handsome afghan, and I can't make head nor tail of 'em. I like to go over everything before I begin, but this is such a devilish mess it's got me fair scunnered from the start."

"Read your tea leaves," said Owen. "Consult your Ouija board. Go into a trance, and it'll all come clear."

She chuckled. She was never offended by jokes about what she considered her particular gifts, any more than she was conceited about them. "I've never been in a trance in my life," she said, "and never want to be. And I'd like to see what tea leaves or a Ouija board could do about this ungodly mess. Besides, those things aren't for daily use like the broom or the teakettle," she added. "They're for special, serious times. . . . I wish you'd take this paper sometime, Jo, and see what you can make of it."

"I'll look now, but if you can't make sense of it, I probably can't either," Joanna said. She sat down beside Maggie. "Carol Fennell could maybe. She knits some pretty complicated things."

"Maggie, did you see Drake coming?" Owen asked curiously.

"Nope. Nor the Mystery Lady either. That's what my girls call her.

See this right here, Jo—" She pointed. Danny sprinted past; his elbows were held into his sides, his fists were clenched, his knees pumped high, his face fierce with resolution, and his eyes were fixed on some distant tape. Sweat shone on his skinny little torso. They all applauded him, and Tiger ran behind him; but nothing diverted him.

"He's training for high school track," said Maggie fondly.

"Well, in eight years he ought to be pretty good at it," said Owen. "Good-bye, ladies." He went down over the lawn to the road, not hurrying, hands in his pockets, and headed for the store. Anne Barton came running past Philip's as if to catch up with Danny, a small ginger-haired girl in jersey and minute shorts, barefoot, and as determined as Danny. Her mother was still far back by the harbor beach.

Anne chugged past the Binnacle, audibly panting, her face screwed up with the effort. "Go it, Sal, I'll hold your bunnit!" Mag called out. And then, just passing the bit of beach beyond the Sorensens' fish house, Anne stubbed her toe on something and went flying forward, landing on her hands and knees. She let out a wail of grief and astonishment, then sat back and bowed her head over her scraped knees, and wept. Tiger frisked and wagged as he tried to lick her ears, but she only bowed lower.

Joanna and Maggie both jumped up involuntarily, but Owen, just a few yards ahead of the child, walked on as if he had heard nothing. It was this that gave Joanna the next shock of the morning.

That's not like Owen, she was thinking while she and Mag hurried down the slope. Not like Owen *at all.*

"Tiger, leave her alone!" Mag called. "Come here this minute!"

All at once Owen turned and came back and reached Anne before the women were halfway. Unsmiling, he dropped to his heels and stood her up, steadying her with one big hand. Sternly he wiped the gravel off her knees and felt her bare foot. "It's not broken," he said. She nodded between snufflings and hiccups and held out her hands to his. He looked at each one.

"They'll be all right," he said. "There." He brushed his lips across one small palm and then the other. The child, quieting, looked into his face and then at her hands. He spoke in a low voice, and Joanna saw her fingers close up as if to hold something tight in each hand.

Maggie, telling Tiger to stay, hadn't seen.

"Here comes your mother," Owen said. Anne looked around, and Owen stood up and went on toward the store, walking fast. Vanessa was now just abreast of Philip's front steps.

"Mommy, Mommy!" Anne called. She rushed back with her fists still tight, Joanna could see that.

"I don't think I'm the one for that pattern, Maggie," she said.

"Thanks anyway," said Mag. "That Owen's some nice with young ones, isn't he?"

Around at the wharf *White Lady* started up, and by the time Joanna walked out on Nils's wharf, the boat was crossing the harbor, with her load of lumber, heading for Eastern Harbor Point. Owen was at the wheel, and he didn't look back. Joanna sat down on a crate and shut her eyes rather than watch the boat out of sight.

She wasn't sure what she had just seen back there on the path; she only knew that she wished she hadn't seen it.

16

By noon the fog lay at a distance, surrounding the island with an opaque lilac-colored wall. In the hot early afternoon Rosa took a drop line and a couple of herring and rowed out into the harbor to try for mackerel. She avoided the harbor mouth, where homecoming traffic would be soon churning up the surface and keeping the skiff bouncing. Beneath Eastern Harbor Point she dropped her little anchor and began fishing.

No one had been around the shore when she rowed out, and there'd be no children fishing in the harbor this afternoon. Richard and Sam had become soccer players away at school, and everyone was meeting in the island schoolyard to be divided into teams. Later their older sisters and friends would be swimming in Schoolhouse Cove and graciously looking out for the younger children. Whatever Linnie was doing, Rosa was glad of it. She wanted to be alone out here. Solitude under a roof could be desolation; it was something very different when you floated like a mussel shell between sky and sea.

There was even a hiatus in the bird activity. When the ospreys, shags, and medricks were fishing, and the mackerel gulls laughing crazily across the sky like a pack of stage witches, the schools of fish were kept too frantic to snap at bait or lure. Only Hank was there today. He paddled around the skiff above his perfect reflection, knowing that when she caught a small pollock she'd throw it to him.

It was hot out here. Rosa had never worn shorts; as a child she'd been self-conscious about her fat. Now as a concession to the moist, windless heat she wore thin cotton slacks rolled up above her knees, a sleeveless blouse, and an old broad-brimmed straw hat she'd found in the house. She brought along a couple of nectarines in a bread wrapper.

Almost everyone used rods now, and some of the men took theirs along and caught mackerel on the way home from hauling. On a fine Sunday they might take the family and make a day of it out by the Rock or down toward Pirate Island. Rosa fished contentedly with her drop line and bits of herring, as she had done for hours as a child. Lying almost without motion on the summery water, she was at peace. She believed that she would succeed in living a life free of emotional dependence on anyone outside herself. She knew that if *Valkyrie* should suddenly pierce the lilac wall of fog, she would be severely tried; but she had won one contest the night she'd kept him out of her bed, and, as they used to sing in Junior Christian Endeavor, "Each vict'ry will help you/Some other to win."

She caught herself humming it now. "Fight manfully onward,/Dark passions subdue. . . . " She smiled without humor. It hadn't been exactly a valiant victory, letting him think it was the wrong time of the month. But it had taken courage to deny herself that night before the storm.

He'd been good-tempered, even philosophical; he'd stayed awhile, smoking his pipe and talking peaceably, not raging about Drake. She hadn't lit a lamp, making it easier for her, because they couldn't see each other's faces. She lay back in one of the rocking chairs with her feet on the low windowsill, looking out at her moonlit spruces, and he had the other rocker. Darby and Joan, she thought nastily. Why does he have to be so *nice* tonight? Because he wants to bend somebody's ear, that's why, and he's forgiven me for being both cussed and simpleminded. Probably blames it on the time of the month now that I've handed him that excuse, and he understands women's frailties. Now he's feeling all secure and comfy because I'm behaving properly: I'm *listening*. But he's not taking any chances in introducing Drake or the Bainbridges into the one-sided conversation. No use stirring her up, she's a woman, and they just don't understand. A *mainland* woman. Two strikes. Three strikes and you're out. *One, two, three, and you're out at the old . . . ball . . . game.*

"Hey, talked you to sleep, have I?" he said, still good-humored.

He got up, and she took her feet off the windowsill and mumbled, "Sorry."

"You don't have to be. I'm ready to crawl under the kelp myself. I just hated to stir myself, that's all." He felt for her head, patted it and then her shoulder. "Night."

After that she didn't fall asleep until she had exhausted herself by planning out just how she would tell Jamie that she was no longer available either to sleep with or to talk to. The trouble was that when you imagined these dialogues the other person always made the right response, so you could extinguish him with your cold reasoning, but in reality you never got past your opening statement.

Something was yanking at her line. She shook herself free of the night and brought in one of the small mackerel she liked best, larger than a tinker but not big enough to have a strong taste. Simultaneously *Sweet Helen* broke through the fogbank hiding Brigport. Here comes Linnie's high-wire walker, she thought, not unkindly. The story had touched her. But Linnie could afford to have poetic dreams; she wished she herself were twenty again and had Linnie's choices.

"However, I'm not and I haven't," she said aloud, turning her eyes from the sight of the mackerel's death struggle.

She was always tempted to throw them back before it was too late, and sometimes did, unless she was fish-hungry enough to be hardhearted. Hank thought she was talking to him and paddled closer.

Sweet Helen approached the harbor, looking twice as big as she really was. Rosa put her oars into place, ready to turn bow to the wake. The boat slowed down, but even then she made a considerable wash that sent large, glistening, green-hearted swells toward the skiff, which rose up on them and dropped into the hollows as nonchalantly as a duck.

Pitt was at the wheel, and Roy leaned out past him, smiling, and waved both arms like a homecoming hero greeting his public. The engine was cut down even more, and *Sweet Helen* came about and moved toward Rosa as easily as if she were drifting on the tide. Hank paddled out toward the ledge off the point usually occupied by shags.

"Hi there, dear!" Roy sat on the washboard. "Some pretty in here, ain't it? Christ, it's thick as lobscouse out there."

"Too thick to find your way to Cash's?"

"Damn right, dear, if your radar's kicking up. And ours is. We're likely to end up at a bullfight in Spain. We found our way in here by smell, for Pete's sake." He thought that was funny; his laughter bounced back from the rock wall of the point. "That good hot land smell. Spruce trees and rockweed, nothing like it." He inhaled noisily, expanding his bare chest. Under the canopy Pitt smoked a cigarette, his eyes half shut.

"How's the mackerel biting?" Roy asked chattily.

"Fair. I've got one for my supper." And that's likely to be all, she thought, with you fubbing around here.

"Seen my sister, dear?"

"Nary a peep."

"She's some depressed." Roy looked suitably perturbed. "We brought her a few goodies. I don't think she eats enough to keep a cat alive."

Pitt ended the conversation by snapping his cigarette overboard and putting the engine into reverse. "Impatient, ain't he?" Roy yelled between his hands as the boat backed away and headed for Drake's wharf. Rosa wondered if they knew or suspected that Drake was probably sleeping with their sister. She didn't know it for a fact and wouldn't repeat it as such, but she was certain of it, as sure as she knew that a red sunrise meant bad weather and that when the land loomed, there would be an easterly wind, if not a storm. It *was* a fact that Drake didn't want her brothers poking around, dropping in; it was also a fact that he had a wife and family back on the mainland, too close to Coates Cove for comfort.

The two Fennell boats came home in company, followed by Philip Bennett's *Kestrel;* the others would be coming along. She was surprised to catch three more mackerel, and then some shags arrived, and the ospreys took position. She pulled up her little anchor and rowed ashore, accompanied on high by Hank, who did some graceful sideslips and figure eights over the harbor and still reached the wharves before she did. He waited on the Sorensen hoisting mast, knowing that she would clean her fish on the beach by Linnie's haul-off and he could gobble up the remains.

As she crouched there on the hot stones at the water's edge, washing the gutted fish with only the gull for company, she thought, I could very happily be a hermit. And I'd better be careful or I'll start acting like one.

"Hi!" Linnie was standing on the wharf. She wore faded blue denim shorts and a yellow tank top. Her hair was just starting to dry after a soaking. "You get many?"

"Enough to hold body and soul together for another day," said Rosa. "What have you been up to?"

"Oh, I went berrying with my mama." She put the accent on the last syllable. "Doesn't that sound hoopskirtish? Then I took a quick swim with the kids." She shaded her eyes with her hand and looked around the harbor and yelped, "Do you see what I see?"

"I dunno," said Rosa. She laid the cleaned fish on a bed of cold dripping rockweed in the pail and put more rockweed over them. "I don't know what your visions are."

"*Sweet Helen*, and I never even heard her come in! I knew when I woke up this morning that there'd be more to this day than thick o' fog. Well, I'm all ready for Pitt. I've been planning out my strategy. Want to hear it?"

"Nope," said Rosa. "I could live happily for the rest of my life without seeing or hearing the Bainbridges again."

Linnie was not offended. "You must have got up on the wrong side of the bed this morning."

"I did. I don't sleep well when it's so foggy, and I get up feeling like a bundle of old dirty laundry."

"God, how ravishing!" said Linnie. "Well, I suppose they're up in the house with her now, so I'll have to lie in wait. I don't expect another soul ever gives Pitt serious consideration as an individual. Oh, probably his mother did at first, but the minute Roy bounced into the world, Pitt was a lost cause. I'll bet Roy was born waving his little fists and saying, 'Hi, there, de-ahs! Hey, this is some nice delivery room!'"

Rosa gave up and laughed. "What are you going to do, run out when Pitt shows up and throw yourself at his feet?"

"Wearing a bikini and holding up a quart of wild strawberries, all hulled. You think that might make a dent? Cause a wee little smile?"

"Maybe, if he's crazy about wild strawberries."

"Fly over her head, Hank, and do something rude," said Linnie. "Anyway, the berries aren't hulled yet, and I don't have a bikini. But all those little high school girls have them. They're lying around Schoolhouse Cove like a bunch of seals. Richard and Sam are either absolutely blasé about it or stunned, I couldn't tell which. Except that they're about killing themselves showing off. And those boys of Ralph's are growing up too fast, if you ask me."

Valkyrie was coming in. With no effect of haste Rosa said, "Well, I wish you luck with the graven image. I'm going home and broil my mackerel."

They went together to where the path branched off past the

Binnacle. "Gosh, I'm so curious about what goes on over there," Linnie said. "Every so often it hits me, the weirdness of it. This woman in our midst, but invisible."

"Well, we know what's going on right now," said Rosa. "Roy is talking."

They laughed and separated. Linnie was going to saunter around the harbor to Kathy's. Rosa walked up past the well, refusing to hurry, refusing to look back at the harbor and watch *Valkyrie* coming to the lobster car. But she began to sweat for the first time this afternoon. When she reached the house, her skin was wet and her hair under the straw hat was damp. She began stripping as she went in the door. She fastened the door and sponged herself with tepid rainwater from the barrel, letting her skin dry in the air. She wrapped the mackerel in foil and put them in the refrigerator and went up to her room. It was very warm up there even with all the windows open, and she lay on her bed as she was, reading, or trying to, because she was as sensitive to all outside sounds as a dog.

17

She woke up chilled. The day had darkened, with the fog moving in again, and a damp wind was blowing through the house. She bundled herself into a bathrobe and went around shutting windows. She was both forlorn and bad-tempered, the usual result of sleeping heavily in daytime. It was only a bit past four, and she had too many hours to get through until tomorrow morning, when she could go to haul again; she looked forward with desperate longing to the hours she could spend on the water.

She'd be damned if she'd stay in now, feeling like this. She got out clean underwear, shirt, and slacks, combed her hair and went out. But she didn't want to go to anyone's house, she'd be noticeably poor company, and people would be asking if she was all right.

She went out on her wharf and looked out at the harbor. Everyone was in, and the boats were seen as through billowing gauze curtains, fairly clear one instant and hardly visible the next. A good-sized sloop was tied up at Mark's mooring. Sam's dory-skiff came out from Philip's wharf, with the outboard held down to a sedate crawl, which meant that Philip was watching. Richard, Cindy, and Robin were aboard with Sam. Before they passed *Sea Star,* they became temporarily invisible, but their voices were clear above the engine. Cindy was happily anticipating at least four new signatures for the large notebook she called the Guest Book, in which she collected visitors' autographs. Richard said callously, "Maybe they can't write." His comment struck him and Sam as exquisitely funny. They were laughing so hard that Rosa was amused in spite of herself.

The outboard stopped. They'd reached the yacht. In the new quiet she heard Hugo speak to Jamie by name farther along the wharves. Now that she knew he wasn't in the store, she went in that direction.

A pleasant whiff of woodsmoke blew down on the wet wind. There was a small fire in the potbellied stove to take off the dampness, and Helmi sat by it, knitting. Mark was working at his desk in the post office; Louis slept by the cash register.

Helmi had never been heard to raise her voice, which made her an exotic in the Bennett family. "Help yourself," she said, nodding at the blue enamel coffeepot on the stove. She kept a tray of mugs on a box behind the counter, not plastic cups that could corrupt the bouquet of fresh coffee. Rosa filled a mug and sat down on a nail keg. She never did that without temporarily becoming the fat youngster who'd sat there as if glued to the keg, eating ice cream with eyes that felt out on sticks.

"If I were nosy," Helmi said, "I'd say a penny for your thoughts."

"Now that's a nosy remark if I ever heard one," Mark said from the post office.

"I was just thinking what good coffee this is," Rosa said. "And with the fire, and Louis, and the water sloshing around under the floor—it's nice."

Comfort was settling around her like a warm cloak to keep out winter. Here she was, a convert, if not a cradle islander, and Jamie or no Jamie, she wasn't about to give it up.

There were footsteps outside, and Mark said, "Here comes Boanerges."

Owen came in. "Afternoon, girls," he said agreeably. He poured coffee for himself and sat down. "Well, I see the Bainbridges are back again. Looks like they're changing the guard. He goes, they come. Woman a homicidal maniac, or what?"

"They were on their way to Cash's, but their radar's acting up," Rosa said. "Or so Roy says. And their sister's depressed. I guess they'd have stopped in anyway to see how she is. Maybe she has melancholia or whatever they call it."

"Well, they're not spending much time with her. Roy's in everybody's mess and nobody's watch, with his shadow trotting around behind him to be sure he doesn't give away state secrets."

"Now that's a thought," said Rosa. "What could they be?"

"Maybe Henry Coates is in the white slave trade," Mark suggested from the post office. "As they used to call it back when I was young."

Owen went on with it. "Maybe he's shipping tender young Maine females out of state in those vans of his, along with fresh fish and lobsters. He looks so damn respectable he could be doing a stavin' business in whores, and nobody'd suspect it except naturally dirty minds like ours."

"He'd be a whoremonger then, wouldn't he?" Helmi said. "Sounds picturesque."

There was a peaceful silence until Owen cocked an eyebrow at Rosa and said, "Melancholia, huh?"

"I'm just guessing," said Rosa. "They call it depression nowadays, I guess."

"Well, everybody's got a theory, so I guess yours is as good as any. But shutting yourself up in the dark sounds like a hell of a poor way to raise your spirits." Rosa considered telling them what she'd seen; she was tempted but resisted. The way Owen was looking at her, she wondered what her expression was giving away; then he gave her a smile that she couldn't resist. Bennetts could look black one instant and blaze out the next.

"Beats me why you're still a free woman," he said. "In my day it'd be a different story."

"I thought your day was still going on," Helmi said.

"Me? A married man all these years and old enough to be a grandpa?" Young Mark came in, and Owen reached out for him. "Now if I had a little boy like this, I'd feel like a young rooster again." Young Mark leaned comfortably against his uncle, smiling with shy pleasure.

"You ever take off those long-legged rubber boots?" Owen asked him.

"Only when his mother overpowers him and hauls them off him," said Helmi.

"When I got my first ones," Owen said, "I was thinking they just might be a pair of those seven-league boots like the ones in the fairy tale. You know that story?"

Young Mark nodded, looking down at his boots. "Well, I could hardly wait to get off by myself, down in Goose Cove," Owen continued. "That's when we all lived at the Homestead, the whole raft of us. So I had to do some sneaking. Anyway, there I was, hoping to get to Schooner Head in just one long step." He paused, and Young Mark gazed into his uncle's face, visibly holding his breath.

"Well," Owen went on, "I swung my leg back hard, then swung it forward with one mighty heave, and rose up on the other foot, and flopped my arms like mad, figuring the next minute I'd be flying through space—and I never went anywhere. Fell on my face, that's all." He gave the little boy a squeeze around his skinny middle. "That's when I first found out that life was no da—no fairy tale. You want to get somewhere, you get *yourself* there. The only good thing about that day was, nobody else in the family saw me down there, trying to take off like a young gull that's not sure of his wings yet."

"There was one other good thing about that day," the child said huskily. "You got your boots."

"You're right. And I was some proud of them, too. Only thing was, my mother wouldn't let me keep 'em in the bedroom at night, 'specially after I'd worn 'em in the bait shed."

Young Mark rolled his dark eyes toward his mother, who smiled at her knitting and didn't speak. Rosa experienced an ache of loss that was almost physical. Boy or girl, it wouldn't matter, as long as it was hers. *And Jamie's* was left unworded but implicit. She shouldn't have come down here this afternoon; she didn't need this wound.

"Your Aunt Jo was some jealous of those boots," Owen said reminiscently.

"Of mine, too," Mark said. "And when Steve got his—and he was the baby—she slatted out of the house in some fine old rage, slamming all the doors on her way. I'll tell you, she saw that Ellen and Linnie got theirs."

Rosa had got her long-legged rubber boots for Christmas one year. Those days looked more and more like Paradise Lost. If she believed one of the poems memorized in high school English, she'd been still trailing clouds of glory at that age, just as Owen had been when he was hoping for seven-league boots, and so was the dark little boy with whatever he dreamed when he played alone.

She stood up to leave, but there was a sudden confused tramping on the wharf outside and a burst of adolescent voices all talking at once with everybody trying for supremacy. Richard made it first through the door, the other three squeezing in behind him, shoving and giggling.

"My God, a buffalo stampede," said Owen. He sat Young Mark on his knee. "You stay put, or they'll run you down."

"We're giving a dance tomorrow night," Richard announced. "Aunt

Helmi, you got anything we can make posters on? We've already got the markers." Sam held up two.

"You been to the board of governors for permission?" Mark asked, coming out of the post office.

"Yes, sir. Sam asked Uncle Philip, Cindy asked her father, and I went up to ask Mr. Fennell. See, we think this is a good time to have a dance because the fog's going to be around awhile, and *Sweet Helen's* here and that yacht. There's three guys and two girls, and they said they'd all come. And," he finished in radiant triumph, "if we're doing it for a good cause, we don't have to pay rent, see?"

"Oh?" said his father. "When'd the club pass that law?"

Richard widened blue eyes. "You mean, the club won't contribute the use of the building for a good cause?"

"Depends on the good cause," said his uncle. "What's yours?"

"We haven't decided yet," Cindy said. "We all have ideas, and we have to settle on one."

"I want to save the baby seals," Robin put in, belligerently. "And the whales, and—"

"Hey, they're good," Sam said, "but there's some other good ones, too. If we do real well, and we ought to, if everybody here comes and a crowd from Brigport, well, we can divide it up."

"Nothing for your own pockets?" asked Owen. "Whatever became of good old-fashioned greed?"

That drew patient smiles from son and nephew, while the two girls looked shocked. "Uncle Mark," said Richard "can we get some cases of soda on credit, pay you after the dance?"

"Yep. Do I and mine get free admission for supplying the poster material and calling Brigport for you?"

There was an exchange of dramatic eye signals among the four. Lips were pursed, or flattened and thinned.

"God, how they hate to let go of that fifty cents," said Owen.

"It's a dollar," said Robin. "Inflation."

"A dollar a family or a dollar apiece?"

"Apiece," said Sam. "Kids under twelve, fifty cents." He sighed. "Heck, Uncle Mark, I guess you three all get in free. I'm glad you don't have eight kids."

"So am I," said Helmi.

Richard approached Rosa with a winning expression. "You want to help out, Rosa? We've already promised that anybody who plays for the dances gets in free and has free soda, up to three cans. Ralph wants you to play," he said with a sweet earnestness. "You and he don't have to play for all the dances, because Hugo's bringing his accordion and Roy Bainbridge can play the banjo with him. If you'll lend him yours," he added rapidly.

"Come on, Rosa," Robin pleaded. "I think the violin and guitar are just beautiful for the waltzes."

"And you can get up to three cans of free soda," said Helmi. "You can't let that go."

"Is this one of those soirees that turns into an orgy after the clock strikes twelve and the old folks and the babes go home?" Mark asked.

"My God!" said Owen. "You mean those things take place somewhere else besides out in the bushes or in somebody's hayloft? All my years on Bennett's Island, I never knew I could've been lewd and lecherous undercover, in comfort. Hell, it never mentioned *that* in the by-laws."

The four older children looked at him in resignation. Young Mark, who had been a solemn, silent witness throughout, resting from a day of long-legged boots, said suddenly, "What's an orgy?"

"When you're old enough to go to one, you'll know," said Owen.

"Hey, Dad," said Richard with a suspiciously straight face, "we have to have somebody sort of in charge, even though we can run it. Could be you and Mother."

"Oh, no, you don't get me in any of them scrapes, as old Tootie Freeman in Brigport said when the schoolmarm asked him to tie her shoelace."

"Hey!" said Sam. "We got this whole thing worked up, promotion, drinks, music, without Betsey and Holly knowing one cussid thing about it. They're so darned bossy," he explained to the adults. They huddled at one end of the counter making their posters, with much discreet argument about the wording and comments about each other's poor printing.

"They don't really need posters," Rosa said. "They've pretty well covered everybody already. Except Betsey and Holly, they hope."

"Putting up posters is what you do when you're giving a dance," said Owen. "Isn't official otherwise."

Mark said, "No time like the present," and went into the back room to call the store at Brigport. Rosa, still under the fresh and vital influence of the children, went home to broil her mackerel.

18

Joanna wasn't at all keen about going to the dance. She'd have rather kept to herself until the aftershocks of revelation had trembled out of existence or until she could convince herself that if there'd been a revelation, it was only that of her melodramatic imagination.

Everyone would turn out for the dance, and she dreaded being in the same room with Vanessa and Owen only a little more than twenty-four hours after the incident on the harbor path. The room would be filled with other people and motion and music, but for her there would be only four: Vanessa, Owen, Barry, and the child.

She was restless the night before, but she often had wakeful spells, especially when the air was so heavy with fog. She slept in naps, got up with the dawn chorus, and went out and walked around the house barefoot in the wet grass and the drenching mist. Pip sunny and loquacious beside her, she was released from the imprisoning pattern of the night. What was wrong with telling Nils? That is, if they had a chance alone before Linnie came down or Jamie crossed the yard instead of making his own coffee? Tell Nils, and it would disappear. Or would it?

There was always the chance that Nils had known something all along, and she'd been put into the category labeled "The Wife." What The Wife doesn't know won't hurt her. No need to let The Wife know about this. She did not want ever to find out that Nils sometimes thought of her as The Wife.

The other possibility was that he would say it was all in her imagination, and she could tell herself that without humiliation. If she did it often enough, it ought to take after a while; she was already feeling better. She explained to herself that she had pounced on an imaginary fact as Pip sometimes pounced with all four paws on a nonexistent mouse. He smelled it, heard it, saw the grass move, but in the instant when he gathered himself together to spring, the mouse had gone. Joanna knew she could have leaped into the wrong place. Laurie could have; Owen had been a rover once, and at the time Laurie specified he might have been having one of those periodical moods of restlessness and dissatisfaction, even of claustrophobia. She'd seen a bit of that yesterday.

And on the practical side, how could anyone as brilliantly visible and strikingly audible as Owen have had a secret affair on either island?

No. Owen and Vanessa just didn't like each other, it was that simple. They'd been getting along all right without anyone's making an issue of their silence, and the incident of the child had been a nothing. What if he hadn't laughed and jollied her when he set her on her feet? What about those kisses brushed across a child's palms and the fingers folded over them? So it wasn't typical of Owen, but where was the unbreakable law that said everyone had to behave according to everyone else's idea of what was typical?

Damn it, Jo, she thought, if all you've got to worry about is something that might or might not have happened five years ago, you ought to be shaken until your teeth rattle for inventing stories you wouldn't give houseroom if anyone else had told them to you.

The dance wasn't quite ready to begin when Nils and Joanna arrived at the clubhouse. Most of the islanders were there, but the dance committee insisted on waiting for two boatloads from Brigport and the people from the yacht. Rosa, Ralph, and Hugo were limbering up with some music of their own. In the poolroom a game was going on in a circle of watchers; Linnie and Eric sat against the wall in deep talk, Linnie joggling Peter Fennell's carriage.

The women visited on the side benches; the small children jigged to the music or slid on the dance floor. The dance committee, all dressed up—blazers, pressed slacks, and ties for the boys, frilly dresses for the girls—was incandescent with importance. They couldn't stand still but kept conferring in pairs, a trio, or all together. They were watched with kindly indulgence by Holly, Betsey, and their friends.

It had finally been agreed that the good cause would be the Limerock Animal Shelter, which had provided several dogs and cats for the island.

A large poster had been tacked up beside the kitchen serving window, decorated with cutout pictures of dogs and cats, and a quart jar invited more contributions.

Nils and Joanna politely examined the poster, Nils put five dollars in the jar, and gave their admission fee to an ecstatic Cindy in blue organdy. Vanessa was across the hall with Maggie Dinsmore and Kathy. Joanna had just sat down by Helmi when the Bainbridge brothers appeared in the doorway. For an instant she saw Pitt's narrow dark face, and then it was gone as Roy filled the opening.

He came in all of a grin and did a little clog dance to "Soldier's Joy" played on Ralph's fiddle. Then he bowed to the amused applause. Until now he'd been seen only in his skin and overalls, but tonight he was dressed in white slacks and a violently printed green and white sport shirt. His ruddy hair and beard were fluffy from recent washing, and his joyous anticipation of a party was as fresh as a child's. He caught up Robin and swung her off her feet, and her ruffled peach skirt spun wide; she was too overcome even to make a sound.

"They must have quite a social life out on Cash's," Helmi remarked, "if he carries his party clothes aboard."

"Maybe he's like the Coast Guard," said Joanna. "*Semper paratus.* He's the kind who's always ready for a party and usually finds one. Or makes one."

He came over to them, children like a comet's tail behind him. "It's a fine large evening, isn't it? Fog or not." He was fragrantly scented. The accordion began "The White Cockade," and he clapped his hands and tapped one foot. "Christ, I'm glad our radar kicked up!" Then he looked contrite. "Excuse me. My mother's always on my neck for that, but I don't mean any disrespect. I mean, I'm a Christian and all."

"I'm on my son's neck, too," Joanna said.

"That Jamie," said Roy, his dimpled smile returning. "He's sure something."

He sure is, Joanna thought. At supper tonight Jamie's opinions on the Bainbridges had been pungent enough to get Linnie mad, and Nils had closed down the subject. "I wish your sister had come with you," Joanna said.

"We tried to talk her into it, but she says she's not ready for people yet. And the fog depresses her."

"We're curious," said Joanna. "Do you always head out for Cash's with your dancing gear in your locker?"

He laughed so immensely that the flame in the nearest wall lamp shivered. "Only when I'm stopping off at Bennett's Island. See, one thing I always heard about this place was you still do square dances with homemade music, and I figgered that sooner or later I'd hit here just right. And by Godfrey Mighty, this time I did! God bless the fog!"

"Even if it depresses your sister?" asked Helmi.

"Well, see, we can cheer her up and have a good time ourselves. Evens out. And our partners on Cash's, they can have extra time ashore when we get out there. Now I gotta try out Rosa's banjo." He whirled around and seized Tammie Dinsmore by the hands and danced her up the hall. The child was scarlet with embarrassment and joy. Joanna saw Jamie in the poolroom doorway, watching impassively, and she nudged Helmi.

"He can't stand it. To think we've raised a curmudgeon!"

Helmi smiled. "Jamie's all right. He just has to have somebody to be mad with when Felix Drake isn't here. . . . And you ought to hear your brother Mark on the subject of Drake. He tried to pay for his gas with a credit card yesterday, and Mark refused it."

There was a surge of noise out in the foggy lane and up over the shallow porch steps as the Brigport people arrived, a mixture of natives and summer people. The thickest of fogs had never kept the islanders from traveling between the islands to go dancing or courting, even in the pre-radar days when they crawled the distance at rowing speed with a lookout on the bow, and frequent stops to listen for breakers.

For an instant, as the Brigporters spilled into the hall, Joanna thought, What would I do if I saw Eloise there? What if Darrell's taken her back, and she has the nerve to come over here? But in the next instant she saw Darrell himself with his arm around a girl who was no beauty but had a wide, happy smile. Darrell himself looked happier than he'd ever been with Eloise.

The cowboy was there in a splendid rodeo outfit, boots and all, and he made a beeline for Linnie. Hannah MacKenzie headed for Joanna and Helmi.

"Who's the dancing bear?" she asked.

"Brother of the mysterious lady in what used to be Foss Campion's house," Joanna said. "The Lady of Shalott, Madame X, or Felix Drake's first girl for his white slave business, according to who you listen to around here."

"He must be hiding her till he makes up his mind," said Helmi.

"Maybe he's going to surprise us some night with garlands of red lights and a honky-tonk piano," said Joanna. "But first he'd have to get the piano off the boat and into the house under cover of darkness."

"Well, as Tom Robey's always saying . . . and saying . . . and saying," said Hannah, "if we just had a good whorehouse out here, the islands would have all the amenities of the mainland. I don't know who'd go to it, though, do you? I mean, why pay when there are plenty of enthusiastic amateurs around?. . . I'm not speaking of this place, of course," she added. "On Bennett's you can't sneeze without the entire population saying 'God bless you.'"

"Which a lot of people have found mighty inconvenient over the years," said Helmi.

"Hey, when do we get going?" someone shouted.

"Five more to come!" Richard shouted back. The color was high in his cheeks. Owen leaned in the poolroom doorway, watching him with a mellow expression, and Laurie was trying not to be too obviously charmed. Holly's friend said audibly that Richard was adorable, but Holly was noncommittal.

"Here they come!" Sam yelled from the porch, and began to applaud, so that the five from *Astarte* entered to an ovation. The captain swept off his Greek fisherman's cap and bowed deeply, showing a beginning bald spot. Otherwise his hair was collar-length, dark, sprinkled with gray.

He straightened up laughing. "Captain Nemo, at your service!" he announced in a bass voice. He was a broad-shouldered man with heavy features and thick eyebrows. His black shirt was open almost to the waist and a belt buckle as fancy as the cowboy's; chains and medallions glimmered amid the hair on his chest.

"Margo and Jennifer!" he boomed, pushing the two girls forward, gripping each by a scrawny shoulder. They could have been interchangeable except that one was straw-yellow blond and the other black-haired. Giggling nervously, they clutched each other's hands. They wore twenties headbands, holding back thick manes that looked uncombed for a week and unwashed for longer. Wide-necked blouses sliding off their shoulders showed prominent collarbones and no bras, but these weren't necessary. Their pants were skintight over small bottoms and thin legs which ended in dirty sneakers.

Two young men lurked behind the captain. "Cal and Shawn!" he announced.

Cal ducked his head with a bashful grin. He was undersized in a large once-white sweater and dingy red slacks, with a meager face and pointed nose and chin, his eyes partly obscured by dull blond hair hanging over his forehead like a terrier's bangs. It hid his ears, and Hannah said, "I wonder if they're pointed. He looks like an elf in disguise."

"And lost," said Joanna.

Shawn, with hair the color and gloss of polished maple, was bigger than Cal, though not as large as Captain Nemo, and vain about his athletic build, if one judged by his tight white turtleneck jersey and extremely snug cream-colored jeans. Dark glasses hid his eyes, but the rest of his face was conventionally good-looking. He was bandbox tidy and fairly sparkled against the other three. He nodded with casual, unsmiling grace.

"Welcome to Bennett's Island, and we hope you have a wonderful time!" Richard said with true Bennett flair. He raised an elderly megaphone to his mouth and announced the first dance. "Everybody choose your partners for March and Circle!"

Nils came for his wife, Bruce behind him for Hannah, Mark for Helmi. Linnie and the cowboy lined up. The yacht people wandered uncertainly around the sides. The girls seemed forlorn. Cal behaved as if he were in Ali Baba's cave but didn't dare touch anything. Shawn looked stultified with boredom. Captain Nemo was genially inspecting possible choices among the females not up on the floor yet.

"Line up," Joanna said to the other four. "Everyone will see you through."

One girl took Shawn's arm. "Come on, let's do it," she coaxed.

"We'd be trampled to death by fishermen. I'm surprised they're not dancing in rubber boots. So let's just watch the show, shall we?"

"Watch, hell!" said the captain. "I came to dance!"

Robin Bennett darted through the crowd like a medrick, dragging Richard and Sam protesting behind her. "I don't care!" she was saying. "We're the dance committee, and it's our *job.*" She arrived, flustered but game. "Hello, I'm Robin Bennett, and this is Sam and Richard Bennett," she told the girls, "and they will dance with you."

Margo and Jennifer were taken aback, but they were also game.

"There's plenty of girls," Robin said to the men, "but you have to move quick."

"Miss Bennett," said the captain, crooking his arm. "I'd be honored."

"How about me, sweetie?" Shawn drawled. Robin's fingers went childishly to her mouth, and she blushed.

Nemo said severely, "Where's your enterprise? Find your own girl."

Shawn suddenly swooped past Joanna and reached Betsey's friend just before a Brigport boy did, and Richard seized a startled Holly by the arm and thrust her toward Cal. Cal reacted like a three-year-old seeing his first Christmas tree. Island manners took care of the rest of it. Richard would pay for this later, but Holly would not be rude to the stranger. She held out her hand, saying, "Come on," with a feminine version of her father's smile, and Cal went to her like a sleepwalker.

Jamie and Rosa were on the floor, and Joanna was relieved that he wasn't one of the diehards in the poolroom or on the porch.

After the quadrille Joanna had the first waltz with Nils, as always; then the Lady of the Lake with Charles, because Hugo was his mother's partner, while Ralph and Rosa provided the music. The strangers were now well into the spirit of the thing. The exotic birds from the yacht were going down the hall like experts before the long dance was over. Cal looked manic with happiness. Shawn wore a fixed satirical grin beneath his dark glasses, terribly amused to find himself romping with the peasants.

While everyone was taking a breather, either inside or outside the hall, Captain Nemo came to Joanna to ask for the next waltz and sat down beside her. Nils had gone to the poolroom.

"You must do a lot of square dancing twenty thousand leagues under the sea," Joanna said. "Is that your real name?"

"I swear it," he said in a funeral bass. "And if you knew the unspeakable name they cursed me with when I was born, you wouldn't blame me for making it legal."

"It wasn't something like Theophilus, was it? Or Aloysius? I went to school in Limerock with a boy named Aloysius, and I was so sorry for him."

"I won't tell you. It has never passed my lips since the day I was born again as Captain Nemo. 'Captain' is my first name now."

"I'm surprised you didn't name your boat *Nautilus.*"

"I should, to complete the joke. It would be worth it when I meet up with one in five hundred or so who knows Jules Verne."

"Your statistics don't work here. Everyone on the island over the age of ten has read *Twenty Thousand Leagues Under the Sea.* If they went to school here, that is. It's one of the staples of the school library, like *Treasure Island* and most of Dickens, and it always has been. You don't graduate from the eighth grade until you've read your way through those bookshelves."

"It's not only Eden out here but a literate one. Now don't disappoint me by asking who *Astarte* was."

"Oh, gosh," said Joanna. "Was she a Babylonian goddess of love?"

"Phoenician. Another version of Ishtar. But that was a very good guess!" The music began. He rose, and took her hand with a courtly gesture. "Your fiddler is gifted, and I suppose he can't read a note of music. This island is full of surprises, like Prospero's. That thick-handed fisherman wouldn't be playing a Stradivarius, would he?"

"I think that violin was made by somebody way up-country in Maine, not Italy."

He laughed and drew her close for the waltz. He was good, as smooth as any of the island men who had learned to waltz back in their days of reading through the schoolhouse bookshelves. Turning, she saw a blond head in the poolroom doorway; turning again, she caught Nils's amused glance past Hannah MacKenzie's ear; another turn, back to the view of the poolroom door. Jamie was glowering at her. She lifted the hand resting on Nemo's shoulder and waggled the fingers at him and saw his scowl deepen. Linnie, dancing with Eric, winked at her mother. The cowboy, to whom the waltz was a complete mystery, fidgeted on the sidelines, unable to stop watching Linnie.

The medley finished; Captain Nemo led the applause, and he walked Joanna back to her place. One of his girls was leaving the floor, still hanging on to Hugo's hand. She said in a piping voice, "I thought all you fishermen danced in your rubber boots."

"Sometimes we do," Hugo assured her, "when we come in from seining, plastered with herring scales. They're as good as sequins on your clothes and give you that good rich fresh herring smell. Only trouble is, if you wear the same clothes in daylight, the gulls'll mob you."

The girl looked both astonished and doubtful. Nemo laughed,

thanked Joanna, and took the girl by the arm. "Come along, my love, my own. I'm going to hurl you through the next square dance."

Hugo grinned at Joanna and went back to pick up his accordion, and Roy joined him with Rosa's banjo. Nils came and claimed the next two dances. "Just in case Sinbad shows up again. I saw the way he muckled onto you."

"So did Jamie. It's bad enough for him to be trying to censor his sister's life without watching his mother like a hawk in case she's seduced in public. Why doesn't he watch Rosa, for heaven's sake? First thing he knows, somebody else will get her. Does he think she becomes visible for only *him?*"

"Well, she's visible enough to somebody else now." A Brigport fisherman was urgently talking to her, and Cal was hovering around them, looking timid and jumpy. Linnie slipped by them while the cowboy was looking elsewhere and disappeared into the poolroom.

"Jamie's got nothing to worry about," said Nils. "Pitt won't even see her. Put a cue in his hand, and he's hypnotized. He never changes expression, just demolishes anyone in his way."

"That'll make him even more fascinating."

"Choose your partners for the Portland Fancy!" Robin yelled through the megaphone. Out of kindness, Rosa picked Cal, who turned into a demon dancer once the music began.

After this dance there was an intermission, and Nils went to look in on the pool players. People were buying soda, talking in groups, or wandering out for a stretch and to smoke. Van came across the room, leading Anne, and sat down beside Joanna. She lifted the drowsy child into her lap. A little more than five years ago she had arrived on the island, a haunted soul forever wearing an old raincoat as if it were her one security; she had looked sidewise at people with yellow eyes, not so much hostile as with the desperation of an animal that knows it is trapped but will die fighting.

"What do you think of the visiting firemen?" Joanna asked.

"You get either boy or the Ancient Mariner in a square dance and you sure get rampsed around. I wonder what Captain Nemo does for a living and what his real name is. Probably something like Oswald J. Newcomb."

"Captain Nemo is his real name. He says the other is unspeakable. I didn't ask him what he did, but it's probably something in an office full of computers."

"His girls look as if they need a good dunking overboard," Van said.
"At least he smelled clean when he pressed me to his bosom."

"Choose your partners for a Liberty Waltz!" Sam called hoarsely
through the megaphone. He had taken off his blazer and his necktie.

"Oh, that Sam!" said Van. "What a happy kid! I hope it lasts forever
for him." Liza and Philip had taken Sam at nine and adopted him at
twelve. "I often wonder," Van said, "what my life would have been if I'd
been adopted." She looked down at the child's head against her
shoulder. "I wouldn't have had Anne, would I?"

"No, and she's a treasure," said Joanna. "But whatever children you
had, they'd be yours as much as she is."

"But not to know Anne!" Van said. "I can't even imagine it. Even
if my life had taken an entirely different tack, I think I'd have always
been missing her. As if she were meant to be born, this little soul flying
around in space like a swallow looking for a nesting place, and somehow
I'd have known that she was out there somewhere but we couldn't find
each other." She didn't look up from the sleeping child.

"Anyway, you and Anne did find each other, and that's what
matters," Joanna said.

The music began, and a few couples took the floor. Barry came in
from the porch. He was at last beginning to look his age, and a few lines
added strength to his small neat features.

"Come on, beautiful," he said to Van. He reached out to take Anne.
"We'll put the baby on the bench, wrapped up in your coat. She's out
like a light."

"Oh, let me hold her," Jo said. "I'd love to. My grandchild is too far
away."

"Jamie'd ought to get busy and give you some," said Barry. He put
Anne into Joanna's lap, where she sagged comfortably, murmuring in her
sleep. Van and Barry joined the circling dancers. Nils appeared in the
poolroom doorway, she shook her head, and he went back to the game.
Linnie was towed onto the floor by Roy. She was in pale blue tonight,
and her hair was silvery pale under the lights. When Joanna was Linnie's
age, she was pregnant with Ellen, and Alec, whose fiddle music could put
the leap upon the lame, as a song put it, was dead. She had never
dreamed then of a Linnie and a Jamie to be born. If Alec had lived,
would she have gone through life missing them? The whole concept was
like imagining space or eternity; one shies away from it with mingled
terror and relief.

The waltzers went around and around like figures on a carousel until Sam ordered, "All join hands!" Partners were relinquished, and the chain began, women circling one way, men the other, their hands briefly clasping, first right, then left. Among the younger dancers there was a lot of hanging on to certain hands and sending signals to Sam, which he ignored, this being one of the few times when he had absolute power.

Finally he shouted, "Everybody waltz!"

The chain stopped, and new partners turned to one another, but also in that instant Vanessa and Owen went on past each other, she to Terence Campion and he to Holly's school friend, who looked as if she couldn't believe her luck. He bent his head to her, smiling and courtly, and danced her away. Terence laughed at something Van said. Laurie was dancing in sweet innocence with Tommy Wiley, and Barry was with Phillida Robey from Brigport.

Joanna wondered, as she had wondered many times, what malicious force had arranged for her to see something which she could have easily missed by a turn of the head; and now, knowing what she had just seen, she wished she had been looking up or down the hall or at any other dancer in the circle besides Vanessa or Owen. They had not touched hands; she was sure of it. What if Terence or Phillida had each taken a new partner too quickly? Would Owen and Vanessa have danced, or walked off the floor in different directions, calling attention to themselves?

Heat bathed her, and she felt sweat on her back and forehead. She looked down at Anne. All children, even the worst little hellions, were transformed by sleep into something as innocent and blameless as those tiny nameless flowers discovered by accident in the grass; seen through the wrong end of the binoculars, they were often more exquisite than roses. Every small child was as unique as a snow crystal. How could there be so many mediocre adults?

Anne had tipped her head back against Joanna's shoulder so her face was lifted, and Joanna, with dismay, caught herself looking for a resemblance to Owen. Anne's coloring was her mother's. Her smile, when she was awake, was all Van's, too. She had a cleft in her chin; Owen had one, but so did Barry. She scowled in her sleep now, brows drawn together, mouth set hard, lower lip rebellious.

Owen. And the fingers closed over the small, hard palms that day? Kisses sent to the mother?

After it all she felt only a dull lack of surprise and then a kind of relief. No more ups and downs. Her next reaction was a desire to escape from the noise and heat and light into the cool, foggy dark. She consciously had to loosen her arms; they had instinctively tightened around Anne.

If this child in her arms were a Bennett, and she felt this way about her, how could Owen go day in and day out through time, knowing this was his daughter but not able to acknowledge her?

Unwillingly she looked again into Anne's face, and the resemblance had gone, if it had ever been there at all. She clutched at the *if*, welcoming all the doubts and wonders back again. Better the ups and downs than the flat "This is it." Oh, God, for one sign of Barry in her!

Nils sat down beside her. "Saying your prayers?"

"Praying for this waltz to be over. She's heavier than she looks, and my arm's going numb."

"Let me take her."

"I can stand it for a little more." She held the child closer. "How was the game?"

"Pitt Bainbridge has just ruined our son's whole year."

"You mean he beat the blond fox?"

"And your brother Charles, too; he's still reeling from the shock. Matt Fennell's mopping his brow. The trouble is we've had it to ourselves around here too long. A little competition shakes us up."

"It's a good thing the club rules don't allow gambling, or he'd be setting up in business."

"Remember the big touse when we were playing poker up here using Necco wafers for chips?" Nils asked. "Grandpa kept me standing at the foot of his bed for three hours, knitting trapheads and listening to him tell me what a sinner I was. I kept thinking if I ever got away from him, I'd live a life of crime just so I could thumb my nose at him from the gallows."

Everything else fell away like a bad dream dissolved by sunrise. "You never told me that before!"

"Well, I like to spring little surprises on my wife from time to time," he said with a smile.

"I just can't imagine you as a criminal. It's fascinating."

"That's why I'd be good at it. I look so honest. Take your brother Owen out there; anybody'd spot him for a con man from the word *go*. But while they kept their eyes on him, I'd be in the bedroom stealing the diamonds."

"Not quite that easy," she said dryly. "He'd be in the bedroom when you got there, with the owner of the diamonds."

The music stopped, and Barry and Vanessa were coming toward them. "Let's go home," Joanna said to Nils. "I hate to admit that I can't stay till the last gun's fired, but I was awake too darned early this morning."

19

While Robin and Cindy sold drinks through the kitchen hatch during an intermission, Sam and Richard sprawled luxuriously on benches in the musicians' corner, sipping cold soda as if it were champagne and they were successful entrepreneurs, which they were, judging by the crowd and the way the contribution jar had been filled. They congratulated each other expansively, as if the girls had had nothing whatever to do with the affair.

Rosa was adjusting a guitar string, only half hearing the boys, when Linnie joined them. "Make the next waltz ladies' choice," she said winningly.

"Why?" said Richard, sounding like Owen.

"Because it would be fun, that's why. We'd all like it. Come on, you're too young to be a male chauvinist."

"A man's never too young for that," Richard said. "It's a matter of self-defense."

Sam snickered. "There's a summer kid from Brigport been chasing him all night. He's scared she'll get him." Richard sputtered on a mouthful of soda. The girl, perhaps thirteen, sat on a bench halfway along one side, solitary in a talkative group. She wore a full-skirted flowered dress, and her hands clasped her little bag. Her toes were turned in, her eyes in big pink-framed glasses were fixed on Richard. She was fattish and reminded Rosa of herself. How cruel these young boys were, without even knowing it.

"What a pair of nitwits," Linnie said with distaste. "I hope both of you get girls who will lead you around by your noses and twist them every

149

five minutes for good luck. And I'm a nitwit, too," she said to Rosa. "I don't have to have somebody else do it. I'll ask him myself, right now!"

She headed for the poolroom. Since it was pretty crowded, it would be interesting to see how she managed to ask Pitt without an audience, but Rosa wasn't about to go and watch. She'd have liked to go home, but she had committed herself until midnight.

Her lassitude must have shown in her face because suddenly Sam said to her, "Hey, Rosa, what about another soda?"

"I've already had my three free ones."

"Oh, heck, you can have another," he said handsomely. "We got to keep the musicians happy. What kind?"

"Ginger ale, I guess." He sped off.

Richard said, "Well, I guess I'll see how the money's piling up." He took the long way around so he wouldn't have to pass too close to the forlorn admirer. The sight of that child depressed Rosa. She'd outgrow this heartbreak, but there'd be plenty more. Start early to make your own life, kid, Rosa silently advised her. It's pretty damn painful to begin at thirty saying, *To hell with them, who needs them?*

It was late. Nils and Joanna had left sometime ago; the older Fennells had gone, wheeling Peter, who had slept in the poolroom for most of the evening. Stephen and Philippa had left Robin for Eric to bring home. Charles and Mark had gone, the Bartons, the older Dinsmores and Campions. The young crowd, Brigport, Roy Bainbridge, and the people from *Astarte* were getting their second wind now and would probably be going strong for a long time yet. Officially the dance would end at twelve, but they'd play records after the musicians were tired.

Cal dropped into the chair beside Rosa. He was streaming with sweat and smelled of it, his hair flattened and damp, his sweater patched with wet. He held a cold-beaded can of soda against his forehead, shut his eyes, and breathed deeply.

"God, this is fabulous," he said. "You people are incredible! So *gracious!* Let's face it, we look like a spaced-out crew, don't we? But do we get met with shotguns? No! Do we get told, 'Stay away from our women?' No! We're welcomed. In this brutal world, we're welcomed!"

He opened his eyes, and they were full of tears. "Four sweet kids row out to tell about this dance they're having for a good cause. Out here on this island in time and space, lost in the fog—" He blinked and snuffled. "It could have risen up out of the depths like Brigadoon. And these beautiful, innocent kids are thinking of other creatures helpless out there in a rotten world."

His trembling voice broke. He began twisting in his chair so he could grope through his pockets, and Rosa doubted there was room for anything in such tight quarters. She pushed forward the box of tissues she'd brought along for her and Ralph to wipe sweat out of their eyes while they played.

"Thanks," he said shakily. He wiped his eyes and blew his nose. "I'd forgotten hearts could be so kind." He took another tissue.

"Corny Cal." Shawn propped an elbow on the cold potbellied stove and looked down at him through his dark glasses. "The Dripper is at it again. He doesn't need booze to get him started. 'Oh, I feel so great!'" He yelped in falsetto. "'People are just wonderful. Let's all have a good cry!'"

"Shut up, Shawn," Cal said in a desperately warning voice. There was no one around at the moment, they were isolated in this rear corner of the big room. "Just shut up and go away, damn it! You've been needling me all night, and I'm fed up." He slumped forward and stared at his feet. "Get lost."

Shawn's arm shot out, he grabbed Cal by the forelock and jerked his head up and laughed into the strained and helpless face. "Christ, what a sight! Left out in the rain too long, weren't you, Dripper, chum? Watch out, your ears will turn moldy."

Rosa looked around for an eye to catch, but of course, neither Jamie nor Eric was in sight. Ralph was telling his boys to stop sliding on the dance floor; Captain Nemo was heard laughing outside; Margo and Jennifer were at the serving hatch being bought drinks by Hugo and Roy.

She looked back at the dark glasses and the sardonic grin. "Knock it off," she said. "If you want to start a fight, go outside."

He laughed, released Cal, and cuffed him not too lightly on either side of his head.

"There'd be no fight. You could insult his mother, and he wouldn't even fight back. I've tried everything, haven't I, Cal baby?"

Cal, wiping his eyes, grinned weakly. He looked ashamed, and Rosa felt disgust; she could have risen up and hugged Ralph when he came. "Hi," he said to the other two with a friendly nod. He put a can of soda on the nearest windowsill and took his fiddle from its case, and he and Rosa began to tune up.

"You two are damned good at this stuff," Shawn said languidly.

Cal leaped up, saying, "There's that black-eyed gypsy!" He darted off under Shawn's nose and reached Holly Bennett. He gave her a bashful dancing-school bow and said, "May I have this dance?"

Holly smiled and nodded. She'd grown tall and had thinned down. The days when she had reminded Rosa of a sturdy little Shetland pony were long gone. The music began, and other couples moved onto the floor; but Shawn remained ornamentally leaning on the stove. When Cal and Holly circled into view, Cal looked happy and quite attractive; he was a good dancer, and Holly was obviously not regretting this waltz.

Suddenly Shawn left his perch like Hank taking off after a flung herring, moved lithely through the crowd, and tapped Cal's shoulder. Cal's head swung back, and Rosa saw the shock and then fury on his face. Holly, taken aback by the surprise move (no one ever cut in at the island dances), was swept off by Shawn. Only the nearest couples noticed, and they were both startled and amused. Cal set his jaw and went after the pair, tapped Shawn's shoulder, and Shawn ignored him, smoothly carrying Holly out of reach. He was laughing.

Sadistic bastard, Rosa thought. Ralph fiddled away, seeing nothing, slumped deep in his chair with his eyes shut, going with the music. Cal left the floor, bumbling blindly among the others. Margo (or Jennifer) grabbed at his arm as he passed her and Roy, but he slithered free of her grasp and went out the front door.

Life must be real fun aboard that yacht, Rosa thought.

At midnight the official last waltz was played, and the instruments were put away. Ralph and Marjorie took their boys and left. Jamie and Rosa had been tacitly left in charge, as a couple young enough to endure, and without children who had to be taken home to bed. Eric stayed on waiting for Robin, and took refuge in the poolroom; the door was now kept shut against the new barrage of noise, as the high school students played their records of unintelligible vocalists destroying their larynxes above a cacophony of indistinguishable instruments.

A door at the outer end of the poolroom opened into the woods and a well-traveled path to Barque Cove, and Rosa wished that Jamie would suddenly say to Eric, "Take over for a half hour, will you? Rosa and I are going for a walk."

It was the purest fantasy. Jamie didn't do things like that; he wouldn't, even if the night weren't dripping with fog. He'd taken her once to Fern Cliff to watch the moon rise, when she had first come to the island, and he must have considered it a wasted effort because he'd never suggested it again.

He was playing against Pitt Bainbridge again, galled by his earlier defeat. Linnie, failing to get a dance with Pitt, had been snatched by Captain Nemo. He hadn't been drinking, as far as anyone knew, but by now he was calling her the Blessed Damozel and inviting her to Come into the Garden, Maud.

"His poetry's from way back," said Eric, "but his ideas aren't. He's giving Roy a run for his money."

"I still think he's either sniffing or shooting something," said Jamie. "Man his age flying around like a fart in a boot. What's he trying to prove?"

"That he's top rooster out there," said Pitt unexpectedly, lining up his shot. "The rest of 'em are just learning how to flap their wings and crow."

"Well, let's hope he sprains his cock-a-doodle-doo," Jamie said dourly, watching Pitt's cue. Then he looked up with one of those spontaneous grins which never failed to startle and stab Rosa, they came so seldom and were so long remembered. He began to laugh and took the rest along with him except for Pitt, who impassively made a perfect shot.

Hugo opened the door just wide enough for him to slide in sidewise, slammed it, and leaned against it, blowing hard and wiping his face. His hair was damply curled with sweat.

"Been learning a new dance," he explained, puffing. "I think the Ancient Mariner picked it up on Venus. Maybe even farther out. Jesus, taking hold of one of those girls is like grabbing a washboard. All you get is a handful of ribs. And I think the blonde wants to rape me." He picked up the nearest can of soda and took a long drink. "Whose was that?"

"Funny you should ask," said Eric. "Somebody really weird came in the end door with it, scuttled around here looking furtive, left it, and went out again. He was pretty dirty."

"Stunk, too," said Bruce MacKenzie. "We put his soda away over there in quarantine, you might say. Just in case. You can't tell what might be crawling on it. Invisibly," he added.

Hugo looked incredulous, a little sick, and then laughed. "Funny coincidence. Jamie's the only one around here who likes lemon and lime, and then this critter shows up with the same—"

"Sophisticated tastes?" suggested Eric.

Hugo sat down and lit a cigarette. "There's a real cunning little thing came with the Robeys. I tried to get her out for a walk, but somebody must've told her it wasn't safe to step outside the Bennett's Island clubhouse."

"With a Bennett," said Jamie. "You want to watch out for those cunning little things they lug over from Brigport." Nobody picked that up; the silence could have been called embarrassed or at least uncomfortable. His cue shot forward; the balls rolled softly on the green and went where they should. Pitt gave him a nod. Under the hanging lamp that cast a yellow glow over the table, Pitt was like a small dark hawk as he sighted along his cue. Jamie's head was as yellow as the light, and the hair along his arms gave off random glints of gold. He always stood straight and square-shouldered, his head held high on his strong neck.

Tired as Rosa was by now, after a long day and a long night, she was not so much battered by that as by the irony of being considered one half of the childless couple automatically expected to stay on and chaperon. She could see it going on for as long as they were able to stiver to the dances. For the first time she wondered about the middle-aged couples she had known, unmarried but always thought of as One. Comfortable-appearing, settled into a snug rut, but how much frustration was merely damped down but still smoldering in one or the other? How many of them cherished little grudges which could give one a cozy case of self-pity when it was needed? How many times had it been a case of waiting, of hoping, of giving a little more time until that little more had become years?

Not for me, she thought now.

The door from the dance flew open, and Linnie was borne across the threshold on a wave of noise. She closed the door behind her and buttoned it.

"I just escaped from Captain Nemo!" she said dramatically. "Either that man has discovered the Fountain of Youth, or else he's killing himself trying to convince everybody he's only fifteen but hairy for his age."

"What's my brother doing?" Pitt asked without looking up from the table.

"Can't you guess? Bounding around as if he's half kangaroo." She was transparently pleased because Pitt had spoken to her. "He just bounded out the door with a girl who came over from Brigport."

Hugo sat up. "Which one?"

"Not the same one you've been dragging your wing for," said Linnie. She couldn't keep her eyes off Pitt. Somebody knocked at the door, and Hugo opened it. Cal slid in, smiling apologetically and pulling Jennifer, or Margo, behind him.

"Do you know where we can get a drink of water?" he asked Rosa. "The soda's all gone, and I'm dehydrated."

"Sure," said Rosa. "Come on, I live nearest." And I won't be back, she thought. Tonight I start not being half of that settled old couple. So long, lover.

Jamie straightened up at once and laid down his cue. "I'll go down with them," he said curtly. "You stay here." He picked up a flashlight.

Damn it, he could always defeat her, even in something so small; she couldn't start an argument here and now. No, he was guarding her as he did Linnie; he wouldn't let her go down the lane with strangers whom he suspected of God knows what. I don't want protection from you! she felt like shouting at him.

"All right," she said agreeably. "There's a full pail of water on the counter you can bring back, unless you want it straight from the well."

"Thank you, you're awfully kind," Cal said, giving her a rather sweet smile. He was the last one out the door. The girl was close on Jamie's heels. Rosa wondered if she'd make a pass at him in the lane; she hoped so. Something ought to jolt him.

"You object to a female opponent, Pitt?" Linnie asked, with an edge of self-conscious belligerence.

"Nope," he said dispassionately.

Hugo went back to the dance. Rosa thought with peaceful detachment that when Jamie returned, she'd leave. And if he stopped by later, there would be a dark, silent house and a locked door.

20

The game finished; Pitt won, but Linnie gave a good account of herself. "You did all right," he said tersely, and disappeared out the end door. Hannah and Bruce MacKenzie went to gather up their passengers and started herding them down the lane toward the wharf. This included the lovelorn thirteen-year-old. The lovelorn cowboy was in the Robeys' group; he pounced upon Linnie when she incautiously crossed the hall and twirled her into a dance that seemed different from what everyone else was doing.

Eric and Rosa walked out into the cool fog to say good-night to Bruce and Hannah. Afterward they stood in the lane listening to the clamor within.

"My head seems to be breathing on its own," said Eric. "Opening and shutting like a sea anemone."

Farther along the Brigporters sang out good-nights to Jamie, and then his flashlight came up the lane, a luminous globe bouncing through the fog, and Rosa prepared to disappear into the dark and the mist. Too late; the light shone in her face.

"*There* you are," he said, sounding so relieved she wondered if Jennifer-Margo had really made a move. She wanted to giggle as if she'd been drinking more than soda all evening. "Hey, come in and get out the paper cups, will you? In a half hour I'm about to close down this hoorah's nest."

Exasperated at being trapped again, Rosa followed him along the side porch to the kitchen doorway, with Cal babbling happily behind her. He addressed the girl as Jen, which established her identity. Jennifer thought outdoor toilets were gross, but Rosa's privy didn't make her want to barf. "Thank you," said Rosa.

"My God, what wonderful water in that bucket," Cal said fervently. "I've had about a quart, and I want more. Never tasted such stuff. Pure, uncorrupted, just like this island."

"That's debatable," Jamie said over his shoulder to Rosa. The other two crowded with them into the galley-sized kitchen.

Jennifer said, "He hasn't drunk straight water since he was in grade school. You were debauched early, weren't you, pussycat?"

"Listen, Jen, I don't want to talk about my rotten past in this place, to these people."

The kitchen was scantily illuminated by the light from the hall through the serving window. Jamie set the pail on the counter and went out into the midst of the dancers. Rosa took a package of paper cups from a drawer beneath the counter and groped for one of the thick white coffee mugs on the dark shelves. "Here, you can use this for a dipper," she said to Cal and Jennifer. She was preparing once more to disappear.

Bedlam suddenly ended in the hall as Jamie turned down the music. The dancers stopped like mechanical toys all running down at once. Cal loudly gulped water.

"All right, everybody!" Jamie said. "In exactly one half hour from now this dance is over!"

"Hey, it's *our* dance!" Richard protested with Bennett volume. "You can't shut it down!"

"Listen, son," Captain Nemo said, with a paternal arm around Jamie's shoulder, "how about it if we put more money in the kitty to save the whales or whatever?"

"Yea, Nemo!" Sam yelled, and it was picked up by the pack.

"I've got a day's work to do tomorrow even if nobody else does," Jamie said flatly.

"Then go home!" said Holly. "We can be trusted to put out the lights, for heaven's sake!"

"I represent the board of governors," said Jamie over the uproar. "I don't go home until the last gun's fired, and that will be"—he looked at his watch—"twenty-seven minutes from now, so make the most of it."

He raised the volume somewhat, but not to where it had been. With fairly good grace most of the dancers flung themselves back into frantic motion, but Richard, Robin, Sam, and Cindy still surrounded Jamie, haranguing him. He was good-natured but immovable. Margo spun away from the Massachusetts cowboy and put her arms around Jamie's neck. "Come dance with me, you gorgeous Nordic blond!" she shrieked.

"Go get him, girl!" Linnie called. "Stick to him like feathers to molasses!" Rosa was distracted from seeing how Jamie shucked off Margo by Shawn's sudden intrusion into the kitchen, dragging Betsey by the wrist, and crowding Cal and Jennifer over against the stove. "I've got me a captive maiden," he announced. "And God, it was thirsty work! She fought me every step of the way." Betsey grinned.

Rosa gave Shawn a cup of water. He tasted it, smacked his lips, and said, "Ah, purest moonshine! Hundred proof." He lifted his cup to Betsey and sang in a light, pleasant voice, "'Drink to me only with thine eyes, and I will pledge with mine.'"

Then his elbow jogged the full cup in Cal's hand just as Cal began to drink. Cal gasped and had a violent coughing spell. Jennifer pounded him on the back. "Damn you, Shawn," Cal wheezed, "you did that on purpose."

Shawn laughed. "You here, little man? Whatever do you want? Don't be always hanging around the grown-ups making a nuisance of yourself, or Uncle won't bring you again."

What a pain, Rosa thought, turning back to the hatch to see if Jamie was still wearing Margo. She hoped he was. Behind her there was a grunt, the sense of something heavy falling, bumping her back on the way, and hitting the floor with a jarring thud.

"My God, Cal!" Jennifer shouted over the music. "You really punched him out! I didn't think you could do it!"

Rosa turned and looked down. Shawn was crumpled between her and the gas stove, and she could just make out the pale glimmer of his face. Cal had withdrawn into the narrow space between the stove and the cupboards, squeezing Jennifer behind him. In the light through the hatch he wore the unblinking stare of a waxwork. Jennifer kept saying excitedly, "Cal, you were wonderful! I didn't think you could do it! Well, he's been asking for it all night!"

Betsey stood transfixed by the counter. "Betsey, go get Jamie," Rosa said. "It's all right; it's not the first time somebody's been knocked out at a dance." She held on to the girl for a moment and said in her ear, "Just tell Jamie I need him. Don't get everybody rushing over here."

Betsey nodded mutely and dodged her way across the hall to Jamie. Margo seemed to have three pairs of arms, and Jamie's expression suggested that he'd have been happy to whack off all six with an ax, if he could lay hands on one. Betsey spoke to him, and he forgot restraint and ripped himself free of Margo as if she were a blackberry bush. He walked rapidly to the kitchen, where Jennifer was still yipping deliriously, still imprisoned behind a silent and rigid Cal.

"Cal knocked Shawn out," Rosa said.

"Just like old times, huh?" Jamie said briskly. "You've got quite a punch for a little feller, Cal. We'll have to haul him outside and pour cold water on him." He stooped down into the shadows. "Come on, grab a hold."

Cal was motionless, still staring blindly into the light. "*Move*, Cal!" Jamie ordered from below.

Rosa knelt. "I'll help you with him."

"What in hell ails Cal?" Jamie asked irritably.

"He's in a trance. Probably never hit anyone before."

"Okay. Each take a shoulder and drag this one out. Where the heck are his arms? It's dark as the inside of a cow down here." Their hands collided, and Jamie said with rare humor, "We've got to stop meeting like this."

She wanted to laugh, but at that moment her fingers touched what she could not believe was there, yet there was no mistaking its ghastly familiarity. Panicked, she felt with her fingertip for a familiar scar on the staghorn handle. Jamie said, "I've got a good grip. How about you?"

She leaned across Shawn and took Jamie's head in her hands, and said in his ear, "Where's your flashlight?"

"Why?"

"My carving knife is in him."

"*Jesus.*" Jamie sat back so abruptly his head struck the stove behind him with a hollow thunk.

"What's the matter?" Jennifer cried piercingly from behind Cal. Jamie lit a match, and they saw the staghorn handle of the carving knife protruding from under Shawn's left ribs. Just as the flame reached Jamie's fingers and he swore and shook it out, Rosa saw Shawn's face. His eyes gleamed with a cold, dead light under half-closed lids. He was breathing in short shallow breaths.

"Maybe we can take him out of here before the place flies apart," Jamie said. "Can you get a couple of guys out of the poolroom without a fuss?"

She was already standing up, glad to be doing something away from here. Cal seemed to be breathing less than the man on the floor. The word *catatonic* came to mind.

"What is it?" Jennifer kept saying. "What's *wrong*? Goddammit, Cal, let me by! You *crazy?*" She shoved Cal out of her way, a cigarette lighter flicked on in her hand; she looked down at Shawn and began to scream.

Inside the tiny kitchen it was ear-shattering. Outside, it brought the dance to a stop as everybody crowded toward the hatch and around to the door. Someone shut off the record. Jennifer went on screaming, her eyes shut, mechanical as a siren.

With the strength of desperation Jamie lifted her over Shawn's body and threw her into the arms of Captain Nemo, who clamped a large hand over her mouth.

"All right, everybody," Jamie said. "There's been an accident. Looks like somebody has to go in to the doctor. You can all help by staying out of the way. Hugo, get the stretcher out of the coatroom."

"I'll let you go," Nemo said to Jennifer, "if you'll shut up." She nodded vehemently, and he handed her over to Margo; they clutched at each other, whimpering, teeth chattering. "Now what's happened here?" he said authoritatively.

"I'm going home for blankets and hot-water bottles," Rosa said to Jamie, and went out.

"Change your clothes and be ready to go in with me," he called after her. She kept on moving. The light touch of the fog on her face was a caress or a benediction; the silence was another blessing. Oh, Lord, oh, Lord, she kept thinking. He is probably dying right now, and there's nothing we can do. And with my knife in him. Her great-grandfather's carving knife with the staghorn handle. Taken care of for generations. Never put the staghorn handle into hot water.

Now she would never want to use it again. What did you do with such a thing? An honorable burial at sea for an old friend, that would be it.

She turned off the lane and moved surefootedly among her own spruces into the yard. In the kitchen she lit a lamp and set it on the table, and then brought in rainwater to heat in kettles on the gas stove. She had two hot-water bottles, and collected all the blankets she could spare; she could sleep in her sleeping bag. She wished she could crawl into it now and sink into a soft, furry blackness.

Somebody ran up onto the back steps and came in. It was Linnie, wearing jeans and a heavy dark sweater. "Hi! Isn't this *wild?* I've been home and changed, and nobody knew a thing except the cat. You're going, too, aren't you? Jamie wants you along. He's bringing the boat in now." Against the shadows around and behind her, she looked as if she were illumined from within. "Hey, we can't miss this! Not that I'm a ghoul," she added hastily, "but it's an adventure, isn't it?"

"What's going on at the clubhouse?"

"Well, Eric's simply great; he's got them dancing again. Phillida and Carol are talking Margo and Jennifer down, and Roy's back from wherever he's been playing favvers and muvvers, and he and Ralph and Matt are guarding doors like Horatius at the bridge so everybody won't go streaming down to the wharf for a bon voyage party. Quick, go change! I'll fill the bottles."

"I don't know if I'm going. What about my knife?"

"Nemo took it out, and Shawn hardly bled at all. They wrapped it in paper towels and then a dishtowel and tied it up. And I've got it; it's in your entry right now. I'm supposed to deliver it to the boat." The water was steaming, and Rosa wrapped a hot-water bottle in a towel and began to fill it from a dipper. "Rosa, if *you* go," Linnie said, "Jamie'll have no excuse to say I can't go. I *know* it's not a joyride," she said appealingly, "but I think I ought to be in on it as much as anybody."

"Well," said Rosa, folding her lower lip between thumb and forefinger. "How's Cal? He looked catatonic when I left there."

"When they took the knife out, he suddenly exploded in all directions, and Nemo flattened him. From the size of that fist Cal could be in worse shape than Shawn. Will you please hurry and change out of those clothes?" If the Massachusetts cowboy could see her now in the lamplight, he'd die of desire.

"Oh, all right," said Rosa. "Fill the other bottle." She took a flashlight and went upstairs, unzipping her dress on the way. *He wants you along.* Can it be that the Granite Man is actually nervous, and wants you there for his security blanket? Never mind. You are going so Linnie can see Life, or whatever she calls it. Let's pray it's not death instead.

21

When they were passing the dark store, the high tide smacked and gurgled around the pilings underneath the planking, stirred into action by the quiet passage of *Valkyrie* from mooring to wharf. She was barely seen; her red and green running lights dyed the fog around them.

The high tide meant that Pitt and Hugo could get Shawn aboard without too much tilting of the stretcher. Rosa went ahead of them into the lighted cabin and spread a blanket on one of the bunks and shook up the dubious pillows. Nemo followed her in and dropped Cal like a rag doll on the opposite bunk. Then Hugo and Pitt lifted Shawn off the stretcher and brought him in and left him on the blanket, moaning.

Nemo took off Shawn's shoes and loosened his belt. "Hardly any blood, Shawnie," he said soothingly. "He must have just nicked you."

"I felt it go in. Straight to my heart." Shawn clutched the big man's hands while Rosa was putting a wrapped hot-water bottle at his feet. "I'm bleeding to death inside."

"If it had reached your heart, you'd be dead by now, Shawnie. Just let the quacks check you over and stick on a Band-Aid, that's all." He put Shawn's hands down and tucked the blankets around him. "These people will take good care of you."

Shawn fought to get his hands free. In the cabin light his face was glazed with sweat, his color unearthly. His dark glasses had disappeared along the way, and his full eyes were wildly staring and bloodshot.

"You're going with me, aren't you? I don't want to die among strangers!"

"You aren't going to die." Nemo forced the frantic hands under the

162

blankets again. Rosa tucked the second hot-water bottle against Shawn's right side. All this while Cal was immobile in the opposite bunk, a boneless sprawl like a dropped puppet, his face turned away to the side of the boat.

"*Nemo!*" Shawn implored.

"You'll be fine, Shawnie. Trust me." Nemo patted the sweat-darkened head and turned away and left the cabin.

"Nemo, please!" Shawn gasped. Rosa leaned over him.

"Are you warmer now?" she asked.

"I'm cold into my guts, where the knife went." His eyes beseeched hers. "Nemo's going with us, isn't he?"

Jamie was asking the same thing, out in the cockpit. "What do you mean, you aren't going?"

Nemo's deep voice had an undercurrent of amusement as if every one were being too childish about everything. "There's nothing I can do for either Shawn or Cal right now."

"Jesus, they're *your* friends that I'm making this trip for in the middle of the night, in thick o' fog! You can at least take responsibility for them when we get there, for God's sake!"

Nemo calmly overrode him. "I also have the responsibility of two hysterical girls." He stepped over the side onto the lobster car as Rosa came from the cabin. "I'll pay you whatever this trip over and back costs you in gas, and more for your time and trouble, whatever price you put on it, but I'm not going in until tomorrow. It's supposed to clear, and I'll start in my own boat at first light."

"What if your boy Cal goes berserk again?"

"He's not my boy, and if you hit him hard enough, he's no problem." He walked across the car and went up onto the wharf.

"Horse's arse," said Jamie after him.

"Boy, what a friend *he* is!" Linnie said loudly.

"Yeah, and who needs him?" Hugo asked. "Stay with your floating whorehouse, man!" he shouted into the fog. "Somebody might snatch a free feel!"

"*Shut up,*" said Jamie savagely. "I need another man in case Little Boy Blue blows his top. He may be more than you and Rosa can handle."

"I'll go," said Pitt from up on the wharf. It was as startling as hearing a voice from out of a well.

"Let's get going then," said Jamie. "You need to tell your brother?"

"Nope, he'll figure it out." Pitt came aboard.

"So long, Linnie," Jamie said pointedly "Give my love to the old folks."

"I'm going with you," she said.

Jamie made a sound impossible to interpret and put the boat into gear. They slipped away from the dark wharf on a carpet of green-white luminescence, and the already invisible village seemed to have never been there at all. They stopped at Hugo's and Nils's boats for extra life preservers, Jamie called the Coast Guard base at Limerock and asked for an ambulance and police to meet them at the public landing in approximately two hours.

Guided by radar and compass, *Valkyrie* rode the easy swell, and the first hour passed quietly. They felt alone and therefore totally secure on the great bay. Pitt sat hunched on the port washboard, smoking cigarettes in silent isolation from the rest. Rosa, Linnie, and Hugo took turns looking in on Shawn and Cal. Shawn needed constant reassuring, so finally Linnie stayed with him until he seemed to relax and fall asleep. Cal remained apparently unconscious, but Jamie was afraid he would come awake fighting and attack Shawn. He let Hugo take the wheel while he went into the cabin, and loosely tied Cal's wrists and ankles.

"That won't cut off the circulation," he said, "but it ought to slow him down a dite."

Rosa put the spare blankets over him. "He could have a concussion. Seems as if he's been out for an awful long time."

"Well, it's not our mess," Jamie said. "We'll hand him over to somebody, that's for sure. Hospital or sheriff, I don't give a damn."

Linnie sat beside Pitt on the washboard; she didn't press him into conversation but seemed to feel she was gaining if he didn't move away from her. She had put an old oil jacket over her sweater, and both the jacket and her hair showed pale in the partial darkness of the foggy midnight. The faintly reddish light cast up by the compass and the greenish glow from the radar screen, like phosphorescence, provided the only light in the cockpit.

The nearer they came to the mainland, the more the fog thinned. The milky luminous circle in which they had moved from the start grew larger and larger. But with Limerock only about an hour away, the trip had become dangerous because they would soon be crossing the shipping lanes used by freighters and small tankers heading up or down the coast. Jamie's radar would show them, but theirs could miss *Valkyrie*.

Hugo stopped talking about food. They all were quiet aboard the boat now, listening and watching for anything to break through the sedative beat of the engine and wash of water, or to blaze through the wall of fog. In the light from the compass Jamie's face was impassive, and his eyes flickered constantly between the compass and the radar screen. Rosa sat on the washboard just outside the canopy on the wheel side, watching the cold shine of the bow wave sliding past and falling away to the stern. She was half hypnotized, realized it, and woke herself with a jolt.

She stood up, took Jamie's five-cell flashlight, and stepped down into the cabin. Shawn was either sleeping or comatose; his breathing was light and fast, but his forehead was normally warm. Cal was sobbing softly. He twisted his head away from the light.

"Would you put that off, please?" he asked thickly. She did so, and he said with a gulp, "I'm sorry. I just can't seem to stop, and my nose is all plugged up."

She found a crumpled tissue in her jacket pocket and held it under his nose and said, "Blow."

He did, and then laughed tremulously. "God, how humiliating. I was awake when he was tying me up, but it was easier to play dead. Saved a shred of pride anyway." His voice broke. "Why did he have to do that?"

"We didn't know what you'd do when you came to. I hear you really exploded up there."

"I just wanted to get away from everybody staring at me and Shawn lying there. I was going to run till I dropped dead or fell off the land and drowned. Then Nemo hit me. I thought when he threw me down here I'd just stay limp and quiet, and when nobody was looking, I'd find a chance to go overboard."

"We thought you might finish up the job on Shawn," she said candidly.

"I never hurt anything before in my life!" he wailed. "I'm so *ashamed!* What have I got to *live* for?" A fresh spate of sobs. "Have you got another tissue?" She put one into his hands, and he brought them both up to his face and blew his nose. "At least I can do that for myself," he said mournfully. "Nemo's turned absolutely against me; he treated me like carrion tonight. It was like throwing something into an incinerator, the way he tossed me down here." He wiped his nose again and hiccuped pathetically. "The girls hate me. 'Shawnie was their darling, their darling, their darling!'" he sang in a weak, cracked voice to the tune of "Charlie Is My Darling." "They never had any use for me, except to get my sympathy when Shawn was making it with the other one. And now I've killed him."

He was overcome again. "Damn it," he wept, "I loved him, too! He shouldn't have needled me, that's all. In front of all those people. All those good, sweet people that welcomed us in. He made me feel like worse than a fool. Something worse than despicable." He heaved himself over onto his side and asked plaintively, "Can I hold your hand?"

Reluctantly she felt for his tied hands, and he clutched them in a hot, sweating grip.

"Shawn isn't dead yet," Rosa said, "and he doesn't sound as if he's dying. Listen, if these people make you feel like such a lowlife, why don't you cast off from them? There must be a few things about yourself that you like." She had said it so often to herself, back in the days of Conall Fleming. "You've had an education. What did you train for?"

"I wanted to be a doctor," he said brokenly. "But I passed out the first time I had to dissect anything." He brought her hand to his face, fondled it and kissed her fingers. It made her slightly squeamish; she was annoyed, uncomfortable, and angry with herself for being disgusted with him. She loathed having her hand slobbered over, and he smelled of stale sweat.

"Tell me about Captain Nemo," she said conversationally. "What does he do for a living?"

"He's rich for a living, I don't know why, just that it's not old money. You know?"

"I know," she said, not sure she did. "And Shawn?"

"Shawn's an actor. He was on a soap till they killed him. But they never found his body, so they'll be bringing him back." He broke into fresh sobs. "They were *going* to. But now he's really dead, and I did it. Cal, the wimp." He held her hand against his cheek. "Feel my tears. . . . Do you know why my name is Cal?"

She didn't care. She was so weary her head wanted to float away like flung foam; she wanted her hand back, to wash in the cold bubbling water over the side of the boat.

"My real name is Draper Smith," he was saying. "Isn't that revolting? I always hated it. I was small and a crybaby, and the other kids called me Dripper. I made the mistake of telling Shawn that, and he's used it against me ever since."

He seemed about to dissolve again, and she said in a hurry, "Where does Cal come in?"

She could feel the surge of energy that vitalized him. "I was Caliban in *The Tempest!* I got it secondhand the way I get everything else. I was the understudy and a big joke to everybody. They never thought they'd have to use me. Then Caliban turned up stoned out of his skull, and they could see the play going down the drain. But I was *great!"* He laughed exultantly. "Nobody could believe it of Draper Smith. *I* couldn't believe it. God, what a feeling! Behind all that makeup I was liberated. *Ecstasy!* And it came from *me*, not from anything I sniffed or popped or smoked. Me, Draper Smith!" He said more quietly, "I had a hell of a hangover the next day, and of course, *he* was back, so I had only that one chance. The good thing that came out of it was people calling me Cal from then on."

"That must have been a relief. Did you get other good parts?"

"I tried out for them, but usually I wasn't even good enough for an understudy. I shot my bolt with Caliban. But he stayed with me, you know. It is like possession by a demon. Most of the time I can keep him subdued, but tonight he came out." He sounded drowsy; the grip on her hand was less fierce. Again that faint chuckle. "It's not everybody who has one of those."

"Listen, Cal, do you have any more family? Besides the demon?"

He didn't answer. He was asleep, his wet cheek against their three hands.

22

"All right in here?" Hugo said from in the cabin doorway.

"Yes, if I can get my hand away," she whispered. "He was in a state." Gently she pried her fingers loose.

"I don't blame him, poor little bastard. His buddy was really carting it to him all evening."

She stood up, balancing against tiredness and a sudden pitch of the boat. She rubbed the wet back of her hand distastefully against her slacks. There was a little breeze now, and they were going into it. Hugo was bending over the other bunk.

"I hope to God he's still breathing. We've had everything else on Bennett's Island but a murder, and I can't say as I want to be in on one. Yup, I can hear him."

The fog had gone on the freshening northwest wind, and *Valkyrie* was cutting across a stiff top chop toward the dark mass of the mainland. The harbor of Limerock was marked by lights, and from this distance they looked like garlands of incandescence.

Jamie nodded gravely at Rosa, as if he were being civil to someone whom he'd met once under formal conditions. Pitt stood behind him, looking past his shoulder and out over the rising and falling bow.

Astern Linnie sat on a life jacket on the floor, huddled in the oil jacket, her legs drawn up, her arms around them and her head on her knees. She didn't stir when the other two came.

"We've seen some pretty queer characters come off yachts," Hugo said, "but this is a different kind of queer, if you get me."

168

Rosa laughed. "Well, you were the one who told Nemo he had a floating whorehouse."

"It was the only thing I could think of right then, but I don't know what professional whores look like. The only ones I know are amateurs," he explained seriously, "and I don't know if you can call them whores when they do it for free because they like it."

"I wouldn't think so."

"Those two of Nemo's looked and felt about as sexy as a couple of tholepins. But I guess you don't have to look sexy; it's what you don't mind doing that counts. Or don't mind having done to you. Sick, ain't it?" he said cheerfully.

"Who's sick?" Linnie sat back, rubbing her neck. "I'll never be able to straighten out again. I *hate* sleeping like that! I hope the toilets are unlocked at the public landing. There's no place on this boat where you can be alone with a pail."

"I could tell all the gents to face forward," Hugo offered.

"No, thanks. I don't want Pitt to think of that in connection with me. Wait till we know each other better before he finds out I have to go like ordinary mortals."

Now the sky was paling, and the boat seemed to fly across the sheltered inner waters toward the chains of light, and Jamie was telling the Coast Guard that he was arriving. Pitt then called *Sweet Helen*, back in the harbor of Bennett's, and eventually Roy answered sleepily.

"We're in," Pitt said curtly.

"Gotcha. How is he?"

"Still breathing. Thanks for the comeback. See you." He signed off with *Valkyrie*'s identification.

The ambulance was waiting at the public landing, and a cruiser from the sheriff's department; there was also a good handful of the curious, both on foot and in cars.

"Jesus, look at the dirty stay-out-all-nighters!" Jamie said in disgust. "They'd all turn out to watch a rape if they could get the word in time on their scanners."

Any idea of simply delivering Shawn, Cal, and the knife to the proper authorities and then going to find coffee and food disappeared like the fog. There were too many explanations, and neither of the two was in any condition to give them.

"Goddamn that Nemo!" Jamie swore. "Believe me, he'll pay for dropping all this shit on us!"

Linnie volunteered to go to the hospital and wanted Rosa to go with her, but Cal was clinging to Rosa's hands and begging her to stay with him; Hugo, looking as uncomfortable as they'd ever seen him, blurted out that he couldn't stand hospitals and would stay with the boat. Linnie looked wordlessly at Pitt, who said without expression, "I'll go."

An onlooker offered to drive them to the hospital behind the ambulance. "We'll all meet back here at the Harbor Edge for breakfast," Jamie called after them. "I'm leaving this place as fast as I can!" Tight-lipped and breathing very hard and loud through his nose to indicate his dangerously attenuated patience, he got into the cruiser with Rosa and Cal. Rosa had insisted on Cal's keeping a blanket around himself; his lips were blue, and he couldn't stop shivering.

At the jail he waived his rights and told his story in a stumbling but persevering rush. He'd stolen the knife from Rosa's house and stabbed Shawn; he was guilty. He was a murderer; that was all there was to it. The sheriff told a deputy to give them all hot coffee and left for the hospital. Cal's teeth clattered on the edge of his mug, and he needed both hands to hold it. He watched Rosa as if he would drop into an abyss if he lost sight of her for a second.

She insisted on waiting until he was booked. When he was about to be led to a cell, he hung on to her hands. "Will you be here in the morning?"

"No. But you turn in and get some sleep, and Nemo will be over to get you a lawyer and bail you out and everything."

"Nobody ever rotted yet in our jail," said the deputy. "It's a real health farm for some of the inmates. Good food, too, and you look like you could use a few square meals."

Cal gave one last appealing look over his shoulder at Rosa, who heard herself calling after them, "Can you give him an extra blanket? And *watch* him? You know what I mean."

"Yes, ma'am."

The door shut behind them. Jamie said, "Anybody'd think you were seeing your problem kid off to summer camp." She ignored that.

They walked downtown in the cool ruddy light of sunrise, with the city waking around them. Pitt and Linnie were at the restaurant, whose windows looked out over the harbor; from their table they could see

Valkyrie tied up below them. Hugo had been in before daylight and eaten, according to the waitress, and had gone back aboard.

Needing a shave, Pitt looked darker than usual; needing sleep, he was even more reticent than usual. Linnie was as bright as the sky over the harbor. She told them at once that Shawn was still alive and likely to go on living. The knife had missed any vital organ; it may have just nicked the outer lining of the heart. The pericardium, she explained learnedly.

She had already washed up and combed her hair, but she went with Rosa to the rest room; the instant the door latched behind them, she dropped her poised restraint and gave Rosa a violent squeeze. "Would you believe it would take an attempted murder to get Pitt and me together? I couldn't get one dance with him all night, and then some odd little critter off a yacht blows his top, and here we are!"

Rosa turned on the cold water and leaned over the sink to toss handfuls on her face and flush the prickles out of her eyes. Linnie's voice came dimly through the splashing.

"It's the damnedest thing! I was perfectly in control riding to the hospital, but when we got into emergency, I practically lost my wits. I fell all over myself with explanations, and then Pitt stepped in. Rosa, he was so *masterful*—that's the only word for it."

Rosa splashed on more cold water, lifted a dripping face with closed eyes, and groped for paper towels. "He told what happened in just a few sentences," Linnie babbled on. "Right to the point. Jamie couldn't have done any better." She put sheaves of towels into Rosa's hands.

"Of course, when he said we didn't know anything at all about these people, but Shawn's friend Captain Nemo would be in to take care of things, they all got this suspicious, sly look, as if we'd just beamed in from outer space."

Rosa blotted her face dry and borrowed Linnie's comb. She saw with a modicum of satisfaction that she didn't look bad for having been up all night, or else the glass had been made especially to flatter.

"Then the sheriff came and backed us up," Linnie said. "Finally he gave us a ride back here. How's Cal?"

"I don't even want to think about him," said Rosa.

"I asked the sheriff to tell him Shawn was going to live. Let's eat. I've never been so hungry."

Jamie had ordered the Fisherman's Special for them all. "You billing Nemo for it?" Pitt asked him.

"Damn right I am!"

Once they were heading across the harbor, leaving the green-bowered city behind, Linnie lost her sheen. "I'm going to turn in."

"He didn't bleed on any of the blankets," Hugo said. "Besides, I've been sleeping in them, and that takes the curse off."

"St. Hugo," said Linnie through a yawn. "Coming, Rosa?"

"I'm not ready yet," Rosa said. "It's too pretty out. You go on, Pitt. You look as if you could use some sleep."

He shrugged and went below.

"Okay, Jim, what happened uptown?" Hugo asked.

"If you don't mind," Jamie said frigidly, "I don't want to think about the whole stinking mess until we have to go over for the goddamn trial."

"I can see the only way to get anywhere near *him* this morning is with a kitchen chair and a whip," said Hugo. "You tell me, Rosa, darlin'."

"Cal waived his rights, said he did it, they booked him, and that was it."

"Short and sweet. Well, I might as well have another soshe. If Captain Bligh wants me to take a trick at the wheel, let me know. I'm not volunteering. God, he looks some savage." He made himself a couch of life jackets on the floor.

Rosa went and stood beside Jamie, her arms folded on the shelf. The mountains behind them and the islands on either side were as blue as iris, and the crest of every little wave was burnished gold. The early-morning traffic ranged from lobstermen through big trawlers and a variety of pleasure boats under both sail and power. The incoming gulls took on the sunrise colors as at night they were tinted by the sunset.

Rosa let herself go in a waking dream, seeing herself and Jamie returning home alone. She saw them walking away from the island wharf up to their house through the wet grass, silently stripping, getting into cold sheets and moving into each other's arms like two halves of a whole, warming each other's bodies, sleeping entwined for hours as the sun climbed and the island came to full life about them.

She was jarred out of this by Jamie's voice. He was trying to raise *Astarte*.

"We should be seeing her by now," he said irritably. "How long ago was first light, for God's sake?"

"Depends on what he calls first light. Maybe the sun has to be well up over the yardarm."

Jamie gave her his sidewise look, the withering effect weakened because he couldn't help blinking his tired eyes. She or Hugo could have taken the wheel to spell him, but she knew better than to mention it. Behind them Hugo slept on his back, one knee drawn up, one hand on his chest, the other arm flung out with the hand palm up, open and defenseless. With his black curls and his face smoothed and softened by sleep, he looked about fifteen.

Jamie began calling *Astarte* again. Rosa looked into the cabin; in one bunk only Linnie's hair was showing from under the blankets. As if Rosa's glance had roused him, Pitt came awake all at once, the way fishermen do. He swung his feet out and stood up all in one motion.

"Ready to turn in?"

"I guess so," she said reluctantly. Jamie wouldn't miss her. He and Pitt made a good pair; let them have it all to themselves.

The rhythmic throb of the engine and the swash of water past the hull put her to sleep without her ever forgetting where she was; when a harsh clanging roused her, she knew at once it was the bell off the northwest shore of Brigport.

She stretched and lay there, enjoying the motion and the sense of deep water beneath her, cradling her in perfect security. She was indeed the ocean child of the song she sang.

Linnie was still sleeping when Rosa went out into the cockpit. The blue-black forests and green fields of Brigport steamed in the sunlight, and men were hauling traps a little distance off the shores. Washed by the fog, dried by the northwest wind, the day was enameled with color.

"Morning, sunshine," Hugo greeted Rosa. Pitt nodded at her.

Jamie, now wearing dark glasses, took his pipe out of his mouth, scowled at it, and spit over the side. "I don't know what in hell they put in that tobacco. Tastes like root beer."

"Any sign of *Astarte?*" she asked.

"He must be going to Limerock by way of Mount Desert," Hugo said.

"Maybe he's taking the underwater route," Pitt suggested. "Back to twenty thousand leagues under the sea." Rosa and Hugo laughed, and Pitt behaved as if he'd said nothing at all.

They went down the eastern shore of Brigport and cut out around Tenpound, the small high island between the two larger ones; black-faced Hampshire sheep grazed on the rich herbage above the reddish granite ledges that shelved or tumbled into the sea; and the animals stopped feeding to watch *Valkyrie* go by.

Linnie emerged from the cabin, smiling, with her hair combed. If

Pitt hadn't been there, she'd have crawled out yawning, squinting against the light, huddled in a blanket and groaning that she was half dead. "I miss anything?" she asked. "Oh, look at the sheep! Aren't they lovely with those black ears against the sky? I always wanted a pet lamb," she said wistfully. "When I have a place of my own, I'll have a half dozen."

"*Jesus!*" said Jamie. "Look at that!"

That was a mast cocked over Pudd'n Island, the craggy islet which stood up from the water like a blunted mountain peak off Steve's cove at the Eastern End. "That her?" Hugo asked incredulously.

"Has to be."

They sped across light-spangled blue ripples toward the shadowy cove in the lee of the great mass of the Head. Steve's boat was gone from her mooring. Up and back from the shore, the wet roofs of the two houses and their outbuildings shone like polished silver in the sun. Philippa was coming down to the wharf, with a black Labrador and Robin's brown Toggenburg doe.

The boat was *Astarte* indeed, high and dry among the boulders, miniature bluffs, and small crevasses. When the tide left her, she had tilted sharply to starboard, exposing her copper-painted bottom. A gull roosted on her askew mast, from which the pennant limply stirred in the wind.

The five aboard *Valkyrie* gazed at her with a kind of reverence, she had been so thoroughly rammed ashore. "Well, now," Jamie murmured with a small chilly smile of satisfaction.

They went into the wharf where Philippa waited, sitting on a crate. The goat was nosing delicately through her hair, and the doe stood looking benignly down at those in the boat.

"How's Shawn?" she asked.

"He'll be all right; the knife missed all the vital spots," said Jamie. "Looks like somebody was in an awful pucker to leave."

"Oh, somebody was! Eric said Nemo hustled the girls back aboard as soon as you'd left. The dance went on for a little while longer, and then everybody left together. It was too thick to see across the harbor, so they didn't notice the sloop had gone."

"When'd you find her?" Hugo asked.

"Early this morning," said Philippa. "The gulls were making a lot more noise than usual, they woke Steve and me up, and Eric, too. We could just make her out with the glasses. . . . Don't browse on my hair," she said to the doe, gently pushing the persistent head away. "Go find some nice grass. . . . We couldn't figure out if anyone was still aboard her or if they'd put off in a small boat at the time it happened. You know how thick it was last night. We all had the same nasty picture of their missing the cove and rowing past the Head right out to sea. Then we spotted the dinghy standing on her tail, and Eric went out in Robin's boat and found them aboard, very uncomfortable, Nemo in a black mood and the girls sniffling and whimpery. He brought them in." She laughed. "Poor Robin slept through the whole thing, and she's still out cold. She'll be furious."

"They still up there?" Linnie poked Hugo in the ribs with her elbow. "Hugo's insane about Margo and Jennifer, aren't you, dearie?"

"Gorry, I don't know how to tell you guys this," said Hugo, "but it's really Nemo that stole my heart."

"Grieve away, poor child," said Philippa. "They're all gone like the snows of yesteryear. We fed them, warmed them up, and the girls were so relieved they outtalked Captain Nemo, and one of them let slip the fact that they had *not* been heading for Limerock. He'd have wrung her neck if he could have reached her across the table. Anyway, he gave up gracefully when Steve told him *Astarte* was on Pudd'n Island to stay until the tide floated her. So then he asked Steve to take them all over to Brigport before he went to haul, so Nemo could call for a plane and get the girls over to Limerock with their bus fare to Boston."

"Anybody spare a thought for Cal and Shawn?" Rosa asked.

"Oh, yes," said Philippa. "The girls talked about them. They worried about Shawn but agreed that he'd asked for it. They intend to see both the boys. Captain Nemo ignored the subject." She looked diverted. "When the girls were in the bathroom, redoing their faces, he got terribly confidential, said he hardly knew the four of them, he'd just invited them along on the spur of the moment, and the sooner he was rid of them, the better. Eric and Steve and I kept straight faces, but we all were thinking the same thing: that's he's scared stiff this will get into the Boston papers. The girls may be minors, and maybe he's like the man in the Harry Lauder song, he's got a wee wifie waiting."

"So where is he?" Jamie was past civility.

"Oh, he'll be back from Brigport at high tide," said Philippa, "and then he'll probably head down east. That's my guess. He thinks he can run away from the mess, but I'm sure if the police want him, they'll be able to find him."

"Well, he wasn't anywhere near the crime," Jamie said sourly. "I don't know how they can haul him in it. But by God, I'll be here when that sloop floats."

They went up Long Cove to the harbor. Roy was aboard *Sweet Helen* with the engine running, and his lifted arms and his grin embraced them all. Jamie left Pitt off there, with a gruff word of thanks. Pitt's nod was noncommittal, but Rosa thought his obsidian gaze flickered toward Linnie. She couldn't be sure, but Linnie was; the aura was all but visible, as if some connection delicate yet positive had been forged during the night.

Rosa walked home through a quiet village, carrying her blankets and hot-water bottles. The men were out, and all the children were sleeping late after the dance; even Sam and Richard weren't up yet to attend their traps. Tiger gave her a perfunctory wag, and Hank stood contemplatively on the Binnacle chimney, uninterested in her if she was not handling herring.

Up in her yard she threw the blankets over the clotheslines and went into the house, shedding her clothes. She dropped the hot-water bottles on the counter and went straight up to her room, where she took off the rest of her clothes and crawled into her sleeping bag. She shut her eyes against the blue radiance filling her windows and at once saw Jamie at the wheel of *Valkyrie*, first by the glow from the compass at midnight and then in the morning light, when they came into the harbor.

So she had gone with him; she didn't know why, he hadn't needed her. She'd been more necessary to Cal, and the thought of all that made her queasy.

One instant she was thinking that she would never be able to get to sleep because of the two of them, and then she was asleep without knowing it was happening.

23

Joanna had expected her thoughts would keep her awake for most of the night that was left, but the recorded music blasting away across the field, amplified by the foggy hush, would have done it anyway. Suddenly, around half past twelve, the noise stopped.

"Jamie's had enough," Nils remarked.

There were the usual shouts and whistles of protest; the music was started again.

"He's just given them the word," Joanna said. "On the stroke of one, they all turn into pumpkins."

This time the volume was muted by closed doors or possibly a masterful hand. A few moments later it stopped again.

"Broken down," Nils said with relief. A series of penetrating female screams soared into the night but were cut off in midflight. "I wonder who grabbed her," Nils murmured.

"And who she is," said Joanna. "Somehow that screech didn't have a Bennett's Island accent."

After that there was a good deal of talk in the lane, and then the records commenced once more, sending a persistent, if subdued, beat throbbing across the field. But it ended in about a half hour, and in the return of quiet, they heard a Brigport boat leaving the harbor, then the hushed conversation of home-going youngsters. Nils fell quickly asleep, and by now Joanna was too tired to lie awake brooding. Nils's breathing was as soporific as the sound of the rote on the shore.

She slept until Pip woke her by patting her face. She opened her eyes and looked into his inquiring ones; he bumped his forehead against hers,

177

rubbed his cheek against her temple and poked his black nose into her ear as he poked it into flowers.

"Hello," she murmured, and he fell over on her in drunken adoration. A mouthful of cat hair will get you up faster than anything, she thought, removing his limp body from across her throat.

Cool dry air blew the curtains into the room, and the dawnlight was as clear as well water. Nils followed her downstairs in a few minutes. She had let the cat out and was making coffee, while leftover fish hash browned in the iron spider, when Nils found the note on the sun parlor table, propped against the big old-fashioned white and gold sugar bowl. He read it aloud to her.

Cal stabbed Shawn with Rosa's carving knife, Linnie had written in a hurry, so Jamie and Hugo were taking them both to the mainland, and she and Rosa were going, too. She signed with her love.

"Do you realize," said Joanna, "that our kid got in here and changed her clothes and left a note without our *hearing* her? Never even bothered to let us know what was going on! Now I call that sneaky."

"You feeling cheated? . . . Now I know what all the screams meant," said Nils. He went out onto the doorstep. "The yacht's gone, too," he called back to her. "She must have followed Jamie in." He returned. "Wonderful morning! How about some breakfast?"

"You sound as if stabbings happened all the time around here," she said crossly. "Aren't you upset? This happening in our clubhouse, ruining the kids' dance—that turns my stomach."

"Just be grateful no islanders are involved. As far as ruining the kids' dance, they'll still be talking about it when they go back to school. They'll be a sensation. Come on, let's eat, and then we'll walk around to see if either of our young ones thought to call Mark."

Jamie had called from the public landing before *Valkyrie* left for home. Shawn wasn't dead and wasn't going to die. Not this time anyway.

"That's all he told me," Mark said. "You know what he's like. When he's that quiet, he's madder than a wet hen. I never heard all the touse down here last night. By God, anybody could have towed the wharf and store away right under my nose. That's what comes of kicking up my heels like a young goat for half the night. I fell into bed and passed out. Too bad us old coots had to miss all the fun."

"Speak for yourself," said Nils. "Rather them than me. I've had my turn chasing back and forth across the bay in the middle of the night."

They walked home in a blinding sunrise. Brigport, having been lost so long in the fog, looked new-painted, almost garishly so. The ospreys were back, fishing over waters turned larkspur blue under the light northwest wind. Filling Nils's dinner box, Joanna was tempted to invite herself along as sternman; but it was Sewing Circle day, and the only way to keep the tradition alive was not to miss meetings.

When she went down to the shore to see Nils off, Roy Bainbridge was rowing out from Drake's wharf toward *Sweet Helen*, shouting at anyone he saw.

"Hey, that was some fine old rumpus last night, huh?" he called to Terence Campion. "Your little girl tell you about it? Gorry, them kids' eyes was out on sticks!"

If Nils hadn't been there, Joanna would have shamelessly beckoned Roy in. Nils had stepped on a sensitive toe when he'd said, "Feeling cheated?" As far back as she could remember, she'd felt swindled whenever she missed any excitement on the island. Nowadays she didn't resent the actual witnesses as she used to—they were so *smug!*—but she still retained the single-minded determination to get all the facts for herself as soon as possible. She kissed Nils at the head of the ladder as if Roy, now hailing Philip, were no more than a gull squawking out there, but in spirit she was halfway to Philip's house, where Liza would be up and getting the story from Sam over his oatmeal.

Sam was still asleep, but he had given his parents a report, somewhat incoherently, before he went to bed. "He was mad because the stabbing didn't take place right on the dance floor. I hope the little ghoul isn't disappointed to find out it wasn't a murder after all."

Needing to do something which required all her attention, Joanna was frying doughnuts when Linnie and Jamie walked in. Jamie was still in his good slacks and shirt, somewhat rumpled, with new beard glinting in the sunlight. The rims and whites of his eyes were stained with pink. Linnie looked as if she'd had eight hours of sleep and were ready to run for an hour. Over a large mug-up of coffee and warm doughnuts, Jamie gave his mother a laconic account of the night, quelling Linnie with a thin-lipped, icy silence whenever she tossed in a footnote. Finally she was allowed to supply the drama and the color. It was a pity she'd missed the actual stabbing, she did so well with everything that happened afterward, beginning with Jennifer's screams.

"Your father and I heard that," said Joanna. "We thought someone was having fun in the bushes."

"Mother, how you *talk!*" said Linnie happily. She went on with her narrative, ending up with the meeting for breakfast. "You'll have to get the stuff about Cal from Rosa. He cried all over her and told her his life story." She jumped up to let the cat in and hugged him. "Was I gone all night, mean old me? Did you miss your bunkie?"

Jamie looked tired and bored. "Now it'll have to go to court. Assault with a deadly weapon, and all that bull—" He cut the word off with a bitter little grin at his mother. "I just hope this frigging mess doesn't keep us going and coming across the bay all summer. Damned foreigners!"

"Jamie'd like to put a chain across the harbor every night," Linnie said, "and let nobody but islanders have keys. You'd think every yacht that came in here was full of weird characters."

"Well, most of them are. And not just the yachts, either."

"If you mean *Sweet Helen,* the Bainbridges came in mighty handy last night," she said. "Of course, Pitt beat the pants off you at pool, so that damns him forever. We all know that, lovey."

"All right, all right!" Jamie waved a hand at her. "I admit he was a help. And now they've gone, so they'll be out from underfoot for a few weeks. Seems to me that radar must have fixed itself. I thought they were having somebody come out from Limerock Marine to do the job."

"Maybe it was just a matter of a loose screw," his mother said.

"A matter of quite a few loose screws is more like it. The whole hoorah's nest across the harbor stinks. There's something about *that* foreigner as queer as a three-dollar bill. It sticks out all over him, and it's not just because he's out here where we don't want him."

"Come on, Jamie," said Joanna, "put it into words. What is it besides the fact that he's got about twice as many teeth as normal and smiles with them all, clear back to his ears? And drives your father into a cold rage by calling him Cap'n? And says he's a biscuit even if his mother didn't have him in the oven?"

Her children looked at her with blue-eyed astonishment tinged with apprehension. She laughed at them. "He calls himself a Bennett's Islander, doesn't he? And the last I heard, that was the crime of the century around here."

"I can't put it into words," Jamie said quietly. "But I haven't forgotten my high school English, so I could say there's something rotten in the state of Denmark."

"Jamie, are you turning psychic?" Linnie was almost respectful.

"*No!*" he snapped. "But I can have intuition, can't I? So let's wait and see how right I am. I can trust you to keep your mouth shut, Marm, but I don't know about Turdheels here." He gave Linnie a sardonic smile.

"Fine, Lillebror," she said composedly. "You'd be surprised what secrets I have locked up in this fair, flaxen head. If you knew some of the things I know, you'd either turn feather-white or have a stroke."

"I didn't know that much was going on around here," said Jamie, "except for a stabbing now and then, and Buttery Ben slithering in and out. You mean this place is a roaring pit of iniquity? Come on, tell us who's bushwhacking with who, and just how they manage it."

"I'm not talking about sex, if that's the first thing that comes to your mind." She rested her chin on her hands and fluttered her lashes at him. "Nobody would guess *you* ever thought about such things. Unless catching herring is a sublimation or something."

Jamie shoved back from the table and got up. "Well, I'm about to catch a nap and then be on deck with my hand out when old Nemo surfaces at Pudd'n Island."

When he had gone, Linnie gave her mother a curiously shy smile. "Pitt and I really talked last night, Marm. In the hospital and while we were waiting for Rosa and Jamie. Know what? He wishes Henry Coates would buy Pirate Island from Ivor Riddell and put him down there to fish it all on his own. It was as if something had shaken loose in him, as if he'd never such the chance before, to talk about himself." She laughed self-consciously, a wild rose color coming up into her face; Joanna thought objectively that she was almost beautiful. The "almost" was a modest qualification.

"And it made me feel sort of humble," Linnie said. "Honored and humble, because it was me he was talking to. And he *smiled.* Marm, what a smile! He doesn't use it often, but when he does—well, all I can say is, I don't know how I'm going to stand waiting two weeks before I see it again."

The wild rose deepened to peony. She laughed again and whirled around and ran up to her room. "I've got to go haul. If I'm lucky, I'll be done before Sam staggers out. . . . Buttery Ben's slithering in now!" she called from her room. "Just coming into the harbor."

"What do we do, swim out to him with garlands of flowers?" Joanna called back, and Linnie hooted.

"He'd probably take it as his due."

24

Sewing Circle was up at the Fennells' today. The house had been changed over so much inside that it held for Joanna few memories of her marriage to Alec. Part of her reluctance to attend the meeting grew from her slight uneasiness about seeing Van today, but she kept reminding herself that she had put all the foolishness behind her. Still, she'd have liked to have skipped the meeting altogether; after years of scrupulous attendance she felt such an enervating lack of interest it seemed impossible to stir herself to the effort of getting ready. She knew this was temporary, but each time it had the smothering weight of a cave fall-in, and it was not always caused by the Sewing Circle.

She went, of course. Staying home would cause more trouble than it was worth. Nobody missed Sewing Circle if she could possibly help it. Only Mateel wouldn't be there today because she'd gone to the mainland and would return with her older children when they came for the Fourth. Mateel never left the Homestead for casual calls around the island or to meet the mail, but she never missed Sewing Circle and always entertained in her turn.

Linnie went off to walk alone to Sou'west Point. She took the binoculars, and Joanna said, "What for? You can't possibly see Cash's from there?"

"Funny Mommy," said Linnie to Pip. "Full of them foolish jokes."

When Joanna left the house, the northwest wind had whipped up into smart gusts, and *Drake's Pride* was just going out, dipping her nose into the tide rip at the harbor mouth. Drake must have finished hauling early and was in a hurry to get back to the mainland.

The Sewing Circle had plenty to talk about today. Rosa wasn't there to add her story; after a long nap she'd gone to haul. Philippa said that Steve, Jamie, and a Brigport boat were helping get *Astarte* afloat, and most of the children were down there to watch. Helmi, usually a reserved, if attentive, observer, was expected to tell what Mark had found out; he'd gone to high school with the sheriff and had talked with him by telephone this noon. Cal had quieted down, and now he was mild as milk and was eating well. The girls had been flown in from Brigport and had seen Cal. The injured man was in no danger, but nobody could afford to post bail for Cal.

"If they're waiting for Nemo, they've got a long wait," Philippa said. "I may be wrong, but I don't think he'll go near Limerock."

"Wouldn't it be nice," said Joanna dreamily, "to find out where he lives and send a news item to the local paper?"

When the subject had been worn threadbare—or been beaten to death, Laurie said—and there came a natural pause around the quilting frame and over the knitting needles, Kathy spoke without looking up from her tiny, meticulous stitches. "Remember what happened to the Lady of Shallot? 'She left the web, she left the loom,' she took quite a few steps across the room, and right out the door, down the wharf, and aboard *Drake's Pride.*"

"You mean she was aboard when he left just now?" Joanna asked.

"She sure was!" Kathy could no longer be offhand. "And listen, she wasn't leaving for good, because she didn't take anything more than a handbag. It was all so quick that if I'd been five minutes later, I wouldn't have seen anything. But I always watch him whenever I can, because he's such a jerk, and sometime I'm going to catch him looking foolish or mad or upset instead of—" She bared her teeth in a hideous grimace, clenched them, and said between them, "'Hello, this is so nice, I admire your husband *tremendously*, and *you're* gorgeous, too!'"

She prevailed over the laughter. "And then I'm always hoping the Easter bunny will come hopping out, holding up her little paws. And *today*—well, it was a good thing all my kids were out, so I could really whoop. Because there she came, and Godfrey, was her hair some handsome in the sun! And hot as it is, she had that big cape of hers wrapped around her like a tent."

Absolutely sure of her audience, Kathy could now afford to pause, and did, just long enough for dramatic purposes. "So there she was standing on the end of the wharf, waiting to be helped aboard the boat, and I was thinking that for somebody who grew up in a family of fishermen, she's some dainty if she needs help to get aboard a boat at high tide. All of a sudden a gust of wind snapped that cape out like a sail behind her."

Most of them guessed what the next suspenseful pause meant, but no one wanted to spoil Kathy's moment.

"She's pregnant," she said solemnly. "Very pregnant. Out to here." She measured with her hand.

"I've been dreaming of funerals!" Maggie Dinsmore said at once. "That means a birth!"

"So Drake has a duckling on the way," Liza mused. "I think I knew it in my bones."

"It doesn't have to be his," Carol Fennell said, turning her large glasses on Liza. "I was just reading this book, about this girl who found out after she was married what a brute her husband really was, and she ran away to save herself and her unborn child."

"Which way did they go, Kathy?" Philippa asked.

"Around Eastern Harbor Point. They could be going either to Limerock or maybe only as far as Stonehaven. She should be seeing a doctor, if she's that far along, and if she's hiding out, Stonehaven would be better. He left Willy painting the trim on the house," Kathy said. "I went over and began talking to him as soon as the boat went around the point. I never *asked* him anything, of course."

"Of course," Van agreed.

"Well, nothing direct. I said I was glad to see her out of the house enjoying the weather, and it was a great day for a sail across the bay. I thought something might help out, but all he said was Ayuh, and kept on painting. I think he's been threatened with boiling oil if he lets her name pass his lips. Anyway, I invited him for supper, lobster chowder, and he said fine. I guess he thinks he'd be safe from me with Terence and the kids there. And he will be," she added gloomily.

"You know," said Liza, "when he brought her out here, I said this was a great place to stash a mistress. But a *pregnant* one—what a mess. I'm sorry for the poor thing." She shuddered. "Lord, I hate to think what her thoughts might be, shut up in that house."

"She ought to be seeing people, having cheerful conversation, taking walks in the sunshine," Maggie said. "I'd be glad to give her a cup of tea any time. No matter whether she's married or not," she added sternly.

"Nobody's condemning her, Maggie," Laurie said. "I guess we're all sorry for her."

"Well, I don't care who the father is or if it's an immaculate conception," said Joanna. "We've got a very pregnant woman on this island, and we're not supposed to know it. We're to avoid the place like a pesthouse, and if she falls downstairs or goes into premature labor, she could die in there. The man's out of his mind, or else he's just plain stupid."

"Or she is," Van suggested. "Maybe this is the way *she* wants it, and he's just carrying out her orders."

"And I thought this was going to be a peaceful summer," Laurie murmured.

"After last year," said Joanna ironically. "Well, the one thing I can safely say is that Jamie's not the father of it. At least I think I can." Everybody laughed.

"Well, we're off to a great start," said Marjorie Percy. "A stranger shows up with a load of gear and says he's a Bennett's Islander. That's enough to stand everybody on their ear. Then he dumps a pregnant woman in our dooryard and tells us to ignore her, which is like ignoring a time bomb. Then we get a stabbing at a perfectly nice dance, and it's just luck it wasn't a murder."

"Captain Nemo was quite a dancer, wasn't he?" Liza said reminiscently. "He clasped me so close I expected to be imprinted with all his chains and medallions. What do you suppose he is back in the world? What are any of them?"

"God only knows," said Joanna. "But whatever goes on with them over in Limerock, it's nothing to do with us unless some islanders have to go to court as witnesses. But we do have to think about Susanna Baird or Selina Bainbridge."

"Why don't I keep shoving notes under her door until she opens up just to get rid of me?" Kathy asked.

"Might work," said Vanessa. "You wore *me* down, and I was a hard character."

Kathy grinned. "I learned young how to make a real nuisance of myself, didn't I, Aunt Helmi?"

"I remember," said Helmi. "Mark was always threatening to keep you in a barrel and feed you through the bunghole."

Kathy happily made notes of all the suggestions offered for her notes; the gist was that everyone respected the woman's privacy but wanted her to know that if she needed help and wanted company at any time, someone was always ready. Nora and Carol went out to the kitchen to make tea, and the talk broke into several separate conversations, none of them about the pregnant woman or last night's fracas.

Joanna heard without listening. The words in her head were Van's: "You wore *me* down, and I was a hard character." She had to strive to keep from watching Vanessa across the room; what would mere looking prove? Even if she could stare at an oblivious Vanessa by the hour, it would tell her nothing. Oh, drop it, drop it! she silently cried, but then she could feel the weight of the sleeping child in her arms and experience again the jolt in her chest when she had looked down at Owen's scowl in miniature.

But in the next instant the scowl had gone; she'd only imagined it, as she'd been imagining so many other things, conjured out of a clear sky. No, not a clear sky. There had to be a cause for that mute enmity.

"*Jo.*"

She jumped as Van took the chair beside her, and Van said in consternation, "What's the matter?"

"Oh, Lord, nothing except remembering." She laughed. "Is that a sign of old age? I'd better watch it. I was thinking of all the babies born on this island in the past. My mother never went to the hospital with any of us, and I had Ellen here, but that wasn't planned; she came early. She was the last baby born here."

"Maybe the Lady of Shalott is planning to leave in plenty of time."

"Oh, probably," Joanna said. "But it won't do any harm to have some contact if Kathy can manage it."

"She can if anyone can. I spent days dodging her before I gave up, and might as well have done it first as last. She got me in the end. Now I don't know what I'd do without her, and Cindy, too. She's got Anne this afternoon, and I don't worry. Listen, can I walk home with you and borrow a book or two?"

With relief Joanna slipped back into their friendship as if into dry warm clothes after a chilling rain. "Do you have to ask?"

25

Mateel Bennett came home on the mail boat the next day with her oldest son and daughter and their families. They brought the fireworks for the Fourth. It was a tradition that it never rained on the Fourth of July picnic, even if they had to have it on the fifth or the sixth. The fireworks had never yet had to be postponed more than a day or so.

The mail boat also brought Rosa a letter from the people who were buying her house at Seal Point. They'd been able at last to sell off some acreage which had been left to the wife and were now ready to pay off the mortgage, or would be by the week after the Fourth. Rosa would have liked to go in at once; she wanted distance between herself and Jamie, the sooner the better, and the next ten days stretched out before her like ten years. No matter how well you were doing, you needed a chance to breathe in a different atmosphere. If she was not seeing him one way or another all through the day, her bedroom and his place at her table were filled with him just the same. He was everywhere, moving against the backdrop of sea and island; he dominated her nights through the low thrumming of *Valkyrie*'s engine as the boat cruised from cove to cove in search of herring.

If she could be free from all that for forty-eight hours or more, when she came back to the island the distance between them should be permanent. The island was her home now, and she wouldn't be driven from it; the way she felt about it, with or without Jamie, meant that she couldn't go ashore now and idle away the time until the Sloanes were ready. The prospect gave her claustrophobia enhanced by suffocation.

She sent the Sloanes a postcard by return mail, saying she would be

187

in on the eleventh of the month. There'd be moonlight again by then, and the seiners wouldn't go out. Would he miss her? If he felt any lack, it would probably be like wondering why a favorite pair of old shoes had disappeared.

The six o'clock news from Radio Limerock informed the islanders that Draper Smith had pleaded guilty to assault, but Shawn Murray had made a statement from his hospital bed to the effect that he had maliciously and persistently provoked Smith, and considered that he had brought the assault upon himself. Two young women friends of the pair bore this out. Smith was given a suspended sentence. All four would leave Limerock as soon as Murray could travel.

Rosa was alone when she heard the news and felt nothing but a dull surprise, as if the weird trip across the bay in the midnight fog, with Cal weeping all over her hands, had happened so long ago it was barely remembered now. Yet she had thought of Cal from time to time, unwillingly, and always put him quickly out of mind. Well, it was over now, as simply as that. She and Jamie wouldn't have to go to court; Cal hadn't hanged himself in his cell; Jennifer and Margo had been loyal to him as well as Shawn, proving that they were more than grimy little racks of bones without brains. Shawn had proved that he was more than a sadistic peacock; he had a conscience. Captain Nemo became a nervous, frightened man scurrying away from scandal. He'd probably lied about his name change, too. Which all went to show that nothing was as it seemed. Time turned like a kaleidoscope, and the patterns kept changing, not only from week to week but from hour to hour.

The only person who missed the picnic in Goose Cove was Selina Bainbridge. She was alone for the holiday, with her brothers still out on Cash's and Felix Drake spending the time with his family. Willy was also ashore.

"Well, it's her own fault if she feels left out," Kathy said callously. "I keep leaving her notes, and she keeps ignoring them. She's probably looking down on us as a bunch of inbred half-wits."

"Anyway, she can watch the fireworks," Maggie Dinsmore said comfortably, as if even Selina Bainbridge should adore fireworks as much as she did.

Afterward there was an impromptu dance, which Rosa didn't attend. Jamie didn't go either, Rosa found out the next day. We could have had the island to ourselves, she thought, but dispassionately, as if she had already moved a long way off. Since he hadn't come near her that night, he was breaking it off, too, and she wouldn't have the chance to say all those things that came forth with such clarity and brilliance when she was alone. She laughed at herself for feeling defrauded. Wasn't the breakup the thing, with or without speeches? Besides, all her fine words would just bounce off him like hailstones off the roof.

The day before she was to go ashore was chilly, with a light west wind working up a light surf along that side of the island. The boys' and Linnie's small boats were bouncing and rocking when Rosa went by them, well outside and slowly so as not to add a deep wake to the chop. A good swash was breaking over the Sou'west Ledges, where there was always a sleek, glistening surge even in calm weather, and she went out around them to find the first buoy of her string leading to Brig Ledge. On this side the island was bordered by a satiny band of calm water; the rocks were blindingly bright and shimmering in the rising waves of heat. To the south, the Rock, sanctuary of puffins and terns, rose glowing from a sea that looked as if it could never sweep over the granite crest and endanger the automated tower. There had been no families at the Rock for a long time now, and no coast guardsmen for a year.

Any boats in Rosa's view were a good distance away, and she relished the novelty of being absolutely alone and absolutely safe on a summer sea—alone, that is, except for the birds, and now and then a seal popping up to watch you with dog-curious eyes. If you were lucky, there might be a small head close to the big one.

Just as *Sea Star* was going behind Brig Ledge, Rosa saw *Valkyrie* appear from behind Schooner Head. "Oh, *damn!*" she said aloud. "If there has to be somebody, why *him?*" But in the next instant Brig Ledge was between her and the sight of *Valkyrie*. He had a few traps out here near hers, but he might have already hauled them and be working ahead of her to the east'ard. But just from seeing him she felt squeezed into too small a space for breathing, and the iridescence of the day was dulled beyond saving.

She hauled her traps, in a hurry now to get the work over with. She tried to slow down; if she were leisurely here, he would be moving away all the time, and perhaps she could get back what he had driven away, or a part of it.

Then all at once *Valkyrie* appeared again, heading straight out past the northern end of Brig Ledge. She could see nobody in the cockpit; he could have ducked below for an instant to pick up his thermos of coffee.

She stopped work involuntarily, her hands resting on the trap she was about to slide overboard, wondering if he would come to her, and then she saw the foot of a black rubber boot showing over the upright in the stern, toe pointed at the sky, and the taut line running from it out into the wake.

She could not make a sound, she could not. She whirled around from the trap on the washboard and opened the diesel to its top speed and went after the other boat. *Valkyrie* was not running at her highest; otherwise *Sea Star* couldn't have caught up with her.

As she came up on the other boat's starboard side and the two bumped and scraped against each other, Rosa jumped onto his washboard and into the cockpit. Jamie was on his back in the stern, or rather up on his shoulders, the free foot braced against the upright. The other leg, being drawn up and out, was caught at the ankle in a loop as tight and as killing as a hangman's noose. He saw her but didn't see her; he was looking at death while his hands clawed space for something, *anything*, to hold on to, and there was nothing.

She had cut off his engine almost before she had both feet in the cockpit, but momentum carried the boat long. Rosa grabbed up a knife from the washboard and ran aft. She cut the taut line to the lobster trap which would have dragged Jamie down with it to the bottom. The loose end whipped free over the stern, and he collapsed flat on the floor, gasping, "Tend to your boat."

Outside the lee of Brig Ledge *Sea Star* was moving swiftly away. Rosa started up *Valkyrie* and captured the running boat and fastened her with a line around the cleat on *Valkyrie*'s stern deck. Purposely she ignored Jamie while he eased his tortured leg back into the cockpit, pulled himself up, and vomited over the side. Then he sat back on a lobster crate, white-faced as she had never before seen him, except on the day Eloise left him; his hair was dark with sweat, his eyes were shut. She kept the engine idling. Up beyond Schooner Head Philip Bennett was hauling, and Terence and Rob were working almost side by side outside the Seal Ledges; but nobody seemed to be looking toward Brig Ledge.

Rosa got out Jamie's lunch box and gave him a cup of coffee. "Thanks." He sounded out of breath. "Anybody around to see that?"

"If they did, they'll think I was overcome with lust and leaped aboard to have my way with you," she said. "How's your leg?"

"Feels pulled clean out of the socket, but I guess it isn't." He shifted it cautiously, stiffening his face, but couldn't hide a wince. "The blood's going back into my foot, and I don't know as I ever felt anything like it. But then, I never got caught in a riding turn before. Where was that goddamn knife?"

"Back there on the washboard."

"I remember. I was cutting away kelp; that last trap came up in a real tangle." He drank some coffee.

"It's a good thing I saw it," she said. "I'm some numb in an emergency."

"*Numb!* What do you think *I* am?" She knew he was calling himself all the brutal names he'd have given anyone else who had been so foolishly, and nearly fatally, negligent.

"Any law says you can't have two or three knives on board, so you won't be cutting kelp with the one you're supposed to have back here just in case?"

"Good idea," he conceded, which was something.

"Are you going to take your boot off?"

"Jesus, I don't dare. It feels as if my foot would come off with it. Did I say 'thank you'?"

"You were too busy worrying about who was within five miles of us."

"Damn right!" he said with passion. "Getting caught in a riding turn like a damn gaum and nearly pulled overboard. I'd never hear the last of it."

"You'd never have to hear any of it if you'd gone all the way," she commented.

"Having to be saved like some fumblefoot idiot." He went on as if she hadn't spoken.

"Why don't you add, 'And by a woman, too?'" Rosa asked. "I suppose you prefer death to dishonor, is that it?"

He looked up at her, his eyes opening wide as if in some new recognition. "You're kind of gray around the mouth. Here." He held the cup toward her. "Pour some for yourself." She shook her head; her insides were beginning to heave and crawl.

"If you can take yourself home," she said, "I'm going back to work."

"Remember the first time you showed up in the harbor? If I'd really discouraged you then, you might not have stayed, and you wouldn't have been around to save my life today."

"You couldn't have driven me off. And if you think fate moved me onto Bennett's Island just so I'd be around today, you're farther out than I thought."

He pulled himself onto his feet by holding on to the upright and sagged back against it. "God, my arms and shoulders are some lame. And look at my hands." He held them up in disbelief as they shook uncontrollably. "I couldn't have held on much longer." Suddenly he began to shake all over. She poured more coffee for him, holding the cup while he drank, his teeth hitting the edge.

"I was an ignorant arsehole way back then," he said. "But I know a little more now. Damn little, but it all helps."

He took the cup into his own hands, steadier now. "Thanks, Rosa. I kind of like living. I'd hate like hell to stop just because I made some numbhead goof."

"Me, too. I'd hate to go through the rest of my life thinking, If only he hadn't been so stupid."

"They'll probably put it on my stone at that, whenever it happens. You know, one reason I made that damn fool mistake, I didn't have my mind on my business. I was thinking about something else."

Eloise? She used to go hauling with him on such days, lying on the bow.

"It was just a lot of crap, but it almost turned me into food for the crabs. Now if knowing *that* doesn't put a man's head back on straight, he's a hard case." He stood up and put his arms around her. "You aren't going to tell, are you? I skidded on a piece of kelp and twisted my leg, · that's all."

"That's all," she agreed, quiet in his embrace, not returning it.

He hugged her with a hurting strength and kissed her. "Thanks again, Rosa. Thanks for being."

She kept herself from responding, she would not be trapped by his touch. "Anytime," she said. "Just as long as you don't bill me for that trap I cut off."

He grinned. "Nope. But I might send you down after it."

"I wouldn't put it past you? Can you manage now?"

"Yep." He let her go. "I have to move around to keep from stiffening up, so I'll finish up here, and when I get home, I'll go over to the house and soak in the tub for a while. Good thing it's the bright of the moon. I don't have to think about going out tonight."

Once she was back aboard her own boat, she felt a stultifying exhaustion. The hug and the kiss at the end had been a gratuitous cruelty; he had embraced her because she represented life at that moment, not a woman he could not live without. But knowing this was not as terrible as knowing that if she, or anyone, hadn't been there, Jamie would now be drowned with the trap. She imagined the empty boat running on this summer sea. She was not nauseated; she was simply drained of strength; she felt as if she could hardly start the engine or turn the wheel.

She did, finally, and went home, leaving her other traps unhauled. There was no one whom she could tell, to diminish the horror, and she was tempted to take herself to the mainland today directly to Seal Point, in her own boat instead of waiting to go in on the mail boat tomorrow.

But Jude and Lucy were expecting her to stay with them in Limerock, and one of them would be meeting the mail boat at the ferry landing tomorrow afternoon. To change arrangements would be more trouble than it was worth.

26

Jamie didn't finish out his workday; she saw him limping home before noon as if he could hardly bear any weight on his left foot, and he was not seen for the rest of the day. So he'd had to give in to human weakness after all. Sprains, twists, bruises, scrapes, and infected fingers all were part of the normal wear and tear of the business, so a painful skid on slippery kelp caused no comment except that he was lucky not to have broken a leg.

Waking or sleeping, Rosa kept reliving the incident all night long and imagining what could have happened, and with each performance it grew worse. She kept seeing the empty boat going in circles, and familiar faces turned unfamiliar with shock; she heard weeping in her sleep and woke to find herself crying. So she was up before daylight, and as soon as she thought she could pick out her buoys on the water in a showery dawn, she went out to finish hauling her traps.

On the way home she met *Valkyrie* coming out, with Jamie on a high stool at the wheel, and Linnie in her oil pants as sternman. Jamie waved, and Linnie shook the gaff over her head. They would not be speaking when they came home; the failed rendezvous with death would not make a saint of Jamie overnight, especially if he ached. If he didn't get a full bait bag in the face before they were half through, it would be almost as much a miracle as his escape had been.

The trip on the mail boat was surprisingly pleasant because for once she was glad to be going to the mainland, and not just to receive a good deal of money. No other Bennett's Islanders were on the boat. They picked up a few passengers at Brigport, nobody whom Rosa knew except by sight, so she wasn't involved in conversation for the next twenty miles. The day was open and shut, with sudden showers falling through sunlight. "The devil is beating his wife," True MacKinnon used to say, and his child, lifting her face to the sparkling, blowing rain, marveled that what the devil did in his fiery kingdom deep in the earth could make it rain in God's territory.

She stayed outside in her raincoat, sitting on a milk crate with her back against the pilot house. The bay wasn't rough, just pleasantly choppy, and the colors shifted from moment to moment as the sky changed. At the end of two hours the Fremont hills looked close enough to touch in a blinding torrent of sunshine. Since she had become an islander, she had always preferred to see them falling astern, but today her spirits improved as *Clarice Hall* approached the great harbor of Limerock and the air became warm and smelled of summer-struck mainland. She could not bear to think of Jamie dead, but it would be a rest to be where he was not.

Her cousin Jude's wife, Lucy Webster, met her at the ferry landing and drove her home for lunch, and she changed into something more appropriate for a meeting in a lawyer's office. The last time she'd been to one had been at the time her divorce was granted. Before that there'd been the frightful day when she'd started proceedings; even now, carrying not an ounce of extra weight, flat of belly and rump, she felt the cruel constriction of a girdle that had ruthlessly tightened on her as her heat and agitation grew, and the torture of the high heels on which she'd blundered down the stairs, feeling as if she were the only mourner at her own funeral. And the green eye shadow. Why did I ever go in for *that?* she asked her now-reflection in the Websters' bathroom mirror. Oh, God, what a sight I must have been!

"Go wash your face, Ro," Jude Webster had said firmly. By the time she left the restaurant with him that day, she was on her way to Bennett's Island.

Today, when she walked into her lawyer's familiar premises, to meet the Sloanes and their check for forty-five thousand dollars, the miserable ghost composed of blubber and tears and streaked green eye shadow made one last appearance—she wondered if the lawyer saw it, too—and left forever.

There was a family dinner at the Websters that night; her deaf cousin Edwin came with his hearing wife and baby son. His wife had worked in the office of the building supply firm where he placed most of his orders, and now she was his partner in his restoration work. She adored him.

"I always liked his looks," she told Rosa, "and his dignity. His silence was a lot more impressive than anything any other man had to say." Edwin, expertly hefting his son to his shoulder to be burped, had an extra sense that told him when he was being discussed. He looked at them past the baby's fuzzy head and smiled.

He drove Rosa to Seal Point after supper; she'd been urgently invited to drink champagne with the Sloanes at the burning of the mortgage. His wife stayed behind, so they had a few minutes alone in the driveway under the maples that had once been Rosa's. She wasn't as expert in hand language as he was, so their talk was half in writing, half in sign.

"You're happy," she told him. "It sticks out all over you."

"But not all over you. What's wrong?"

"You with your sixth sense. Stop showing off."

His eyes granted no quarter. She shrugged. "Okay. I want to marry Jamie Sorensen and have some babies. But he's the most cautious bachelor I've ever known since you. Once bitten, twice shy. It's that damned Eloise."

The best thing about Edwin was that he never told you what you shouldn't have done, should have done, and must do in the future. He simply gave you his unwavering attention, in which there was no clue whatever to his opinions.

"So I've decided to stop thinking about it," she said defensively. "If a baby's the most important thing, I could leave the island and find a man somewhere who'll give me one. But it's Jamie Sorensen's baby I want. If I can't have that, and him, I'll have nothing. There's no second choice."

She had rarely put it so succinctly even to herself, and the part about babies had come up out of nowhere, as if the sight of Edwin's son had unlatched a secret door unknown or ignored by her until now.

"But if Jamie didn't want children, I'd still want him," she said. She didn't know if she felt better or not, but at least she'd told someone who'd never repeat it.

They kissed good-bye with a deep, lingering affection; at one time when they both felt like castaways, flung away from life as if by centrifugal force, they had shared the unspoken thought that they should hang together.

One of the Sloane relatives who lived near the Websters would drive her back to Limerock. She went into the house with which her last tie had been cut, expecting to feel the strangeness of the amputation, but she experienced nothing but pleasure; a baby was going up the stairs on her hands and knees, egged on by two slightly older children in pajamas. A mongrel terrier distinguished only by his cheerful nature was running up and down the stairs, barking.

The other guests hadn't all arrived yet, and Jed Sloane took her around to show her what they'd been doing to the house, while his wife got the children to bed. When they came back to the living room, Con Fleming was coming through the front hall. He always looked dressed up even in work clothes; tonight he was elegant in ice blue corduroys and a matching shirt, with a sleeveless argyle pullover. He looked on his way to a party. She suspected that it was this one.

"Hi, everybody!" He saluted them. "I knocked, but nobody heard me. Hey, Jed, congratulations." He put out his hand. Jed shook hands with him, slanting an embarrassed glance at Rosa, who smiled reassuringly.

"Taken to crashing parties, Con?" she asked.

"Hell, who's got a better right to crash this one? I used to be married to this lady," he said to some out-of-town Sloane relatives. "The worst day of my life was when I lost her."

"Don't you believe his blarney," said Rosa. She was angry with him for barging in like this and showing off; she knew now that he was a little drunk, but she wouldn't risk a scene that would spoil the Sloanes' evening.

"Christ, but you look good, honey," Con said. "Damn handsome woman I married. I should've hung on to you."

"You look good too, Con," she said amiably. "But you're thickening. You want to watch that."

Involuntarily he put his hand to his midriff, then brushed it quickly over his thick coppery hair as if to reassure himself about his crowning glory. He grinned at her. "Take a walk with me? Fifteen minutes, that's all." *If you dare* was unspoken but there.

"All right," she said, wanting to get him out; she'd see that he didn't get in again and make an ass of himself over the champagne. "We'll be down back," she told Jed. "Give a holler when you want me."

They walked out the back door into the sunset light, along the boardwalk past the lilacs and across a grassy yard with swings and a seesaw. The Sloanes had fenced in the yard and put in a gate with a latch too stiff and too high for the children to manage. Rosa and Con went through the gate and down to the wharf, which had recently been rebuilt. The fish house had been reshingled and wired.

A crude bench had been set against the end of the fish house facing the harbor and out of sight of the house. They sat here, and Con lit a cigarette and sighed heavily. He sat forward with his arms braced on his knees and stared at the planks. Children were rowing their skiffs across water streaked gaudily with cloud reflections in purple and flame. The gulls were flying high in groups of twos and threes, with a few solitaries. When they came in the morning, they called aggressively or sociably back and forth, waking up dreamers as they banked past open windows down to their favorite checkpoints. But at night it was always this high and silent flight on sunset-colored wings out to the nesting sites.

Con sighed again, shook his head, and continued to stare at the planks. There'd been a time when she couldn't have resisted stroking his back. She'd begin at the crown of his head, on that thick, wavy red hair she'd loved; her hand would linger on his nape and then make the long sweep down to his belt. Tonight her palm had no residual itch.

"So this is it," he said with dramatic gloom. "The end. It's really gone, a whole chunk of my life. To tell you the truth, I never thought you'd do it."

"You never thought I'd keep the boat or go through the divorce either," she said placidly. "Con, you really did me a favor when you walked out on me for the honor of your little woman."

He threw down his cigarette and ground it viciously into the plank with his heel. "That little whore!"

"Gosh, I kind of like her," Rosa said. "Because she liberated me. You know, when you told me you wanted to marry her, I had to start running my own life. So I owe you something."

"Huh?" He sat up and looked at her with gratified surprise. "Listen, get away from here as soon as you can. Call me first and I'll pick you up. My place is real quiet, off by itself. You remember that place of Clem Blackett's—"

She burst out laughing; she couldn't help it. "Don't you ever get your mind above your belt? I just meant I should thank you, and I do. Tomorrow maybe I'll order flowers for Phyllis," she said mischievously.

"I'll write on the card, 'With heartfelt thanks for getting him out of my hair.' What's her name now?"

He stared glassily. Then shock gave way to unwilling admiration. "Christ, you're a cool one. You *have* grown up. Who's the lucky guy?"

"What guy?"

"There has to be one. I remember you in bed." He whistled. "You're a normal, healthy woman, and you're getting plenty. Anybody can tell. It puts a shine on a woman. Is it one of those Bennetts, or are they all past it?"

"If you were in a roomful of them, you wouldn't be wondering," she said. "You'd be too busy feeling like the little man who wasn't there. And they have sons, too. I'm going back to the house, and you'd better go back to your nice quiet little house and quack away for another duck."

She started to get up, and he gripped her arm and pulled her down again. "Don't think I can't. I was just making a gesture for auld lang syne."

"It's the spirit that counts. So let's take it that we're friends and be glad of that. I'll always wish you well, Con."

He blinked rapidly, and she thought in dismay that he never used to get sentimental when he'd been drinking. "I wish you well, too, darlin'," he said. "So roost a dite longer. They don't need you yet. I won't muckle on to you, if that's what you're scared of."

"I'm not afraid of that," she told him. She remembered the days of the physical ache to have Con's baby, how often she had found her hand unconsciously shaping to cradle a little red head. She recalled a fantasy of Phyllis's death in childbirth and Con's bringing the child home to her. She was still Con's Rosa then, as helplessly bound to him as a hostage to her captor.

He was sitting back now, lighting another cigarette. Over the lighter flame he crinkled his eyes at her; this used to devastate her, first with adoration and then with hopeless grief. "How's the lobstering there?" he asked.

"Good. How's the herring?"

"So-so. Hey, I hear you got a gentleman lobster catcher out there these days. Doing it for fun, like one of these big-game hunters."

"Oh, all kinds wash up there and then wash out again the next high tide."

"He won't wash out that fast, as long as he's having fun." He was alert with suspicion. "There's no hanky-panky with *you*, is there? I hear that Drake's as horny as a billygoat. His wife supplies the money, and he flits from flower to flower."

"That's some goat. Got wings, has he?"

Con was always a gossip, and he usually described men as womanizers or eunuchs. Himself excepted, of course, and a handful of men for whom he had a real and almost superstitious respect. But anyone with money was automatically marked down as a secret satyr, a roaring bull, or hopelessly impotent and a collector of pornographic films. She had stopped believing his yarns long before she stopped being in love with him.

He was rambling on now. She heard the last few words: "The wife found out, raised holy hell, girl went back to Boston or New York or somewhere—"

"If you're ever called to swear on the Bible to all these stories of yours, Con, you'd probably fall down in a fit or be struck dead by a thunderbolt."

"You don't believe me?" He looked bewildered.

"I don't *care* about all the garbage you and your cronies swap over your booze."

"The trouble with you is," he said kindly, "you don't want to face the real world. You never did."

"Oh, brother!" She threw back her head and laughed. "Con, you can always come up with *something*. Even," she added wickedly, "if it's not what you'd like to come up."

"By God, I'll have you know I'm as good as I ever was!"

"Well, you don't have to tell the whole of Seal Point. I'm going back to the house." She started to rise, and he held on to her wrist.

"Don't go yet. I'll talk about something else. But you hadn't ought to make cracks like that about a man. It's like kicking him in the balls."

"All right," she said. "So talk."

He made a self-righteous effort. *See, I'm trying.* "I'm thinking of going into dragging full-time. I rigged her for shrimping the last two winters and did damn well. But I hear some fellers are doing stavin' out on Cash's, catching lobsters. I'd like to try that, if I could get a partner I could stand to be stuck with for two weeks at a time aboard a boat, way out there."

"Mmm," she said.

"These guys going out there now, the ones I know about—they got partners and spell each other. Two on and two off. Been mighty lucky in their weather so far."

"Somebody from Seal Point?" she asked.

"Nope, from Coates Cove. A pair of brothers named Bainbridge and a couple of guys named Rouse and Wilcox. I know 'em all by sight. One of those Bainbridges could talk the hair off a dog. The other's named Pitt, and he's as deep as one. Never says a word." He chuckled. "Never gets a chance. They sell to Henry Coates. You ever heard of him?"

"Maybe," she said vaguely. "There's a lot of talk in the store sometimes, you don't remember who says what. Got a big seafood-peddling business, hasn't he?"

He laughed. "Him and his peddling! You'd think he had enough to do, with the size of his lobster business and shipping them out all over the world. But that man's dabbling in more pies than he's got fingers for. It must keep him up all night trying to figure out how to take care of everything. He probably pays some genius to keep two sets of records, one for him and one for the IRS."

"You think he's a crook?" she asked idly. "A man of his standing?" She wished Jed Sloane would call her.

"Listen, we all know the big buyers get rich at the fishermen's expense, but the way he's exploded over the top in the last few years is pretty sickening. Three planes in the family, two Mercedes', trips to Bermuda, Hawaii, and it can't all be coming out of buying lobsters and peddling fish."

"Real estate," Rosa suggested. "Good investments. Lucky in the stock market."

Con threw his cigarette butt overboard. "I'm thinking," he said in a lowered tone, "that it's something else. Where's the big money along the Maine coast these days?"

"Real estate, I said."

"I'm talking about the kind of money you don't have to pay taxes on because you ain't supposed to have it."

"Henry Coates smuggling pot? You're not smoking that stuff, are you? You'd better be careful. He'll be getting you for defamation of character." She stood up. "The mosquitoes have found me," she lied. "I'm going in."

He stood up, too, and put his arms around her. "There's nobody like you, Rosa," he said emotionally. "All the rest are sluts and bitches. You were such a good person; you *are* one—" He burrowed his face in her neck, kissing and nibbling the way he used to do.

And I just put forty-five thousand dollars in the bank, she thought. "Yes, I know, Con," she said. "I was the great earth mother. Made nice hot soup for you and warmed your bed. A real treasure." She wrestled herself free with some difficulty, but was equal to holding him off. "Con, go home."

"There's no one there," he said mournfully, trying again.

"Keep your hands to yourself, or I'll shove you overboard, so help me. Go *somewhere*—anywhere—but not back to this house."

"Why can't I stick around? I got feelings! We had some good times in that house, Rosie, darlin'." Who but Con would get weepy over the good times he'd smashed?

"It's a private party, and you weren't invited." She walked away from him up the wharf, and he followed her.

"You're hard, Rosa. Who's the man?" he asked jealously.

She slapped away his hands, first from her and then from the gate. "Take the outside path around to the road, Con. So long, and take care. Oh, and watch the liquor. It's ruining your looks."

She went through the gate and left him staring at her as if he were six and his mother had inexplicably slapped his face and then abandoned him. But a stunned six-year-old would have been a tragic sight. Con wasn't even pathetic, but annoying, like the mosquitoes.

With the strong gate between them she repeated, "Take care, Con. And don't try to come in, or you'll be put out. There'll be enough men to do it, if I ask them to."

Melancholy rather than vicious, he called her an obscene name and walked away along the path, smoothing his hair as if for comfort. She had put him from her mind by the time she entered the house from which any psychic residue of their good and bad times had been exorcised.

27

When she left the island, she had planned to stay away a few days, to keep time as well as distance between her and Jamie. The champagne had given her a good sleep in a strange bed, but she woke very early the next morning and lay listening to the unfamiliar and obtrusive sounds of the mainland, heard even on a quiet street well out of the city. She was so homesick that if she'd obeyed her body, she'd be up and out of here in ten minutes, walking the three miles to the ferry landing to make sure *Clarice Hall* hadn't sunk or blown up during the night.

She had become an islander, and when she was away from the island, even the recollection of her worst moments there were nothing compared to her physical and emotional longing to be back.

Jude was already downstairs, talking to the cats and starting to fry bacon. The coffee was ready. "I knew you couldn't hang to your bed past the crack of dawn, Ro."

"I'm going home. The boat's going out again today with a jeep for a Brigporter. I love you and Lucy, but I'm homesick."

"That doesn't surprise me. I lived out there once, remember, and I know how it can put you under a spell. I just hope things go better for you than they did for us. . . . How do you like your eggs?"

"Any way you do them." She carried a mug of coffee to the table and tipped a cat out of the chair, scratching behind its ears by way of apology. "Jude, sell me the house now. I can make you a good down payment and monthly payments a lot higher than the rent I've been paying. Or I could pay for it outright right now."

Without answering, he brought her loaded plate to the table and fixed another one for himself. Then he sat down across from her and gave her the patient, kindly look over his glasses that signified opposition.

"Look, Ro, you could be out of there in another year, and if you can't sell the house, you're stuck with it."

"I won't want to be out of there in another year." To show she wasn't being impulsive and thoughtless, she began to eat. "It's really my home now."

"What if you married someone who isn't an islander? You'd want to go where he made his living. You're a young woman, Ro. Good God, you shouldn't set out to be a hermit! It's not right for a woman."

"Is that why you don't want me to buy the house?" she asked. "Because I'm a woman and I need to be taken care of whether I want it or not? You're a male chauvinist, Jude. I love you, but that's what you are."

He smiled. "I get called that all the time. But you're part of my family, and I can't help feeling responsibility. I want you to be sure, that's all."

"Jude, if you tell me you and Lucy can't make yourselves give up the house because you might want to go out there again sometime or any of your kids might want it, I'll understand," she said. "These eggs are perfect. Eat yours before they get cold." She yelped as two double paws' worth of claws sank into her thigh, with fourteen pounds of cat behind them.

"He does that," said Jude fondly.

"He sure does." She gave the cat a piece of bacon and tossed a bit to a shy calico. "Breakfast in the tiger cage. Come on, Jude. Give me a straight answer."

"I've given it to you, my girl. I just want you to be positive."

"If I don't know my own mind now, I never will. Listen, Jude, it's easy to sell Bennett's Island property if there's a shore privilege with it, and to lobstermen, not summer people. They think it's Eldorado out there. Somebody made Philip Bennett an offer of a hundred thousand for his house, wharf, and fish house, a thousand traps, and an eighteen-year-old boat. I don't know how much Foss Campion got for his place, but there was a waiting list. It's getting so crowded in here, those islands are the last frontier."

Jude nodded now and then, apparently giving most of his attention to his food. But he was listening.

"You put a good price on it, Jude," she said, trying to hold back the full spate of her desire for the house. "I don't expect any special consideration. And if I ever have to sell it, and I get one of those fancy inflated prices, I'll share with you. That would be only fair."

"There'd be no need of that," he said severely. "Listen, I've been getting rent out of it for a long time, and you've kept it in repair besides. Anything you get more than you paid for the place, it would be your own. Eat your breakfast now, and stop talking."

"Can't you give me a promise to think about it?"

"I'll think about it." His thin face creased into the deep lines of his smile. "But no more promise than that."

It was the best admission she'd had from him in two years, and she knew when not to push. Besides, Lucy was coming downstairs.

"The sheriff wants you to pick up your knife," he said.

"I don't want it," she said.

"Call him anyway, so he'll know I gave you the message." He kissed her good-bye and went off to work on the house he was building across town.

The sheriff told her that she had to take the knife and give him a receipt for it. After that she could do anything she wanted with it. Lucy drove her around to the courthouse on the way to the ferry landing, and a woman deputy gave her the knife, neatly wrapped. She wondered if she could drop it overboard in the bay but decided that wouldn't work; there'd be likely too many people taking a ride out with the jeep. She could hold private ceremonies at home.

In the morning calm the sea was as blue as blue-eyed grass, striped with the dark lines of currents and paler lustrous bands like satin ribbon. The southwest wind suddenly kicked up an exhilarating chop just before they reached Brigport.

There was a good audience to watch the transfer of the jeep to the main wharf, and Rosa hired one of the boys to take her across to Bennett's in his substantial eighteen-foot dory with its ten-horse outboard. When they came out by Tenpound and she saw the island lying before her in the sun and wind, she felt as much joy as if she'd been gone for weeks.

Sea Star was the only boat on the mooring in the brimming harbor, and no children were in sight; there were only the empty skiffs and the birds. The boy charged her five dollars for the trip, delivering her to her own wharf, and while she was picking the money from her billfold, he was craning his neck, searching in all directions. "Where is everybody?" he asked finally.

She guessed that *everybody* meant all girls over fourteen. "Probably swimming over in Schoolhouse Cove."

"Oh." He took off, whistling as if to disguise his single-minded intentions.

The store was quiet. "I'm back," she called to Mark in passing. She arrived in her own back yard without being seen, or at least hailed, by anyone. There was something entirely suitable about this unnoticed entrance into a new chamber of her existence. She was able to contemplate undisturbed her relationship with the island. All mainland ties were gone except those of blood. For better or for worse she had married the island. They had been living together for a long time, but now she was about to commit herself for the rest of her life. With or without Jamie. Apparently it had to be *without*. But not because he was dead, and she was so grateful for that she trembled at the memory of an apparently empty boat.

He was alive because of her, and she'd settle for that. If you honestly recognized yourself as a loser, like recognizing yourself as an alcoholic, your honesty made you a winner for once, didn't it?

In the same anthology where she'd found the poem about "the Ocean Child," she'd come across a line that stuck in her mind like burs on a spaniel's ears.

Two souls may sleep and wake up one,
Or dream they wake and find it so,
And then—you know.

Know *what*? It had never happened, the dreaming *or* waking, to her and Jamie. He had forced her to make the effort to accept him as a friend; she had saved his life. Debts had been paid, and that's all they were, obligations, not passages between lovers. Admitting it was not the beginning of an end, but the end of a beginning, if she chose to look at it that way, and she so chose.

In the afternoon Rosa delivered the purchases she'd made for Helmi and Marjorie, and refused to visit, saying she needed a nap. She wanted to keep on relishing a day which she felt to be unique in her existence. She knew this euphoria couldn't last, that she could come flapping down in a heap like an old sail, but she intended to get the most out of it.

But by sunset she needed fresh drinking water, and she re-entered the world by taking her pail to the well. The evening baseball game was going on, with Maggie Dinsmore as umpire and Tiger hysterically chasing all runners and pouncing on the ball whenever he could; it was too big for him to pick up, but he guarded it with growls. Linnie sat on the well curb cheering. When she saw Rosa, she grinned and said, "Welcome back! Hey, you actually *look* rich!"

"Ayuh," said Rosa.

"You mean you're tired of it already?"

"A million here, a million there. Peanuts, kid."

Jamie came out of his house, still limping. She did not think his appearance was anything more than coincidence, but he smiled as if he were glad to see her; well, why shouldn't he? He'd been damned glad to see her two days ago, even if he wasn't making it public.

"How's your leg?" she asked.

"Better. I'll be on my own tomorrow and glad to be rid of that." He jabbed a thumb at Linnie. "It's like having a tall flea aboard. A talking one."

"Some gratitude," said Linnie.

"Well, they say offered services stink," Rosa said.

"Offered, hell," said Jamie. "She got her twenty percent. Insisted on it. I'd have had Eric go with me, but he's painting Uncle Steve's boat."

"Oh, for the peace of my *Dovekie*," said Linnie, "where I can talk out loud if I want to without getting a dirty look. Rosa, did you ever notice that whenever he grouses about somebody, the first thing he finds fault with is they talk too much? He ought to join the Trappists."

Uncharacteristically Jamie put an arm around her. "You did fine, kid, and I appreciated it. How's that for handsome? And in front of witnesses, too."

"Out of this world, handsome." She gave his cheek a loud smacking kiss. Maggie applauded, and the nearest boys groaned as if one of their heroes had plummeted into disgrace. Jamie took Rosa's full pail and started off with it.

"He's a real mellow fellow tonight, Rosa," Linnie said. "Must be your influence."

"Hmm," Rosa said cryptically. She went after him, intending to take the pail and say good-night at the bridge. But he was going faster than she'd have expected, lame as he was. She caught up with him in time to open the back door for him, and he set the pail on the counter by the sink.

"Thank you," she said formally. "I'm much obliged."

"I heard Jed Sloane talking this morning," he said. "Telling some pals of his how they burned the mortgage last night, had champagne and everything. He was some happy, and you're a hell of a nice woman. He said that about ten times."

"Well," she said modestly. She waited for him to go.

He limped across the kitchen to the windows and stood looking out, his hands in his pockets. "Con show up?"

"Didn't Jed mention that, too?"

"Looking for a slice of that big check, was he?" Jamie was extremely casual.

"No, he never mentioned money." She stayed by the sink, so as not to behave as if she expected him to stay.

But he didn't move. Still looking out at the trees, he said, "The bastard upset you?"

"Why should he?"

"I just wondered. But maybe you've got regrets about selling the old homestead. I could understand that. It would be natural for it to hang over you for a while."

"I don't have any regrets about that."

"Well, you're acting funny," he said. "So is my mother. You two know anything the rest of us should know?"

"I don't know about your mother, but I know about me, Jamie, and I'm fine."

"Good," he said absently. Then, still without looking around: "Fleming's still single, isn't he?"

"Yes." She was tempted to add, just for the hell of it, "He invited me to go to bed with him," but Jamie would certainly not bristle possessively at the thought, like Tiger with the baseball; he would probably look at her as if she were a round-heeled moron.

She took a long drink of cold water. "My, that's good," she said chattily. "Want to know something funny? Con thinks Henry Coates is smuggling dope; that's why he's so rich."

It was like setting a match to dry shavings, the way it ignited him. "By God!" He was jubilant. "I never thought I'd ever give Conall Fleming any credit for anything but being a son of a bitch, but that makes sense to me!"

For this he lights up, she thought. Not for me.

"Listen, he'd had a few drinks, and like you, he's been depressed about the herring. So he thinks anybody making a good living these days has to be so crooked he could hide behind a corkscrew."

"A good living or a Henry Coates kind of living?" Jamie sat down and took out his pipe. "Dope is what I had Felix Drake pegged for. They're old buddies, I keep hearing. They could be in it together."

"Felix Drake's wife is rich," she said. "And as for Coates, there're plenty of ways to get rich without smuggling drugs. He could make a million selling off waterfront property. He ships out Maine lobsters for more than their weight in gold. Probably the fish peddling doesn't hurt, keeps the plane and the two Mercedes' in gas."

He didn't answer. He was a man seeing visions while he got his pipe going. "He could have people raising marijuana for him inland and processing it, and then he ships it out in his trucks. Or it could be something worth a hell of a lot more. Something that comes by sea in small packages."

"Heroin? Cocaine?" Rosa said skeptically. "It's all those paperbacks you hand around. Tell you one thing, nobody's yet come up with one about running drugs off the Maine coast. If you could turn your ideas into fiction, it ought to do well. I'll try to think up some good titles for you." You'd better quit, Rosa, she warned herself, but she went careening on. "The hard thing for you would be to write up the sex. You ought to let Hugo do that. Just the covers of his favorites make me blush."

Jamie stood up and limped out past her, either too preoccupied with his new idea or too peeved to speak.

As twilight was coming on, she took the wrapped carving knife and walked out to the water. It was quiet now after the day's boisterous wind.

She untied and unwrapped the knife. "Good-bye, Gramps," she said, and threw it as far as she could. She heard the faint splash, though she couldn't see it, and wished Cal well wherever he was. She found herself rubbing the back of her hand against her slacks, as she'd done after Cal had held it and wept on it.

28

A curved section of blood-orange sun appeared behind the uneven sawtooth rim of the spruces and cleared the highest peaks in two minutes. At first it was easy to watch, a perfect globe of color suspended against a gray velvet sky, but quickly its fire intensified from within as it rose. No, it's not rising, Joanna thought. We're tipping toward it, rolling over, and tonight we'll be hanging by our heels in the dark underneath, and Australia will be up top. When she was small, this was another reason for being horrified by a round and constantly turning earth.

She went back into the kitchen to pack Nils's lunch. He was filling his thermos bottle at the sink. The early-morning weather summary finished, and news began.

Two men, returning late last night from offshore lobstering, found a local fisherman drowned in Coates Cove. Ira Beecham, twenty-four years old and the father of two, was discovered floating face down by brothers Roy and Pitt Bainbridge when they were rowing ashore from their mooring. They had taken him in, and resuscitation was begun while neighbors called for police and medical help; but Beecham was pronounced dead by the county medical examiner. His wife said he had gone down to the shore to put his boat off on her mooring at high tide; he'd had her beached to scrub and copper the bottom. Since the lobster boat was found on her mooring, and his skiff drifting, it was believed he had slipped on the wet deck or lost his balance somehow while stepping from the boat into the skiff. He could swim, his wife said, but he might have struck his head and knocked himself out. The Bainbridge brothers were friends and neighbors of the dead man.

"That's awful!" Linnie came into the kitchen. "Poor Pitt!"
"Poor Ira Beecham," said her father.

"I mean that, too, and I'm sorry for his wife and those little kids, but imagine finding someone dead like that, somebody you know, and thinking maybe if you'd been a few minutes earlier, you could have saved him—" She disappeared into the bathroom, still talking.

"Well, a pretty grim start to the day," Joanna said, conscious of a wooden stiffness around her mouth as if she'd just come from the dentist's and the anesthetic hadn't worn off. "I'll walk you to the shore," she said to Nils. "And you be careful." He put his arm around her and kissed her, soberly; sensation came warmly back to her mouth.

When she came back to the house, Linnie said at once, "Marm, I owe you an apology. I forgot all about what something like this must do to you. It must have really smacked you in the stomach."

"For a moment. Anything like that always does. But I don't dwell on it."

"I hope I don't ever lose anyone like that," Linnie said, "but if I do, I hope I'll be as strong as you were."

"I didn't feel very strong at the time, but I had all the family, and being pregnant helped. It meant somebody was depending on me." Linnie's flare-ups of admiration, though nice, were disconcerting. You didn't know whether to agree that, yes, you had been very brave, or to be silent with a sort of smug and martyred smile.

"You just keep on breathing," she said. "That's all. You live one hour at a time. . . . I'm going out to tend my girls."

She always enjoyed feeding and talking to the hens and gathering the eggs in a particular blue bowl. She could never resist holding at least one warm brown egg to her cheek. When she came back across the yard, a goldfinch in the alders beyond the birdbath called over and over again in a plaintive, upward inquiry, "Her-bie? Her-bie?"

Linnie had gone to the shore, and Jamie was limping out onto the wharf. Ralph Percy's whistling challenged the birds; Rosa claimed the catbirds were going insane trying to imitate him.

Fending off any thought of the drowning and the young widow, she went upstairs and tidied her and Nils's room. Linnie's room was in a state of inspired disorder, but that was her own affair. After a token trip around the house with the dry mop, Joanna sat down at the sun parlor table and wrote a letter to her eldest child. The Lady of

Shalott was in the letter, and Felix Drake, but she did not mention the drowning.

When she went out to mail the letter, everyone had gone to haul, and Mark's wharf and lobster were enticingly empty even of young Mark. The mail boat wouldn't be due for at least three hours. She stopped at the fish house to get her fishline, her old knife, and a corned herring from the bait shed, dropped into a plastic pail. Hank planed past her ear, and she gave him two herring.

Mark was alone, doing paperwork in the post office. She mailed her letter and went out onto the wharf and down the ladder to the lobster car. Louis padded behind her on his big feet. Unlike Pip, he was monumentally silent. One could never imagine Louis making frivolous talk or even scampering. He sat at the edge of the wharf, observing her and the harbor birds with the same impersonal attention, neither menacing nor benevolent.

The green and silver harbor pollock that swarmed about the lobster car snatched at the bait as soon as the hook dropped. Hank flew over to watch from the top of the hoisting mast. It was a muggy morning, with the sun burning white-hot through haze, adding to the oppression caused by the news.

Over at the Binnacle, Tiger barked and then stopped. Joanna looked across the exposed harbor ledges and saw the tiny figure of Anne Barton in bright red overalls, patting the dog. Van was walking to Maggie on the doorstep. She was carrying the canvas tote bag she always brought to the store.

"Oh, *damn!*" Joanna whispered. "Why can't I just once have it to myself?"

To feel this way when she saw Van coming depressed her even more than she was. She tried to let herself go again with the tiny sounds of the water around and under the car, and the hypnotic effect of triangular flakes of light on the endlessly rippling water. She thought of the big-boned boy named Jamie Bennett who had bought South Brigport for a hundred and fifty dollars in 1826 and got his brothers to help him build a log cabin at Bull Cove. Why there instead of this big deep cove that made a natural harbor? Maybe it was to get away from the sight of Brigport over there. Maybe it was for what she craved now: the experience of being absolutely alone, except for the lover, in one's own kingdom by the sea.

Linnie maintained that Jamie Bennett's spirit must be at Bull Cove, where he had been young and in love. The ghost of his first wife would be there; she hadn't lived long enough in the Homestead to make it hers. Charles pointed out that he'd be more likely to be hanging around the harbor beach, where the sloop and dory fishermen used to stand at the splitting tables, cleaning each day's catch of the big cod you never saw now in these waters. Old Jamie had been down there on the beach two days before he died in his sleep, ninety-three years old. His life-span had been the nineteenth century, less seven years. Joanna's father, Stephen Bennett, had remembered his great-grandfather; he had sat on the old man's knee and learned his first letters from the family Bible.

Hank came down past Joanna's head with a blast of wind from his wings and landed a few feet from her pail of fish, and Louis looked mildly interested. Joanna returned resentfully to the present, like someone being dragged out of an absorbing dream. Yawning, finding the diffused sun uncomfortably warm now, she threw Hank the smallest pollock and began cleaning the others. She cut up one and put the pieces on the wharf for Louis, who accepted with dignity. Down on the car Hank gobbled up all the entrails.

While she knelt there, washing the cleaned fish and laying them in a rinsed pail, someone came down through the long shed, in which all footsteps were echoed and magnified. By a quick sidewise glance she saw Vanessa come out into the glaring light. Joanna went on washing her fish. She heard footsteps come to the head of the ladder, but Vanessa didn't speak. After a moment Joanna heard her returning through the shed.

Instantly she wanted to shout after her, "Van, come on back!" But then what would she say? Whatever it was, even offering Van some cleaned pollock, would sound false, at least to herself; she felt as if she'd lost some faculty of ease, like suddenly going lame or partly deaf. Being at a loss for words wasn't natural with her. And what was Van thinking now, for heaven's sake? What new self-consciousness had kept her from speaking as she always did?

She waited on the car until she saw Van stop at the Binnacle to collect Anne and go on. Then she took her pail and her fishline and climbed the ladder again. She carried the fish home, wrapped them in foil, and put them in the refrigerator. Then she went out to hoe weeds in the garden. She'd have to go back to the wharf again to say good-bye to Pierre and Donna and their families; if Van was back there, too, the crowd should be enough to keep them naturally apart.

Pip lay on the warm soil between the rows, rolling over whenever he caught her eye but not needing eye contact to keep his questions and comments going as long as she said, "Mm," or "Uh-huh," or "Is that so?" at frequent intervals. The swallows came in low over him, and he batted a lazy paw at them but without malice.

Linnie came home from hauling and stopped by the garden, slinging Pip around her neck. "How are the lobsters coming?" Joanna asked.

"Great. But now I'll never know whether Pitt likes me for me or my money."

She went in by the back door, still wearing Pip. She would sit down at the table before she changed her clothes and write in her account book her catch, her earnings, and her expenses.

Presently she came out again, in shorts and a fresh blouse, smelling of soap and water. She was carrying a glass stein of milk in one hand and a doughnut in the other, while Pip wreathed dangerously around her ankles, trying to keep his eye on the doughnut.

"What are you mad about?" she asked her mother.

Joanna said in genuine surprise, "Nothing! Why?"

"I've been watching you out the window. You look severe. As if you'd like to give somebody a piece of your mind."

"Not me. I need to hang on to every bit I've got."

Linnie sat down on the wheelbarrow, and Pip got up beside her. "You're sure you're all right? I've seen those long looks a lot lately."

"Maybe because I've been thinking a lot lately that I'd like to take a trip down east or over into Vermont, but we can't walk out on the lobsters in shedder season."

"Leave Bennett's in *summer?*" Linnie was aghast. "I didn't know you'd ever do that. Now I'm really worried." She laughed, but her eyes were anxious.

"Oh, for heaven's sake," said Joanna, dropping her hoe. She sat down on the grass by the wheelbarrow. "Look, I don't have a string of traps, I'm not on the seine gang. I've heard what everybody has to say at Sewing Circle, and except for that touse at the dance, and Felix Drake, and this insane woman who's shut herself up across the harbor, there's nothing new to discuss with friends and relatives. I think I'm just plain bored."

"Bored? *You?*" Anxiety gave way to shrewdness. "You weren't bored last summer. You'd have settled for boredom then."

"I know. Never satisfied, that's me. Part of it's the weather." Joanna gathered the cat up in her arms and rocked him. "Isn't it, old Pippin? Linnie, as soon as we see the gang off, let's take our lunch out somewhere."

"Goose Cove," said Linnie at once. "There might be something good coming in."

29

They came back in midafternoon, their sneakers soaked from sloshing around in fresh rockweed, their hair damp and curling from the moist wind. They had found a new lobster crate and tied it to a tree, piled good boards and pieces of two-by-four above high tide, picked up a tennis ball—whose point of departure was most mysterious—and some buoys, with initials and colors unknown to them, which had been in the water a long time. The styrofoam buoys were shriveled into ugly insignificance, whereas a wooden buoy, no matter how scarred, maintained its integrity. These they saved. There was also a green wine bottle thickly grown with small mussels. There was always at least one whole work glove, its fingers poking up in macabre fashion from a drift of weed. Linnie saved these compulsively, though they never came in useful like odd oars. Once she'd found a hand-knit sweater of Shetland wool, soaked it for days in rainwater to get out the rockweed stain, and had worn the sweater until it fell apart.

This time there'd been no dead seal or gull, which always ruined everything.

Linnie went to the shore to bait up, and Joanna intended to indulge herself further today by reading for the rest of the afternoon. She was washing out the thermos bottle at the sink when she saw *Sweet Helen* coming into the harbor, and remembered for the first time since this morning that the brothers had found the dead man floating in Coates Cove the night before. They'd been just getting home from Cash's; they wouldn't be going back out again now; they must have come to see their sister.

Linnie came running the way she used to race home from school when she had something to tell. "Pitt's here, and we're going down to Pirate Island right now. They look *terrible!* Even Roy's dimmed right down, and Pitt looks so sad. It must have been awful for them." She took up a jacket. "I asked Pitt right off if he wanted to go to Pirate and take a walk on it, and I thought he'd snub me, but he acted as if he really wanted to do something to take up his mind." She was on her way out, still on the run.

Joanna went up into Jamie's room and opened the carton of books Ellen had bought at a sale in her town. They'd been intended for fall and winter reading; but today was the time for breaking resolutions, and this form of escape couldn't be equated with an alcoholic's return to the bottle.

She picked the first six paperbacks off the top and carried them into her own room; she took off her damp sneakers, piled up pillows, and lay down to choose luxuriously. Four had possibilities, and Anne Tyler's *Searching for Caleb* was the pick of these. She sighed with anticipation, wiggling her bare toes pleasurably in the soft air. *Sweet Helen* went out, and presently that engine sound was lost in the eternal duet of surf on the shore and wind through the spruces.

"'The world forgetting, by the world forgot,'" she murmured, opening her book.

Then Roy Bainbridge spoke, and she jumped. He sounded as if he were directly under her window. She sprang off the bed to look out. He was at the well, hauling up a pail of water, watched by Tammy and Diane, while Tiger bristled about his heels.

Now was a perfect chance to speak to him about his sister, if she hadn't sworn to forget all about the woman. She stood by the window in uncharacteristic uncertainty; did she or did she not want to get involved? No, she did not. But there was this goweling, officious little insistence that she had to do something, or she'd regret it. At worst she'd be called a busybody, perhaps to her face, but she'd have salved her conscience.

She ran downstairs in her bare feet, and out to the gate.

"Roy!" she called. "Will you come here a minute?"

"Aye-up!" he boomed. "You need a pail of water?"

"No, just wanted to ask you something."

"You got me." He left his brimming pail on the cover of the well. "Just so Tiger can't lift his leg," he explained to the girls. "Short as he is." They went into spasms over that. He came rolling up to Joanna, thumbs in his overall straps as usual. He wasn't too depressed to beam at her, but his broad smile in his red beard was in no way as offensive to her as Felix Drake's.

"Come on in," she said. He smelled of clean sweat; his freckled shoulders and back were damp with it. "Would you like a cold drink?" she asked. "Soda, beer?"

"No, thanks. Been drinking enough cold stuff, I'm about to founder. You want me to fix something?" He looked around him with bright-eyed interest. "Refrigerator gone out? Those pilots are hellish sometimes."

"Nothing's wrong. Sit down a minute, will you?" They sat on opposite sides of the sun parlor table. Pip smelled Roy's shoes and then sat back and stared at him.

"Roy," said Joanna, "there's no way to say this but straight out."

"Mrs. Bennett, if you're worried about Pitt, don't be," he said solicitously. "My goodness, he's a real gentleman. He don't muckle on to a girl the minute he's got her alone, and he won't take any chances landing on Pirate Island if it don't look good. He's so cautious he's like to drive me crazy sometimes."

"It's not Pitt," she said. "It's your sister."

His smile went out; the dimples disappeared. The shine of his greenish blue eyes became glassy. She said quickly, "We're all concerned about her. I'm not being meddlesome, unless you think that's meddlesome. Mr. Drake told me flat out that she didn't want to be disturbed, and we've all respected that; but we didn't know then she was pregnant and close to her time."

He breathed loudly, and his full mouth became oddly compressed. I don't give a damn how mad he is, Joanna thought.

"Over the Fourth," she said, "you were out on Cash's, and Drake never came near the place for five days. He took Willy ashore, too. Your sister could have been in trouble behind those drawn curtains and locked doors. She could have had a fall and gone into premature labor. How do you suppose we feel, having someone in our midst we're supposed to ignore when she could be in danger? And another life, too? A *little* one?"

Roy's cheeks became like hard red apples; his big front teeth clamped down hard on his lower lip.

"She's on all our minds, Roy," Joanna went on. "We're islanders, and we're used to being responsible for each other. We're twenty-five miles from the mainland. Now, if you can tell me she's got firm plans for leaving here in plenty of time—"

He cleared his throat explosively before he spoke. "What do you want her to do?" he asked hoarsely.

"We'd just like to be able to keep a neighborly eye on her. Nobody wants to run all over her, poke around, pester her. But she needs that contact right now, and if she doesn't think so, maybe you can convince her. If she cares about the baby, she should be willing. Kathy Campion's been shoving notes under the door, telling her they could arrange a signal, but she never answers to a knock or shoves a note back."

"I'll talk to her. Pitt and me both. Pitt's a man of few words, but that might make 'em worth more than mine." He pulled out a handkerchief and wiped his face. "She come back from Boston like this, and our folks don't even know it." There was a doggy appeal in his eyes. "They think she's still up there, happy as a clam, and her partner mails her letters home. It'd kill 'em if they found out."

"That's awful, Roy," she said sincerely, and he seemed grateful for her sympathy.

His words fell all over each other on the way out. "Drake, he'd got this place out here, and he met her at the plane in Portland and brought her up the coast in his boat. Nobody's supposed to know she's back." Sick grin. "He's some numb, you know that? Thinking she could hide out in a place where she sticks out like a sore thumb."

Joanna was tempted to ask what interest Drake had in the matter besides being a kindly landlord, but it would have been too nosy altogether, besides taking advantage of Roy's eagerness to confide.

"We weren't even supposed to know about it," he said. "I figger *he* figgered we couldn't keep our mouths shut. Well, me, anyway. Pitt's different."

"How'd you find out?" That was permissible, he'd started it.

"Willy," he said, "but we never gave him away. Drake sure gave us hell when he caught us out here. Jesus, he's got some command of language." He was almost admiring. "Had me dumbfounded. Well, Pitt says, after he run down, 'She's our sister, and we'll see her when we feel like it.' So we kept on dropping in, but we don't reckon to be here when he is. That upsets her awful. When *she* tells us to up killick and head out, we will."

"He's mighty protective of his tenant's rights," Joanna said.

"Oh, he always liked Sheena," he said vaguely. "I guess he wants something to fuss over. His wife's got all her things she does, and the girls got their horses. Trouble is, some people don't think anybody's own family is good enough, or smart enough, to take care of anybody. They always know better. We could've found a nice place for Sheena."

"I know what you mean," she said, "and it can make you so darned mad. How about that drink now?"

"I'd appreciate it, but it better be soda. If I'm going to talk serious to Sheena, I don't want to be blowing a beer breath in her face. She hates liquor," he said solemnly. "So does Drake. He used to like it pretty good, when he and Henry Coates were young goats. Nowadays butter wouldn't melt in his mouth."

They drank ginger ale. "I want to assure you and your sister that we can all be pretty closemouthed out here," Joanna said.

"I believe you," he said solemnly. "We'll talk to Sheena, tell her she's got to let somebody check on her once a day. How's that?"

"Perfect. Tell her nobody'll expect to come in or have any talk; they'll just knock to see if she's all right, and she can call out. But it will be only on days when you or Felix Drake aren't here."

"You Bennett's Islanders are good people," he said respectfully. "I always heard so, and now I know so. It's real heartening to meet with something like this after some of the bad things going on in life."

"I forgot you and your brother met up with one of those real bad things last night," she said. "It must have been heartbreaking."

"You know it *was.*" His eyes watered. "Christ—I mean, Godfrey, we could hardly believe he was dead! Ira Beecham! It's just like somebody *here*—you know how you'd feel."

"Yes, I know. It's happened here, more than once."

He cleared his throat again and stood up. "It's one friggin'—excuse me—mess. Thanks for the soda, Mrs. Bennett, and being so kind and all. I'll take my pail of water and go on over to Sheena's." The old sparkle came back into his eye. He said in a stage whisper, "Drake, he brings out fancy springwater for her. We dasn't drink any of it in case he keeps strict records."

She laughed with him and saw him out. He had just disappeared past Philip's house when Jamie came out of the fish house and headed home, walking as fast as his limp would allow. "Am I crazy?" he demanded, "or did I just see Roy Bainbridge come out of here?"

"You're not crazy. Coming in?"

The two soda cans were on the table, a glass beside hers. "You were drinking with him?" he asked incredulously.

"Ginger ale, dear heart." He was not amused.

"What did he want?"

"I asked him to come in and talk about his sister."

"I hope they're taking her out of here, and then we can get together and clean out Drake."

"I know you're working under difficulties, Jamie," she said, "and you probably feel like telling everybody to go to hell. I know, I've been through it. But sit down and rest your face and hands; have a cold drink, or I'll make you some fresh coffee, and—"

"Jesus, it's bad enough to have my sister out running around with one of that pair, and me getting the jokes on everybody's radio about what they went ashore on Pirate for, and then I get home and find the other one coming out of my own home, and he's been cozily having soda with my mother."

She didn't move. "Who can have soda with anyone she likes. What are *you* drinking?"

"Coffee. Real stuff, none of that decaf you old folks go in for. Please," he added as an afterthought. He limped into the kitchen and washed his hands. She turned the gas on under the teakettle.

"You might as well make a pot; the old man was right behind me," he said.

"Why do you hate the Bainbridges so?" she asked conversationally, measuring coffee into the drip pot.

"They've got no business hanging out here."

"Their sister's here."

"The way I see it, she's not their business any longer; she's Drake's, and has been for close onto nine months."

"We don't know that for a fact, and it doesn't matter anyway. She's pregnant, she's *here*, and Roy's going to try to convince her we're honestly concerned."

"Roy! Talk about gustaleering! Tongue hangs in the middle and wags at both ends. But the other one's worse. I don't trust him as far as I can see him, and when he's out of sight with my sister, that's enough to turn my stomach."

"I didn't know you were so dainty." She poured boiling water, left it to drip, and sat out matching Swedish mugs. "Is it just because they're not islanders, or is there any special reason you aren't telling me?"

"Anybody hears things," he said vaguely.

"Anybody can hear anything. Depends on the source whether it's worth listening to or not. Like what you've been hearing aboard the boat."

"Oh, hell." He dragged his hands angrily over his face. "It's the whole setup! You know what I think of Drake; I told you I had a feeling about him. Well, there's something about the whole gang that stinks like rotten bait, and Linnie's off to hell and gone with one of 'em."

"I know what it's like to have those feelings. But use some common sense. Linnie's not sixteen, she's twenty, and she's not likely to be raped this afternoon. She took a karate class at school last year. I remember seeing you on the floor a few times."

His mouth twitched, but he wasn't giving way any more than that.

"It'll soon be time for Selina to have the baby," she went on, "and she's not likely to be back. So the Bees won't be dropping in anymore."

"If Pitt thinks he can talk Linnie into the bushes, he'll keep coming back till he makes it. If he hasn't done it already."

"*Jamie*, that is enough," she said icily. "You're insulting your sister's character and her intelligence. And while you're so busy working up a case against a couple of men because you don't know their life history down to the last detail, and foaming at the mouth because you can't keep your sister locked up in a tower, someone else is going to get fed up and just move quietly out of your life for good."

"Meaning?" They were squared-off adversaries.

"Meaning you'll look across someday and see that the next wharf is empty and that nobody's home anymore where you like to spend some of your nights when the fancy takes you. Or the house will be occupied by another stranger for you to foam at the mouth about. Maybe that's what you like, Jamie. Maybe that's what you feed on. But I don't like it in a son of mine."

Jamie walked out of the house, exactly as he had turned from her as a child when he didn't dare answer her back. She was not overcome by affection for the back of his head and the square set of his shoulders, she wasn't moved by the limp; but she was trembling inside as well as out, and she took five deep breaths, counting.

When Nils came in, she had coffee poured for them. "I just got a dirty look and a grunt," he said. "What's eating him now?"

"I lambasted him."

"Who's got a better right? He must have needed it."

She took Nils's face between her hands and kissed him. "Am I glad to see you! Ten minutes with that boy when he's in one of those spells is like ten years in a hairshirt. Or what I imagine it to be. I'd like to shake him till his teeth rattle."

"Let's drink our coffee and relax, and you can tell me about it."

"Pitt took Linnie down to Pirate Island this afternoon, and of course, somebody hauling down there had to mention it, so Jamie came home steaming like some Sicilian carrying on about his sister's virtue and the family honor." Nils looked entertained. "Then he saw Roy just leaving here, where I'd been plying him with ginger ale, while I asked him if he could persuade his sister to let us check up on her the days when nobody comes. Well, I told Jamie to stow it, and that if he didn't watch out, he'd lose Rosa. And he left."

"If Rosa wants him bad enough, she'll manage to get a line on him."

"Rosa has plenty of pride. She'll go just so far and no farther. Who wants a man who's always looking just past you at some new cause? If it was a useful cause like saving the lobster industry and the herring business, it wouldn't be so bad. She could make herself part of it. But those vendettas of his! Before he's thirty, he's going to be a tough, antisocial old bachelor, so touchy you'll have to watch how you *breathe* in his presence."

"Calm down, calm down." He hitched his chair around close to hers. "You can't do anything about him. If he loses chances, it'll be his own doing. You can't change him. He's Jamie; he's *himself.* Remember last year? The word is still *survive.* You and me."

"I *am* thinking of you and me. He's going to be so damned hard to live with, and we don't deserve that in our old age."

They both began to laugh. "Now," he said, close to her ear. "Do you think if we locked all the doors and went upstairs we could get away with it?"

"In the middle of the afternoon? I doubt it. Now if we had that cabin at Bull Cove—"

"The rest of the population would be beating a path to our door."

"I was thinking of barbed wire and disguising Pip as a Doberman."

30

*L*innie came home full of the afternoon with Pitt. Nils had gone back to the shore again, so Linnie bubbled on in full spate, woman to woman. "You should have seen Pitt, Marm. When we walked up on the ridge, he was looking all around him as if he were Moses and he'd gotten into the Promised Land after all. Oh, gosh, I hope Henry Coates buys it and lets him fish it!"

"Did you warn him he'd have to fight off Brigport?"

"Oh, sure. Tom Robey was hauling down there and gave us this big wave and a grin. I told Pitt Tom was a pretty hard case, and he said he was one himself."

"How about scrubbing some potatoes to bake?" asked her mother.

Linnie filled the colander with potatoes from the bin under the cupboard and had to pull Pip out by the tail. "He'd like to build around the chimney where Eloise burned down the love nest. He was so depressed about finding that poor guy floating; he wouldn't talk about it, but I *knew*." Brush in one hand, potato in the other, she turned from the sink to get Joanna's eye. "He's crazy about Pirate Island and so hopeful. You know, when he's happy, he looks so vulnerable; no one would ever believe it without seeing it."

Listening, Joanna imagined the two of them climbing about the treeless island. She and Alec had gone there once on a warm day in spring and had made love in a grassy hollow, in sunshine, under a blue sky. Ellen had been conceived then, but Alec hadn't lived to find out. She wondered how much Linnie was leaving unsaid about what had passed between her and Pitt: implicit understandings, unspoken but guessed-at promises? All you could do was pray for common sense on both sides, but to expect that of new lovers puts you in a class with Canute trying to hold back the tide. Just remember that Linnie always ran on like this about her new enthusiasms.

". . . knows the medricks' part of the island is supposed to be left alone," she was saying. "We just took a *look*, and my gosh, they came for us! We ran. He's all for the wild things. They see a lot of whales between here and Cash's, and porpoises."

"I'm glad you had such a nice afternoon," Joanna said, reminding herself of her own mother, who'd had six to listen to.

"And it's not over yet. We're taking a walk after supper."

"A word to the wise," said Joanna. "Keep it all under your hat at the supper table."

"Don't worry." Linnie patted her on the shoulder. "In Jamie's presence my lips are sealed. About the Bees, anyway."

The sealing wasn't necessary. When they were ready to sit down in the dining room to Joanna's crisp-fried pollock, baked potatoes, and new spinach, Jamie hadn't appeared. Linnie offered to go see why, but Nils said, "I'll go."

"For some reason I'm not to be trusted," Linnie said without ill feeling. "Lillebror's temper must be in a delicate condition tonight."

"And maybe your father just wants a quiet word with him, man to man," said Joanna. "Here, you can fix Pip's fish." She'd boiled one pollock. Linnie broke it into pieces and kept blowing on them and stirring them up, while Pip leaped from chair to chair, chirruping, trying to get closer to his dish.

Nils came back looking much as usual. If they'd had words, it didn't show. "He's on the couch reading, he says he's pretty lame tonight, and he'll make a sandwich later."

"Here." Joanna put a full plate, foil-wrapped, on a tray, with a nectarine and a handful of peanut butter cookies. "Tell him his mother loves him."

Linnie was as predatory as Pip was for his fish.

"What's the special message for? Is he really rotten tonight? More than usual, I mean?"

"Oh, I guess he thinks that wrench he gave his leg should have cleared up in twenty-four hours. Will you give that cat his fish before he starts on ours?"

"If I were a dear, kind sister," Linnie said, "I'd go over and play cards
with him tonight. Or chess." She smiled reminiscently. "The last time I
won, he was quietly furious. Women cannot play chess, period. So the
spectacle of me across the chessboard twittering, 'I just love this little
horse!,' and calling my king and queen by name—that should make him
forget his aches and pains."

"I don't think you'd better try it," said Joanna. "You might end up
with the chessboard around your neck."

"That bad, huh? Anything to do with Pitt and me?"

Nils came in. "Nothing the matter with his appetite, anyway. He
sent you a message. 'Thanks, Marm.'" Solemnly he kissed her forehead.
"That's from me. Now can we eat?"

Joanna was moderately curious as to whether or not Pitt would call
for Linnie after supper, but the instant the dishes were washed Linnie
took a sweater, put a can of mosquito repellent in the hip pocket of her
jeans, and went out to meet him at the anchor. Hugo came in the back
door, using the sun parlor as a shortcut on the way to play cards with
Jamie.

"Want to go anywhere?" Nils asked Joanna.

"Nope."

"TV?"

"Still nope," she said. "You watch if you want to. I've got a good
book upstairs."

He went up with her.

The morning was cool and bright after the humid, hazy day before,
and Joanna walked to the shore with Nils, prepared to go rowing. Jamie
had already gone out; Linnie was still eating breakfast. She said she and
Pitt had talked for hours last night, but she didn't say what they had
talked about.

Joanna waited in the skiff, paddling around the wharves, until the
wakes had quieted somewhat and then set out for the harbor mouth. She
saw the Bainbridges walking down Foss's wharf. They might have been
leaving an empty house behind them. They went down the ladder into
their dory, and Pitt took the oars.

She turned the skiff's bow and rowed toward them. Roy saw her
coming and spoke to Pitt, who glanced over his shoulder and then swung
the dory in her direction. As the two boats approached each other, she
shipped her oars and took out the oarlock on the side that would have

grazed the dory's strakes, and Pitt impassively shipped his own oars. She took hold of the dory's gunnel.

"Good morning!" she said. Pitt answered civilly, unsmiling, and Roy depressed was painful to see. Pitt mutely offered her a cigarette. When she shook her head, he lit one for himself.

"I talked with her, Mrs. Bennett," Roy said, apologetically. "So did Pitt. But she says she's fine, everything was all right at her last checkup, she never felt better, and she's going for another one right off." His eyes shifted almost with apprehension toward Eastern Harbor Point, as if *Drake's Pride* were already coming up Long Cove. Pitt blew smoke from his nostrils and gazed back at the island. For a glimpse of Linnie? Joanna wondered.

"She just doesn't want to be noticed," Roy said, actually blushing with embarrassment.

"Well, that's it then," said Joanna cheerfully.

"We're sure much obliged to you for worrying about her."

"As long as she's feeling all right, that's the important thing. She must be planning to leave in plenty of time."

"If it was up to us, she'd leave today," Roy blustered. "We have to go back in and be pallbearers for this cussid funeral. I'd dump her aboard and put her in a nice room in a motel somewhere. Hell, if she ain't stepping outside the door, what the frig does it matter where she is? Excuse my language!"

"Excused," Joanna said. "Look, we're drifting ashore. I'll let you go." She pushed away from the dory, Pitt put the oars back in the oarlocks, and Roy nodded sheepishly at her.

She gave him an encouraging smile. He seemed honestly worried about his sister, and now he had to take part in the funeral of a man whose body he had found. She was sorry for him. But was it possible that Pitt could look vulnerable, or happy, or enjoy watching porpoises and whales? Was it possible that he could move his face at all?

She was rowing up Long Cove when *Sweet Helen* came around Eastern Harbor Point, caught up with her, and passed her slowly on a parallel course. Once the brothers were well ahead, they sped up and were gone around Tenpound before she reached Steve's cove.

She spent most of the morning with Philippa, both in the house and climbing up on the Head and around the massive rocks of the outer shore. When she rowed home near noon, the southwest wind was picking up, as it did most days. She felt very lighthearted, whether from the change in the weather, or from crossing Selina off her list, or from her own natural buoyancy, she didn't know, but she wouldn't muddy her good mood by trying to analyze it. Linnie was making pizzas for their lunch, and after that she went to the shore to bait up for tomorrow. She took her swimming suit and a towel along, intending to go swimming in Schoolhouse Cove later. Joanna went back upstairs to her good book; she hadn't read much of it last night.

She came downstairs later, planning to make the most of what remained of a perfect day. When she took the usual survey out the kitchen window, *Drake's Pride* was just coming in, and then Vanessa came around Liza's, with books under her arm, and turned up toward the house. Anne was ahead, wheeling her doll carriage.

Without stopping to think, Joanna went out the back door, and she didn't stop until she was through the woods and out in the Homestead meadow. She felt both guilty and irked; she wished she hadn't run. But what if she'd stayed? She could only imagine labored conversation and miserable silences, conditions which had never existed between her and Van. But Van would think nothing of her absence.

Or would she? Supposing she'd glimpsed Joanna in the kitchen before Joanna saw her? Had somehow caught the rapid movement in the sun parlor and the slam of the screen door? It's done, forget it, Joanna thought, but watch out next time. One of these days you're going to be cornered.

She walked up to the Homestead and drank tea with Mateel.

31

The next day the weather stopped just short of being a smoky sou'wester. Only a fanatic would go to haul on such a day, to try to keep his footing in a boat roughly jostled by opposing seas, wasting gas and punishing his eyes while he tried to find buoys pulled under by the tide or made invisible by the dull glare on turbulent water.

The island had had such fanatics in the past and would have them again; they were driven by desperation for money or the senseless daring of inexperience. One good scare usually doled out a big enough dose of common sense to last quite a while. A boy could acquire a lifetime of sophistication in ten minutes when his engine stopped dead and his boat was blown helplessly toward a ledge exploding in surf, and no other boat in sight. He would know, when the engine finally coughed back to life just before he was swept into the breakers, that next time he might not be so lucky.

This mail day no one went out. Felix Drake had taken Selina Bainbridge away yesterday afternoon but had come back after dark, and now his boat lay on her mooring, waiting out the blow; Drake was in the house with his tenant. Willy was apparently left free to visit around the shore, where most of the men were working on gear or tidying up workshops; the pungency of old rope burning blew erratically from fish house stovepipes. A few had strolled around to the wharf just for the sociability of it or because someone was expecting a special piece of freight.

A stiff sou'west wind would not keep *Clarice Hall* in Limerock Harbor, as long as it wasn't officially classified as a gale, and everyone on the island had made plenty of these trips across the bay. Some swore they'd never once had a good chance over. There was a good deal of reminiscence in the store this morning as they waited for the boat to whistle. Betsey's and Holly's friends were supposed to leave today, but they had already called their families to say it was too rough. Now they all were out on the wharf, handily close to the cluster of young men; Linnie was with them.

The younger children were as excited as cats by the wind and were whooping up and down in the long shed, chasing each other among the hogsheads. Whenever they burst out at the far end, one of the men growled at them to stay the hell away from the edge of the wharf.

Joanna was in the store when Van and Kathy came in. Kathy was talking as usual, and Van went to the post office window with mail. Joanna left unobtrusively while Kathy was holding everyone's amused attention.

The radio in the Sorensen house hadn't been turned on all day until someone put it on for the six o'clock Maine news and weather, and heard that Ira Beecham had not been buried yesterday. In fact, while the Bainbridges were on Bennett's Island, dreading the return to the mainland to be his pallbearers, the county medical examiner and a state pathologist were giving Ira Beecham a good deal of attention. No explanations were forthcoming yet, and the funeral would take place in a few days.

"*Damn!*" Linnie exclaimed. She stood by the dining room table, plates in her hands, gazing accusingly at the radio. "Poor Pitt!" Fortunately Jamie wasn't there to hear. "He had the horrors about that funeral, and now it's still ahead of him."

"The pallbearers will be walking away from the cemetery, but Ira Beecham won't," her father said from behind his newspaper.

The tone was gentle; the reproof was not. Linnie resumed setting the table, careful not to slat the silver about. Joanna wondered again about the mysterious Pitt, who could illuminate her daughter like a roomful of candles and extinguish her as quickly.

"What do you think?" she called in to Nils.

"Must be some mark or bruise they want explained. They just want to be sure, I suppose. Maybe he had a scrap with somebody that day."

"Pitt kept saying if they'd been only ten minutes earlier," Linnie said. "They feel so guilty. But I think talking to me was a help." She gave her mother a sidewise look of gleaming satisfaction. Then Jamie came in, and the subject was changed.

They woke up to rain; no wind, but a steady summer rain dimpling the green and silver glass of the harbor—it hindered neither birds nor fishermen. When Joanna went out to feed the hens, it delicately touched her face and hands with warm drops almost too light to feel. Pip followed her back into the house, fastidiously shaking his paws.

In her mind she sorted out projects saved for rainy days. Look up the boxes of quilt pieces she'd promised Marjorie and Kathy for a joint project. Start cable-stitch pullovers for Ellen's child and stepchildren, for next Christmas. She could write letters; she was the only one in the family who kept in touch with their uncle Nate's sons. She could pick out a corner of the attic to go through; pleasant, with the steady rain on the roof close to her head and the rich gurgle of water running down the spout into the cistern.

She could make herself a second breakfast right now and read all the way through it. But at once she was reminded of how many times Van had come in wet weather, with books sheltered under her poncho, wanting to swap. Reading had been the first link between them, safe ground on which the alien creature could approach and be approached. Those strange eyes. Not strange now, but one would always remember them that way, as if they had belonged to someone else who had come and gone. What had *really* been behind them all these five years?

So much for waking up feeling snug. She couldn't indulge herself in the simple luxury of reading at the table without worrying about an unwelcome tap at the door. And it was her own fault; she'd gotten this obsession, like Jamie's bee in the bonnet, and she had given it dominion over her. That's a nice biblical touch, she thought cynically.

"Oh, the hell with it!" she exclaimed. "What was *was*. That's it. Not *is*." She put on her yellow rain pants and hooded jacket, thinking irritably, The trouble with this place is that you can't get away from anything or anyone. Why didn't she accept the standing invitation of her cousins' wives to visit them in Connecticut or San Diego? But leaving the island in *summer*? If she could do it—which she couldn't—it would send the whole family into the high fantods; they'd be sure she was gone around the bend with menopause.

"Maybe I am," she said to Pip, who was watching her yank on her deck boots as if he'd never seen such a sight in his life. "If I did take off, for me the jolt would be like one huge shock treatment, stopped just short of frying the patient. . . . Behave yourself now, and take care of the house."

As the back door latched behind Joanna, Pip transferred his avid interest to the front door of the sun parlor; even his whiskers looked attentive.

The henyard was empty this morning, but there was a cozy clamor from inside. Joanna went past the barn, and her oil clothes rustled so loudly she had to stop moving to hear the patter of rain on the leaves and the voices of the small birds working through the alders. She went out into the Homestead meadow and she turned off to her right on the shortcut to the Fennell house, whose wet gables she could see ahead of her. Then she went to the left into the old orchard planted by one of Jamie Bennett's sons.

It was surrounded by spruce woods now, and the trees were descendants of the originals, but old in themselves. They blossomed extravagantly each June, turning this into a sheltered alley of pink-and-white bouquets, fragrance, bees, and birds. Once in a while they surprised everyone by bearing a fair amount of fruit, which the children ate up as fast as they could. Joanna always tried to make at least one pie, for tradition's sake, but the trees which had the firm, tart pie apples must have long since rotted into the earth without issue. She remembered a tree of small sweet pears, but that was gone, too. Still, the blossoms came; if a tree rested one year, it outdid itself the next.

The cemetery was kept neatly fenced as a matter of propriety, the graves kept mown, and the stones cleaned of lichens. The graves of the unknown drowned sailors from the past were marked by the progeny of the original apple tree that had sprung up there.

She sat down in the wet grass under one of the orchard trees outside the gate, with her back against the rough trunk, her knees drawn up, her hands thrust into the opposite sleeves. She felt snug as a snail, with the rain tapping on her hood and shining on the green leaves. Chickadees were undisturbed by her; in one of the sailors' apple trees a woodpecker drove a steady tack hammer. From over in Goose Cove the sound of the long easy swell was like deep breathing. Close to her the Queen Anne's lace and wild roses were gemmed with moisture.

Happiness began to spread through her with the inevitability of a returning tide. She looked about her with satisfaction and saw a figure entering the orchard at the far end. "*Oh, damn!*" she whispered. With a dose of ice in her stomach she recognized the dark green poncho which had replaced Vanessa's threadbare raincoat. She wore a yellow sou'wester. She came straight to Joanna as if she had known where to find her. Framed in the fastenings of the sou'wester, her angular cheekbones and long jaw were emphasized. Joanna's mind was alarmingly blank; her tongue refused to move.

Unfastening the sou'wester, Van dropped down on her knees before her and then sat back on her heels. The color of the sou'wester accentuated the yellow-tawny eyes. "I came in the front door as you went out the back."

"Have you been following me?" Joanna tried to sound amused.

"Yes," Van said. "I came to find out why you're always running away from me, and I'm going to find out, come hell or high water. I think it'll be high water, if this keeps up. It's not St. Swithin's Day, is it?"

"I don't know," said Joanna. "When *is* St. Swithin's anyway?" All at once she experienced a releasing sense of resignation which quickly became a reckless exhilaration. "Here I go to sea in a sieve. Why don't you and Owen speak when you meet in doorways? Why won't you dance when you come face to face in a Liberty waltz? Why do you turn aside when you pass on a path?"

"Because we can't meet." Her lips hardly moved, and the eyes were unwavering. "And we can't dance because we can't touch. Do you understand, Jo?"

"Yes." Her own mouth felt almost too stiff to move. "I don't want to understand, but I do. Is it going on now?"

"No. Not for almost five years. I could tell you the day and hour it ended."

"I don't want that."

"What *do* you want?" Van asked courteously. "The answer to the question you didn't ask? Anne isn't his. That must be a relief to you." It was said without sarcasm.

"Yes," said Joanna, "but only because I feel it's a tragedy for a child to live among her own family and not know it or be known to them. For her own father not to be able to show it."

"The last time Owen"—there was a slight but noticeable difficulty with the name— "and I spoke, it was when I was beginning to show. We met by the anchor, and all he said was 'Is it mine?' and I said no. We have never spoken directly since."

"How could you manage it?" Joanna asked.

Van shrugged. "How did we ever manage anything? It wasn't for long, after we knew it couldn't go anywhere." She slid over onto one hip and braced a hand against the wet grass while she stretched out her legs to ease them. A flurry of chickadees overhead in the apple tree sent a miniature hard shower down on the hood and sou'wester.

Joanna began shyly, "Did Barry—"

"Yes. My fault. Your brothers were all gods to him when we came out here. Still are, in most cases. Well, he was doing a lot of loud hero-worshipping one day when I was trying to come to terms with the truth that it was over, and I was desperate enough to feel suicidal." Humor flickered around her mouth and eyes like the reflection of a flame. "Sorry to load you with this, Jo, but you're the one who opened Pandora's box. I had to shut him up one way or the other, and I didn't have anything to kill him with, so I told him. He was shattered, and that very nearly shattered me."

"My God, Van!" Jo said. "What hell was going on in that house for both of you, and nobody ever guessed!"

"There was some going on for your brother, too," Van said. "Anyway, Barry wanted a child, I owed him that much, so—"

"And so Anne." Joanna spoke tenderly, as if the child were there with them.

"All the time I was carrying her, I didn't think this baby would mean anything to me, even when it began to kick. I was just paying a debt, that's all. But once she was here, when I heard the first yell, I knew I had something to live for."

"You fooled everybody," Joanna said with awe. "You pulled it off under our noses, and I always swore nobody could have a secret affair on this island." She was ashamed of herself and blushed. "I'm sorry, Van." She leaned forward and touched Van's knee. "I'm not making light of it."

"Well, it's not an accomplishment I can brag about," Van said. "When did you suspect anything? I don't want us to settle down for a cozy girl-to-girl session, but I'd really like to know if you're psychic, or what."

"I noticed the bit about the dances several times and avoiding each other on the path and in my house, but I thought you two just couldn't stand each other. Then one day this summer Laurie mentioned a time when Owen seemed so distant, and she'd been frightened, she thought there was another woman."

For the first time Van looked away from her. Joanna went on. "Then he had the heart scare, so she thought that was it. Well, right after we had that talk, I saw Anne fall down in the path just behind Owen, and she was crying, and he walked on—which wasn't like him."

Van nodded. She was a little pale around the mouth.

"He turned and went back to her," said Joanna, "and I can't describe his expression except to say it was black. But when she showed him her hands, he kissed the palms and closed the fingers over them."

"She showed me." Her voice trembled, but she allowed it no leeway. "She said, 'For you, Mama.'" Joanna felt the tears coming into her eyes. She was unbearably moved, and she hadn't expected anything like that.

"Do you hate me, Jo?" Van asked calmly.

"No! And that's the truth." Joanna got a clammy tissue out of her jacket pocket and blew her nose. "I had to ask. Now I know, and I won't think about it again or mention it. Our friendship's not flawed, for me anyway."

"Are you sure of that? Because if I could have taken him from Laurie and the island, I would have."

"But you didn't, so why should I hate you for something that didn't happen? Besides, it wouldn't have been all your fault. I know my brother. Nobody can be taken who doesn't want to be taken." Eric's words. "But after all these years, you're still not—I mean, it must still be hell in some way."

"We've managed. Let people think we can't stand each other. One contact would be like that fatal first drink. Even talking about it is pretty awful."

"I'll never say anything more," said Joanna, "after today. But there's something I have to tell you. I respect you because you have to live as you do and you do it so damn well. And I have more respect for Owen than I ever thought possible."

It's the punches you take at fifty that kill, he said once. And now she knew what he meant and took the punch in her own gut, for the two of them. Afraid to let eyes meet. Afraid to speak each other's name. Terrified to be in each other's arms at a public dance, for fear their torturously constructed lives would collapse and bring down other lives with them.

"Don't you ever want to scream, or run?" she asked.

"Take Anne away from Barry? No. And he'd never leave the island; it's heaven on earth for him. Also, he knows just where I am, practically every minute," she added wryly. "Besides, it's where *he* is." As if stitches in a lacerated artery had suddenly broken, words spurted out. "Sometimes I feel we are looking at each other from safe distances. Like half the island or the width of the harbor. We look and look, but we never dare get any closer. Too close is not close enough. Far is best. Meanwhile, I remember at night in my sleep, never in daytime. I don't allow memories in daylight."

"No," said Joanna. "I never did, after Ellen's father died. But I know about the dreaming."

With the first dream that comes with the first sleep
I run, I run, I am gathered to thy heart.

She could not have spoken the words aloud, but she had not been able to forget them for months after Alec's death. Vanessa would know them, too, or something very like, both comfort and torment.

She loosened her grip on her knees and shook her clamped fingers and arms, rocked onto her knees, and stood up. "If we sit here any longer, we'll mildew. How about a good hot cup of coffee or chocolate to get the damp out of our bones?"

Vanessa stood up. "I'd better not. I left Anne at Kathy's, and she'll be needing a nap. She woke up too early."

"Don't they always, on a nice dark wet morning, when you'd think they'd sleep?"

Van walked back with her to the house. They talked about other things, striving to sound natural, and parted with a spontaneous embrace by the dripping lilacs.

When Joanna got into the house, she felt light-headed and tremulous in her limbs. She wanted something sweet and hot, she felt as if she could drink a quart of hot chocolate; she wanted company, and yet she didn't; she was too full of what she knew, she was actually shaken by it. Her hands shook as she pulled off her boots and hung her wet rain clothes on hangers on the rack at the back end of the sun parlor. Pip followed her around, and she picked him up and squeezed him; he vibrated in her arms, purred deafeningly in her ear.

"How did they stand it, Pip?" she asked him. "All these years. How can they stand it now? What their days and nights must be!" He rubbed his cheek against hers. "You know I've got to hide it in the attic, Pip," she said, "and never take it out to look at it again."

Linnie came in and caught her at it. "What are you telling him?"

"Something he'll never repeat," said Joanna. "That's why he's so satisfactory. How were the lobsters?"

"Crawling like mad. They must love this weather; it was my best day yet." She kicked off her own boots. "Felix, alias Buttery Ben, is back. Any more news about the Beecham thing?"

"I've been out. I haven't had the radio on."

"I keep thinking about Pitt. I can't help it. Marm, did you ever fall hard for anyone before Alec?" She always spoke of him familiarly, a young man little older than herself. "Ellen's father" sounded strange to her, since she had always regarded Nils as Ellen's father. "I know you were married at my age, but what about before that?"

"Oh, I had my moments," she said lightly. Talking about first loves should be quite a diversion through lunch, but the very word *love* had changed radically for her in the last hour. She was belittled by her colossal ignorance of a whole area of experience in which two other people were silent experts.

32

The Beecham funeral finally took place, but the investigation would be continued since the police weren't ruling out foul play. They said they were following leads. *Sweet Helen* came into the harbor of Bennett's Island in the late afternoon; the Bainbridges had left Coates Cove right after the funeral. They stayed at the island all night, and Linnie and Pitt went walking, and Roy played cribbage with Barry Barton. They left early the next morning for Cash's.

"They could hardly wait to get away from the mainland," Van said in the store before mail time. "They were so depressed by the funeral. Roy kept sighing and shaking his head all evening, except when he skunked Barry. That cheered him up considerably."

"Did he say anything about the police leads?" Marjorie asked.

"Oh, he looked as mysterious as anybody like Roy can look," Van said. "Then he said Ira took somebody's girl away from him and married her, and every time the somebody got drunk, he made threats. But Roy wasn't naming any names, no, sir! Casting no stones. No blackening a feller's name. Besides, sometimes when there's smoke, it don't mean there was ever much of a fire. Just a little smudge."

She managed uncannily to put Roy among them. "Seems to him those boys in the State Police are just trying to make themselves important. Show they're earning the taxpayers' money by doing more than wearing those fancy uniforms and cruising up and down the roads."

"When I saw the boys come ashore," Kathy said, "I was tempted to rush right over and see if they'd ask me in. But I resisted. The day before, when Drake took her away for the afternoon, I was even more tempted to face him and her right on the wharf, before he got her aboard the boat, and let's see them get out of *that*. But I didn't," she said desolately. "I'll probably hate myself till my dying day. I must be getting old. Next thing it'll be liver spots on my hands." She lifted them, inspected them, and sighed. "But I'm getting so I don't give a damn about Selina Bainbridge."

"I'm a charter member of the club," said Joanna. "I think I founded it."

"Even her brothers didn't spend much time with her," young Carol said. "She must be weird."

Mark cleared his throat from behind the post office window, attracting everyone's attention, and Philippa said, "Did you ever notice what happens when there's one rooster in a yard of hens? One sound from him, and everybody gets *so* respectful."

"I don't know whether that's a compliment or not," said Mark.

"Oh, take it as one, dear," said his wife.

"The boys stopped in here for cigarettes and gas this morning before they left for Cash's," he said, "and Roy was gustaleering about Henry Coates maybe buying Pirate and recruiting carpenters to work down there for twenty-five an hour, and get carried in for the weekends. Of course, he could be the biggest liar outside Congress."

"Gorry!" said Maggie Dinsmore. "We all ought to take our hammers and sign up."

"Over on Brigport they must be sharpening up their machetes and oiling their shootin' arns," said Joanna. "Henry Coates had better not leave the place alone on weekends."

"It may be all scuttlebutt," Mark warned. "Henry Coates is no fool. I wouldn't believe anything till I saw them working down there, and even then it might not be camps for fishermen; it could be somebody's idea of an exclusive summer resort. A thousand a week to get away from it all, even trees."

"And a chance to listen to a few hundred medricks screaming their heads off," Laurie Bennett said.

Out hauling this morning, Linnie had exuberantly waved her gaff at Rosa, who expected she would be up early in the afternoon to talk about Pitt. Rosa considered escaping this. Why did someone else's love life sound so boring, if not idiotic, when you didn't have one of your own?

She ate her lunch at her backyard table. Hank always knew when

and where anyone was eating outdoors, and he had eaten more at the
Fourth of July picnic, proportionately, than anyone else. Now he took a
sharp dip past her head and landed on the end of her table, settling his
wings.

"Quark," he said hoarsely.

She gave him a piece of bread and said, "When do you get past
puberty?"

After lunch she did her washing outdoors, in a galvanized tub of
sun-heated rainwater, another tub of rinse water beside it. A little soap
powder went a long way in the soft water, and she used old-fashioned
yellow soap on the worst places, scrubbing them on the washboard.
Anyone who had a generator had a washing machine; she had neither
and didn't miss them. Washing by hand was drudgery only when you had
to do it indoors. She spread her jeans out on the long table and scrubbed
them with a stiff brush. Towels and sheets were laid on the grass to
bleach as they dried. To sleep in such sheets the first night after that was
a sensuous experience.

Linnie didn't come; whatever had happened last night must be too
precious to share yet, and it might never be shared, only guessed at. On
the practical side Rosa hoped they'd been careful. Linnie was a romantic,
and probably Pitt wouldn't even recognize himself in her picture of him.
Women could create lovers the way a spider spun her web and then be
wounded enough to die when the gossamer ripped and showed the man
as he had always been: dolt or scoundrel or a perfectly ordinary critter
who was unwilling, afraid, or unable to be someone's creation. How *could*
he be? He was himself, whatever that self was, and everybody else but the
woman had known it all along.

Rosa had not made that mistake with Jamie; the young girls were the
ones who saw him as a romantic enigma, the source of mystery opening
into mystery, the way Linnie saw Pitt.

But what of Jamie himself? It wasn't only women who created dream
lovers. Offer him his first vision of Eloise, the Eloise who never was, and
Pirate Island, the Bainbridges, and Felix Drake would be less to him than
the mist dissolving over the woods in the morning sun.

Linnie came after supper, when Rosa was taking in her washing. It
was still as calm and warm as it had been all day; the sea was still the
palest aquamarine from horizon to horizon. "Why don't you coax
Lillebror over to Fern Cliff to watch the moon rise?" she said. "He might
just do it, where it'll be too bright to go seining."

"Nice to know you have your brother's priorities right," said Rosa. "Too bad he couldn't marry a mermaid. That's the closest he could get to a herring. You and Pitt have a good walk last night?"

"Did we!" Linnie hugged herself. "We watched the moon rise from Sou'west Point. And I got up at the crack of dawn this morning to see them off. When Henry Coates buys Pirate, Pitt will be only five miles away instead of all that distance to Cash's. And he *is* buying, Pitt swears to it. I wish everything was all settled and Pitt was already living there, while there's so much summer left." She folded dish towels in slow motion. "I want something solid between Pitt and me before I go back to college, something to make a tie that'll hold."

"Meaning what?" said Rosa. "A ring?"

"Gosh, no! I'm not out to hook a husband. I want a declaration. I know I love him, and from the way he acts I think he loves me; but he's still an unknown quantity. I'd have to know an awful lot more about a man before I went to bed with him, no matter how much I wanted to."

Rosa was relieved to know that Linnie was much more of a realist than she'd believed. "Has he mentioned it? Made any moves that way?"

"No," said Linnie, "so he's cagey, too. Maybe it's all to the good. But we've kissed and kissed, and I couldn't have stood a lot more of that. . . . He's so easy, he doesn't grab, but he's sure of himself. I like that, don't you?" She didn't wait for an answer. "For him to commit himself that far is something I'd never dreamed of, the first time I saw him."

"That mainland oaf," said Rosa. "It was hate at first sight, I should have known."

She brought out her guitar so as to keep Linnie off the subject of Jamie; any discussion of herself and Pitt always ended up with her brother and Rosa. Tonight the guitar reminded Linnie that she wanted Rosa to set a favorite love poem to music, and this occupied them until twilight and mosquitoes drove Linnie home, humming the new tune.

Rosa went upstairs in the warm gloom and changed into her pajamas. There was a slight rustling among the treetops, a slow stirring of the curtains, signifying that the tide had turned; she could smell it. The thrush still sang in the dusky, echoing depths of the woods, and there were a few isolated, sleepy chirps from other birds. A white-throat began his song but broke off in the middle as if caught by a yawn. Everything was quiet next door at the Percy house.

She had finished a book last night, and the one she wanted to read

tonight was downstairs. Without stopping to light her lamp, she went
back for it. The air moved pleasantly between her cotton pajamas and
her body.

She enjoyed that as she enjoyed the feel of the bare floor under her
feet, and because she could enjoy such simple things, she thought she
was doing very well in her new life.

On the stairs she met the scent of pipe tobacco, and when she crossed
the living room in the dusk, she heard the faint creak of a rocking chair
in the kitchen. The moon had cleared the trees toward the east, but it
still had the pale copper cast of its rising. It shone feebly into the
kitchen, on Jamie in the rocking chair, with his feet on the windowsill,
his pipe in his mouth, and his hands behind his head.

"Gosh, don't be so shy," she said acidly. "Make yourself at home.
We're all friends here."

Without moving he answered, "Come on ashore with me."

For one insane moment she thought he was going to add, "And get
married." But he didn't.

"What for?" she said to the top of his head.

"I want to do some nosing around Coates Cove. Not now, but when
the Bees are due in again. I want to be under a handy spruce tree with
my binoculars when they're unloading those crates at midnight."

"Oh, Lord," she said. She went around him and sat on the
windowsill by his moccasins. "Just what do you think you'll see?"

"We won't know till we see something with our own eyes, will we?"
He was too gentle.

"You're crazy," she said.

"Okay, now you've got that said, you coming with me or not?"

"Are you telling me," she demanded, "that you believe Con
Fleming's garbage enough so you want to go fubbing around strange
territory in the dark, in the hopes of seeing something you can't prove
and that you've probably got wrong in the first place?"

He took his pipe out of his mouth and nodded at her. "That's a good
question."

"As they say when they want to kick the questioner in the teeth.
Well, can you answer it?"

He pointed the pipe at her. "Answer *this*. You know they always get
back to Coates Cove in the middle of the night. Why?"

"For heaven's sake," she said crossly, "it's cooler traveling for the lobsters, the later they haul those crates aboard and start in from Cash's. The crates won't be stacked up in the sun all day."

"Now that makes a perfect excuse." He was irritatingly patient. "And Coates's trucks then have to start out in the middle of the night to deliver all that good fresh seafood to poor fish-hungry New England the next morning."

"Do you really believe the Bainbridges and their partners are bringing in cocaine and maybe heroin? And Henry Coates is shipping it out?"

"You have to admit it's a perfect setup. Who'd suspect those trucks going out? And these vessels coming up the coast looking like trawlers— maybe they even fish like trawlers—and who's out there to see what's going on?"

"Don't you think the Coast Guard has already thought of that?" Rosa asked. "They may have boarded the Bees already."

"Sure, and found nothing that time. But they can't be everywhere at once. Drug running is getting bigger by the day. That's a fact of life. I just want to see for myself. Who knows what I might pick up? How many times does something happen by accident?"

"And what if you see one of the Bees hand a package to Henry Coates? What does that prove? I can just imagine taking that bit of news to the police. Ho-ho-ho! Roy won't stop laughing for a month."

"Who said I'd take it to the police?" This good temper was unnatural and patronizing. "But I can use it against them to keep them away from here. I have a gut feeling that Roy's some jumpy under all that ho-ho-ho stuff. And here's something else." He took his feet off the sill and sat up straight. "No wonder they found Ira Beecham floating in the harbor. They probably put him there. Maybe he was too close at the wrong time, and just happened to see something funny under the lights on Coates's big dock. He might even have been nosing around, because the talk's getting pretty common if Con's picked it up."

It was hideously vivid, and hideously possible, but she did not want to accept it as probable. "I wish I'd never told you what Con said!" she exclaimed. "You grab any excuse to foul-mouth them because Linnie's so crazy about Pitt."

"Wrong," he said equally. "She's got as much right to make a fool of herself as I had."

"You're still doing it if you go around suspecting the Bees of murder and Henry Coates of running a big drug-smuggling ring."

"And Felix Drake. Don't forget him." He was maddeningly good-humored. "They're all in it together. The Bainbridge girl is his woman, and this feud between him and the brothers is all a big act. I don't know what in hell *for*, unless they think it would look funny if they were thick. Well, it'll take us a day to clean out Drake's gear, and a delegation can meet *Sweet Helen* when she comes in and tell the boys the frontier's closed."

"This happens after you've been in and seen the stuff being transferred," she said sarcastically. "What happens if you don't see anything? Or maybe *you're* seen? If they're all criminals, you could end up floating like Ira Beecham, or at the bottom tied to a well-ballasted lobster trap, which you almost managed to do to yourself awhile ago."

He laughed at that, and this genial mood was more irritating than his bad ones. *Unnerving* was more like it. "I don't plan on having my skull bashed in. Or yours."

"I never said I was going," she said.

"Then I'll go alone."

"Take Eric."

"I wouldn't even mention it to him. He thinks I'm crazy, too."

She saw the empty boat heading out past Brig Ledge. The picture still had the power to make her want to double up with stomach cramps.

"All right," she said. Maybe something would happen between now and then to knock it out of his mind.

He showed no relieved gratitude; he'd taken it for granted all along that she'd go. If it hadn't been for that damned riding turn, she wouldn't even consider it, and she still might change her mind, even if nothing else interfered. He'd be all right, because there was nothing to discover; she'd better hold on to that thought, or she'd be as paranoid as he was. It all came back to Pitt and Linnie, she was sure of it.

Jamie stood up and put his arms around her. "What's this?" he said softly. "All ready for bed?" He dropped one hand to her hip and let it slide back and forth over her buttock. His hands were hard and warm through the thin cotton. "He's so easy, he doesn't grab, but he's sure of himself," Linnie had said about Pitt. "I like that, don't you?"

She didn't move or speak as he opened her pajama jacket and pushed it back so her breasts glimmered in the strengthening moonlight. He stood looking at them, while his fingers gently pushed down inside the elastic at her waist. She wanted to take his head between her hands and press it down to her breasts so he would kiss them. Without him she occupied, in solitude, a desert, yet she had never really had him. Not as Eloise had. She swallowed to wet her throat and said, "Yes, I'm ready for bed, and that's where I'm going. Alone."

His hands jumped against her ribs as if she'd nicked him with a lighted match. "*Jesus!*" he exclaimed. "It's not the wrong time of the month again, is it?"

"It'll always be the wrong time from now on, Jamie," she said steadily.

"But what the hell is going on all of a sudden?" He stood off from her, and she buttoned her jacket again.

"It isn't all of a sudden," she told him. "Jamie, we're friends, that's the way we want it, and that is the way it has to be."

"But what's it got to do with now—with this—" He was frustrated into fragmented speech; he sounded bewildered. "Sure we're friends! That's what's so good about it! What do you *want?*"

"Don't worry," she said, "it's a little late for me to say I'm saving it till I get married. No, I'm not holding you up. I just never expected to be casual about going to bed with anybody. I've never been comfortable about it, so I decided to stop. If we're friends, you ought to accept that. Of course, if you only come around here for one thing—"

"Jesus, you know better than that!" he flung at her. He was red enough for the darkening to show in the moonlight and breathing fast. "But I'm not just *anybody!*" He made a clipped military turn away from her and walked out.

33

The wild strawberries were long gone; there were scatterings of blueberries the color of young kittens' eyes. The first raspberries were ripening in the heat of old cuttings in the woods and along the lane among the wild rose bushes. The dawn chorus now belonged mostly to crows and gulls and the early-to-work ospreys, as the land birds gave their attention to raising and protecting their young. The new swallows were already flying, and by August they would be going south.

The older Joanna grew, the more she was appalled by the speed of time. Even as a child she'd always hated the ones who croaked on a cool day in July, "Feels fallish, don't it?"

It had infuriated her, as if they were trying to steal her summer from her. Now she was stealing it from herself by fussing about time. "Next thing I'll be pulling out all my gray hairs," she told Pip. He answered with a rising inflection, stretching up as far as his front paws could reach on her thigh. She put him over her shoulder and let him ride as far as the gate. He always behaved as if he appreciated the view from up here and tried to look everywhere at once, an avid sightseer.

When she put him down, he sat and watched her go, then turned and trotted back past the house. There were no cats up at the Homestead now, which meant the meadow, Goose Cove, and the adjacent woods were all his.

It was around nine in the morning, another flat-calm day with the supernal pastels and exaggerated hush of a weather breeder. Yesterday had been one, too. A tropical storm was trying to wind itself up into a hurricane off the Carolinas. Those fishermen who still had wooden traps were moving them away from the rocks out to deeper waters; wire traps didn't shift on the bottom like wooden ones. Linnie, Sam, and Richard were all helping each other.

Out on their family wharves the Dinsmore and Percy children were collaborating on chores, picking up everything loose that could blow overboard or against a window and break the glass. Tiger ran around with his nose to the planks, tracking mice. Hank flapped back and forth between ridgepoles and hoisting masts. Young Mark was helping his father on the big wharf, tramping up and down in his long-legged rubber boots. Across the harbor Cindy Campion directed her younger brothers and Anne Barton like a drill sergeant, her commands clearly heard across the water.

Liza spoke to Joanna from her porch. "Where are you bound?"

"Well, I should be doing something around the wharf, but once the wind hits, it's likely to be rough for a week afterward. Come for a row while it's quiet."

"You're on. Let me get my glasses."

"Bring some newspapers; the seats may be wet." She chucked Leo under the chin.

The tide was about halfway in, and the harbor was like a three-dimensional watercolor which they would presently enter, and row away into the subtly tinted transparencies of distance.

"You want to row first?" Joanna asked.

"No, I'd like to look at those ospreys. Aren't they magnificent? When they plunge, it stops my heart. And I'd never even heard of them until I became an islander." As the skiff moved out across the quiet water, she followed one bird with the binoculars. "A three-pound body and a five-foot wingspread. God, what power in those wings! To lift up dripping from the water, with a fish in the talons—I never get over the marvel of it."

"And they belong to themselves," said Joanna. "The whole world over, the osprey is in a class by itself. Those two up there are the actual lineal descendants of the first two ospreys, and how did *they* evolve?"

"And how did *that* bird evolve?" Liza asked, looking past Joanna's shoulder. Joanna glanced around. *Drake's Pride* was coming past Eastern Harbor Point, loaded with new wire traps. Her engine was so quiet that it had blended into the muted background medley of other engines. Joanna veered toward the granite blocks of the breakwater.

"I won't even make a stab at answering," she said. "I try to imagine his parents, but I can't. I think he's of himself, too."

She turned the skiff bow to the wash. "I guess he's not happy playing with his two hundred traps," Liza said. "Looks as if he's going to be ready for fall fishing. My goodness! Which won't be what Philip says when he sees that wharf loaded with more gear."

"You know, twenty-five years ago the words *Bennett's Island* would have been painted off that stern the first night she lay in here."

"You sound wistful," said Liza.

"I am. I don't want any feuds, I don't want any violence, but I can't stand that man. Thank God he couldn't see us past all those traps, or we'd have had to wave. And *smile.*" She leered toothily, and they both laughed. The skiff bounced lightly in the remains of the wake as they went out around the end of the breakwater. The oars dipped and rose almost without sound. The skiff glided onward over quivering reflections of the shore. The oar blades softly shattered them, but they grew together again as soon as the skiff had passed. Loquacious eider groups moved out of the way without flurry. At the far end of this shore there was the activity of three small boats as Linnie, Richard, and Sam shifted traps, but here the women floated along in a private world of water and birds.

Yesterday at the Sewing Circle Philippa had told them that Eric was giving up the ministry and going into the Peace Corps. "If I had my heart set on anything for Eric, it was that he'd find something satisfying to do with his life. Sometimes I thought he'd decided on the ministry because he felt he owed it to his father," she said candidly. "If he doesn't feel right in it, it's certainly not the thing for him. He could be a good teacher. He really lights up when he talks about working with kids."

"Do you cancel an ordination?" Liza wondered now. "Become *un*ordained?"

"I don't know," Joanna said, bemused. Eric knew now what he wanted, and he was going for it; she could only wish the same for Jamie. If only he'd want something within his reach. Of course, there was the saying that a man's reach should exceed his grasp, but Browning had never known Jamie.

"I still think it's too bad we can't have a summer wedding while we've got a minister in the family," said Liza. "Maybe Jamie'll surprise you."

"The surprise would come afterward, with Rosa showing up wearing a wedding ring. And maybe pregnant. That's how we'd find out, but I'd jump up and down with joy. If she loses patience with him, I don't know what will come next. Another Eloise would be the last straw even for Nils."

"Another Eloise can't strike in the same place. It can't be!" said Liza dramatically. "Oh, Lord, I hope there isn't one in training right now to snag Sam." Suddenly she leaned forward with her hands tightly gripping her knees. "Jo, his mother showed up at the school one day this spring. They were having soccer practice, and she was on the sidelines. She spoke to him when he came off the field."

Joanna stopped rowing. "What did he do?" She imagined Sam's round face going white and blank.

"He was floored, of course, but he kept his wits about him. He said she was well dressed and had a nice car, with Connecticut plates. She wanted to take him for a hamburger, but he told her it was against the rules." She shivered a little. "I get cold just thinking about it. Maybe she wouldn't have tried to steal him, he's too big for that, but I keep wondering. He may have wondered, too. What a position for a kid to find himself in!"

"When did you find out about it?" Joanna began rowing again.

"He told us right away, the first day he was home. When Philip asked him how he felt about it, he said he wasn't sure, just 'kind of funny.' I've been feeling that way ever since. My first impulse was to never let him off the island again. She gave him up freely, she wanted to be rid of him, so why did she come back?"

"Maybe some maternal feelings stirring?"

"Where the hell was the maternal feeling when she let her boyfriend nearly kill a five-year-old child? He was taken away from her, and she never tried to get him back, never showed remorse, went on living with her man as soon as he was out of prison. . . . I just wish I knew what Sam meant by 'funny.'"

"He must remember the beatings and that she let them happen. Maybe that's what he meant."

"But what a burden for a child to carry. Perhaps hating her for it and all torn up because you *have* to hate your own mother."

"It might not be so with Sam," Joanna said.

"Well, Philip says if he sleeps well, and eats well, and seems to think only of getting the most out of every minute, he must be all right. But is he as sunny as he acts? Should we be doing something, and *what?* That's what keeps niggling at me."

"He was in a good foster home for a long time before you got him, you said. That counts. It was probably more healing than you know."

"Yes, they were like loving grandparents to him," Liza said. "That's how he still thinks of them, and we encourage it. We let him visit on weekends from school. He just wrote to them the other day and sent some snapshots. I'm fussing about *nothing*," she said decisively. "Whatever she tries now, there's no room for her. He's got Gramps and Gram, Philip and me, and all this huge family here plus my good Italian clan. What chance does *she* have? She gave it up years and years ago."

"There you are," said Joanna. "Maybe what he meant by 'funny' was that he didn't feel much of anything."

"You know something I've never told anyone, even Philip? It's always felt so *right;* it's as if we were really his parents but somehow lost each other, the way families are separated in a war and go on looking for a long time. His being born to someone else was just an accident."

She wiped her eyes on her sweater sleeve. "Gosh, I'm glad I came out with you today. I was beginning to let that woman get to me, and I hated to keep on at Philip all the time. So thanks for listening. How about letting me row for a while and using up this adrenalin?"

"Not being like my son, who never lets *anybody* take over his boat, I'll be glad to swap places." Joanna rowed into the shallow water of Old Man Cove, and they carefully changed seats.

They didn't go all the way to where the young ones were working but turned around and went slowly back to the harbor. Owen's *White Lady* was just leaving, with Tommy Wiley at the wheel and Betsey and Holly up on the bow. They waved and shouted at their aunts, and Tommy's euphoria was obvious.

"Heading for Brigport, looks like," said Joanna. "Wonder what brought brother Owen in so early." She felt queasy.

"The kids didn't look worried about anything," Liza said.

"Owen puts up a good front." And you don't know how good, Joanna thought.

But when the skiff came in to the Sorensen wharf, he stood at the top of the ladder, looking benignly down at them.

"Good morning, sisters fair," he said. "You pull a strong oar, Liza, love."

"Why are you standing around with your hands in your pockets," asked Joanna, "when everybody else is working, working, working?"

"Living in that house for so long, you sound just like old Gunnar," said Owen. "Standing around with your hands in your pockets was a worse crime than attempted murder."

"Standing around with your hands in your pockets, spinning cuffers," said Joanna, "and gustaleering."

"You have to take your hands out of your pockets for that," Owen corrected her. "Wave your arms around and so forth. The Bennetts were always great at that. Father told me that Gunnar used to thank God out loud he never had daughters to be swept off their feet by them." Laughing, he took each woman by the arm and walked them up the wharf. "I miss the old bastard, don't you, Jo?"

"I miss the times," she said, "but I wouldn't go so far as to say I miss Gunnar."

"I'd like to meet him just once," said Liza. "Couldn't we bring in somebody to raise him up? Maybe Maggie could get him on her Ouija board, and I could talk to him."

"You'd rue the day, you Italian ex-papist," said Owen. "He probably hasn't stopped spinning in his grave since you set foot on the island."

"Now I feel even more cheated. I never met up with one of those."

"Tommy looked out of his mind with happiness, being trusted with White Lady," Joanna said.

"Well, the girls got a couple more friends coming out on the plane this morning, so we came in early. He's a good boy, and it doesn't take much to make him happy. He's careful with the boat, treats her as if she's eight months along with quintuplets. I hope Richard's that easy someday. Right now I don't know. These kids are all speed-mad."

"Where's your long gray beard, Gramps?" Joanna asked him. "Things were different in my day," she quavered in a cracked voice. "If you'll excuse the expression, Skipper, like hell they were."

"Oh, yes, they were. Our mother," said Owen severely, "never said hell in her life."

"I'll bet she thought it plenty of times."

They left Liza at her front steps, and Owen walked home with Joanna. "You making a pot of coffee?"

"So you can tell me all the criminal ideas you've had in your head since you saw the new load of traps coming in."

"They aren't fit for you to hear, let alone saying them at the table."

At the gate they heard Linnie's outboard, recognizable without a sight of *Dovekie*, but Joanna turned anyway for a glimpse of Linnie standing up in the stern in her yellow oil pants and old plaid shirt, her hands on her hips, steering by shifting her weight from one foot to the other.

"And the hell of it is," Owen was saying, "if you cut off every damn pot of his, you'd just be helping to ruin the bottom and trapping lobsters down there that'd never—"

His voice shut off in mid-word and was succeeded by such a profound stillness that it was as if he had suddenly vanished. She turned to him to speak and saw Van just coming away from the sun parlor door.

In the sudden terrible silence which lay about the three of them, Hank's voice went pealing and echoing over their heads. Joanna's mind was blank. She did not know where to look; she shrank as if in shame and guilt from seeing either face.

Then Owen was walking away, and Van was looking after him as if witnessing a final departure. It must have always been like that whenever she saw his back going away. How many times in five years? How many times more? *Forsaking each other for as long as you both shall live.*

She wet her lips, but it was Van who spoke first. "I left some books on the table. Yours and a couple I thought you'd like." She sounded perfectly natural; after all, she'd had much more practice in this than Joanna had.

"Come on back in again," Joanna said. "I'm just about to make some coffee. I'm parched."

"Not this time, thanks. I wasn't going to stay anyway." Vanessa's gaze shifted a fraction away from hers, and she blinked quickly two or three times, and Joanna knew that Owen must have just gone out of sight, either between the fish houses or past the Binnacle on the way to the big wharf. Now they had been set free and could breathe again; she felt her own breath go out in an involuntary sigh.

Van gave her an ironic half smile and a slight shake of the head. No words were called for. Van knew how it was best handled; she could at least take pride in her stoicism and would not cheapen it by wanting or accepting pity.

For Joanna, the price of knowing the truth was never to admit that it had been spoken.

34

By midafternoon Tropical Storm Alan had been promoted to hurricane rank and was off the New Jersey coast. Penobscot Bay might have been enclosed in a giant paperweight, it was so quiet. The children went to Schoolhouse Cove to swim, the women picked what they could save in the gardens. The men did the heavy work around the shore, moving stacked traps onto the land in case the wharves were damaged. Skiffs were pulled up well above high water and made fast. The ground lines, chains, and pennants of the moorings were kept routinely checked for signs of wear, so this wasn't an immediate worry.

Willy and Felix Drake were taking turns wheeling Drake's new gear up the wharf. "Real comforting to think Drake's raising a sweat just like us lower classes," Ralph Percy called across Rosa's tidy and vacant wharf.

"Well, I suppose he deserves some credit for coming out to be with her during the storm," Joanna said.

"I thought you didn't give a damn anymore, Marm," Linnie teased her.

"I don't, but there's such a thing as common decency." She got out of the way as Jamie's wheelbarrow came toward her with three empty lobster crates precipitously stacked on it and Jamie invisible behind them. It was Linnie and Hugo, not Jamie, who'd helped Rosa move gear, and he was working in a silence more threatening than that of the calm before the storm. She'd have called it a sulk when he was ten or so. Come to think of it, she observed now, it's still a sulk. A super sulk. Rosa must have set him back on his heels.

"I wonder when *Sweet Helen* will show up," Linnie said. "They must

253

have started back in when they heard the hurricane warnings. I'll bet they'll come in here to ride it out."

"They won't be welcome in sister Sheena's house, that's for sure. Not with the dragon in residence."

"We could let them have Jamie's room, couldn't we?" Linnie said. "It would be pretty mean to make them stay out aboard in a hurricane, and we have plenty of room."

"You can keep Pitt out for half the night," said her mother, "but do you want to wish Roy on the rest of us?"

"Heck, he'd be making the rounds all evening. When he was little he heard that Jesus wanted him for a sunbeam, so that's what he tries to be." Jamie, coming back with the empty wheelbarrow, hadn't heard the subject but distrusted the way Linnie smiled at him.

"We're working around here," he said. "And I want that crate you're roosting on, so you can either fish or cut bait. I can put that plainer if you want."

"My, my, aren't we touchy," Linnie began, but her mother gave her the Bennett look.

"Let's get out of here, and leave them to it," she said.

"All right," Linnie said amiably, following her up the wharf. "Listen, Marm, I'll do the work, make up the bed, cook their breakfast tomorrow morning, and so forth."

At the land end of the fish house, where the traps were piled, Nils had stopped work to wipe his forehead. "Coffee or beer, love?" Joanna asked him.

"Beer. It's hotter than love in summertime. I'll be up for it."

Walking toward the house Joanna said to Linnie, "It's Jamie's room. We can't let anyone sleep in it without his say-so."

Linnie groaned. "Well, that's that. He'd rather let Typhoid Mary use it than them."

"He wouldn't want anyone in it," said her mother. "They might move something an inch from where he had it. Besides, they'll probably want to stay with the boat. We won't get the worst of it till sometime tomorrow anyway."

"You're probably right," Linnie said grumpily. "I guess I'll see if anybody's going swimming while it's so calm. Anybody over sixteen, that is." She took her suit and a towel and went out the back way toward the Homestead.

By suppertime the sky was what the islanders called smurry, and the still heat was oppressive. *Sweet Helen* didn't come. Linnie fidgeted in and out of the house, down to the harbor and back, all evening; fortunately Jamie was playing pool at the clubhouse, so he could not make unkind remarks.

"They probably went straight home," Joanna said. "They got the word that Drake was out here, so they know their sister has company for the storm, and they'll ride it out with their parents, and that's proper. What if a tree falls on the house and somebody gets hurt?"

"Oh, I suppose so," Linnie mumbled. She went up to Rosa's finally but came back looking cranky. "She's going to bed," she said indignantly. She went to bed herself, carrying a plate of crackers and cheese, a peach, and a glass of milk.

"Going away to starve, I see," said her father over his book.

"Yup! I'm going to eat myself into a decline." She was followed by Pip, who thought cheese was one of the finer things for which he'd been born. He said so, all the way up the stairs.

"Ah, love!" murmured Joanna. "Reading poetry in bed amid all the cracker crumbs."

"What do you think about this?" Nils asked her.

"What is there to think about it? All we know is what she tells us. She's impressed, but she's been impressed before."

"We'll just have to trust to her common sense," said Nils. "Let's go to bed. Without the saltines."

The upper room had cooled, and the curtains moved quietly in a noiseless breath of breeze. The island was unusually quiet tonight. Nobody seemed to be staying up and running a generator for a late television show. Everyone had put in a long day, and tomorrow would be hard and long in a different way. Joanna knelt at the front window. Only the brightest stars could be seen, dulled, through the thin cloud, and the moonlight was diffused into a clear, colorless medium, like that of the hour before dawn when everything close at hand is distinct but all in shades from black to white. The beacon on the end of the breakwater was as weak in it as a candle flame.

Because of the hush, they heard an engine begin in the harbor and travel across it. Nils came to the window and looked out over her head. They saw the running lights and the glow under the canopy as the boat turned to head out, with the wake glimmering astern and a momentary

flash of her side from the beacon light. Then she was going discreetly out
around Eastern Harbor Point.

"Felix," Joanna said. "Good, he's taking her ashore. I hope this is the
end of that little mess."

She slept well and awoke at daybreak to a skyful of tumbling, boiling
clouds and the roar of the wind through the trees, drowning out the bell.
Occasionally a random gust slammed against the house. Nils was already
up, scrambling eggs in one pan and cooking sausage in another.

"I see we're going to keep up our strength," said Joanna. "Any news
on it yet?"

He shook his head. "We don't have to be told it's on the way; we can
hear it. I was awake around midnight, and it was already kicking up a
good row. Came on fast. Why ruin a good breakfast listening to the
disaster reports? We'll know when she gets here."

"*He*," said Joanna. "*Sweet Helen* come back?"

"Nope. Grab your plate."

Jamie came in, sniffing. "Thought you might be cooking up a real
John-Rogers breakfast," he said, with gloomy satisfaction. He went
straight to the small radio on the shelf beside the harbor window and
turned it on, but low. Joanna began taking plates out of the cupboard.
She was pleased that Jamie had come in; it was when her children
skipped meals that she worried. He was standing with his ear close to the
radio now, his head bent.

"Listen!" he hissed suddenly, and signaled to them to come and
listen too. The small, disembodied voice of the newscaster crackled in
the room.

> "*During the night, as the coast of Maine battened down the hatches against the
> arrival of Hurricane Alan, a joint operation by the State Police, federal narcotics
> agents, and the sheriff's department resulted in a raid on the premises of Henry
> Coates, a well-known seafood dealer, realtor, and community figure.*"

Nils impassively turned off the gas under his frying pans. Joanna
thought stolidly, I must not drop these plates, and she tightened her grip.
Jamie stared at his mother, but she knew he was not seeing her; she could
have been a transparent cutout. His mouth opened in incredulity at
hearing his suppositions made fact, as if by giving voice to them, he had
also given them substance. The radio voice went weirdly on.

> "*Coates was arrested in the act of receiving from the captain of a dragger a small
> package which was found to contain cocaine. The dragger captain and his crew of*

two were also arrested, and four men on Coates's wharf at the time. Two were truck drivers, and two were fish handlers for Coates."

All the names were given. Clay Fosdick, the dragger captain, said he had received the package from the captain of a New Jersey menhaden seiner but had had no idea what was in it. He said he had picked up such packages before for Coates but thought they contained tapes of pornographic material.

"The raid was the result of an exhaustive investigation into the death of Ira Beecham ten days ago. The combined forces of the law had received several pieces of information from unnamed sources. While the arrests were being made, an offshore lobster boat, Sweet Helen of Coates Cove, entered the harbor, made an abrupt turn, and left. Sweet Helen is owned by two brothers, Pitt and Roy Bainbridge, twenty-six and twenty-three years of age."

The voice went on. *"They have not answered all night as their father, Micah Bainbridge of Coates Cove, appealed to them to come in. The air search will begin this morning, weather permitting."*

The announcer added that since Alan was upon them, the air search would probably not be possible. However, a land search was already in effect, in case the two brothers had gone ashore somewhere. It was doubted that drugs would be found aboard the boat; that cargo would be easily disposed of. The Bainbridge brothers were primarily wanted for questioning about Ira Beecham's death.

"And now," said the announcer with obvious relief and a dry throat, *"we will hear the latest hurricane advisories from the National Weather Service."*

"I knew it! *I knew it!"* Jamie said just above a whisper. "I knew it in my bones! But damn it, I wanted to be in on it! Goddamn the luck!"

"Be in on *what?"* asked Linnie from the doorway. The other three looked at her, and Jamie had the grace to blush. Joanna wished she could take Linnie in her arms, but this was no child, this young woman who spoke so precisely.

"Pitt never carried drugs. He hates them. And he's not a murderer either."

"They shouldn't have panicked, Linnie," Nils said. "It makes them look guilty."

"Roy was the one who panicked," she said with bitter contempt. "Never Pitt. That stupid Roy has made them look terrible. I'll never forgive him." She came into the kitchen and picked up a cup with a perfectly steady hand. "Coffee ready?"

"I wonder if they've picked up Drake yet," Jamie said in a subdued voice.

Linnie turned on him so fast Joanna thought she was going to throw the cup at his face. "You're glad about all this!" she accused him. "You hope it's true, you *think* it's true, but it isn't!"

She ran toward the back door, and Joanna started after her; but Nils caught her by the arm and shook his head. He went out himself and disappeared past the thrashing lilac bushes.

"Oh, *Jesus*," Jamie muttered, and for once his mother didn't rebuke him. She was staring stupidly at the empty wooden walk. It was as if Linnie and Nils had vanished into an immense booming gulf. Jamie said, "Well, there goes a good breakfast all to hell." He took a couple of sausages and walked out the front door of the sun parlor.

Pip attempted to climb Joanna's leg, and she picked him up automatically; his purr roared in her ear like a conch shell. The radio was still babbling on about the weather, and she snapped it off. She kept seeing Linnie's white face, a stranger's face contorted with rage and anguish. She had often seen Linnie's grief, disappointment, and anger, but it had all been childish compared to this. She paced the sun parlor, thankful for the sinewy, ardent life vibrating in her arms while she waited for Nils to come back. Everything had happened so fast she suddenly found herself marooned, wanting to act, needing to act, but not knowing how or where.

Nils came in, and Pip squirmed to get down and meet him. Nils let him out, and he raced along the walk with his tail up and crooked sidewise.

"He'll find her," Nils said with a half smile.

"Where is she?"

"Out in the barn. She just wants a chance to howl in private. Mostly it's rage with her brother, but I think she's scared that it could be true."

She went to him with her arms out. "How about a hug?"

"Any time, kid." Wrapped in a close embrace, they kissed like lovers just meeting after a long separation. "Don't worry," he said into her neck.

"For a few minutes there," Joanna said, "I thought everybody had fallen off the world. My favorite horror. What do *you* think?"

"Why did they turn tail? As the man said, if they were carrying drugs, they could have tossed them overboard on the way in, and chances are they hadn't even had time for a rendezvous this time. Come on, let's have breakfast. Sausages ruined?"

"We can start again," said Joanna. "All of a sudden I want to drop tons of food onto those eggbeaters in my stomach so they can't move. Poor Linnie. This is going to be a wild day in more ways than one."

They had just settled at the sun parlor table when Jamie returned, silently fixed a plate for himself, and sat down with them. "Linnie still out?" he asked abruptly. "I suppose it's my fault."

"Not necessarily," said his father. "I think we can safely blame the Bainbridges. Just pipe down on the 'I knew it' tune."

"I will," said Jamie. "When the kid gets an idea somebody's perfect, it just about kills her to find out he isn't."

"Remember, they're innocent until proved guilty," Joanna reminded him.

"Why wouldn't they be guilty if somebody like Henry Coates could be caught in the act? If they didn't kill Ira Beecham, why run away with a hurricane coming up the coast? Wherever they duck in, somebody's going to recognize that boat, unless they know some hidden cove with nobody living in it but some old codger who doesn't believe in radio. And the minute the storm's over the search'll be on again."

"Pretty hard to hide a boat that size," Nils commented. "You can't push her into a quarry, the way they do stolen cars. And the whole coast's alerted."

"They've sure got their arse in a sling," Jamie said with satisfaction. "I'll bet Old Teddy Bear Roy is between a shit and a sweat right now. Excuse me, Marm."

"I don't know if I will or not," said Joanna coldly. "Sometimes I wish you weren't too big to have your mouth washed out with soap and water. Remember what your father said. Just try not to be so happy about this out loud."

"I promise, I promise! But won't you grin just a dite," he cajoled, "when they haul Felix the Fart in on this?"

"I'm not grinning at any bit of it," she said. "Not with a death involved."

"I'm going back to the fish house," Jamie said. "Good morning to sort through some of that cultch up in the loft. Thanks for the chow." In a gesture foreign to him he lightly ruffled Joanna's hair in passing, leaving her bemused.

35

Nils followed him to the shore in a few minutes. Joanna went out to tend the hens and looked into the gloomy barn, where the ghosts of Gunnar's cows and the scent of past hay harvests still lived. The barn swallows came and went through their entrance high in one gable end, and they provided the only life there this morning. Pip did not appear. So Linnie had gone to the outer shores or into the woods, as they all did for solace or refuge, to walk off a rage, hoard a joy, try to make woe manageable. Linnie was not a fool; she would be back before the wind reached its hurricane strength.

When Joanna was returning to the house with her blue bowl of eggs, Pip came running from the alders and went into the house with her. He was a cat of great common sense.

Thinking that Linnie would rather find the house empty when she did come home, Joanna went down to Philip's, and found Philippa there, up from the Eastern End with Robin. Laurie came in; Kathy and Vanessa stopped on their way to the store. Everyone was on the move this morning in spite of the gale blowing across the open spaces of the island.

The Bainbridges were now in everybody's mind. They could hardly have been more so if they were on the island in the flesh; the emptiness of Drake's mooring contained not only *Drake's Pride* but *Sweet Helen*. The women gathered in Philip's kitchen listened silently to new bulletins about the storm, the drug raid, and the missing boat. In their collective consciousness Roy leaned back against the counter in the store with his thumbs in his overall straps, always talking, and Pitt was the shadow who made his point by silence.

"I wonder if Felix Drake's in this, too," Liza said. "Or is he too smart?"

"All I know," said Kathy, "is I'm some relieved he took *her* off last night. At least I'm assuming he took her; I don't know why he'd leave her here in a hurricane when she looks just about ready to pop. Willy's here, though; he was down on the wharf this morning. He'll probably be over to see us today."

"She must be frantic worrying about her brothers," Laurie said sympathetically. "Maybe she's with her parents now."

Everybody hoped so. The first spatters of rain, a sharp increase in the wind velocity, and a certain relentless note in its voice, sent the women home. Pip came down the stairs to greet Joanna, and she heard the soft closing of a door up there. So Linnie was back.

Joanna assembled a corn chowder, which all the family liked on stormy days. Jamie came home with Nils; he didn't offer to turn on the radio. They had one in the fish house and had been tracking the hurricane and getting the latest bulletins on the drug arrests. "No news on the boat yet," Nils said. "The partners, Rouse and Wilcox, have rushed to give themselves up and offer to tell all, naming more names. They say they were going to get out of the business as soon as they had their boats paid for. Makes you want to shed a tear for them, doesn't it?"

"Nobody's mentioned Felix Drake yet," Jamie said glumly. "Shows you what money can do."

"Well, it didn't do much for Henry Coates," said his mother. "Dollars to doughnuts Felix isn't involved, doesn't know a thing about it. Or didn't until this morning, like the rest of us."

"Oh, *Felix*, is it?" He grinned. "Hear that, Pop? Next thing she'll be asking him in for coffee. She's already had Roy in."

"You're a fresh mutt," said Joanna. "In the words of your uncle Owen, how would you like your face pushed in?"

She went upstairs and asked Linnie if she wanted her meal on a tray.

"I'm not an invalid," Linnie said composedly. "I'm over my fit. I don't know why they ran, except it must have been Roy's doing, and Pitt couldn't control him. But I *know* Pitt hasn't committed any crimes."

When she came downstairs, she had changed into sea-blue denim slacks and a blue gingham shirt, and tied her hair back on her neck with a blue ribbon. Jamie obligingly whistled, and she gave him a small, constrained grin.

They ate in the dining room, which was quieter than the sun parlor, though the whole house was invaded by the tumult of the storm. The Bainbridges were not mentioned in the conversation around the table. Jamie did his part, and even Linnie contributed.

"The Dinsmore kids are worried about Hank," Jamie said. "Rob told them he was snugged down in the lee somewhere."

"What *do* gulls do in hurricanes?" Linnie asked. "And medricks, and ospreys, and all the rest?"

"Well, you never hear of them being blown away," said her father. "But nests can be damaged, I suppose."

Everyone must have been relieved when the meal was over. Now there was nothing to do but wait for the hurricane to reach its peak and pass over. The men would collect at the shore to watch the boats, either from the store or from someone's fish house; Owen would be keeping an eye on *White Lady* in Schoolhouse Cove; Steve and Eric would watch the action in their cove. If a mooring gave way at the height of the storm, in spite of all precautions, there would be nothing anyone could do but watch a boat, or boats, go onto the rocks and be destroyed; but they would never turn their backs on the deaths even though they felt each blow in their own bodies.

Holly Bennett and her new mainland guest came in, bundled up in rain clothes, exhilarated after fighting the wind across the long flat stretch between Long Cove and Schoolhouse Cove; they wanted Linnie to go up to the Homestead with them, to spend the afternoon with Betsey and her friend making popcorn, playing records, and watching the surf batter the shore as far as Schooner Head. The old house stood foursquare to the winds, with no lee on any side except where the big barn stood between it and the east wind. Since 1836 it had been riding out the worst weather any season had to offer.

Its hand-hewn timbers were fastened with trunnels, and it creaked in the strongest gales like a ship at sea; generations of Bennett men had said, "As long as she creaks, she holds."

Linnie, showing no strain, got into her oil clothes and boots and went out with the girls through the back path. Joanna was left alone with Pip.

"I don't know about you," she said to him, "but I feel as if I'd been dragged through about ten knotholes. I'm going to forget everybody else's troubles, including my children's, for the next hour. Maybe two."

She went upstairs. Before she lay down with her book, she looked out at the harbor. The rain blew like smoke over the lunging boats, and across a mile of white water Brigport was a long, dark, blurred shape in the mist.

She settled down to read, and Pip curled up on her midriff, purring himself to sleep.

This house had the lee of a substantial forest which stretched to Sou'west Point, but that didn't count today. The noise went on without letup, with higher gusts thudding against the house and making it shudder. Sudden bursts of heavier rain hit the windows with enough noise to make Pip lift his head. When the clamor lessened for a few moments, there were mysterious taps, creaks, rattles, vibrations, and a peculiar keening that got Pip up to prowl from room to room, staring for a long time into certain corners.

With all this racket there was no pleasant escape in a book, and the atmosphere inside the house was oppressive. Joanna gave up and went downstairs. There was a brief lull in the rain and the wind, one of those moments when the storm holds up a bit to catch its breath. She went out on the front doorstep. The warm wet air was scented with beaten earth and grass, and she thought regretfully of her garden. She wondered where Hank was, but he'd gotten through the winter storms all right. Willy came around the corner by Philip's house, carrying a water pail; head down, he plowed along in his oil clothes and rubber boots. While he was hauling up his water with the long pole, he looked all around from under his sou'wester and saw her up by the house. With his missing teeth he resembled a gaunt jack-o'-lantern when he smiled. He left his full pail in the lee of the well curb and came up through the gate.

"Hi, Mrs. Sorensen! Some storm, ain't it?"

"Wild. How'd you get around here without being blown away?"

"Oh, I saw she was backing off a dite, so I grabbed a bucket and come around the beach all aflukin'. She'll be over the seawall anytime now, and she's already up the beach almost to the anchor, and I wanted me some good old Bennett's Island water while I could still get across. I ain't a bit partial to that fancy water Mr. Drake thinks is so arrigorical." He grinned at the nonsense word. "You need a fresh pail?"

"No, thanks. Did Mr. Drake take Selina in?"

"Gorry, no! I was some surprised! But he never offered, and she never asked. Of course, she don't know it's a hurricane, she never listens, but

he knew it." He looked anxious. "He says to me, 'I got to be with my wife
and girls, Willy. They expect it.' Just like they didn't have plenty of folks
over there, and here *she* is, all soul alone. Some folks puzzle me, Mrs.
Bennett," he said sadly.

"Me, too, Willy," she said. "So she's here now. She must be pretty
sure she's got plenty of time."

"*She* may be sure," he said. "I wish I was."

"How is she?" Joanna tried to rein back her exasperation; she
reminded herself she still didn't give a damn.

"Good's anybody can be in her condition, with this wind shaking the
place fit to make your teeth rattle. She don't seem nervous, I'll say that
for her. Mr. D., he gave her this little TV"—he pronounced it like a
babyish nickname, Teevie—"five inch screen, runs on flashlight batter-
ies, and comes in real good, but she never uses it. Told me to take it up
in my room. She reads an awful lot. She's a real nice young woman, Mrs.
Sorensen," he said. "She keeps telling me not to worry about her, so I
figger she wants me to give her plenty of elbowroom. I wouldn't mind a
good game of gin, though. I get some tired of solitaire."

This would be a good place to end the conversation, but Willy
obviously did not want to, just yet. So she could not avoid the question
she loathed asking.

"But has she heard about Coates and the boys? She can't have," she
answered herself, "if she's as calm as you say."

"Nope, but *I* got it, first thing this morning." The storm, having
caught its breath, was beginning to shriek again, and Willy had to shout
at her. "I sleep upstairs; she's down, has a hard time with the stairs now.
I got my little radio right by my pillow; she never heard nothing." He was
goggle-eyed with horrified amazement. "If that ain't some goddamn awful
mess! *Henry Coates!* I still can't believe it!"

"Nobody can," she shouted back. "So she doesn't know about her
brothers yet."

"No, and I ain't gonna tell her. And I won't let nobody else."

"Good for you, Willy!" She patted his arm, and he smiled proudly.

"She don't know nothing about this drug business!" he yelled against
the noise. "I'm sure of that! Way she talks, she hates drugs!"

Wind slammed against the house behind her. "You'd better go!" she
told him. "Do you have plenty to eat over there?"

"Lashins of grub!"

"Good. I hope he takes her off here as soon as this is over."

"He better. I never 'prenticed for a midwife!" He gave her a cocky grin and set off. He got his pail from the well curb, and the wind was blowing the water off the top of it. She hung on to the porch post until he'd gone past Philip's, shoved along by the gale.

An erratic gust whipped around the corner of the house, loaded with rain, and doused her in the instant before she could get the door open behind her. She put the teakettle on to heat, changed into dry clothes, and took a towel to her hair. She turned on the radio to the Limerock station, but it wasn't time for news or weather. There was only music and not the kind she liked even when her skin and her stomach weren't crawling with nerves.

To know that a boat was missing, no matter whose, was always a matter of intimate significance to those who had nearly been lost themselves, or who had lost, or almost lost, someone. In the island's history some men had come home after narrow escapes, and some had never returned. Young Charles Bennett would be in the family's collective mind today, and Ralph Percy would be thinking of his older brother; the two young men, hardly more than boys, had set out for the mainland one winter day, taking along old Gregg, who lived in one of the camps that used to stand near the anchor. It had begun to snow and blow, and the three had never been seen again.

Alec had gone out to Cash's with Nils and Owen, to make a killing in lobsters; a storm struck, and Joanna had never forgotten that night, and their return in a wild-rose dawn with no gear, no lobsters, only their lives. Alec had lived to be drowned after all, in the harbor on a clear summer evening.

The impact of the news that a respected man like Henry Coates could be involved in drug trafficking, that the Bainbridges were probably involved and might have committed murder, was dulled by a powerful and superstitious dread because of the missing boat and the men aboard. *It could be happening to me or mine* would be the unspoken but universal thought, with an acerbic modifier; *I should hope none of mine would be that stupid or have been so criminal.*

For the sake of the Bainbridge parents, Joanna hoped the boat was tied up in the lee, if there was any real lee anywhere. Maybe they *hadn't* killed Ira Beecham. The drug traffic was bad enough, but Pitt and Roy could very well argue that if they weren't pushing drugs in schoolyards, and Henry Coates was selling his cocaine to adult customers who knew what they were doing, they weren't in the same class as arsonists, muggers, vandals, or the city thieves who broke into houses and drove away with the contents. "Doesn't everybody laugh about the rum-running days now? What's the difference?" She could hear Roy saying it in the store, leaning back against the candy counter with his thumbs in his overall straps, beaming at his audience.

She had a cup of tea and measured out the dry ingredients for hot biscuits for supper. Pip sat on a chair to watch her turn flour into the mixing bowl as if he'd never seen such a thrilling spectacle. She found the music station she liked and sang along with Jo Stafford and Bing Crosby. Pip was even more enthralled by this.

She was giving her best to "Dancing on the Ceiling" when Linnie came in the back door. There was so much din outside that even Pip hadn't heard her until she was there in the sun parlor, getting out of her dripping foul-weather gear.

"Did you nearly blow away?" Joanna asked her.

"Wow! I ran like mad in the lulls, but they lasted only about one second apiece. I went on my hands and knees in some places." She looked oddly gaunt, as if years, bad ones, had passed in an afternoon. Her conscientious smile made it worse. "Nice to hear some decent music. Those kids go in for the absolute worst."

"Seems as if this ought to be passing by pretty quick," Joanna said.

"Maybe the peak hasn't even got here yet. Have you heard any news lately?"

She didn't mean the weather news. "No," Joanna said, as if it weren't important. "I can hear it out there; I don't need to be told what it's doing. I haven't even looked at the barometer. Have a cup of tea and a cookie?"

"No, thanks, I'm going up and change. My rain pants have sprung a leak." She ran upstairs in her sock feet; to turn on her own radio, Joanna knew. Pip followed her, and her door shut on them both. So she wouldn't be alone up there with the cold comfort of her radio and the hubbub of the storm to feed her tormented imagination. Pip was the most attentive and most undemanding companion that anyone could want.

It was worth fighting the gale to get out of the house for a while; Joanna could make it to the fish house, on her hands and knees if she had to. She was just going upstairs to tell Linnie where she was going when someone pounded on the front door. A figure in oilskins and sou'wester was looking in through the window at her. Willy's knobby face, red and distraught.

"Come in, come in!" she called.

He opened the door and stood dripping on the threshold. He had to gulp a few times before he could speak, and she thought with a vast, stunned calm, *She is having the baby. Of course, she would have to have it during a hurricane. What else?*

"She's gonna have it," he shouted at her as if they were outdoors. "She's been havin' pains, thinks I don't notice. They're comin' awful close together."

"All right," said Joanna. Was this how people felt under the influence of tranquilizers? No, this was the comfortable numbness of shock. "I'll come. It would have been quicker if you'd got Kathy." She began getting into her rain clothes.

"She's too young; she don't seem hardly older than Cindy to me. I'd have got Mrs. Steve, but I'm scared to take the time to walk to the Eastern End."

"What is it?" Linnie called. "Is it—?"

Joanna went to the foot of the stairs, and Linnie looked down at her, aflame with the hope that *Sweet Helen* had somehow made it to the harbor.

"Selina's about to have it," Joanna said.

"Oh, my God." Linnie sank down on the top stair. "What do we do?"

"Pray that nothing goes wrong and the baby and Selina can do it all by themselves," Joanna said.

"I'll come, too—"

"I wish you'd wait to tell your father what's going on."

"But listen! Aren't you scared out of your skull?"

"*Scared* isn't the word." Joanna sat on a step and pulled on her boots. "I'll send Willy for Kathy and Van. Between the three of us we ought to have one complete set of brains. I hope."

"Who was the last baby born on here?"

"Your sister, and that doesn't make me any expert."

Linnie followed her into the sun parlor and maternally helped her zip up her jacket and fasten her hood. "You going to assist, Willy?"

"No, sir!" Willy said passionately.

"I feel as if I ought to be taking something, but I don't know what," Joanna said, with a longing look about the place as if she were going into permanent exile.

"If I know Kathy, she's been ready and hoping for a month." Linnie kissed her mother on the cheek. "Good luck, and keep the old cool."

"You keep *yours*," Joanna murmured, looking into her eyes, and Linnie nodded.

"I'm tougher than tripe, Marm. Go catch that baby."

Joanna groaned, and Linnie winked and slapped her on the shoulder; it was a comforting way to leave her. Off the doorstep, Willy gripped her arm. His hands were large for his slight build and strong like all fishermen's hands.

"Take quite a wind to blow the two of us away!" he yelled in her ear. "I'll hang on to ye like you was my last nickel!"

"What about the beach and the marsh?"

"We can wade across all right. I found a good place."

She didn't know if Liza saw them go by her house or if anyone saw them passing the fish houses. She was too busy to look around and wave sociably at a face in a window. When they came to the harbor beach, she had a good, and disturbing, view of the rearing boats. From the opposite direction white-crested waves were racing across the marsh. The seawall above Schoolhouse Cove looked like a long breaking ledge; water swirled around the swings and broke in bursts of spray against the schoolhouse steps.

On the harbor side the tide was up to the anchor, a heaving mass of floating rockweed. Holding her like a vise with one arm around her middle, and other hand clamping her nearer arm, Willy walked her across the shallowest strip where the two waters met. The flow from the marsh pulled at their legs; the thick layer of weed dragged at them; the undertow sucked at the very ground under their feet; the wind beat at their heads and shoulders hard enough to make them stagger.

When they reached higher ground, the harbor tide was well up over the ledges and flooding the wharves, but the houses were just enough higher to be safe. At least they always had been, Joanna thought. But today she expected anything.

"Tip-top high water!" Willy called. "Should be falling back now!"

Foss Campion's house, now Drake's, was the first one on this side.

They went in through the shed. "Go get Kathy and Van," she told Willy. "You don't have to wait around to introduce me. And tell them she doesn't know about the boys and Henry Coates, any of that stuff."

He was so relieved to be dismissed he grinned like a happy drunk. She laid her rain clothes on some old chairs, took off her boots, and went into the kitchen, which was just as Helen Campion had left it, and almost as neat.

"Hello in there!" she called sunnily on her way through. The house was out in the open, so the pandemonium was much worse than it was at home, and she couldn't tell if anyone answered. She walked into the small sitting room, dim because the front curtains were drawn against the view of the harbor, the flood tide, and the plunging boats as they'd been drawn against sunshine and blue water. On the other side of the steep stairs there was a small bedroom, and she went to the open door. Selina Bainbridge lay on the bed, staring at her through the artificial twilight as if she were a hallucination. Her face was very thin, coming down to a chin like Pitt's, and the fiery cloud of hair was damply darkened, flattened, and tangled. Her belly was enormous under a light coverlet.

"Hello," Joanna said. "Willy came over to say he thought it was time."

Selina lifted herself on her elbows. "Mrs. Sorensen, isn't it?" She had a low husky voice, but that might have been caused by pain and effort. "I guess Willy's right." She spoke with hopeless resignation. That makes two of us, Joanna thought. "While he was gone, my water broke. I'd gone out to the shed to the toilet."

Her face contracted in a grimace, and she fell back on the pillows. "Otherwise I'd have flooded this place, and poor Willy would have died of embarrassment." She ran out of breath and waited until the contraction had passed, and then said, "I apologize for all this. I'm not due for about three weeks. I was going to be in Stonehaven in plenty of time."

"You don't think it wanted to miss out being born in a hurricane, do you?" Joanna said. "There's a song one of the girls sings about the Ocean Child. You'll have to hear it sometime." Hurry up, Kathy! she thought crossly. You could hardly wait. Now get here.

"I hope you know something about this," she said conversationally, "because I don't. I've had three, and I've seen movies, but I'd hate to set up a practice on that basis."

There was a faint chuckle. "I've done a lot of reading and looked at a lot of diagrams, and Dr. Poole says I'm fine. But I'm so scared—" She caught her breath at another contraction. "And I don't think he'll wait much longer."

"Are you sure it's a boy or just hoping?" *For heaven's sake, Kathy! Get here!*

"It's a boy. I'm over thirty, so I had amnio—oh, God—I can't—" Her legs writhed under the coverlet, and her head twisted back and forth on the pillows. "I'm sorry, but—"

"Don't try to talk," Joanna told her. "I know about the test. And here come the Marines."

36

They had left Willy with the children, and Cindy was making cocoa for them all. Barry and Terence were somewhere around the harbor.

Linnie had been right about Kathy. A large new plastic bag gave up a stack of newspapers to go between sheet and mattress; sheets, towels, soft old diapers; a large apron; a length of new cotton twine and her best shears, sealed in a freezer bag. "I sterilized them *before* I put them in there," she said. She radiated self-confidence. Her fair hair seemed charged with extra electricity, you expected to see it sparking off her fingertips. "Come on, let's fix this bed, no sense ruining the mattress if we don't have to. Can you kind of roll over, Selina?"

"Call me Sheena," Selina gasped, rolling onto her side with Joanna's help. "If we're going to be so intimate. . . . I'm sorry to make all this trouble. . . . I'm sorry I've been so aloof—"

"But it's so nice of you not to disappoint Kathy," Van said dryly. "This will make up for everything." She had brought crib blankets and a pan to wash the baby in.

"We'd better scrub," said Kathy efficiently.

"*You'd* better scrub," said Van. "You're going to catch him."

"Oh, gosh!" said Kathy, looking about as old as Cindy. "Hey, I don't want to act like the head hooter or anything. I mean, just take over, and—"

"You don't think we'd deprive you of it, do you?" asked Joanna. Kathy grinned and went out to the kitchen.

"Shouldn't somebody be boiling water?" Selina asked breathlessly.

"You mean for coffee afterward?" said Joanna. "Or would you rather

271

have tea? I'm taking the orders now." Selina tried to laugh, and it came out as a shriek.

"*Oh, God!* I didn't—I don't want—" Her eyes went wild. She gathered up the bedclothes in her white-knuckled fists.

"Take my hands," Joanna said. Selina's grip was so frantically strong that Joanna had to clench her jaws to keep back a grunt of pain; she had visions of ending this adventure with broken fingers, if not two broken wrists. She wondered if she could possibly look as composed as Van, who was tucking an extra pillow behind Selina's back. *Are you nervous?* she mouthed over Selina's rolling head.

Van looked up at the ceiling and blew hard, then winked at her, and immediately she felt better. The house trembled in a blast of wind, reminding them that the storm was still going on. Joanna had forgotten the storm entirely until this moment.

"Yell if you want to, Sheena," she said. "Who's got a better right? And it may help."

"I doubt it." Selina gave her a twisted smile. "I thought because I wanted him so much, somehow it wouldn't hurt so much."

"That's the great mother trap," said Van. "We all think it'll be a breeze, but it's more like a hurricane."

Kathy returned. "I missed my vocation," she said happily. "Why didn't I ever want to be a doctor? And it's too late now. I could never pick enough crabmeat to put me through medical school. I think we need more light in here." Van pushed back the curtains. Joanna prayed alternately to be able to endure Selina's grip and for everything to go all right.

Selina cried out just once more. "*Felix!*" she shouted as if for him to rescue her from assassins. "Felix, help me! Save me!"

The three looked at one another across her arching body, and no one spoke. After that she gave herself up to pushing, resting, breathing, pushing again, and the baby came fast.

"Red hair!" Kathy said. "Now if he comes out talking we'll know he takes after his uncle Roy—" She stopped herself and gave the others an appalled glance. Selina didn't notice. With sweat and tears streaming down her face, she was able to smile as her red-headed broad-shouldered son was born. He was *there* protesting through the vane of the storm pounding about their heads. Selina let go so quickly Joanna almost lost her balance. Kathy, still professional though she was very flushed and she had to blink her glistening eyes, laid the baby on his mother's stomach, tied off the cord in two places, and cut between them. "I watched the whole thing when Danny was born," she said to her fascinated audience. "And I asked questions. I *should* have been a doctor, damn it! Now let's hope the afterbirth comes right along. You want to save it and bury it, Sheena?"

"For heaven's sake, why?" Selina asked faintly.

"It's supposed to make the baby smart, or lucky, or something."

"He's already that," Selina said. "Listen to him. You didn't even have to clean out his mouth so he could cry. He came out all ready. And he's lucky, being born here with all of you."

Kathy sat down abruptly; she had gone very white, and suddenly she burst into tears. Van washed the baby, who stopped crying in the warm bath; she diapered him and put him into one of Anne's baby nightgowns and into Selina's arms. Immediately she put him to the breast, and he began to suck.

Kathy stumbled her way to the kitchen, sobbing. Joanna understood the reaction. The last hour seemed to have been one of the climactic ones of her own life. Van stood looking out the window at the harbor. "The lulls are longer," she said. "It's passing." Selina was oblivious of everything but the sucking baby.

Kathy came in with her face washed and said as if nothing had happened to her, "We'd better make this bed up fresh."

"I don't know how I can thank you all," said Selina. "I just regret all the time I shut you out, but I—" Her eyes went back to the small red-gold head.

"I've done the same thing myself," Vanessa said. "And it's your own business, so never apologize, never explain."

"I think we should thank *you*, Sheena," Joanna said. "You didn't intend this, but you've given us quite an experience."

"Did you ever see such blue eyes?" Selina murmured. "He's looking right into mine. I think he sees me."

Kathy stuffed the laundry into her plastic bag, saying she had to leave now to tell the children and Willy. "You shouldn't do my washing," Selina protested.

"We've got hogsheads of nice soft rainwater over there," Kathy said. "And I'll be back to stay with you tonight. Willy can sleep at my house."

"I'll bring you supper tonight, Sheena," Van said. She leaned over to touch her finger to the baby's cheek. Then she and Kathy left.

"Would you like that coffee now?" Joanna asked Selina.

"Could I have a cup of tea? I'm parched."

Joanna made tea for them both. The baby slept, cribbed by pillows on one side of the double bed. Selina, leaning on one elbow, said, "I haven't tasted such good tea in nine months. It's pure heaven." She sipped and lay back, smiling at Joanna. There was a wraith of resemblance to both brothers, different as they were from each other. She had the long face, the prominent cheekbones and narrow jaw like Pitt, on a finer scale, and Roy's coloring, with the hair softer and brighter.

"I wish my brothers had come in here to ride out the storm," she said, "so they could see their new nephew right away. They'll be mad about him. But I suppose they went straight home. They'd be thinking Fe— Mr. Drake was here." Color flashed up her white throat and into her face. Joanna tried to think how to get the conversation away from the brothers.

"You must have a name picked out for him," she said.

"Yes, but—"

"You don't have to tell me." She sensed that Selina didn't want to name the baby aloud until the father was present. Did she know that she had called for him? Well, nobody would remind her of that.

Felix, Joanna told him, you rushed inshore before the hurricane, leaving your unborn son in the care of a terrified girl and your handyman. You should have been in this room for her to wring your hands off at the wrists. Unconsciously she rubbed her own.

"I apologize for that," Selina said.

"Never mind, they're still whole. I'm glad I could be useful."

"I have been so scared for nine months!" Selina blurted out. "From the minute I found out! Dr. Poole kept telling me we both were perfectly healthy and all I had to do was to eat right and exercise. I walked miles at night on this place when everybody slept—"

"Good Lord!"

"Oh, not on the rocks, but back and forth along the road between the school and your brother's place over there. And around the harbor, out onto the big wharf and back. Sometimes halfway up the hill to the Homestead. I'd always stick to the roads, but I'd stay out an hour at least."

"It's a wonder nobody saw you and started believing the island was haunted."

She smiled. "I *have* dodged out of sight a few times when somebody came down in the night to put a boat off. And I used to sit on a swing in the schoolyard and listen to the sea breathing in the cove and the gulls calling out on the ledges. Now I think of all I missed by being the way I was. . . . But I didn't know what anybody would think of me, an unmarried woman, pregnant."

"What do you think we are out here?" Joanna asked good-naturedly. "The pregnancy was all that mattered. We knew we'd have the responsibility if anything went wrong."

"Roy and Pitt tried to talk to me, but I think I was a little crazy. I was so positive something was going to happen, and the baby and I both would die." Her hand hovered over the baby's head without quite touching it. "Never mind what the doctor said, I knew better."

"But *why?*"

"Retribution. I'd sinned with a married man. That's what my parents would say, and I guess I believed it. I wasn't that liberated, even if I was living in Boston and owned half a good business. My parents think I'm up there now. My partner mailed them notes and cards from me every so often, and they were never ones to make long-distance calls or expect me to make them, so it was all right." She faltered. "And Fe—Mr. Drake thought I shouldn't mix, that it would be hard on me to be looked at and feel like an object of curiosity."

"Aren't you tired?" Joanna asked. "Maybe I shouldn't sit here and keep you talking."

"I'm keeping myself talking; my strength is as the strength of ten." She laughed. "I feel so wonderful about my baby, but I feel so awful about my parents. Do you mind listening?"

"Not if it makes you feel better." They knew by now that she wasn't in Boston; someone had surely tried to reach her by now, and her partner would have had to say *something;* Joanna wondered what.

"The boys will never tell them about this summer, my being back in Maine and so forth," Selina said confidently. "They resent him, but they're loyal to me." Always *him* or Mr. Drake, never the sacred name. "And the next time I see my parents, I'll be a married woman, and it won't matter to them so much that the baby was born out of wedlock, as long as I'm married to his father." She raised herself up and drank more tea. "Of course, his being divorced will bother them, but they never really approved of his wife. She rather looks down on the natives."

"How soon will that be? Your marriage, I mean."

"Just as soon as possible. I'll go back to Boston, and when the divorce is final, he'll come there for me. It will be for irreconcilable differences. She's not the kind to want a messy case, especially for the girls' sake."

"Have they already talked it over?" Joanna asked.

"Yes. They are going to wait until the girls go back to boarding school in September, and they'll have so much to take up their minds; it will be better for them. I *hope*," she added uncertainly. "I would never want to come between him and the girls. He's a wonderful man!" she exclaimed. "I've always admired him, ever since I was a kid, and now, to know I'm—he's—" She turned to the baby again, tears on her lashes. "It's just *incredible*. He helped me with the business, you know, and he'd come up to Boston to see how I was getting on, and—and—isn't it silly, I get all fussed up like a teenager talking about some movie star she's always worshipped?" She was blushing. "It's the Cinderella syndrome, I guess. Could I have some more hot tea?"

Joanna went out into the kitchen. She could hear Selina murmuring to the sleeping baby. The noise outside was perceptibly less. The search would resume in the morning for *Sweet Helen*; she might never be found, or else there would be wreckage and perhaps a body floating. Or if she *had* ridden out the hurricane somewhere, the brothers would be facing charges of drug trafficking and possibly murder. Whichever it was, the bliss enveloping their sister right now would be savagely ripped away. All one could wish for her now was that it wouldn't happen until tomorrow.

She took in two cups of fresh tea and some Scottish shortbread she found in a tin. "I thought you needed some soul-and-body lashins," she said. "Van will bring you a good meal tonight, but have something more now."

"You have a piece, too." She watched Joanna with bright blue-green eyes, so much like Roy's. "I *hate* thinking what I've missed by being so crazy all these months. People do such ghastly, unspeakable things. Why did I think *I* was such a sinner? And Fe—"

"You might as well say his name," said Joanna.

"I guess it springs from our both being so closemouthed about this whole business. But now it doesn't matter!" she said ebulliently. "The baby is here, and by the time the leaves turn, we'll be a real family. You know," she said with ingenuous self-consciousness, "it was my fault, getting pregnant. I couldn't take the pill, but I thought I had everything under control. Turns out I wasn't that smart. And from the moment he *knew*, and when I said I would never have an abortion—"

Wait a minute, Joanna thought. Did *he* want you to have one? Selina was going on. "And there was never any question in my mind that I'd keep it, no matter what, even if I had to lie to my parents and tell them I'd adopted it, because singles can do that now. Though," she said wryly, "with that hair I'd have a pretty hard time passing him off as a stranger— well, anyway, I had amniocentesis, just to be sure he was all right, and found out he *was* a he. And the next time Felix came to Boston he said we would be married. And I never asked it of him! That's what makes it all the more wonderful!"

At last she was calling him by name. "Was this when he found out it was a boy?"

"Well, of course, that made him pretty happy; he'd always wanted a son. His wife had had two miscarriages, both boys. But the way we felt about each other, it must have been in his mind for a long time. His marriage was going nowhere. They've been keeping up appearances, quietly waiting for the girls to grow up. If there's anything that bothers me about it, it's the girls. But once they find out they aren't losing him, and they must know how things have been between their parents, don't you think?" she appealed.

"I should think so," Joanna agreed.

There was a knock at the kitchen door. She went to it and found Nils and Linnie there, blond heads bare, both smiling. "Terence has been in the store handing out cigars," said Nils. "He said somebody ought to."

"Yes, it's over, and he's beautiful," said Joanna. "And his mother's fine."

"Can we see him?" Linnie asked.

"I shouldn't take you into Selina's room, and he's sleeping now."

"Everybody should have a chance to see him," Linnie said. "He's our baby in a way."

"I'm sure everybody will have a chance," said Joanna. "Look, Van's sending over supper, and Kathy will stay the night, so I'll be home pretty soon."

"How was it, Marm?" Linnie asked. "Terrifying?"

"Once it began, we were all too absorbed, and he came too fast for any of us to be scared." She put an arm around each of them. "But gosh, I'm glad to see you two! It feels like a year since I saw you last!" She kissed Linnie's cheek and then Nils's. There was an impromptu three-way hug.

"Mark's set up a jar in the store," Nils said, "and there's sixty dollars in it already. A present from the island to the new islander."

"That will start a good bank account," said Linnie. "Even Jamie put something in," she added. "Can you believe it?"

"Watch out for flying pigs," said Joanna. She dropped her voice. "Nils, will you call Dr. Poole and tell him? He was expecting her over there. She ought to be gotten off here as soon as possible, and I hope to God she doesn't find out anything about the boys until she's near the doctor. I don't know what could happen. She's so happy now it's heartbreaking."

"I'll try right now," said Nils, "and if the telephone is out in Stonehaven, we'll raise him through the Coast Guard if we have to. They could get a helicopter out here tomorrow."

They kissed again. Linnie's embrace was the nearly strangling hug of a grief-stricken child who wants to hold on to something hard. Then she walked away from them over the wet path with her head down and her hair blowing out in the wind, her hands in her hip pockets.

Her parents stood out on the ledges, letting the soft wind push and pull at them; it was still boisterous, but no longer roaring; the boats were bouncing in the harbor now, instead of fighting their mooring chains. Gulls were busy over the windrows of rockweed piled deep on the shores, and Hank was belligerent among them. The scent of the fresh weed and of the soaked marsh filled the air as the rote filled their ears.

"It won't be as tough for Linnie as for Selina," Joanna said. "But bad enough."

"But she's tough, too," said Nils, "and she has spirit."

"Nils, Felix is the father," she said softly. "He said he'd marry her when he found out it would be a boy. She had the test to be sure the baby's all right, and they find out its sex. She's so damned grateful and adoring, but I keep wondering if he'd have offered if it was a girl. . . . Yes, I know it's none of our business. I'm just thinking out loud."

37

When she went back to the bedroom, Selina was asleep, her pale, narrow face open and defenseless. One arm lay over the pillow above the baby's head. I don't give a damn, Joanna had said, and meant it. Now she felt as protective as if Selina were one of her daughters, with the difference that the instinct could go nowhere, and this was no young girl but a woman who had been free to choose an affair with a married man. But the innate dislike of Felix Drake was still there, as unreasonable as Jamie's, and she knew she could be wronging him. Perhaps he was an honorable and loving man who had endured a dead marriage for the sake of his children. Perhaps he had always intended to marry Selina, baby or not.

Perhaps Selina didn't need pity for adoring him, perhaps he was worthy of it. But she was to be pitied for what lay outside the sleep of innocence. Her tomorrow was going to be dreadful indeed.

Joanna felt the reaction in her own legs; one never forgot what it was like to hear the words that could never be taken back, because the fact could never be erased. *It had happened.* You cannot believe it, and at the same time you know it is true. Someone is dead. Why am I assuming that? she thought angrily. Because Alec drowned, because Young Charles and Fort Percy disappeared, that doesn't mean that Pitt and Roy are dead. Even to be disgraced by them, seeing them go to prison, would be better for their family than forever imagining how they died.

She raised the shades in the living room. The boats were only rocking now, and there were lightning bursts of sunshine between the rapidly moving clouds; swatches of forget-me-not blue splashed across the water to reflect the suggestion in the sky. The heaped rockweed glittered blindingly in those instants, the boats flashed like glass. Along the outer shores the unremitting thunder of the sea went on, but the hurricane was now heading for Nova Scotia.

Gulls flew low over the harbor waters, Hank among them. An eider flock rode the surge, the ospreys were already back circling and piping, the shags black on the ledges of Eastern Harbor Point; everything as charged with excited greed as the youngsters would be to go stravaging around the shore, and not just the youngsters. She could feel the old urge in herself, that atavistic warlike drive to get there *first*.

Kathy passed by the front windows, carrying a casserole between padded mitts, a canvas tote bag hung over her arm. Joanna went to meet her in the kitchen. She'd scrubbed her face, but it was still pink around the nostrils and the lids. "I couldn't help it," she said defiantly. "It was just too—I don't know if *wonderful* is the word. Awesome, the high school kids say about everything, even a new soft drink. But this was *truly* awesome. It just broke me up. How is she?" She set the casserole on the stove. "Van just brought this over. Lobster stew."

"She's sleeping as hard as the baby is."

"So it's really Felix," Kathy whispered. "I guess none of us was surprised." Her eyes were watering again. "Damn it, I keep wanting to dissolve. All I can think now is, that world across the bay is going to be pretty brutal, once she leaves this place."

"And there's not a thing we can do about it." Joanna put her boots on in the shed and gathered up her rain clothes to carry over her arm. "What did the kids say? And Willy?"

"Willy's all of a grin, he can't stop it. The little ones can't believe it. You mean there was a *baby* in this house, and they didn't *know* it? Where did she *hide* it all this time? Eyes like saucers, and they wanted to come right over and see it. Cindy tried to act bored, but she's thrilled, too, and wants to give him a present but she can't figure out what." She began unpacking her tote bag. Besides her pajamas, she had a bedpan. "Do you think I should let her up to go to the bathroom?" she asked earnestly. "They do in the hospital."

Joanna smiled and shrugged. "Figure it with her. You two are the experts."

Kathy blushed. "I was scared foolish," she confided. "I hope nobody gets caught again like this. Or if they do, I hope I'm *off* the island."

Van was taking over for her in the morning. Joanna walked slowly home, savoring the hour as if she'd had a miraculous escape this afternoon, as if more than Selina and the baby had been at risk. Liza came out to hear the news, Maggie Dinsmore ran across the sodden path. Ralph Percy was at the well and shouted that Marge would beat him over the head if he didn't find out all he could.

"He came without any trouble, very fast, he weighs about eight pounds, and he and his mother both are fine," Joanna told them. "I don't know if I can say as much for the midwives." Nobody mentioned Felix.

Linnie had the pan of biscuits ready to go into the oven when her mother came in the door. She had opened a jar of last summer's raspberry jam and was cutting cheese. Nils was slicing cold pot roast. "Well, Marm, ready to hang out your shingle?" he asked her.

She held up her hands, spreading and flexing her fingers. "As something to hang on to, I'm an expert. Better than a knotted towel anytime. But you should have seen Kathy cutting the cord and tying it with bait bag twine."

Nils had reached Stonehaven by telephone from the store; the doctor would call the Coast Guard about getting the helicopter out there early tomorrow. It was being used in the renewed search, but he thought this would be a special case because it involved the sister of the missing men, a mother with a newborn infant.

Linnie set the table in stoic silence while he talked. Apparently she had come to some resolution within herself: Either Pitt was dead or, if he had survived, he was in serious trouble. She was no longer rejecting the probabilities with outrage and tears.

Jamie came in, carrying Pip. "I thought you might bring Rosa home for supper," his mother said.

He didn't look directly at her. "Didn't see her around. How they doing across the harbor?"

"Fine, for now. Ignorance is bliss."

"You find out if Drake is the father or not?"

"I don't see any need to keep it a secret. Yes. And she says he's going to marry her."

"Hey, somebody ought to call him!" Jamie's face lightened with mischief. "Tell him, 'Congratulations, you've got a fine son.' Or maybe give the message to his wife. That's when the you-know-what hits the fan."

"Thank you for restraining yourself, Jamie," said Joanna.

"I thought you'd appreciate it, after your afternoon."

"Well, I can truthfully say it was the most interesting hurricane I've been through."

"So he's going to marry her, huh? She'd better have it in writing. Notarized."

"Come on, why can't you believe he really loves her?" Linnie flared at him. "Maybe you can't stand him, but that doesn't mean anything. You can't stand most of the people you know, and you accuse them of every crime in the book. You must make up these things to excuse your own craziness!"

Jamie reached over and patted her arm, and she jerked away from him. "Don't patronize me!" She left the table and went out, saying loudly, "I need some good, fresh, *pure* air!"

"Well, I tried," Jamie said to his parents. "I haven't mentioned those two poor bastards all day, at least not where she can hear me. As for Drake, I'll bet he'll never marry that girl. I told you there was something rotten about him, and it's not just this drug business."

"Nobody's named him yet in that," his father reminded him.

"They will," Jamie said confidently. "You don't think the rest will stand for seeing him skating around free and clear, do you? Do you think Henry Coates will keep quiet? No, by God! If he's taking it, he won't take it alone, he'll bring everybody down with him."

Joanna said wearily, "I would just like it all to be over with. I'd like Selina and the baby to be somewhere else when she finds out what's been going on. And then maybe we can get back to what passes for normal around here."

She went to bed early, appreciating the lack of wind. The seas still resounded on the outer shores, and some islanders had gone to see the surf in the rich evening light. Children played ball in the field, Hank squawked, Tiger barked; voices sounded from across the harbor, the usual birds sang around the house as if there'd been no interruption since yesterday. Joanna lay with her book on her stomach, luxuriating. She grieved for Linnie, she winced away from what Selina must know tomorrow; but her bed felt good, and for tonight she was not going to think about anything else. She was done with this day, and tomorrow was twelve hours away.

Nils came up to bed before dark and was blessedly willing not to discuss anything, except to say that Linnie was downstairs drinking cocoa and eating cold buttered biscuits.

The helicopter came in midmorning of a day burnished by storm to a diamond brilliance. It landed in the meadow between Schoolhouse and Long coves, and all the children and mothers collected to watch; Sam and Richard had stayed in for the event instead of rushing out to see how their traps had fared, and even Linnie was there, for a chance of seeing the baby.

The corpsmen carried the stretcher along the back path to the schoolhouse, out across the recent flooded schoolyard, and between the old stone gateposts for Hillside Farm, along the road and into the meadow, where the field flowers of late July were already erect again and dancing in the northwest breeze. Van, Kathy, and a stiffly proud Cindy walked beside the stretcher, carrying Selina's luggage. For traveling, the baby was dressed in Peter Fennell's first clothes and wrapped in Anne Barton's blankets.

The corpsmen were genial and praised the baby extravagantly, but meeting Selina's smile must have been as hard for them as for the other watchers; they knew who she was and that she didn't know yet about her brothers. They waited a few moments before putting her aboard, so everyone could get a glimpse of the island's new baby and wish her well.

"I just wish I'd known you all before," she said emotionally. She squeezed the hands of the women who had attended her. "I can't ever thank you enough," she whispered. "Never in my life. You all made it a wonderful experience, not a terrible one. My boy is going to grow up knowing all about it. His middle name will be Bennett."

Kathy leaned down impulsively to kiss her cheek, and after a moment Van did the same, a rare gesture from her. Joanna was the last; she was carrying a sealed envelope containing one hundred and fifty dollars and a card Liza had drawn early this morning. It showed the stork trying to find Bennett's Island in a hurricane and being flagged down by three stick figures labeled "J.," "K.," and "V." There was also a message: "From the old Bennett's Islanders to the brand-new Bennett's Islander, with all our hopes and prayers for a good life for him and his mother."

"Open this when you get settled in your bed at Stonehaven," Joanna told her. "And don't lose it on the way. Where's your handbag?"

"Here." Van held it up, and Joanna slipped the envelope into it. Then she, too, kissed Selina's cheek.

"Selina, if ever you want to come back here and really get acquainted, you *come*. You'll have your pick of beds."

It was all she could say to someone heading so innocently, so happily, into tragedy, carried by the same helicopter which would soon return to the search for her brothers.

"Oh, I'll be back," she said merrily. "Don't forget, Felix and I have our own house here. Next time I won't keep the doors locked and the shades down."

She was loaded aboard, and everybody hurried back out of the way. The helicopter lifted off, watched with awe not only by the children; it was so huge, so exotic, rising out of this flowery meadow. It took off over Long Cove, then over Tenpound and the northern end of Brigport, heading for Stonehaven. The children rushed off to their own affairs; the women walked home singly or in groups, as the gulls flew out at night. They spoke quietly, if at all.

Linnie went out to look after her gear. Joanna had a mug-up with her sisters-in-law in Liza's kitchen and gave them a detailed account of the birth. Then they separated to the day's occupations, and she and Pip went to see what was left of her garden; she'd refused to look at it when she'd gone out earlier to feed and water the hens. She was agreeably surprised to find her tomato plants still standing and other plants muddy but intact. The lettuce had suffered the most.

The light wind brought a familiar engine sound to her, and she walked around to the front of the house to look. *Drake's Pride* was coming in. So he'd returned as soon as he could. She went back to the garden. When he'd seen Willy and heard about Selina, he'd doubtless take off for Stonehaven at once. It would be a help if he could be with her when she heard the news, whatever it was. Then she was going to have to meet with her parents, who, on their side, must cope with their sons' disappearance and their daughter's illegitimate son by a married man. Whether the baby would be curse or comfort, there was no guessing.

I'm sorry for them all, Joanna thought, but now I can truthfully and thankfully say that it's none of my business.

Now she was free to take off for Bull Cove. Under the northwest wind the seas were flattening, all the boats were out; but there was still a deep swell, and there would be good surf on the ledges. She could eat her lunch within the spell of that particular island voice. Pip was watching her pour tea into her thermos bottle; he knew the signs. "You can't go," she told him. "You get too close to the surf when you're chasing sandpipers." He leaned seductively against her legs. "No," she said. "NO."

"You sound very emphatic," someone said from the sun parlor. It was Felix Drake, with his Greek fisherman's cap in his hand, smiling at her surprise. He was spotless in tan sailcloth slacks and a madras shirt. His gray curls had been freshly cropped to a glossy plush, his skin had the smooth texture and roseate flush of a nectarine, and he was spicily scented. "I knocked; but you were talking with your friend, and you didn't hear."

But Pip would have heard, she thought. You came in without knocking.

"I'd like very much to talk with you," he said. Automatically she waved him to a chair by the table and sat down opposite him, prepared to be fair and see him only as the man whom Selina had described to her. It would be easier if he didn't try so hard; too much molasses was worse than not enough. Pip sniffed appreciatively at his shoes.

"I suppose you're on your way to Stonehaven to be with Selina and break the news about her brothers," Joanna said. "Have you heard anything at all about them this morning?"

"Not a word. My God, Mrs. Sorensen, what an appalling mess!" His eyes rounded and bulged; his voice burned with affronted astonishment. "My old friend Henry Coates! I couldn't believe it! But when he was caught in the act of receiving cocaine, what can anyone do but believe it? Henry Coates! He's the last man on earth I'd ever connect with drug dealing. The community is reeling over there. Absolutely reeling. His family has gone into seclusion, my wife tried to reach Sophie, but—" Again the spread hands and a hopeless shrug.

Jamie would say this all was an act. Joanna was not concerned with that. "Selina," she said, and he was off again.

"Of course, I'm not surprised at the boys. If they were lobstering for Henry, they were part of it, there was no way they couldn't be. And Beecham's death by foul play, their finding the body—it all hangs together." He took out a linen handkerchief and wiped his forehead. "Shocking. Ghastly. We're mature people, Mrs. Sorensen; we can be objective about this. You'll understand I'm not cold-blooded when I say it would be better for everybody if they *are* lost. It will save the family untold grief."

"Well, I don't know about that," said Joanna. "But I'm sure you and the baby will help Selina a lot, and her parents, too, once they can accept the situation."

"Oh, Lord! I forgot what I came for! I wanted to thank you for your kindness to Selina, for being there for her."

"Mrs. Barton and Mrs. Campion were there, too," she said. "We were all together. But it was Kathy Campion who had the tools ready, you might say. And Carol Fennell came up with the going-away outfit for the baby."

"Oh, I intend to thank everybody, and properly, you can be sure of that. But I wanted particularly to have a word with you right away."

Stop nodding and smiling, she thought, and get on with it. *By the pricking of my thumbs, / Something wicked this way comes.* Now why did she think of that right now?

"Selina talked alone with you?" he asked. She nodded. "Well, I don't know what she told you—" He lifted his handkerchief to his forehead again, then thought better of it.

"Nothing to your discredit," she said politely. His relief was perceptible. He stood up.

"Thank you again for being so kind to her," he said. "You island people are the salt of the earth. Now I must see how my gear stood the storm."

"Aren't you going straight to Stonehaven to be with Selina and see your son?"

Half turned toward the door, he went immobile; the hand with the handkerchief stopped on the way to his hip pocket, the smile was left on his face like a fossil imprint in split rock, and his eyes became opaque. If he was startled, she was startled even more by the response to her question.

"I didn't think your planning to marry her was to your discredit, Mr. Drake," she said gently. "And anyway, we'd have known you're the baby's father because she cried out for you when she was in labor."

He sat down again and looked at her blankly. This time she actually saw the sweat spring out on his forehead, and he reddened dangerously; she saw a vein became prominent on his forehead. "I don't intend to ask my wife for a divorce, Mrs. Sorensen. Not that it's any of your business."

"Then don't tell me about it," she said sharply. "Tell Selina." She wanted him out of her house. *Something wicked this way comes.* But he didn't move.

"You don't understand. It's this drug business. I can't taint my daughters' lives with this scandal." No smiles now, no molasses, unless that was what he was choking on so his words bolted out in uneven bunches. "They were my children first, you know. But I'll look out for Selina. You see"—he sat forward eagerly—"I've talked everything over with my wife, and we've decided there is too much good left in our marriage to throw it away, and we owe it to the girls to try to hold it together. She's been absolutely *wonderful.*" He was almost tearful about it. "This magnificent woman wants to take that baby and raise it! And no child could ever have a better mother."

"Except for its own mother," Joanna put in.

"That's a moot point." Relaxing, he sat back, and put one ankle up on the other knee. "Selina's no fool; she'll be reasonable. She is basically a career woman, who wouldn't be satisfied giving twenty-four hours a day to a child. My wife is all mother."

But she was boring, wasn't she? Joanna thought. "Selina's basically a woman who adores the man she thinks is going to marry her."

"She'll understand." That smile, that unguent ease were sliding back again. Buttery Ben. "She'll have to understand that I have a responsibility to my daughters."

"It didn't seem to bother you much before," she observed.

"That was before this drug scandal. I can't take the chance on letting this filth touch them in any way."

"You mean that Selina's involved?" Joanna asked. "That she *knew?*"

"Of course not!" he said testily, getting up again.

"So about the time she finds out what her brothers have been up to, whether they're alive or dead, she'll also find out that because of them you can't marry her." She stood up. "If you ever intended to, which I doubt."

"Naturally I'll wait till she's stronger—" Then her last words caught up with him. He turned on her with open animosity. "I don't have to listen to this! And she didn't have to get pregnant, the little fool. Or keep it! She owes me, by God. I set her up in business, and it's time she remembered that!"

Joanna felt a manic urge to hurl something—anything—into his face. She was saved by a footstep outside the door and Nils's cool voice. "Hello!" he said in mild surprise, and Drake's cap flew out of his hand. "Too loppy to stay out there," Nils said, coming in. "No sense wearing myself out trying to keep my footing. But I've got a mess of lobsters for us in a crate off the wharf."

Drake's smile came back like a nervous tic. "Good morning, Skipper."

"Would you mind," Nils asked courteously, "calling me Nils or Mr. Sorensen if you want to be formal?"

"Mr. Drake," Joanna explained in a careful monotone, "was just telling me that he isn't going to marry Selina because of her brothers. She's not good enough for him now. But he's going to take the baby, and he and his wife will raise it."

Nils nodded. "Agreed to that, has she?"

Joanna could see Drake's relief at escaping from her to this reasonable man. "No, but she will," he said with assurance. "She knows what kind of life my wife and I can give my son."

"That's right," said Nils. "Seems to me I heard it was your wife who has the money."

"*That is a lie!* Not that it's any of your"—he bit back the profanity— "business."

"No," Nils agreed, "but we all sort of feel that the baby is because he's a citizen of Bennett's Island. He didn't have to paint a name on a boat to convince us. He was born an islander."

"You narrow, hidebound, inbred rednecks have never gotten over that, have you?" He was nearly choking on it. "Do you think this rockpile is *sacred?*"

"In a way. We're all pretty fussy about what comes onto it. It's a matter of self-defense. We're scared of pollution." Nils opened the screen door and handed Drake the Greek fisherman's cap. Drake snatched it and walked out, fitting the cap on his head; even irate, he automatically cocked it with both hands.

"Mr. Drake," Nils said quietly. Felix stopped, staring straight ahead for an instant, then pivoted.

"*What?*" The effect was of a snarl.

"It might be a good idea for you to take up your gear as soon as you can."

"Is that a threat?"

"A suggestion," Nils said politely. For Joanna the meeting of the eyes lasted unbearably long. Then Drake swung himself around and walked off down the path, stiffly erect.

They kept silent until he'd turned off past Philip's house. Tiger received no blandishments this time.

"Can you *believe* him?" Joanna said in awe.

"That is one of the biggest SOBs I've ever met," said Nils. "I'm only sorry I didn't arse him off the doorstep with my boot."

"Why, Nils!" she said with pleasure, and he grinned.

"You know, Jamie was right all along. We'll have to tell him that and make his day."

38

That afternoon Joanna invited Rosa home to supper for baked stuffed lobsters and, taken by surprise in front of Maggie Dinsmore and Marjorie Percy, Rosa couldn't think of an excuse not to go, at least not one that she cared to give in public. She wasn't keen to be alone tonight, even though sitting at the same table with Jamie wasn't what she might have chosen for company. She told herself it was the letdown after the tremendous excitement of the hurricane and the drama of the birth. She hadn't seen the baby, she'd been out checking on her gear when the helicopter came, but she had contributed to the jar in the store. She heard that it was red-headed, the way she used to imagine Con's baby would be, and how proud and happy the mother was, so whenever and whatever Selina heard about her brothers she would still have this.

Depression sat on Rosa like a wet fog, blinding, muffling, suffocating, stupefying. And frightening, when you realized you'd been sitting staring at nothing, hearing nothing, for at least five minutes. She plunged her face into cold water again and again. She changed into a fresh shirt and slacks and looked around for something to contribute to supper at the Sorensens. She had nothing to take but a poetry anthology she had borrowed awhile ago from Van, to look for new songs, and it had some of the old classics in it like *Lochinvar*. Joanna had been trying to remember that one day on the wharf when Hugo went out of the harbor on his way to Brigport and someone said, "There goes Young Lochinvar."

She picked the book up now and opened it to a marked verse in a poem called "A Forsaken Garden." She wondered again why Van had marked it; had she known such a spot? Maybe there'd been someone before Barry. For Rosa it was very sad, and not with the rich sentimental sadness that helped make up good tunes.

All are at one now, roses and lovers,
Not known of the cliffs and the fields and the sea.
Not a breath of the time that has been hovers
In the air now soft with a summer to be.
Not a breath shall there sweeten the seasons hereafter
Of the flowers or the lovers that laugh now or weep,
When, as they that are free now of weeping and laughter,
We shall sleep.

She saw the fields, cliffs and wild roses of Sou'west Point and suddenly desired to go there now and stay through the long summer evening, alone, and make her way home in the twilight over the pale rocks still holding the day's heat, with the sea gleaming and rippling at their feet.

She took the book and went down to the Sorensen house. Nils was pleasant as usual; he always seemed glad to see her. Jamie gave her one of those formal nods. Linnie, setting the table, said wanly, "Hi, Rosa." Her eyes seemed larger than usual because they looked so hollowed. Joanna took the book and at once found *Lochinvar*. "Gosh, how I loved that," she said happily. There were a few minutes to wait before the lobsters were ready. The conversation stayed away from the Bainbridges; everyone but Linnie worked at this, and she was so unnaturally quiet she dominated the dining room simply by being in it. Pip, driven into a mild frenzy by the presence of lobster, walked back and forth, emitting loud cries whenever he caught someone's eye. Joanna had boiled one lobster for him and picked out the meat; he would have it when the family sat down to their meal.

Hurricane damage along the coast was a good safe topic, interrupted when Sam came up with a plate of hot yeast rolls wrapped in a clean dish towel. "Mom just took these out of the oven. She thought they'd go good with baked lobsters." He was keyed up about more than hot rolls. "Hey, you heard the news? They just found *Sweet Helen*!"

From the corner of her eye Rosa saw Linnie, in the act of picking up the cat, turn into stone.

"Where?" Jamie asked.

"Gorry, I don't remember the name of the place. Little island way up in the bay. Nobody lives on it now." He sobered so quickly it was as if he'd just exchanged a laughing mask for a grim one. "She was broken up. That big pretty boat all chowdered up on a ledge in this cove." The tip of his tongue ran over his upper lip. With a frightened glance at his cousin Linnie he said almost inaudibly, "They found *them*, too."

"You might as well tell us the rest of it, Sam," Nils said. Linnie had put down the cat. She leaned against the table, her hands behind her holding to the edge.

"Roy was floating facedown; he had on a life jacket, but he was tangled up in some kelp, kept him kind of in one place." Sam looked as if he felt a little sick. "Pitt was rolled up in the rockweed on the shore. . . . Some fishermen went around there today to see how their traps were after the storm, and they found 'em. They'd tied up on this old mooring, see, and they were in the lee all right; but the mooring was weak and couldn't stand the strain on it. She went on this ledge, and they must have tried to make it ashore."

The screen door at the end of the sun parlor closed almost silently behind Linnie. Joanna moved, and Nils stood up; but Jamie was the quickest. He had gone out behind her before she could have escaped across the yard.

Sam was almost tearful with distress. "Well, you asked me, Uncle Nils," he said plaintively.

"Yes, I did, and you did all right, Sam," said Nils. "Linnie had to hear it sometime."

"I guess I'll go back," Sam mumbled.

Joanna put an arm around his stocky shoulders and gave him a hug. "Are you too big to kiss now? Guess I'll chance it." She kissed his cheek. "Thank your mother for the rolls. They look elegant."

"They *are* elegant. So long, everybody." His dark eyes moved timidly toward the back door, and then he left. He jumped off the doorstep and ran.

Joanna blew out a long breath. "Well, now we know. And now Linnie has to get over it. . . . I wonder about Selina. Dr. Poole said he'd try to keep all of it away from her till a close friend could break the news, but. . . ." Her voice trailed off. "Dead," she murmured. "In the kelp and the rockweed. Why do you always feel it can't be true? I know it must be, but it's not sinking in."

"If nobody minds, I guess I'll go home, too," said Rosa.

"I'm not heartless," said Nils, "but I'm hungry, I can't help that, and the food's ready. Come back and sit down, Rosa. We all feel pretty bleak, but there's nothing we can do for the boys now, and nothing for Linnie, but maybe Jamie can."

"Yes, sit down," Joanna said. "You'll be doing us a favor. Otherwise we'll sit here staring at each other. If we're not bleeding for one child, it's for another one. And if it's not enough to suffer for your own, you can always suffer for someone else's. Selina, for instance."

"Drake must be with her," Rosa suggested, and at Joanna's expression she added, "Isn't he?"

Joanna mimicked Drake's smile. "Sit down and I'll tell you all about dear Felix."

Jamie and Linnie hadn't come back when Rosa left, around eight. "I hope this means something," Joanna said. "I hope they're together. I couldn't believe it when he took off after her."

The nightly baseball game was going on when Rosa walked home on the other side of the spruce windbreak. Marjorie called from her front porch as Rosa crossed her own lawn. "You heard the news?"

"Yep. Awful." She went on into the house and took her guitar down and began working out a tune.

It was absorbing enough to keep at bay, almost, the vision of *Sweet Helen's* destruction and the two deaths. To be pounded to pieces on a ledge was a hideous death for a boat, but to drown, fighting it and knowing while you struggled that you were going to die—she could not imagine it without wanting to vomit not only her baked stuffed lobster but everything she had eaten for the day. She lost track of her tune, couldn't remember the words, and switched desperately to old hymns known by heart from her childhood.

Dusk came into the kitchen, and with it Jamie, as quietly as the shadows filling the room. He leaned against the counter without speaking. "Well?" she said hoarsely. She laid the guitar on the table and got herself a drink of water. "How's Linnie?"

"She's back at the house. We went all the way to Bull Cove, and we talked enough to make up for the last ten years and do for the next."

"Good," she said tersely. "Want coffee, soda, or a beer?"

"Nothing yet." He went across the kitchen and sat down by the window, tipped back in the rocker, feet on the sill. She remained by the sink.

"Your mother told me about Felix Drake and how your father showed him the door."

"God, I wish I'd seen that!" he said fervently. "Except I wouldn't have let the bastard into the house in the first place. Maybe he's not mixed up with the drugs, but he's just as rotten. Telling her he was all haired up, couldn't wait to get married, and then backing off because of her brothers." The rocking chair creaked; his feet came down off the windowsill and struck the floor hard. "The son of a bitch never intended to get a divorce! This shit came along just in time to be a handy excuse for him. She wasn't supposed to get pregnant, she wouldn't have an abortion, and I'll bet he was hiding her out to save his own skin. He sure didn't want her to show up like that around Coates Cove."

"She wouldn't go there, I understood," Rosa offered. "She didn't want her parents to know."

"Yep, but if she married the kid's father, it would be all right. Now he doesn't want her, but he wants the kid. *His son*, for God's sake! As if he did the whole thing! And he'll pressure her, the horse's arse. You can't get rid of that kind short of shooting them. Telling her she can't do anything for the kid, and he can do everything." He sprang up from the chair. "A man who'll try to steal a baby from its mother is as bad as a woman who'll steal it from its father before it's born."

The words plummeted through the dim silence like stones down a well, and with a curious light-headedness she knew what they meant.

"*Eloise?*" she said.

"She told me she was pretty sure she was pregnant. That was the day before we went on that famous picnic to Pirate Island."

She could hardly believe she was hearing this, and she hardly dared take a good breath or shift her position for fear of stopping him. His voice rushed roughly on, headlong in the dusk.

"I wanted her to get a divorce. Hell, I'd been wanting her to do that from the start, but now I began really talking it up so we could get married right away. Well, she kept saying she couldn't have it, she'd die, she was too young to be a mother, she'd be ugly. Pregnant women were gross. Everything was gross with her. Christ, how I hated that word!"

"What happened?" Cautiously she unfolded her aching arms.

"You know what. Before we could argue it out, all hell broke loose. I came over here in all innocence to ask Charles about giving me a piece of land to build on, Riddell shows up to say I burned down his cottage, and I went back to Brigport, and she'd gone out of there like the devil in a gale of wind. A good thing. I might have strangled her. I felt like it."

He stopped to get his pipe started and to try to calm himself, she knew. She wondered if there was a tremor in his hands like the one in his last words.

"But after the smoke died away," he said finally, "I started wondering if she really was pregnant and if it was my kid that got flushed down a drain somewhere, or whatever they do with them." Another short silence. She shifted her weight from one foot to the other.

"Times when I'd feel half crazy for not knowing, not able to find out, but not wanting to either. She went away somewhere. Did she have it and give it away? My kid? Or did she have an abortion and kill my kid?" His voice went thick on the last word, and she knew he was feeling in his pockets for a handkerchief. Not speaking, she handed him a paper towel, and he blew his nose.

She wanted to weep with him. She wanted to take him in her arms. She said, "Marry me, and start a baby you'll be sure of."

She was as thunderstruck as he was, but she had passed the point of no return. "I wish I could tell you there was one on the way now, but we've been too careful. We don't have to be careful now." And maybe someday I'll tell you what I think: that she wasn't pregnant at all but it was a good way to make you throw a fit. She was getting bored with steady old Jamie, and Ivor wasn't doing too well by her either.

The silence in the room had a peculiar quality that made her ears ring, as if she had been caught inside a giant conch shell. She expected him to leave, aghast, in the next instant and avoid her hereafter. He said something, but she couldn't hear it, or wouldn't. "Come on out," she said. "I can't breathe in here." He shrugged and followed her.

They went along the path she had taken with Linnie, toward the steady cannonade of surf. The darkening woods were aromatic from the fresh green tips ripped from the spruces and thickly covering the ground. Broken branches dangled or lay across the path, and a few old trees had been toppled. Jamie and Rosa climbed over bristling trunks and tangled boughs, and he said in a perfectly ordinary manner, "I'll clean up this mess with the chain saw." She heard him through the havoc in her head; waves of heat and chill broke alternately over her. When they came out on the bluff into the fast-fading pallor of the afterglow, she was sweating in anticipation of the way he would handle this. He might even try to be kind. That would be much more awful than if he had simply said, "No, thanks," back there and walked out of her house. She was afraid to look at him now.

The sea was all in motion, an expanse of crests luminous in the oncoming twilight. All along this shore from the breakwater to Sou'west Point the combers rolled toward the rocks, broke into gleaming chaos, withdrew, and drove shoreward again, but without the ferocious energy of the storm. From up on the bluff the two heard the heavy rattling of the stones in Barque Cove as they were drawn out by the force of tons of water and then hurled in again. The pungency of the ocean's upheaval and the fresh detritus thrown clear of the surf was strong enough to cause a prickling in the nostrils.

Jamie stood with his hands in his pockets, looking out over the sea. She knew he was trying to think what to say to her, and she couldn't endure this.

"Look!" The word jumped out like a shout above the roar of water. "Look, I was a little crazy back there, and—" She wished she'd brought a dipper of water with her; her throat felt like a dried-out and splintery spruce lath. "So I'll forget it if you will. I mean—oh, *hell!*"

He turned toward her, smiling. "But I've already accepted. Why not? That's not what you'd call romantic, but I mean it." He pointed his finger at her and said severely, "I'm not marrying you just to make babies. I'm marrying you because it's time I did, and I can't see myself settling down with anybody else but you."

"Now that *is* romantic," she said, feeling a little giddy.

"Life's too goddamn short for me to go fubbing around forever like something just out of the egg. Roy and Pitt thought they had it made, and tonight where are they? Come here." He pulled her down beside him; it was too early for dew, the turf was still warm and dry, but she wouldn't have cared if it had been soaking.

They lay silently in each other's arms, watching the stars appear. After a time he said drowsily, "Me, married. Eric will bust a gut laughing. He can marry us if he can keep his face straight. Me—*married?*" he repeated, sounding half stunned. "Good God!"

"Are you praying or cursing?" Rosa asked him. He laughed, and nuzzled in her neck.

"Will Jud sell us his house, d'you think? I'm kind of fond of it."

39

The next morning was fine and warm; the seas had subsided into long, slow, amiable swells, and as long as it didn't breeze on it would be a good day to make up lost work. Everyone was up early, and a few boats were heading out at first light. Unexpectedly Jamie came across to the house for breakfast, and afterward he and Linnie walked to the shore together. Nils and Joanna purposely stayed back.

"Something good has come out of this mess," Nils commented. "If it lasts."

"If it's happening now, it can happen again," Joanna said. "They're growing up. I just wish Linnie didn't have to do it this way. Knowing what Pitt had done, and was doing, is as hard on her as the drowning."

"You survived worse," he said, watching the two pass the well, fair heads bent; Jamie talking, Linnie listening, or appearing to listen. It was hard to tell about her now. Her father said, "We have to think there's something ahead for her that's a hell of a lot better than Pitt Bainbridge."

Linnie had been quiet enough to keep a constant ache in Joanna's throat. She herself was haunted by the picture of the young bodies entangled in the kelp and rockweed, and she knew from experience how the two could people Linnie's nights. She had spoken with such tender bedazzlement of Pitt's smile; now she had a choice between contemplating what Pitt had really been behind that infrequent smile and imagining how his drowned face had looked when the fishermen found him.

It was as if Linnie in a sense had gone down to death with him and left this hollow-eyed, politely remote changeling in her place. But this morning she had eaten a respectable breakfast, and even in her silence she seemed almost eager to be out with *Dovekie*, looking for her buoys on the blue seas of summer, below richly littered shores where the rising sun alchemized wet ledges and windrows of torn rockweed into blinding glory.

Now, while Joanna and Nils watched from behind the screen door, with Pip twisting around their ankles pleading for attention, they saw Rosa coming down from the lane; Jamie and Linnie waited for her by the Binnacle. Tiger rushed out as he always did, and Hank hailed them from the chimney. Jamie put his hand on Linnie's shoulder, swung her toward him, and said something. Suddenly she threw her arms around him just as Rosa came to them, smiling, and Linnie laughed aloud and reached out to her. For a moment it was a close three-way embrace. Then they went on, arms linked, Linnie in the middle, and disappeared between the fish houses.

"What do you think that was all about?" Joanna asked.

"Whatever it was, I'm glad of it."

"I know what I hope," Joanna said, "but I suppose that's too much to expect."

Drake's Pride, loaded heavily with wet traps, came around the breakwater and crossed the harbor without slowing down, ripping the pastel silk of the surface. Boats rolled deeply in her turbulent wake, and Rob Dinsmore, standing on the bow of *Beautiful Dreamer* to cast off his mooring, was almost thrown overboard. From out of sight beyond the fish houses Hugo yelled a profane threat.

"Pride goeth before a fall," Joanna said. "I'd like to be the one to give him the fatal push." And maybe I *will* give him a little shove, she thought, but kept it to herself.

When she had seen Nils off, everyone else had gone out or was leaving. Mark was down on the lobster car, bailing lobsters out of the compartments with the big dip net and putting them in crates for the smack, and Young Mark was with him. Helmi was alone in the store, doing needlepoint. Across the harbor Drake came roaring away from his wharf. Willy was knocked off his feet by the violent start and was seen picking himself up off the cockpit floor.

"Looks as if Felix is taking up his gear," Helmi murmured. "It didn't take long for the island to lose its charm, did it? I wonder who gave him the word."

"I guess he's heard it often enough by now so he can pick it out of the air," Joanna said. "I'm going to see if I can find out how Selina's doing."

The woman who answered at the small Island Medical Center on Stonehaven told her that Selina and the baby were doing fine and would be leaving tomorrow.

"Does she know about her brothers?" Joanna asked.

The woman lowered her voice, "Yes, poor thing."

"Could I speak to her?"

"Of course, dear. I'll get her."

Joanna waited, gazing out over Helmi's smooth ash-blond head at the scallop of azure harbor beyond the screen door. From the past she retained her earliest concept of voices crawling along inside the cable across the ocean bottom. The calls weren't transmitted by cable now, but she preferred the old image. Perhaps it was just loneliness for the past, the time before Alec, when there'd been no gray in her black hair. It hadn't been an especially peaceful time; there was always some struggle going on in the family or in the community, if not her own private war for some cause or other; but at sixteen she'd still had all those years ahead, and now they'd gone by as if in one long restless night full of fragmented dreams.

"Hello," said Selina huskily.

"Sheena, it's Joanna. We all want to know how you are."

"I'm all right, Joanna." She sounded very tired. "And Micah is wonderful. He eats like everything and sleeps like a happy little pig."

"Micah? As in the Bible?"

"Yes, for my father, but his middle name is still Bennett."

"We're all so sorry here about the boys," Joanna said. "I wanted you to know." She was attacked by a weird self-consciousness which almost destroyed her resolution, but she had only to remember Felix back in her sun parlor. "Felix is here," she said.

"Is he?" Selina asked tonelessly. "He hasn't been here. Hold on a minute." In the pause Joanna heard a door shut, and then Selina returned. "I heard it by accident, on another patient's radio," she said, still in that dull voice, "and I'm trying to make it real. You knew they were missing, didn't you? All of you, when the baby was being born." It wasn't an accusation, just a statement.

"We all were hoping for the best, Sheena," Joanna said. "Naturally we wouldn't tell you; you had enough to worry about. Willy had been keeping the radio away from you, and his mouth shut, from the first."

"Willy's a dear," Selina said with more color in her voice. "Give him my love and my thanks. Give them to everyone, for the help and the reassurances, and that fantastic card with the money, and the message—" She broke off. After a moment she said, "I called my parents as soon as I could speak, after I heard. They had to take in a lot of woe all at once, but they're strong. They're coming for me tomorrow, and I will be at the funeral with them."

"What will you do, or is it too soon to ask?"

"I'm not sure, but I *am* sure my parents won't hold my sins against the baby. They need us both right now. I suppose Micah and I will go back to Boston in time; after all, I have a business there." Suddenly the words came in a rush. "He hasn't even *called!* I think I knew all the time I was telling you about us that it would never happen. It was too perfect."

"It wouldn't have been any good at all," Joanna said, "unless he was the man you described to me. . . . Sheena?" She looked around at Helmi, out at the harbor, listened for the tramp of feet up through the shed. None came.

"Sheena, I want to tell you something. I *need* to tell you." The sound of her own words restored her conviction that this was right and necessary. "It's not meant to upset you, but it will. It's a warning." From the corner of her eye she saw Helmi's head come up. "He wants Micah for him and his wife to raise. He's told her all about it, and she's willing. He thinks you can't refuse because you owe him. It sounds insane, but that's what he told Nils and me."

The silence at the other end terrified her. Had Selina fainted? Helmi was now making no pretense of doing needlepoint. Waiting, the two women stared at each other, expressionless with suspense. When Selina answered, her voice came so strongly that Joanna jumped.

"So that's it, is it? Well, I am going to do just fine raising my son, and we'll want nothing *at all* from Mr. Drake. I've paid back almost all the money he lent me for the business, and I'll get a bank loan for the rest of it. And if he ever comes near us, either in Maine or in Boston, I'll take him to court."

Joanna said faintly, "I'd be cheering, but I'm winded. What a relief! I hated to tell you about him, but I didn't want him to take you by surprise."

"He can't do it now; I'm ready for him. Am I ever! Thank you, thank you, thank you!"

Joanna came away from the telephone with sweat drenching her back. "Dear God," she said prayerfully. "I need something for a quick fix." She took a candy bar from the case and made a note of it on the pad beside the cash register. Her hand was shaking.

"How is she?" Helmi asked with commendable restraint.

"Valiant and all primed for Felix. Her parents know about the baby now, and they're taking her home. She sent her love to everybody, including Willy."

"Willy came over to gas up early this morning," said Helmi, "looking pretty forlorn, and old Tough-as-Tripe Mark suddenly decided to hire him to paint the house this summer. He thought Willy was going to cry at first, but now he's happier than a dog with two tails, though I never could figure *that* one out. . . . So Felix thought he could foreclose on the baby, lacking an old homestead."

"Aye-up! After he carried on about the scandal and protecting his daughters, he told us he was taking the baby and didn't expect any trouble. He didn't even realize how it sounded. Well, according to his thinking, it probably sounded perfectly logical. The critter *has* to be an egomaniac."

"I think I know now who gave him the word," said Helmi.

"Well," said Joanna, and they left it at that. "Now maybe we'll have some good news for a change. We can stand it. I know what I'm hoping for," she said again. She stood by the screen door, eating chocolate and looking out. Three ospreys circled high above the harbor, soaring up or dropping down through blue space, drifting sidewise, hovering with cocked head and beating wings to watch the water below. They kept whistling to one another.

"I love them," Joanna said. "I'm glad they're back."

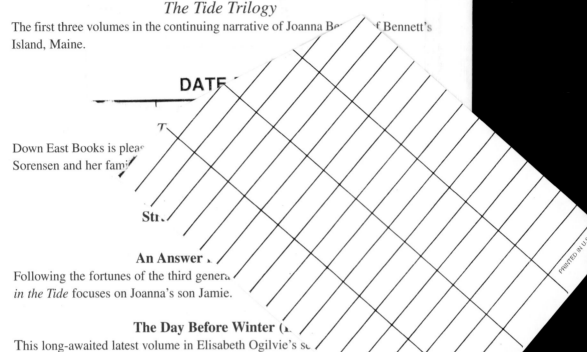